CAMPARI CRIMSON

(FRANKI AMATO MYSTERIES BOOK 4)

TRACI ANDRIGHETTI

Limoncello
Press

FREE SHORT MYSTERY OFFER

Sign up for my newsletter at traciandrighetti.com to be the first to know about my new releases, deals, and giveaways. And I'll email you a link to download "Fragolino Fuchsia," a Franki-goes-to-Rome short mystery, for FREE!

CAMPARI CRIMSON

by

TRACI ANDRIGHETTI

***

❀ Created with Vellum

For my ex-colleagues. Thanks for the love and laughs. I hope this book gives you both.

BOOK BACKSTORY

Campari Crimson began as the intentionally bad idea of two of my ex-colleagues, Gregg Charalambous and Josh Santo. They wanted to be werewolves in a Franki Amato mystery, but I can't remember their plot idea because it was so absurd that I erased it from my mind. But werewolves made me think of vampires and all the Anne Rice novels set in New Orleans, and it occurred to me that there were probably a lot of vampire legends associated with The Crescent City.

To find out, my husband and I went on a New Orleans vampire tour. As it turns out, not only does the city have vampire legends, it has also witnessed true vampire crimes, which I hadn't expected. Another surprise—there was a female vampire on the tour, and she wasn't a prop. She was a tourist from New York on vacation with her husband. I didn't talk to her, but she looked at me and smiled, revealing sizeable fangs, and she wore white-blue contacts that made her eyes glow. Other than that, she looked like any other NOLA tourist in a T-shirt, jeans, and Mardi Gras boa.

The woman was my first experience with a "real vampire," a person who feeds on blood—human or animal—or physical energy. Apparently New Orleans and Buffalo have the largest vampire populations, but my hometown of Austin has an active group too. While I was researching these communities, I learned that an Italian occult watchdog group had warned the Vatican of the appeal of "sexy vampires" portrayed by beautiful actors and actresses on television and in movies. Besides the *Twilight* series, they were most concerned about the influence of *True Blood*, a TV show filmed in New Orleans. That's when I knew I had to write *Campari Crimson*.

And yes, the vampire I saw on the tour is a key character in the book, as are a lot of my ex-colleagues and friends. Rather than identify them, I'll let them tell you if they're real or not. Of course, you already know about Gregg and Josh. They're characters in the mystery (and in life), and I had some fun with them. You'll see what I mean when you read *Campari Crimson*.

Speaking of real people who became book characters, Marissa Maggio (you know her as Veronica, Franki's BFF and employer) lent her legal expertise to *Campari Crimson*. *Grazie, amica mia.*

And thanks to all of you who support me in this crazy book-writing adventure. Even though I'm mostly in front of a computer, I'm having the time of my life.

Now, as the say in New Orleans, *laissez les bons temps rouler!*

Cin cin (Cheers)!
Traci

1

"That vampire is staring at me." I clenched my jaw and tipped my head at a fanged female standing among parade-goers at the gates of Jackson Square.

Veronica Maggio stood on tiptoes and gazed over the crowd. "The one with the curls and blue dress?"

"Uh-huh." I pulled up the collar of my peacoat. "Every time I look at her, she's ogling my throat."

She gave a get-a-grip gasp. "Franki, she's barely twelve years old."

No matter how hard I tried, I could never convince my best friend and employer that danger was a daily concern. Sometimes it seemed like she clung to her perky-positive Elle Woods worldview to spite me, and the proof was in her *Legally Blonde*-inspired pink Playboy Bunny costume. "Go ahead—scoff. But she reminds me of Claudia, the blood-thirsty kid Kirsten Dunst played in *Interview with a Vampire*."

"Well, this little vampirette isn't going to bite you, especially not at a Halloween parade."

I looked to the voodoo doll beside me for support, but she looked away. "How does that make any sense?"

Veronica shot me the side-eye. "You're one to talk about making sense. I don't know why you're always so suspicious of people."

"Uh…" I blinked, incredulous. "Because we're private investigators, and we're in New Orleans?"

"We both know vampires aren't real." She turned toward Decatur Street, resuming her wait for the first float. "And no one comes to the Krewe of BOO! parade to bite anyone. They're here to have fun."

Judging from the way the buzzed Betelgeuse to my right had been baring his teeth at me, I wasn't so sure about the biting part. "Maybe, but as soon as Glenda gets here, I'm heading home."

She glanced at her phone. "It's six-thirty, so I'm expecting them any minute."

If I hadn't been sufficiently spooked by the vexing vampiress, the realization that my sixty-something ex-stripper landlady was bringing a companion did the trick. "*Them?* I thought it was *her.*"

"Carnie's coming too."

Dread filled my veins like a bad transfusion. As her stage name implied, Carnie Vaul was a carnival-clown-turned-drag-queen friend of Glenda's who once hired me to investigate a homicide involving her priceless amber necklace. And even though I technically worked for Veronica's PI firm, Private Chicks, Inc., Carnie had thrown her weight around—all three hundred fifty pounds of it. The worst part was that I'd solved the case six months before, but she was still hanging around like an albatross from my neck—or a big boobie-bib. "I would've appreciated a heads-up."

"You just got one." She stood on her tiptoes and scoured the crowd. "Try not to pick a fight with her, okay?"

"Me?" I said, shocked. "That devious diva has targeted me from day one."

"She's difficult, I know. But you played right into her hand."

I snorted. "Maybe it's because her hands are so huge."

The crowd gave a collective gasp followed by cheers, and Veronica and I strained to see the float.

"Oh." She covered her mouth. "It's Count Dracula."

The old phrase, "I vant to suck your blood," came to mind. With a grimace, I turned to eye my toothy little friend but came face-to-face with Glenda.

"How do you like me, ladies?" She struck a pose in a floor-length black feather dress and matching cabaret shoulder collar. "Miss Carnie and I decided to go as each other this Halloween season."

"Local celebrities trade places," Veronica said as Carnie waddled into view. "What a cute idea."

"Creepy" was a better term. Glenda looked like an old crow with clown hair, and Carnie, in a white, plus-sized halter-top and boy shorts, bore an unsettling resemblance to the New Orleans Pelicans' King Cake Baby mascot in his giant bib and diaper—except for the platinum wig and cigarette holder.

"You know me." Glenda flapped her two-inch purple feather lashes. "I love an excuse to dress in costume."

I suppressed a smirk. Glenda O'Brien, in art Lorraine Lamour, had worn a stripper costume every day since she'd started dancing some fifty years before. And everyone in The Crescent City was acutely aware of it.

"Franki likes costumes too," Carnie said in a fierce falsetto. "And hers is so realistic—a worn-out working girl who's given up on her looks and her life."

A float of Chucky and his axe-wielding bride came into view, which was appropriate since I was feeling stabby.

"I'm not wearing a costume because I was working." I straightened my coat. "I had to finish my notes for an employee theft case."

Carnie's eyes lit up like a jack-o'-lantern. "What did he steal? Your femininity?"

That burned, especially coming from a queen.

Glenda gave a raucous laugh. "If you need a costume, Miss Franki, you know I'll do you right."

Wrong. Glenda was an avid stripper costume collector who'd provided me with outfits for a couple of cases. And thanks to her creations, I'd had wardrobe malfunctions that made Janet Jackson's Super Bowl nip slip seem demure. "I don't need a costume, thanks." I hit Carnie with a direct stare. "But now I need a drink."

Veronica pulled some cash from her bunny suit. "I'll buy us a round."

Before I could refuse, she took me by the arm and led me across the street. We walked along the gutter to bypass the partiers, and the Chucky float pulled up beside us.

Glenda looked at its krewe. "Throw me something, Monster," she shouted, using the Halloween variant of the Mardi Gras cry, *Throw me something, Mister.*

A zombie chucked a painted oyster shell, but it sailed over Glenda and conked me in the head.

"Ow!"

The zombie looked dispirited. "Sorry, lady!"

Carnie cackled as I checked for blood—and did a quick scan for the canined kid. Once I'd located her, I turned to take on the float. "You guys should stick to soft throws like Aunt Sally's Pralinettes."

"Let's get you to safety." Veronica ushered me into Big Easy Daiquiris, and maybe it was the possible concussion, but I could have sworn I saw her smiling.

Despite the crowd outside, there were only a handful of people in the shotgun-style establishment.

"You have a seat," Veronica said as she, Glenda, and Carnie approached the bartender.

Following her advice, I sat at the bar and glanced at the TV hanging in the corner of the room. There was a *Breaking News* banner at the bottom of the screen, and it was clear from the gold New Orleans PD shield behind the empty podium that the police were about to hold a news conference.

Glenda pulled out the barstool beside me and hiked her dress to her thighs before sitting down. "You going to meet your banker beau tonight, sugar?"

The mention of my boyfriend, Bradley Hartmann, made my lips pucker—and not for a kiss. The day before he'd surprised me with the news that he was going on a two-week trip to New York for Pontchartrain Bank. The trip had been a surprise to him too, so I didn't blame him for the late notice. What I did blame him for was not inviting me to come with him, not even for the weekend. "He's wrapping up some things at the office."

She patted my knee. "I used to be like him, you know."

I couldn't wait to hear how.

"Hustling twelve-hour days, seven days a week."

"It must be tough being a stripper," I said to commiserate. "And a bank president."

She gave a grave nod. "One day I realized that all of this"—she pointed to her body—"was no good to my clients if I wasn't good with myself. So I made time to live a little."

Based on the stories she'd told me about her stripping days, she'd lived a little *a lot*. "Bradley can't always control his own schedule. He just found out that he has to leave town tomorrow for work."

"And he's not making time for you before he goes?" Carnie put a hand to her bogus bosom. "How telling."

I hit her with a don't-go-there stare. "We're meeting for brunch in the morning."

"Sounds about as sexy as a date at a grocery store." She flopped onto the stool next to Glenda.

Although I knew better than to fall victim to one of her jabs, it still hurt. I was sensitive enough about Bradley not inviting me to New York, so I didn't need her picking apart our plans. "He has to be well rested for the trip."

"Well, you can hardly expect him to catch up on his beauty rest during a three-hour flight, can you?" Carnie had raised her falsetto an octave to sound innocent.

I lowered my voice an octave to sound incensed—which I was. "He can't sleep on the plane because his secretary's going with him."

Glenda and Carnie exchanged arched brows.

"It isn't like that," I protested. "Ruth Walker's at least sixty years old."

One of Glenda's eyelash-wings lowered to mid-flap.

"I think someone's throwing shade at mature women, Glenda," Carnie said, using drag speak for *insult*.

"'Sixty' and 'sexy' are practically the same word, Miss Franki. You'd do well to remember that."

I gave a three-second sigh. With Glenda's feathers all ruffled and Carnie's boy shorts in a bunch, I would've been better off at the parade with the vampire. "I wasn't 'throwing shade' at anyone. All I meant was, Bradley's not into older women."

Glenda flipped her Bozo hair, but it didn't budge. "His loss, sugar."

Veronica walked up behind me as the bartender delivered our drinks. I started to compliment his Captain Jack Sparrow costume, but then it occurred to me that it might be his normal look.

"Three Zombifieds and one Vampire Bite," he announced, placing orange-colored drinks and a blood-red concoction on the bar.

I didn't have to ask which one was mine. I frowned at Veronica, who raised her fleur-de-lis–shaped cup in a toast, and wished I'd gone home as planned.

"Look, Miss Carnie." Glenda pointed at the TV. "It's that handsome hunk of man meat, Detective Sullivan."

Carnie licked her Lucille Ball lips. "Gurrrl, you know I'd like to take a bite of that beefsteak."

I dosed myself with my drink and glowered at the screen. The superintendent of police and the chief were on either side of the podium, and Detective Wesley Sullivan was right where he liked to be—front and center. I knew because I'd made the mistake of getting in the way of his glory while working on Carnie's case. And because his ego was as inflated as his biceps, he'd done everything he could to sideline me, starting with throwing me in jail.

I made eye contact with the bartender, who poured a daiquiri from one of the machines. "Could you turn up the sound, please?"

"F'sure."

Veronica looked at the TV. "What's going on?"

"I'll bet it's about the blood bank, Miss Ronnie." Glenda held her straw like a cigarette holder.

The cold, red liquid I'd sipped took on a ghastly chill in my mouth. I held it there for a second and then swallowed, hard. "Blood bank?"

The bartender aimed a remote control at the TV, and the murmur of reporters chatting in the background became audible.

"As you may know," Detective Sullivan said, quieting the crowd, "last night there was an attempt to break in to The Blood Center on Canal Street at eleven forty-five p.m. We believe the culprit or culprits were scared away by officers responding to an unrelated call near the scene."

"Send those officers my way, Detective. I don't scare easily." Glenda arched her back to emphasize her sex, not her strength.

Detective Sullivan shot a somber look at the camera, matching my mood exactly. "The security camera outside the building was disabled. Fortunately, a security camera across the street captured an image of a suspect, who we'll show to you now."

Video footage of a caped figure aired.

"A *cape*?" I was dumbstruck—and disturbed. "A guy goes to steal blood from a blood bank and wears a *cape*?"

Veronica shrugged. "Who said it was a guy?"

"Um, the point is the cape?" I glanced around the bar, surprised that no one else was freaked out by the suspect's choice of outerwear. "It's awfully vampiric, don't you think?"

Veronica bit her straw and turned away.

"It's too much clothing." Glenda scowled at the screen. "The public doesn't want to see that."

"And capes are out of style," Carnie chimed. "They need to put the camera back on that delicious detective."

Detective Sullivan reappeared, and Glenda and Carnie clinked cups.

"If you know this individual, or if you have any information about the break-in, you can call us at the number on the screen." He read from a sheet of paper on the podium. "If you'd rather remain anonymous, you can call Crime Stoppers, send them a text, or leave a tip online."

"What about your phone number, Detective?" Glenda cooed.

As Sullivan left the podium, a young male reporter appeared on screen. "Do you have any active leads?"

The detective looked annoyed. "We're following up on some tips, but at this time we do not have a suspect." He nodded at the gathering of reporters. "Yes, Bill."

An older man stepped forward with a notebook. "Do you have any reason to believe this attempt is related to the break-in at the Metairie blood bank last month?"

"I'm not at liberty to discuss that." The detective pointed to someone off camera. "Ann?"

"Do you have any idea what the motive would be for stealing blood?" she asked.

The superintendent leaned into the microphone. "I'm afraid we're out of time. This concludes the press conference."

I glanced at Veronica. "The superintendant skirted that question, didn't he?"

"Yeah." She sat on the stool next to me. "I wonder why."

"I'm not sure I want to know." I reached for my Vampire Bite but then decided to leave it be. "Had you heard about the break-in at the Metairie blood bank?"

"M-hm." Her pretty pout thinned. "They wiped out their entire supply of B Positive."

My blood type. I scratched my neck. "Bizarre."

Glenda plucked a few feathers from her breast area. "Stranger things have happened in New Orleans, sugar."

After a year and a half in the city, I knew that was true. "But why would anyone steal blood? And only one type?"

"I say it's a fetish." Glenda pulled a cigarette holder from the heel of her stripper shoe. "When I was dancing at Madame Moiselle's back in the '90s, we had this VIP room regular we called The Podiatrist. He took pictures of our feet with a Polaroid." She laughed and slapped my leg. "Then he rubbed the pictures between our toes before putting them in individually marked plastic baggies."

I pulled Veronica's drink from her grip and took a gulp.

Carnie, nonplussed by The Podiatrist, leaned back on her barstool. "Maybe it's a wounded criminal in hiding."

A mobster or a drug lord was a possibility—one I didn't want to consider.

Veronica twisted her ring, staring into space. "Or maybe it's for voodoo or witchcraft."

That was my cue to leave, or rather, flee.

"Whatever the reason, I'm glad it's Detective Sullivan's problem and not mine." I hopped from the barstool and, without thinking, chugged the rest of my Vampire Bite. And when I put the glass on the bar, I had a bitter taste in mouth, but not because it reminded me of blood.

It was because something told me that I'd jinxed myself and that the blood bank problem was about to be mine.

I AWOKE, shivering. The temperature in my bedroom had dropped at least ten degrees since I'd gone to bed. Too exhausted to open my eyes, I rolled onto my back and reached for the hot pink velvet duvet, pulling it over the sheets. Then I waited to drift back to sleep.

A blast of hot air hit my neck.

And another.

In my semiconscious state, I realized the blasts were coming in rhythmic bursts.

Like breathing.

In a flash I was alert, frozen with fear. It was ludicrous to think of vampires and blood bank thieves, but I did.

As well as deranged drag queens.

I couldn't get my gun, because it was in the nightstand. My only option for taking on the intruder was the self-defense training I'd received during my year on the Austin PD.

Corralling my courage, I opened my eyelids a crack. And the blood drained from my body.

A hairy face hovered at my throat.

Was it a big bat? A werewolf? An unshaven Carnie?

The creature's mouth opened, as though in slow motion, revealing pointed teeth and emitting a putrid odor.

The smell of death.

I whimpered, and it...barked?

My body went limp.

The creature was my cairn terrier, Napoleon.

"Bad boy," I shouted, supine. But I was madder at myself than at my dog. I didn't know what had gotten into me—all I knew was that I wanted it to get out.

He barked again.

"Ugh." I raised my head. "What do you want?"

In reply, he jumped off the bed and trotted to the doorway. Then he turned and looked over his shoulder.

"This had better be important business." As soon as I'd said it, I thought of Bradley's trip, and then I was doubly annoyed.

I dragged myself from the black bordello-style bed and grabbed my gut. I'd been in a bad state before hitting the sack, so I'd gone out with a bang—an alligator sausage Dat Dog and crawfish étouffée fries topped off with a quarter jar of Nutella. The problem was that the alligator and the crawfish sought revenge, swimming in the muddy swamp of my stomach.

Lumbering Bride-of-Frankenstein-style through the living room, I reached the front door and peered through the peephole. Satisfied it was safe, I opened the door. "Shake your tail fur."

Napoleon darted into the yard, and I lost sight of him in the darkness. I wasn't sure what time it was, but it was after two a.m. because the lights were off at Thibodeaux's tavern across the street.

A cat howled from the cemetery next to the bar, and Napoleon growled.

"Stay," I commanded, although I still couldn't see him. "You go in there, and you're on your own."

The ghoulish graveyard had been the bane of my existence ever since Veronica had talked me into renting the apartment next door to hers on the first floor of Glenda's fourplex. Because I lived in

Austin at the time, my best friend had mailed me the lease. And she'd stayed as mum as a corpse about the macabre tombs, crypts, and mausoleums across the street. Otherwise, I would've run for my life. Even the locals knew how disturbing their aboveground cemeteries were, which is why they'd nicknamed them *cities of the dead*.

And, as far as I was concerned, there was nothing uplifting about living by the dead, especially in one of Glenda's apartments. Veronica described the décor as bordello chic, which was fitting since Glenda had furnished the place from brothel fire sales, but it also had a disturbing funeral parlor feel. When the day came that I could afford to move out, I was going to write a book about the experience—*The Little Whorehouse of Horrors*.

The cat started caterwauling, and I heard my cairn "terror" tear across the grass to save the cemetery from the feline infiltrator.

"Damn dog never listens to a word I say," I muttered, slipping on my soccer sandals.

The alligator and the crawfish switched from the freestyle to the butterfly the second I set off for the cemetery. When I got to the gate, I cursed whoever had left it open. The musty scent of decay assailed my nostrils, and I covered my nose and mouth. There was no way to know whether the odor was from the damp earth and thick carpet of dead leaves—or from something else.

"Napoleon! Come. Here. Right. Now."

Nothing.

As I debated whether to enter, a gargoyle glared at me from atop a tomb. Gritting my teeth, I took a step forward and stopped.

The leaves were rustling—a lot.

"That's a big cat," I said to the gargoyle, shifting my weight to the other foot. "Like, lion-sized."

A hiss sounded, and a yelping Napoleon dashed past me with his tail between his legs.

I cracked a smile at his cowardice and glanced in the area of the cat commotion.

And what I saw scared the smile from my face.

Moving among the mausoleums was a caped figure—like the one on the press conference video.

Following Napoleon's lead, I turned tail and ran to the apartment in Olympic time.

After checking on Napoleon, who was holed up beneath the zebra-striped chaise lounge, I peeked through the gold fringe of my drapes.

There was no one in sight, but I wasn't about to relax because I finally understood why I'd been so spooked. I'd lived in New Orleans long enough to know that people and things were connected in this city in ways they weren't anywhere else. In unthinkable and unknowable ways.

The vampire, the press conference, the caped figure—the uneasy feelings they'd given me had been no accident. One way or another, they'd come back to haunt me during Halloween.

2

My phone alarm went off, and I sat straight up in bed, knocking heads of garlic to the floor. It seemed silly in retrospect, but since I'd had the garlic in the house, I'd surrounded myself with it in case the caped creeper came in. It wasn't that I really believed in the supernatural, but when faced with something spooky like a suspected vampire, my standard operating procedure was to play it safe rather than sorry until I had all the evidence in hand.

After gathering up the garlic, I stumbled to my automatic coffeemaker. As I stood at the kitchen counter stirring the black brew into a half-cup of Baileys Crème Brulée coffee creamer, Napoleon pressed a paw to my foot.

"You want breakfast, do you?" I grabbed his bowl and gave him a glare while dishing up his dog food. "You know what I want? A cairn terrier who doesn't live up to his breed name." I placed his kibble on the leopard-print linoleum. "So the cemetery excursions stop today, feline foe or no."

Swallowing some coffee, I scooped up my phone and returned to my room to get ready to meet Bradley. I should've been looking forward to our date, but part of me wanted to cancel, and it wasn't because I was pouting about the trip. After the previous day's events, my instincts were telling me to get back in bed—and pull the covers over my head.

I stepped into the bathroom and onto something foreign. "What the—?"

My behind hit the floor and the coffee went flying—all over my one clean dress I'd hung in the doorway before going to bed.

So much for listening to my instincts.

Sprawled on my back, I lifted my head to see what had caused me to slip. There beside the pink claw-foot tub was the culprit—a bulb of garlic.

"Seriously?" I put my head down.

My ringtone sounded.

Thinking it was Bradley, I reached for my phone and tapped answer as I pulled myself to my feet. "Hello?"

"It's your mother, dear."

"Yeah. Hi, Mom." I resented the implication that I didn't talk to her enough to recognize her voice. "Listen, I'm getting ready to meet Bradley. Can I call you tonight?"

"This is important, Francesca." Her typically shrill tone had turned snippy. "And Bradley can wait on you for once. After all, you've been waiting on him to propose for almost two years."

I exchanged a look with myself in the oval-shaped mirror of the red Louis XVI vanity. *When was I going to learn to screen my calls?* "What's going on?"

"Anthony quit the deli."

Maybe that was why I'd been getting the vampire vibe. My older brother Anthony had been sucking the lifeblood from my parents since the day he was born. At thirty-two, he was still living at their home in Houston and, until recently, "shirking" (a more applicable word than "working") at their business, Amato's Deli. "Wow. What's he going to do for money?"

She sighed a lifetime of exasperation. "That's what I'm calling to talk to you about."

I didn't like the sound of that, but I didn't like the sound of another receiver picking up even more.

"*Ciao*, Franki," my nonna said in her thick Sicilian accent. "You got a ring-a yet?"

I returned to my sprawling position on the floor. A combined call from my martyr mom and matchmaker grandma carried the physical impact of a one-two punch. "No, Nonna. Bradley hasn't popped the question."

"But you steal-a the lemon six-a months ago," she protested. "If you ask-a me, that-a Bradley is-a the lemon."

"She's right, Francesca," my mother singsonged. "When we were there in March, I told him all about the tradition—a single woman steals a lemon from a St. Joseph's Day altar, and within a year she's engaged."

The reference to the cockamamie Italian-American custom and my unwilling participation in it curdled the creamer in my stomach. There would be no lemonade made from this batch of lemons. "Right. So he still has six months to propose."

"Your Nonna and I think you need to move on. At thirty, your eggs are already old," she reminded in her ticking-time-clock tone. "You can't afford to put them all in Bradley's basket."

I stood up and mouthed "help me" in the mirror. Only my mother could take an innocent idiom and turn it into an insulting indictment against my reproductive system.

"What about that handsome detective we met at your house?" she trilled.

My reflection and I rolled our eyes. *What did everyone see in Sullivan?* "Just so we're clear, I'm staying with Bradley. And even if I wasn't, I wouldn't date the detective."

"What's-a wrong-a with you?" Nonna yelled. "He gave-a you a five-a dollar bill-a."

Bradley had given me a ruby and diamond necklace for my birthday, but my mom and Nonna were placing their bets on a man who'd tipped me five bucks when I'd performed a striptease to crack a case.

"Getting me married is not a family project, okay? I can find a husband for myself."

"You haven't found one so far." My mother stated the painfully obvious.

I watched the corners of my mouth leap to their deaths. "Can we get to the news about Anthony, please?"

She snorted, as though I were the one being rude. "He's decided he wants to work in the hospitality industry."

I almost hit the floor again—this time from laughter.

"What's so funny?" The snippiness had resurfaced.

"Mom, Anthony doesn't greet customers when they come into the deli—he grunts at them. So how the hell is he going to work in hospitality?"

"Francesca Lucia Amato!" She went from snippy to snarly. "You watch your language, young lady."

That was my mother. When it came to having kids I was verging on menopausal, but when it came to anything else I was forever a child. "Fine. But even you have to admit your son is severely lacking in people skills."

"I most certainly do not," she snapped. "Anthony can be very charming."

"Sì." Nonna cackled. "Like-a the ass of a bull-a."

"Go ahead. Make fun, you two," Mom shouted above our snickers. "But it's all settled. Your father has given him his blessing to move to New Orleans."

I choked on a chuckle. "Who?" I whispered, hoping I'd misunderstood. "Who did Dad give his blessing to?"

"Anthony," she replied. "It's a tourist city, and you know we have connections there."

There was no way I could forget. My nonna and nonnu had emigrated from Sicily to New Orleans where they'd raised my dad and his four brothers. And ever since I'd set foot in the city, my nonna had been trying to set me up with her Sicilian friends' sons, grand-sons, nephews, neighbors, and assorted acquaintances—some of the saddest suitors in the South. "But Houston has tons of tourists. Why come here?"

"Your father got his start in the deli business in New Orleans," she said for the thousandth time. "And Anthony has seen how well you've done for yourself after moving there. He wants a chance to do the same thing."

When she put it that way, I couldn't begrudge my brother a shot at a new career. But I could begrudge him everything else. "Honestly, I think it's a dumb idea. But whatever."

"I'm glad you agree." She twisted my words to suit her worldview. "Now that it's all settled, he'll be at your place within the week."

The bathroom began to spin.

"Wait a second," I wheezed, returning to my safe place on the floor. "He's not living with me, is he?"

"He won't be there long, Francesca. Just until he gets on his feet."

"*Uff*," Nonna pffed in Italian. "He never get off-a the couch."

For once I was glad my nonna was on the phone. "She's right, Mom. Anthony doesn't *get* on his feet. And don't forget that I live in a one-bedroom apartment. I don't have room for him here."

"Your father and I lived in a one-bedroom house with all three of you kids when you were small," she shrilled, making her maternal misery known. "God knows we've sacrificed for you. It's your turn to sacrifice for us."

My eyes narrowed. *Was this some kind of parental payback for being husbandless and childless? They unloaded their freeloading son on their single daughter?*

"Goodness, I'd better get off the phone." She verbalized my sentiments all along. "I need to get a move on if I want to get Anthony packed."

I wouldn't swear to it, but I thought I heard her squee.

"Goodbye, dear."

The line went dead. And so did my hopes for the future.

I'd been a fool to fear the caped figure.

Anthony was the one coming to suck my blood.

"Where are you?" Bradley shouted into his cell phone above the jazz blaring at The Court of Two Sisters restaurant. "I'm going to have to head out in about twenty minutes to make my flight."

Disappointment joined the hunger already chewing at my insides as I clutched my phone and mentally cursed the red light. "I'm about to turn into the Quarter. I'll be there in ten."

"We'll have a few minutes together, then," he said, sounding content.

Carnie's comment about the grocery store date came to mind, and my disappointment turned to annoyance. *Was that all Bradley needed with me? A few measly minutes?*

"Franki? Are you still there?"

"Yeah. See you in *a few*." I tapped *End*, which symbolized how I felt about the whole situation—not seeing him the night before, not warranting more than a brunch date that morning, not being invited to New York for the weekend. And "a few minutes" was all the time I needed to tell him that.

The light turned green.

I hooked a right onto St. Ann Street, and I flinched.

The scene before me looked like the college textbook pictures I'd seen of San Francisco's Summer of Love—but in the French Quarter in the fall. And judging from the look of the hippies hanging out on the sidewalks, they were the same flower children from the summer of '67—only they'd matured into flower fogies.

The light at the next intersection was red, so I slowed to a stop. Wondering whether the hippies were getting ready to rally for pot or protest a war, I looked around for their picket signs while I waited. Not seeing any, I glanced at the light.

Then I looked down.

A pair of black go-go boots had caught my eye because the wearer was marching up the middle of the street. The next thing I knew, "These Boots are Made for Walkin'" played in my mind. But when I raised my gaze, it wasn't Nancy Sinatra's face I saw but Nancy Reagan's—with long black hair and gray roots.

The woman reached the cross street, and I realized she wasn't alone. Shuffling behind her slight frame was a chubby dachshund in a tie-dyed T-shirt and a band of merry—and hairy—men.

As I looked on perplexed, she paraded to the front of my 1965 cherry red Mustang convertible, lowered her peace-sign sunglasses, and stared straight at me. Then she raised her bell-sleeved arms, and her entire entourage sat down.

Unsure how to react, I sat immobile as the haughty hippie draped her arms around a sixtyish male with gray chest hair sprouting from his suede-fringed vest and proceeded to swap spit.

Then I remembered that I, too, was wearing boots. I threw open my car door and stomped up to the impassioned pair. "Listen, I hate to break up your love-in, but you need to clear out."

The fringed flower fogy broke the lip lock. "This is a sit-in, man."

"Well, could you sit in somewhere else? Like on the sidewalk?" I pointed at my Mustang. "Because I need to get through here."

"That would defeat the purpose." The hippie chick's tone was hoity-toity. "We're sitting in to protest the cruel and inhumane practice of boiling live crawdads."

I looked at her like she was high, which was a definite possibility. "Um, good luck because they've been boiling them here for hundreds of years."

"Don't listen to her, Pam," a frizzy-haired burnout in bell-bottom jeans and Jesus boots advised. "She's part of The Establishment. You can tell by her cream-colored pants."

"What's wrong with cream?" I protested. "It's an earth tone."

Pam leaned back on her palms and tilted her head. "Yeah, I'll bet she wants to break us up so she can go to brunch."

My head retracted. "I *am* going to brunch."

"Boo, hiss," the hippies heckled.

I recoiled again. I'd never heard anyone actually say "hiss," and it seemed kind of harsh.

A car horn blared.

We turned and saw an elderly male in a Mercedes behind my Mustang.

"See?" I shouted. "I'm not the only one you're blocking, so why don't you keep on truckin' and get out of the street?"

Pam's old man rose on well-worn flip-flops. "We're not moving, dig? So flake off."

Based on the context, I was pretty sure he was telling me to leave. But he *did* have a skin condition.

Pam stood on scrawny legs. "Like, get back in your car and split."

"Like, I would, but you're blocking my way." I scrutinized the not-so-dynamite duo with a surly stare. "And whatever happened to promoting peace and love?"

She grasped her live-and-let-live locket. "The times they are a-changin'."

Her comment reminded me that the times they were also a-wastin'. With mere minutes to meet Bradley, I balled my fists and stormed over to the man in the Mercedes. "You might as well turn around, sir." I cast a glare worthy of a brunch-eating Establishment member at Pam and her people. "Those hippies are downright hateful."

Without further ado, I jumped into my car, pulled over to the curb, and parked. I might've revved my engine too.

The hippies watched as I climbed from the car and slammed my door. Flinging my bag over my shoulder, I set off on the three-block walk to the restaurant.

"Righteous," Pam said.

My boots practically screeched to a halt. What I really wanted to do was "rap" with her—and I didn't mean "talk." But at least ten minutes had passed since I'd talked to Bradley, so I decided to mellow out and keep on keepin' on—and to stop using hippie lingo moving forward.

After a couple of blocks, I emerged from the hippie hotbed into the usual tourist traffic. The strange thing was that the queasy-uneasy feeling of the night before had returned. I told myself it was nerves about confronting Bradley, but even I knew that was a lie.

Because something was up. I just didn't know what.

"Hello, Franki."

The gruff Boston accent was familiar.

A couple of buildings further ahead, I spotted a balding, beer-bellied guy in an orange island shirt and blue toe shoes that looked like gloves for feet.

"Lou Toccato." I flashed a sincere smile as I made my way over to greet him. I got a kick out of Lou and his kooky last name, which was Italian for "touched," as in "crazy." The irony was that Lou was sane while his psychic wife, Chandra, was the loon. But I was indebted to them both because they'd bailed me out of a bad place on a homicide case. "I haven't seen you since the plantation investigation."

"That's right." He gave me a hearty handshake and then hiked up his sagging shorts.

Even though I was in a hurry, I had to stop and chat with Lou, especially since I didn't have to deal with Chandra. "Hey, so how's business? Are you still in Mid-City?"

"Nah." He shoved his hands into his pockets. "Chandra and I formed an LLC."

"Huh," I said, surprised. "A plumbing and psychic services company?"

"Yup, yup."

In a weird way, it made sense. There were plenty of people in New Orleans who would equate overflowing toilets with misdeeds from the dead. "Where are y'all at?"

He jingled the keys in his pocket and rocked back on his heels. "Over on Frenchmen Street."

I nodded, impressed. "That's prime real estate. The plumbing business must be treating you right."

Lou rocked forward to his toes. "Actually," he said in a confidential tone, "Chandra's the breadwinner in the family."

If he'd hit me upside the head with a pipe wrench, I could not have been more floored. As psychics went, Chandra, aka the Crescent City Medium, was just plain sad. Not only was she phasmophobic, she was also a flat-out fake. "Where is she, anyway?"

He jerked his shoulder toward an open door.

It was unmarked, so I read the overhead sign. "Boutique du Vampyre?" Startled, I took a step back. "What's she doing in there?"

"Buying supplies," he said with a shrug. "They sell candles."

"And custom fangs," I added, reading from a placard on the wall. It was probably a psychosomatic reaction, but my neck throbbed. "I'd love to pop in and say hello to her, but I really have to—"

"Why, Franki Amato."

Chandra's honeyed voice hit me like a hammer. And I rued the run-in with the hippies at the sit-in. Thanks to their concern for the crawdad, I was going to be sidelined by the psycho psychic.

She studied my face as she stepped from the store, and I eyed her outfit. She was dressed like a Dallas Cowboy cheerleader but built like the Pillsbury Doughboy. Since I'd seen her last, she'd toned down the size of her Chanel bag, but she'd ramped up the breadth of her frosted bouffant bob.

I mustered a polite smile. "Lou and I were talking about you."

"I know you were." She raised a blood bag with a straw to her tiny lips.

For a moment, I was relieved because it finally dawned on me that I was having a nightmare. How else would I explain the blood bag— and the hippies? But then Chandra shoved the bag in my face, bringing me back to my bizarre and bitter reality.

"It's not a real blood bag. It's an energy drink," she said, as though reading my mind. "Cute, huh?"

Like a leach on a baby's bottom.

She put a pudgy hand on Lou's chest, causing the suns, moons, and stars on her charm bracelet to jingle. "They have a blood clot spread that would be perfect for your cooking class."

The queasy feeling intensified. I wasn't sure what kind of class Lou was taking, but I was positive I didn't want to sample his cooking.

"Boy, I need to get a look at that." Lou headed for the door. "Nice seeing ya, Franki. You'll have to drop by the house sometime."

"Will do, Lou." I watched him go inside with regret. The thought of being alone with Chandra and her psychic shenanigans reminded me why I hadn't kept in touch with her. "I wish I could stay and chat, but I'm super late for a date with Bradley."

Chandra put a purple paddle-shaped fingernail to her lips and giggled. "Oh, you're not going to make it."

"Is that a prediction?"

"No, reality."

I remembered another reason I hadn't kept in touch with her.

My phone vibrated.

"Must be Bradley." I looked into my purse.

Jingling started, and the blood bag hit the ground.

I watched as red liquid squirted onto my cream-colored pants, ruining my chances of making it to the brunch—and of being an Establishment member.

Then I looked up.

Chandra's eyes had rolled back in her head, and her left arm was raised, both signs that a spirit was in the process of inhabiting her.

"Nope. This isn't happening today." I tried to pull her arm down. Chandra might've been a fake, but she was no flake, to use the term in the proper idiomatic sense. If she was pulling the vibrating act, then she knew something—something that most likely had to do with me. And whatever it was, I wasn't ready for it.

Ever.

The vibrating stopped, and her eyeballs returned to their places.

I held up my hand. "Whoever is talking to you, I don't want to know."

"But a young man is in distress." She dug her nails into my arm. "You have to help him."

"If he's dead," I said, pulling her paddles from my flesh one by one, "then it's too late to help him. And no offense to your spirit clients, but at Private Chicks Inc., we only work with the living."

"The human thing to do is hear him out." She began to pace in her white platform boots—the second pair to walk all over me that morning. "But I can't quite understand him. It's like he's drunk."

"Well, if I were dead and calories were no longer a concern, I'd be drunk too." I pressed my back against the building. "Who is this guy, anyway?"

"He won't tell me." She flailed her arms. "He keeps going on about drinking and sex."

I eyed a guy who was two-fisting foot-long drinks and escorting feather boaed–women on either arm. "That doesn't exactly narrow the playing field in these parts."

Chandra gave a ghastly gasp and put her hands to her moon-pie face. "He's not just talking about booze. He's saying something about someone drinking his blood."

This time *my* eyes rolled back in my head. It was obvious Chandra had seen the police news conference the night before and was using it to push her services. Doing my best to sound serious, I said, "Oh. If this is about a bloodsucker, ask the guy if it's my brother."

She blinked. "How did you know? He mentioned Anthony."

My head snapped back. I'd never uttered my brother's name to anyone besides Veronica. Some things—like Anthony—were best kept in the family. "In what context?"

"He said he'll be in danger when he comes here." She stopped pacing. "And he's not the only one."

I knew she was probably guessing my brother would visit me at some point, but I decided to play along—just in case. "What kind of danger are we talking?"

She pressed a palm to her cheek. "The same thing that happened to this poor young man."

"Which is?"

Her eyes were as round as full moons. "He'll be strung up like an animal and have his blood drained."

Maybe it was because she was talking about my brother, or maybe it was because I'd been in this situation with Chandra before, but I believed her.

And, as if to back up the blood-draining business, the blood promptly drained from my face.

3

"You ou went home and went to bed?" Veronica gaped at me from her seat at the two-top table in our office kitchenette. "At ten thirty yesterday morning?"

"Why else would I be here at eight a.m. on a Monday?" I hoisted myself onto the counter and pulled a beignet from a Café du Monde bag.

Her gaze didn't waver from my face despite the doughy distraction. "But why would you do that?"

"Were you not listening to my Sunday saga?" I set the pastry on the bag, so I could tick off the awful events of the previous day on my powdered sugar–encrusted fingers. "First my mom announced that she's sticking me with her slacker son, then those high-and-mighty hippies hijacked the street, and after that Chandra shook me up with her psychic shtick. So, I missed brunch with Bradley, and he didn't even try to seem disappointed."

Veronica's forehead wrinkled. "I still don't see why you didn't go to the restaurant."

"To do what?" I picked up my pastry and pouted. "Wave goodbye?"

She stood and snatched the beignet from my hand. "To inform

Mr. Bradley Hartmann that you'd be taking him to the airport, so you could discuss your relationship during the drive."

My mouth twisted to one side. I hadn't thought of that.

"Wait a minute." She shook the beignet at me, and I lamented the loss of the powdered sugar that fell from it. "Did you avoid The Court of Two Sisters because Anne Rice set one of her books there?"

"Do you really think I'm that paranoid?" I feigned outrage. Because we both knew I would've stood outside the restaurant wielding a cross if I'd so much as suspected that the author of *The Vampire Chronicles* had set a story in there. "The thing is, I was already frustrated when I ran into Chandra, and then she got me so freaked out that I wanted to go home."

Veronica smoothed the back of her brown leather pencil skirt and returned to her seat, taking my beignet with her. "Why would you listen to that medium when you know she's a fraud?"

I pulled another beignet from the bag and bit off half to buy time to think. After chewing it over, I replied, "Sometimes Chandra knows things that make me wonder if she does have a sixth sense."

"Because she pays attention and uses the details she picks up to draw you in?" Not only did her tone leave no room for disagreement, it practically called me a dummy. "But if it makes you feel any better," she said, picking at my pastry, "I watched the news last night and this morning, and there were no reports of vampire attacks."

When she put it that way, it didn't make me feel better. And it definitely confirmed that I was a dummy for sleeping surrounded by garlic. "I guess Chandra's spiel about that spirit does sound pretty silly."

"You think?" Her stare was so pointed it could've drawn blood. "Now let's forget about her and focus on Bradley. What are you going to do about the brunch incident?"

"He called last night while I was asleep." I brushed powdered sugar from my red V-neck sweater and leaned my head against the cabinet. "But I think I'll wait until he gets back to talk to him about it."

Veronica looked like she'd seen a vampire. "Please don't wait, for both our sakes."

"How do you factor into this?"

"Whenever you let things fester, it doesn't turn out well for anyone." Her pitch was low and steady, as though treading through a minefield. "And as your friend, neighbor, and boss, I bear the brunt of it."

I shoved the other half of the beignet into my mouth. Clearly, I was the one who bore the brunt of it, as this conversation attested.

"Now, I have some business developments to discuss with you." She reached across the table for her laptop. "Do you want to talk here or in my office?"

The business bombshell shocked me out of my pastry pity party. Private Chicks Inc. wasn't making either one of us rich—or even comfortable—but I'd been under the impression that our finances had been steadily improving. And with my brother on the way, the last thing I needed was a pay cut. "Can we go to the couches? I want to lie down."

She gave a sly smile as she walked past me. "Change is good, Franki."

"Like Anthony-moving-in-with-me good?" I slid from the counter with my bag of a dozen beignets and followed her into the hallway. "Or Bradley-leaving-for-two-weeks good? Because, frankly, I'm not sure how much more good change I can take."

"I've hired a new PI."

The second she said it, Glenda came to mind—in a Sherlock Holmes hat and stripper shoes. "Before you say anything else, remember that I'm fragile right now."

Veronica stepped into our waiting room and took a seat on one of the two opposing couches. "It's not Glenda."

Overcome, I collapsed onto the opposite couch and tossed my beignet bag onto the coffee table.

"But she was a huge help during Carnie's investigation." She opened her laptop. "If we ever take another case involving a strip club or any other area of her expertise, I'll hire her to consult again."

I stretched out on my back. Glenda's only other area of expertise was men, which left the consulting door wide open, especially on spousal infidelity cases. "Let's get this over with." I clasped my hands across my belly like a corpse. "Who is this new PI?"

Her lips spread into a satisfied smile. "David Savoie."

"But he's in college." I propped myself on my elbows. "He's not quitting school, is he?"

Veronica held up a hand to silence me. "He'll continue to work part-time, like he has as our IT consultant. And since I could've hired him full-time, we also have the funds to bring on an occasional consultant, as needed."

Glenda got into my head again, and this time she was shaking her spyglass-shaped pasties. I promptly shook her out—right onto her partially tweed-covered tush. "But David's a computer science major. Why would he want to do PI work?"

"His experience at Private Chicks has convinced him that he'd rather use his computer skills to fight crime than sit at a desk programming all day," she replied, her fingers clicking her computer keys.

I lay down again. The news of positive change was both unfamiliar and unsettling. "Well, I'm happy it's David. Although I am going to miss having him help me with research."

"You won't have to because I've already hired his replacement." Her eyes sparkled. "Standish Standifer."

Maybe it was the surprise or the repetition of "stand" in that name, but I stood straight up. "You mean, the vassal?"

She did a combination arm-cross and head-tilt. "We're not going to call him by a fraternity pledge nickname. He's our employee, and we will show him the respect he deserves."

"Which is why I'm sticking with 'the vassal.'"

"I'd stick with the medieval servant too," Chandra said. "They work so much harder than regular help."

Veronica started, and I stumbled and fell backwards onto the couch.

Chandra was standing at the reception desk in a shiny silver-skirted suit that looked like something an A-list astronaut might wear in outer space. And I didn't know what was more disconcerting—her loony lunar look or the fact that the lobby bell hadn't buzzed when she'd entered.

"Hi, Chandra." Veronica rose to her feet. "How can we help you?"

She pulled a big silver Chanel bag from her shoulder. "I came to talk to Franki."

Veronica gave me an I'll-get-rid-of-her glance. "We're in the middle of a business meeting. Can this wait?"

She shook her oversized head, but her oversized hair didn't move. "This is business too. I need to hire her for a case."

Visions of vampire bats flapped in my head. "You do?"

She nodded—still no movement from her hair. "I wanted to talk to you about this yesterday, but I couldn't in front of Lou. That's why I sent him inside the boutique to look at the blood clot spread."

Veronica's mouth opened, but no words came out.

"Then that spirit butted in." Chandra rolled her eyes at the heavens. "Talk about bad timing."

Relieved the spirit wasn't the basis for the case, I returned to my reclining position. "Give the guy a break. He'd just had his blood drained."

Veronica shot me a smirk and returned to her seat. "Why don't you come tell us about this case, Chandra?"

"Glad to." She emerged from behind the desk in platform boots that sparkled like stardust and high-stepped as though she were on a spacewalk. She settled in next to Veronica and placed her bag on her lap. "It's about my Lou's cooking class."

I turned toward her. "He's the family chef?"

Her whole body stiffened, like her hair. "I cook for my husband. But he's an adventurous eater, and there are some things I won't allow in my kitchen."

That was a surprising statement coming from someone who'd been drinking from a blood bag. "Like what? Organ meats?"

"Bugs," she replied, bug-eyed.

Creepy-crawlies slithered beneath my skin. "What kind of culinary school is this?"

"It's Bayou Cuisine in the French Quarter," she replied. "They're offering a course in waste cooking."

"*Waste* cooking?" The creepy-crawlies squirmed into my stomach. "Isn't that an oxymoron?"

Veronica clicked her keyboard. "According to this website, it's a movement aimed at protesting food waste. Followers dumpster dive for ingredients."

Chandra shivered, and her solar system earrings started to rotate. "Including the bugs."

"It's a noble cause, but it sounds unhealthy." I reached for my beignet bag.

"The meals featured on this site might change your mind." Veronica scrutinized her screen. "They're balanced and gourmet quality."

"Another oxymoron. Garbage can't be gourmet." I sat up and placed the cushion behind my back. "So what's this case about? Solving the mystery of why Lou would take the class?"

Chandra's lids lowered. She didn't appreciate potshots at her Lou. "It's because he's socially conscious." She paused. "And thrifty." Her grip on her bag tightened, and her chin rose. "What I want you to find out is who's undermining him."

Veronica looked up from her laptop. "I'm not following you."

She sighed as though irritated we couldn't read her mind. "The students put their personal touches on a recipe selected by the head chef, and at the end of each class he picks the best one. The student with the most wins gets to be on the school's Mardi Gras float next year." Her nostrils flared as her upper lip curled. "But someone is making sure it's not Lou."

"How do you know?" I asked. "I mean, maybe he's not the best cook in the class."

Her upturned nose turned up. "Lou knows his food. And he says one of his classmates is slipping bad ingredients into his dishes."

"Are you sure that's what's happening?" I pressed. "Because garbage, by definition, is bad."

Chandra's eyes turned murderous, and it struck me that she was the spitting image of Chucky's bride.

"My Lou doesn't lie," she growled.

"All right, I believe you," I said—but only because I was afraid she'd pull a blaster pistol or sonic screwdriver from her bag. "But this isn't the kind of case we usually take."

"Franki's right." Veronica closed her laptop. "We normally investigate more serious crimes."

"Sabotaging my husband *is* a serious crime." Her honeyed voice had turned hard. "Whatever this one's paying you," she head-jerked at Veronica, "I'll double it."

The irritation on my best friend's face captured my feelings exactly—dealing with Chandra was no walk on the moon. But it was hard to turn down twice my pay. "Let me think about it."

"Um, Franki?" Veronica stared at me like *I* was the space cadet.

"Well I *am* working for two now," I justified, referring to Anthony. "But what's Lou going to think if I show up in his class?"

Chandra's eyes shined like stars. "I'll tell him you called and asked about his class because your Bradley is an adventurous eater."

It was plausible, and under the circumstances I wouldn't have minded serving Bradley a waste sandwich, to put it politely. "Okay, but I doubt the school would let me enroll since the class has already started."

"Nonsense. I called them, and they're still taking students."

I pictured myself pulling the lid off a pot of turnip greens and tarantulas. "You know what? If this were any other kind of class, I'd be happy to help you. But I can't do entomology eats."

"My Lou's going to be on that float come February." Her tone was guttural, and her teeth were gritted. "I'll triple your salary."

"On the other hand," I said, sitting forward, "I *did* grow up in Houston, so I'm fairly comfortable around the cockroach."

"Perfect." She pulled a checkbook from her bag. "Because tomorrow's recipe is Creole Cockroaches."

Houston, we have a problem.

The lobby bell rang as the door burst open. David blew in with the vassal in tow.

"David!" Veronica admonished.

His long, lanky body skidded to a stop, and the vassal, who was shorter and nearsighted, face-planted into his proton pack backpack.

Veronica shifted to face David. "Now that you're a PI, you need to enter the office like a professional. We're with a client."

At the sight of Chandra's space suit, his brow rocketed up his forehead. But the vassal, who sported a Stormtrooper shirt and an R2D2 lunch box, smiled as though he'd found a kindred spirit.

"Oh, uh, sorry." David hung his head and looked at Veronica from beneath his lashes. "We're freaked out."

The vassal didn't look freaked out. He just nodded, and his jaw went slack, but then that was his signature stare.

His open mouth reminded me that it was time for a second beignet. I snatched the bag from Veronica's hand. "What's going on?"

"A Tulane alum we know is missing." David slid his backpack off his shoulder and let it drop with a thud. "It's all over Facebook. And the news."

"Was he in your fraternity?" Veronica asked.

The vassal pushed up Coke-bottle glasses. "No, a rival frat."

I pulled out a pastry. "How do you two know him?"

"He still parties at his frat house, even though he's, like, forty." David pushed his brown bangs to the side. "And he pranked our frat before the semester started."

The boys fell silent.

"Well?" I looked from David to the vassal. "Is one of you going to tell us what this guy did?"

The vassal gripped his backpack straps. "He nailed a gamma and a sigma on either end of our fraternity house sign."

Something told me the result would be classic. "What's the name of your frat again?"

David cleared his throat. "Uh, Epsilon Epsilon Kappa."

Chandra giggled. "From EEK to GEEKS." She pulled a pen from her purse. "I've got to write that down."

David and the vassal exchanged an embarrassed look.

"Sorry, guys, but your frat left itself wide open for that one." I bit into the beignet. "Which frat is the missing alum in?"

The vassal's slack jaw lifted into a smile. "Delta Upsilon Delta."

Chandra snickered as she wrote in her checkbook. "The DUDs."

"DUDs is right." David flipped his bangs. "They've had more scandals than any fraternity in the school's history. And they were just suspended."

Any frat with a forty-year-old member should've been suspended. Not only was it morally unconscionable, it was massively uncool. "What for?"

David shrugged. "No one knows, and the university hasn't released an official statement."

"That's odd." Veronica tapped a finger on her cheek. "I wonder if this alum's disappearance is related to whatever the frat was up to."

"I dunno," he replied. "He was last seen on a vampire tour."

Chandra's charm bracelet jingled, and I jumped.

"If that's a vampire contacting you," I said, tossing my beignet on the table, "you tell him you're in a meeting."

She bolted up in her boots. "I hate to hire you and run." She handed a check to Veronica. "But the undead give me the heebie-jeebies."

This from the psychic who talked to spirits.

We all watched Chandra spacewalk to the door, where she turned and shot me a laser look.

"The cooking class starts at six p.m. on Tuesday." She pointed a paddle-shaped nail at me. "And remember, you're there to investigate a crime, so don't get any big ideas about being in that gumbo pot."

I blinked. "What gumbo pot?"

"I'm paying triple for this?" she huffed. "It's the school float. What else?"

Considering the garbage theme, the choice of float was a low blow to my beloved gumbo, not to mention me. "Don't worry. The only thing I've got big ideas about is my fee."

Her lips puckered, and she left.

I leapt off the couch. "Lock the door, David."

Veronica stopped him with a stare and then turned to me. "What's the matter with you? You know we're open for business."

"Exactly." I grabbed my bag and my half-eaten beignet. "We always get the crazy-creepy cases, and my gut's been telling me one's on its way ever since I saw that ominous vampiress."

"Say what?" David said, and the vassal's slack jaw slackened even more.

Veronica did a head roll and put a hand on her hip. "The second I heard the words 'vampire tour,' I knew you'd start. Now I hate to play the boss card, but we all have work to do."

David and the vassal scurried to their desks.

She picked up her laptop. "I could use your eyes on a workers' compensation case—if you can reign in your sanguivoriphobia."

"My what?"

"Fear of blood eaters." She held up her hands and curled her fingers like Bela Lugosi going in for the bite. "As in *vampires*."

"Don't confuse me with Chandra," I sassed as Veronica turned and headed up the hallway. "She's the one with the ridiculous phobias."

Before following her to her office I looked back over my shoulder, and I clutched my cross necklace the entire way.

AFTERNOON RAIN BEAT a soothing rhythm on the roof of Private Chicks. My eyelids succumbed to the sound, closing and opening like automatic garage doors gone awry, and I dropped my head to my desk. It was amazing how tired twenty hours of sleep and a belly full of beignets made you.

Through the haze of my post-lunch stupor, I heard heavy breathing coming from the doorway. For a second, I thought it was a vampire, but my mind reminded me that was ridiculous. The more likely culprit was the vassal, whose slack-jawed style made him a committed mouth breather.

With my forehead on my forearm, I asked, "What is it, Va—" That didn't sound right. "I mean, Sta—" That didn't sound right either. "Just, what is it?"

The breathing stopped.

"Josh Santo is here to see you."

My head popped up. "Who?"

His gaze darted up the hallway. "A...man?"

The name was unfamiliar, and, judging from the way the vassal had said "man," I would've preferred to keep it that way. "Is Veronica here?"

"Yes."

This internship was off to a stellar start. "Yes, what?"

He looked to one side. "Ma'am."

"Thanks for that." The sarcasm rolled off my tongue as I rolled backwards in my chair. "What I meant was, where is she?"

"With Mr. Santo." His eyes enlarged behind his lenses. "In the conference room."

A clap of thunder shook the three-story building, and the news that Veronica was in the conference room shook me. It was a large space across the hall from our third-floor office, and we reserved it for private client meetings—the kind where the crime was either extremely delicate or especially dreadful.

The mouth breathing resumed.

"That'll be all, Vassal," I said as I rose to my feet, because that time the nickname seemed appropriate.

He turned and ran, which did nothing for my nerves.

I headed up the hallway as though I were going to my own blood-letting. And as I crossed the lobby, David and the vassal eyeballed me from their desks like I had a date with Darth Vader. To stop their stares, I lanced them with a laser-beam look and exited the main office.

I grasped the conference room door handle, and lightning flashed, and the rain intensified.

The weather had to be some kind of cosmic joke.

Steeling myself for whatever was to come, I opened the door. When I caught sight of the twenty-something male at the head of the table, I understood why the vassal had stumbled on the word "man." With his thick brown hair and facial fur, Josh Santo looked part human and part werewolf. And his torn plaid shirt didn't help.

Veronica smiled, but it was strained. "Josh Santo, this is Franki Amato."

"Excuse my appearance." He stood and extended a veiny hand. "I've been at the police station since eight p.m. yesterday."

Before going in for the shake, I checked his fingertips for claws. Then I took his hand. It was cold and damp, and I wondered whether it was from the rain or from guilt. Not everyone who sought our services was innocent. "Did the police do that to your shirt?"

Josh grimaced, embarrassed. "These are my work clothes." He returned to his seat. "I was sanding a fireplace in my bedroom when the police showed up."

"Mr. Santo was questioned in a homicide that took place on Saturday night," Veronica said as I sat across from her. "Apparently, Wesley Sullivan is in charge of the investigation."

My pulse picked up, probably because my blood was trying to make a break for it. That was the same night Sullivan had given the news conference, and I had a sick feeling the case was related. "Why are you a suspect?"

Josh looked at the table and laughed. "You're not going to believe this."

I didn't reply. By then, I was willing to believe anything.

His gaze sought mine, and his ice blue eyes seemed to glow from their dark-circled sockets. "It's because the guy's blood was drained."

My six beignets almost came up, and Veronica seemed shocked. Chandra's psychic surmises didn't seem so suspect anymore.

"Why"—I stopped to catch my breath—"why would the police connect a crime like that with you?"

He pressed his knuckle to his lips. "This is where it gets funny."

Neither Veronica nor I came close to cracking a smile.

"A few months ago," he said, clasping his hands on the table, "I bought the Compte de Saint Germain's old house at the corner of Royal and Ursuline. And now the police think I'm trying to be him."

I had no idea who this count was or why anyone would try to emulate him, but I scooted my chair away from Josh nevertheless. "Why? Who is this guy?"

He grinned, revealing a mouthful of wine-stained Osmond teeth. "An eighteenth-century vampire."

His words hit me like a stake through the heart.

4

"Is there any chance you said eighteenth-century *umpire*?" I knew he hadn't, but I'd been dreading this moment for three days, and now that it had happened I was going to do my darnedest to undo it. "Or maybe *empire*?"

Josh glanced from me to Veronica, who was still speechless. "I get that this sounds incredible, but Jacques de Saint Germain was definitely a vampire."

I sunk low in my seat. Since moving to New Orleans, my creepiest cases had involved freaky figures with French names—like legendary voodoo queen Marie Laveau and the voodoo loa of the dead, Baron Samedi. "I take it de Saint Germain was from France?"

"Well, the count was vague about where he was from and how he got his money, and the history books aren't much help." He leaned back in his chair. "What we know for sure is that he worked in London as an opera composer in 1745, and after being accused of espionage he showed up in France in the court of King Louis XV. Toward the end of his life, though, he started telling people he was the son of Francis Racoczi II, a Transylvanian prince."

And I'd been worried he was French.

Veronica's wide-eyed surprise had been replaced with narrow-eyed skepticism. "Why do people think he was a vampire?"

Incredulous, I looked at her like she'd lost it. "Does Transylvania mean nothing to you?"

Her narrow-eyed skepticism slid into slit-eyed sarcasm.

"All right, so vampirism isn't an ethnicity." I straightened in my seat. "But it *is* suspicious that this guy initially covered up being from Transylvania. And let's not forget that he was a count, like Dracula."

Veronica swallowed a sigh. "Please continue, Mr. Santo."

"Call me Josh." He flashed a too-toothy grin.

The second he said it, I realized that "Josh" was similar to "Jacques" and that "Santo" was Italian for "Saint." I tried to scan his neck for bite scars, but his collar was suspiciously buttoned.

"Josh it is," Veronica obliged.

He took a deep breath. "So, people think de Saint Germain was a vampire for a lot of reasons. For one thing, he had amazing talents. Famous people like Marie Antoinette, Voltaire, and Casanova were blown away by his skills. I mean, the guy spoke twelve languages, played the violin like a virtuoso, and painted like a master. And supposedly, he could turn metal into gold."

"So he was a prodigy," I said, holding out hope the man was merely a misunderstood mortal. "That happens."

His furry brows furrowed. "Yeah, but he never seemed to age past forty. And when people asked him how he stayed so young looking, he told them he knew the secret to eternal life."

I shrugged. "Maybe he had good genes."

Josh laughed like I had to be joking. "Good genes wouldn't explain how he managed to show up in New Orleans in 1903 when he was born in 1690."

That little detail was disturbing, but I was determined to veto the man's vampirism. "Whoever showed up in NOLA was an imposter, like that woman who claimed to be Anastasia."

He flashed an I-wouldn't-be-so-sure smile. "The locals were convinced it was the count because he had a lot of habits consistent with vampire legend. Like, he loved to go to the city's best restaurants, but no one ever saw him eat. He just drank red wine."

Refusing to eat at restaurants was a red flag, and not pairing wine with cheese was all but hard evidence he was inhuman.

Veronica chewed her cheek, unconvinced. "What happened when he came to New Orleans?"

"This is where it gets good." Josh's eyes were eerily aglow. "He got a reputation around town as a ladies' man. Then one night passersby heard a scream and saw a woman jump from his second-floor balcony. She died at the hospital, but she managed to tell police that she'd been having a drink with the count when he suddenly rushed across his living room with super-human speed and tried to rip open her jugular vein with his teeth."

My hand went to my all-too-exposed neck. That did it for me— the dude was undead.

"Was the count arrested?" Veronica asked.

Josh gave a slow shake of his head. "By the time the police showed up at his place, he was long gone. But they reported that the house reeked of death, and there were bloodstains on the floor that were too old to be from the woman." He pressed his palms on the table. "Not only that, there was no furniture or food, only wine bottles filled with human blood."

I swallowed hard, but the spit lodged in my throat like a lump.

After a sickening silence, Josh began to cough.

Veronica touched his back. "Could I get you some water or a soda?"

"I saw a restaurant downstairs." His voice was husky. "Any chance I could get a Bloody Mary?"

My arm hair stood at attention. Given the circumstances, it was a peculiar choice of beverage.

"Certainly." She rose from her seat. "I'll run down to Nizza."

"So will I." I flew to my feet. I wanted to get out of that room—and into a bar.

Veronica opened the door, and David and the vassal fell backwards. They lay frozen with their hands pressed to the floor. But it wasn't a ruthless vampire they feared—rather a wrathful Veronica.

"I don't know what's gotten into all of you," she whisper-shouted after closing the door behind us, "but I'm over it." She turned to me. "You need to go back in there. And you two"—she glowered at David and the vassal—"get up and go back to your desks this instant."

"Stay where you are." I pointed at the petrified pair. "I'm not going in there by myself, especially not in this red V-neck sweater. The name alone is an open invitation for a vampire bite."

Veronica balled her fists. "Franki, this nonsense has gone too far. Josh is a harmless young man who needs our help."

"And who's been accused of imitating a vicious vampire," I said, balling my fists right back. "So on the off chance he gets the urge to tear open my throat with his teeth, I'm taking the guys with me."

David's jaw went slack to match the vassal's.

"Fine," she huffed. "But don't keep him waiting any longer. We don't want to lose his business." She flipped her hair and headed down the stairs.

I grasped the door handle and turned to David and the vassal. "You two can stop holding down the floor now."

They pulled themselves to their feet and followed me into the conference room. "Josh, these are my associates—"

"We met in the lobby." His tone was friendly, as though we were there to hang out.

"Super." Skipping the introductions spared me from saying "Standish." I took Veronica's seat and tapped a key on her laptop to bring it back to life. "They're joining us for, uh, training purposes."

David and the vassal slid as stiff as cadavers into their seats—at the far end of the table.

"You mentioned that the police accused you of imitating Jacques de Saint Germain." I stressed "Jacques" and "Saint" and paused to let that sink in. "What did you do to get on their radar?"

"It has to do with my research," he replied. "I'm writing a book about the count."

Sensing a safe subject, the vassal's chest swelled. "Biography or paranormal fiction?"

Josh revealed impressive incisors. "Comedy."

The vassal seemed paralyzed, and David went pale.

Stifling a shiver, I typed *thinks bloodsuckers are funny*. "How does one research a vampire, exactly?"

"I walk the streets around my house at night, retracing the count's steps." He paused. "I'm not trying to *be* him. I just want to get a feel for what it was like to walk the Quarter hunting a victim"—his eyes widened—"for my book."

I scooted my chair back like I needed more room for my legs. And I did. In case I had to run from the room. "That reminds me, property in the Quarter is pretty pricey. Mind if I ask how you got the money to buy it?"

"Some savings, stock investments." He crossed his ankle over his knee. "You know."

No, I definitely didn't. There were no stocks or savings in my portfolio, unless you counted my Leaning Tower of Pisa piggy bank, and that was never going to tip over at the rate I was filling it. "Not a lot of people your age have that kind of money. What do you do for a living?"

"Programming, until the company I founded was bought out for fifty million. Now I'm retired."

Air escaped from the vassal's open mouth, and his chest began to deflate. And David let out a high-pitched whine, probably pained by his decision to trade programming for PI work.

Normally, I would've smiled, but I was a little shaken by that sum myself. "Are you from New Orleans?"

"Nope." Josh pulled a phone from his pants pocket and studied the screen.

"O-kay." I typed *vague about where he's from—like the count*. "Going back to your research, did you do anything unusual? I ask because plenty of people walk the French Quarter at night, so that wouldn't be suspicious from a police perspective."

He pocketed the phone and folded his arms. "Apparently, the

problem is that I dress like the count when I go out. In a top hat, tails, and a cane."

The vassal snorted, proving his nose could work, and David turned a laugh into a cough, as though Josh was the nerd, not them. And I couldn't argue with that. In comparison to the could-be count's clothes, their sci-fi wear seemed like haute couture.

But no matter what kind of clothes the kid wore, his story wasn't adding up to a trip to the police station. "I don't see how wearing an eccentric outfit in the Quarter, of all places, would qualify you as a murder suspect."

"Neither do I." He looked thoughtful as he smoothed his mustache. "But the cops kept asking about my cape."

The room fell so silent that we could've heard a top hat pin drop.

My mind replayed the video of the caped figure from the news conference, and I typed *possible suspect in blood bank business.* "Why do you think they focused on your cape? Was the murderer wearing one?"

"They didn't say because they were trying to keep details of the murder under wraps." He looked at me from beneath long lashes and grinned. "Get it? Under *wraps*?"

The vassal gave a laugh that sounded like a cross between a donkey bray and a clown horn, and Josh lit up, as though his career as a comedy vampire writer was clinched. When he saw that I wasn't laughing, however, his smile faded.

"Anyway," he said, adjusting his collar, "I told the detective that I wore a cape for book research, and he seemed to believe me. But when I mentioned where I'd bought it everything changed."

I looked into his icy blue eyes. "Where *did* you buy it?"

"Boutique du Vampyre," he replied, like it was Macy's or Sears.

I casually pulled my V-neck closed, and with my free hand I typed *he's a cape-wearing vampire wannabe.* "Do you shop there often?"

"No, it was just the obvious place to get a cape."

Obvious if you're into vampires. "What did Detective Sullivan say to that?"

Josh stared into the distance and tugged at his beard. "He asked me if I'd tried to break in to the blood bank on Canal."

I'd suspected as much, but what I didn't expect was his failure to deny the crime. "And did you?"

He winced like he'd been bitten. "I never went anywhere near the blood bank." He shot me a wounded look. "That hurt my feelings, by the way."

Not wanting to provoke the ire of a would-be vampire, I opted to change the subject. "Let's move on to the murder. You mentioned that the police are trying to keep the details on the down low, but were you able to glean any specifics?"

"A couple of things, yeah." He rubbed his mouth. "A patrol car stopped me in the Quarter at around eleven last night. When I asked what I'd done, they said they wanted to talk to me about a murder that had happened the night before."

My blood chilled at the news that someone had been killed on Saturday night, because it begged an awful question—actually, two. *After unsuccessfully trying to get a fix from the blood bank, had the caped figure preyed on a live victim? And, was the caped figure sitting at the table with me, trying to throw me off his scent?*

I swallowed, but the spit was still stuck. "Where'd they find the body?"

"At Saint Cecilia Cemetery." His tone had turned deathly quiet. "And from what I could tell, the crime scene was gruesome. The killer took all the blood from the guy's body."

The door opened, and we jumped. But it was just Veronica with the Bloody Mary.

At the sight of my best friend, I got a surge of courage, and I decided to go in for the kill. "Did you have anything to do with the murder?"

"Gah! So distrustful." He flailed an arm in my direction. "I'm not a blood-sucking killer, and if I was I wouldn't drink a *guy's* blood. That's just wrong."

Instinctively, I held out my hands. "I'm sorry, but I had to ask."

And then I typed *he's a homophobic cape-wearing vampire wannabe.* "Did you get the name of the victim?"

His eyes bore into mine as he stroked his beard. "Gregg Charalambous."

"Whoa." David's frame went as slack as the vassal's jaw. "That's the dude from DUD."

Josh's lip curled at David like he was the weird one.

"The victim was a member of David and Standish's rival fraternity," Veronica explained. "Delta Upsilon Delta."

"And he was last seen walking the Quarter." I met Josh's gaze—and held it. "During a vampire tour."

"Rest easy in The Big Easy." My tone was decidedly uneasy as I stood on the damp sidewalk of Rampart Street, reading the Saint Cecilia sign.

And it wasn't only because the cemetery had a slogan.

From what I could see, rest didn't come at all easy at Saint Cecilia. Smack in the center of the graveyard was a giant skeleton sculpture crouched atop a crypt that beckoned with a bony hand. And if that wasn't enough to scare the dead, the mausoleum wall that ran along the front of the cemetery was so deteriorated that rotting coffins—and their residents—were being evicted from final resting places.

"This place must be a real scream on Halloween," I said under my breath. Then I zipped my jacket and headed for the entrance.

Cecilia was the patron saint of musicians and a fitting choice for a cemetery in Tremé, the historic African-American neighborhood credited with the invention of jazz. And as I pushed open the main gate, it groaned a quasi-musical tune. But it didn't sound like any jazz I'd heard. It was more like a slasher soundtrack.

"Nothing foreboding about that," I lied and entered the maze of graves.

The rain had stopped, but dark clouds hovered over the cemetery. And the grounds were dead silent, making me wonder whether whatever had happened to the victim had happened to the responding officers too. Picking up my pace, I skirted the skeleton and spotted crime scene tape wrapped around a columned, walk-in crypt and two statues, one of a winged woman and the other of a male with winged sandals, on either side of a Greek-key-adorned door.

Although I was sure the body had already been taken to the morgue, I still needed to get a look inside the crypt. I glanced over my shoulder for cops, and crooks or creeps, and pulled my phone from my pocket. After I'd snapped a few photos of the exterior, I switched my phone to my left hand and rummaged in my jacket pocket for a hair tie and gloves.

"What took you so long?"

The flat, disembodied voice sent my cell and my shriek high into the heavens.

But it wasn't a slasher.

It was Sullivan.

I yanked down my jacket to stop myself from yanking him down —to the hallowed ground. "I'm sure you get a real charge out of sneaking up on people in cemeteries."

He stood before me in a fitted black suit and mirrored sunglasses that glinted like steel. "I do when they're about to contaminate my crime scene."

"Look, I've been hired—"

"Save it, Amato," he interrupted. "I know you're working for Santo because I referred you."

His statement was so shocking that I would've flung my phone again if I'd known where it was. And I realized that I'd been so unsettled by the crime, I'd forgotten to ask Josh Santo how he'd gotten my name. "Why would *you* refer *me*?"

"This is a sensitive investigation." He folded his arms against his broad chest. "Mass hysteria is an understatement for what'll happen if the details get out about what went on in that crypt."

His comment did nothing to quell my concerns about the case. For the sake of my skin—and bones—I decided to play nice. "Was it that bad?"

"The victim was strung up by his heels, and his jugular was slit."

My stomach turned upside down like I'd been strung up by my heels. And I thought of that supposed spirit's words to Chandra about Anthony, not to mention the jugular-obscuring scarf I'd left lying on my dresser. "Is it true that his blood was drained?"

He nodded. "Down to the last drop."

Coffee came to mind—and I resolved to switch to black tea.

The detective's phone rang, and he pulled it from his inner suit pocket. "This is Sullivan."

While he listened to the caller, I started searching for my cell. I didn't see it around the crypt, so I checked a neighboring tomb. A tree was growing from the top, and it had been there for so long that its roots had shattered the concrete on one side. I kicked a pile of leaves at the base of the broken wall, and I found something.

Not my phone.

A bone.

A human bone.

The scream took root in my belly and sprouted from my mouth like the tree from the tomb.

A pair of arms wrapped around me—strong and, gratefully, flesh-covered.

"It's all right." Sullivan's tone, like his embrace, was strangely soothing. "That kind of thing happens in these old graveyards."

I stayed still for a moment, suspended in the surreal scene.

Why was Sullivan holding me?

Was this a trick?

A precursor to a takedown?

And, whatever it was, why didn't I detest it?

My phone began to ring, and I jerked from his arms as though I'd been burned by the fires of hell. I turned and resumed the search for my cell so he wouldn't see the heat spreading to my cheeks. It wasn't my reaction to the bone that I was embarrassed about—it was my reaction to him.

"Bradley Hartmann." Sullivan sounded like he was reading the name.

I spun around and discovered that he *was* reading it—from my phone display.

He shot me a wicked smile and put the device to his ear. "Wes Sullivan here, Brad old boy. I didn't think we'd get a chance to chat again after I arrested you for sucker-punching me in that strip club. You been staying out of trouble?"

Bradley had seen Sullivan slip the infamous five-dollar bill into my stripper thong, and his punch was proof that he didn't share my nonna's appreciation for the tip. So it went without saying that he would appreciate hearing his arresting officer answer my phone even less. Before the dastardly detective could do anymore damage, I wrested the device from his grip.

"H-Hey, Bradley," I said, surprisingly—and suspiciously—breathless. "We were, uh, investigating a homicide."

"You didn't tell me you were working another murder case." His tone was a lot like Sullivan's had been when he'd caught me at the crypt.

"I was only contracted for the case a couple of hours ago."

"That must be why you're out of breath," he said as dry as that old bone I'd uncovered.

"What? I don't understand."

"Because you ran right to the scene." The sarcasm that dripped from his voice seemed to seep through the receiver.

My body went as stiff as one of the cemetery statues while I processed his implication. *Did he think I'd been kissing Wesley Sullivan when he called?* "Wait a minute—"

"I already waited—make that *wasted*—a minute listening to that damn detective." He spoke like he was talking through his teeth. "Now I'm being called back to my meeting."

Classic Bradley—all work all the time.

"Then I'll let you go," I huffed. And puffed. "I wouldn't want you to miss a single second of a meeting on my behalf." I practically punched *End*, trying not to note the symbolism of the gesture, and shoved the phone into my pocket.

Wanting to look anywhere but at the detective, I stared into the distance, and a withered rose on a tomb caught my eye. *Was it a sign of the state of my relationship with Bradley?*

Dying?

Or...dead?

"Trouble in paradise?" Sullivan asked.

That was an ironic choice of words given our surroundings, and I was in no mood for irony. "You had no right to answer my phone."

He gave a low chuckle, but it might as well have been a mwa-ha-ha. "It sure was fun, though."

"Is that why you referred me to Josh Santo? To have some laughs at my expense?"

"Maybe I like the way you shake things up." He did a shimmy, mimicking my striptease.

My fingers formed fists. "I stripped to solve a *strip club murder*. I hardly think that applies in this case."

"From what I've read, funeral strippers are pretty popular in China and Taiwan." He lowered his lenses and leered. "The people of New Orleans would take to them too, if you were taking it off."

My huffing and puffing turned to spitting and sputtering.

But Sullivan just grinned.

"Hidey-ho," a burly male bellowed as he pushed a wheelbarrow full of chains to the crypt. Except for his purple tank top and beige cargo shorts, he looked like a thirty-something Santa. And he was every bit as jolly.

"Hey, Phil, I've gotta run." Sullivan jerked his thumb in my direction. "But do me a favor and keep this one from crashing the crime scene, would ya?"

"Happy to oblige, Detective." Phil grinned and tugged at his tool belt, revealing a tattoo of a cat in pajamas. "I am the crypt keeper."

I took a step back. A merry crypt keeper was not the cat's pajamas.

Sullivan pulled his keys from his pants pocket. "Hey, since I won't be here when your boyfriend calls back, give him a message for me."

I refused to respond.

"Tell him I said it's time to get his priorities straight." He gave my arm a tap and walked away.

I stood there, stoic. But I was reeling from his remark. *Was the situation with Bradley so obvious that even Sullivan could see it?*

The detective stopped short. "Oh, and Amato?" He turned and pointed at me. "You be careful around that Santo character."

A statement like that was worth breaking my stony silence for. "Why? What do you know about him?"

Sullivan removed his steely sunglasses and slayed me with a steely stare. "He was here at the cemetery the night of the murder."

5

"So you referred me to a homicidal vampire?" I shouted after Sullivan, but he'd already disappeared among the tombs.

Phil tapped me on the shoulder, and I spun on him like a Tasmanian Devil.

"Hoo! Someone's jumpy." He chuckled. "Before you go, I'd like to call your attention to a rare opening at Saint Cecilia." He grinned and gestured game-show-host style to a crumbling crypt with a *For Sale by Owner* sign like it was a prize trip to the Netherlands instead of a one-way ticket to the netherworld.

My upper lip fled to my nostrils. "You can *buy* a *used tomb*?"

"You can rent them too." He tipped the wheelbarrow, and the chain hit the ground with a ghostly rattle.

New Orleans had a lot of unusual customs, but renting graves was beyond bizarre even for The Big Easy. Because, last I'd heard, death was permanent. "Why would anyone do such a thing?"

He shrugged. "They have to rent if the family crypt is already cooking a loved one."

My stomach burned like an incinerator. "Mind clarifying that?"

"These babies are like pizza ovens." He patted the top of a tomb. "They cook bodies for a year and a day minimum per Judeo-Christian mourning rituals. When a new body comes along, we empty the bones into a bin below."

My passion for pizza fizzled. "It's a great opportunity and all, but I'm not here to, uh, shop. I came to see the crime scene."

"You heard the detective. No can do." Phil picked up the end of the chain and dragged it around the side of the crypt.

I followed, checking the area for anything unusual. "Could you at least give me some information about the murder?"

"Since I found the body, I'd say so."

Sullivan seemed to trust Phil, but his sunny disposition made me suspicious, particularly since he'd found the deceased. "When did you find it?"

"Late Sunday night."

I recognized the irony of my next question, but I had to ask. "Do you work the graveyard shift?"

Phil shook with laughter, and I half expected him to *ho ho ho*. "Nice one." He wiped a tear from beneath his glasses. "By the by, that expression came from the Victorian practice of putting a bell called a Bateson's Belfry in the coffins of the deceased to make sure they weren't buried alive. Relatives stayed at the cemetery to listen for the ring. Same with 'saved by the bell' and 'dead ringer.'"

I'd had my fill of Phil and his cheerful chatter. "That's fascinating. But why were you here if you didn't have to work?"

He clamped a padlock on both ends of the chain, securing the crypt. "I popped by after spending the weekend at a Do-It-Yourself taxidermy workshop in Texarkana. I'd forgotten my dissection kit at the office." He rubbed his hands together. "And I was ready to get to stuffing."

Alibi aside, the dissection kit was a cutting reminder that he and I were alone—in a place bodies were buried. From the corner of my eye, I scanned the cemetery for a visitor or an escape route. "So, what prompted you to look inside this crypt?"

He put his arm around the statue of the winged woman. "Nike had been moved. When I straightened her, I noticed the door had been pried open."

"What did you see inside?"

His eyes narrowed. "*Chevals-diable.*"

I assumed it was a Cajun curse word. "That bad, huh?"

"The crypt is crawlin' with 'em."

My head tipped forward. "With bodies?"

He looked at me like I was looney. "With *chevals-diable*. It's French for devil's horses, but around here we call 'em graveyard grasshoppers."

My skin prickled at the lexical lessons—and a possible insect infestation.

"It was no coincidence that they chose this crypt."

I looked at Phil like he was the loon. "The bugs?"

"No, the killer. Because we don't know who did this, I used the colloquial singular 'they' to avoid the gender discrimination inherent in 'he' and 'she'."

Yes, we wouldn't want to discriminate against a murderer.

"What I meant was, a Greek-American man wearing a Greek fraternity shirt in a Greek Revival tomb?" He pursed his lips and shook his head. "That was intentional."

When he put it that way, I had to agree. "How do you know the victim was Greek?"

"Sullivan mentioned his surname, Charalambous. Clearly of Cypriot origin."

To me it just sounded like one of those fancy names they gave to cheap booze. "What was on his shirt?"

"The letters Delta Upsilon Delta, which is apparently the fraternity that reported him missing."

The frat house was my next stop. "Are there other Greek Revival tombs in St. Cecilia?"

"Not many. In choosing a final resting place, locals went for architectural styles that were fashionable for houses and public buildings at the time." He winked and stroked his beard. "You know NOLA. We put the 'fun' in funeral."

Phil wasn't wrong about that, especially considering the jazz funeral phenomenon. But still. "What can you tell me about the body?"

He held up a finger. "You mean, what can I *show* you. Before the police came, I took pictures of Gregg. I do that for all of our departed residents and guests. I find it promotes a sense of family."

I tried to close my mouth but couldn't—until I remembered those devil bugs. "Can I see them?"

He twisted his mustache à la Dick Dastardly. "The detective didn't say anything about pictures, now did he?"

His devious behavior did nothing to quell my concerns, and it didn't help that dusk was descending on the cemetery. But I had to get a look at the crime scene one way or another.

He led me to a caretaker building that wasn't much bigger than the crime scene crypt and opened the door. "Ladies first."

Desperately hoping he'd left that dissection kit at home, I stepped inside the dim room, keeping him in my peripheral vision.

He entered and rummaged through the drawers of his desk, and I studied my surroundings. The office had the musty odor of a mausoleum, but it looked like an armory. Antique weaponry adorned the walls, and there was an anvil and a variety of tools scattered around the floor. Even more unsettling, there was a shelf with books on anatomy, embalming, and zombies.

Phil pulled out a cleaver.

I went rigid.

Was he about to siphon my blood?

And stuff me?

"Might I interest you in a charcuterie board?" He grabbed a salami from the clutter on his desk.

My body went slack, and I sunk onto the anvil.

He whacked off a salami slice. "Not to brag, but I cured the meat myself in a casket buried underground."

My saliva went on strike. Given the cemetery setting and his taxidermy hobby, I didn't dare ask where the meat had come from, not to mention whether the casket he'd cured it in had been occupied. "My parents own a deli, so I'm good."

"Fine profession. If I wasn't already living the dream, I'd be a deli owner. Or a butcher." He chewed the meat with gusto and kissed his fingertips. "Mm. *Buonissimo!*" Then he removed a photo album from the bookshelf and flipped the pages.

I stood, and my stomach seized both because of the oily salami smell and the content of the photographs. For most of the "residents" and "guests" he'd taken two pictures, one in the casket and another after he'd removed them from the tomb. And he'd posed with each one as though they were at a party.

"Here we go." He tapped a Polaroid.

I took the album and sunk back onto the anvil. I'd seen some awful crime scenes before, but this one would haunt me. The victim was kneeling and slumped face forward in a pool of black grasshoppers. "Are they eating his blood?"

He gave a happy *ha*. "Good grief, no. *Chevals-diable* are herbivores. They eat moss and the like. And most of his blood had been drained from the gash on his jugular and the two holes on his wrist."

A jolt went through me, and Josh's Osmond teeth flashed before my eyes. "Holes? Like the blood was sucked out?"

"Or drained. You can't see it from the way he's sitting, but his ankles were bound with a rope, and he'd been hung upside down from a hook."

Chandra's words shook me all over again—*he'll be strung up like an animal and have his blood drained.* "How...how did he get to the ground?"

"My theory? He got himself down, which was quite a feat considering his age." He bent over and turned the page. "I cleared the *chevals-diable* to get this shot."

The camera angle of the second photo made two things clear. The victim was facing the wall when he died, and his right index finger was stained red.

Why?

Because he'd used his own blood to write a message on the wall, just above the floor.

Campari Crimson.

THE FRONT DOOR of Delta Upsilon Delta opened, releasing a waft of dirty laundry, marijuana, and stale pizza that practically knocked me off the porch of the Greek Revival mansion. My eyes stung from the stench, and when my tears cleared, I blinked at the twenty-something bleached blonde who stood before me in a sheer black chiffon robe and pink teddy. "Maybe Baby?"

"Who's askin'?" her helium-pitched voice squeaked.

"Franki Amato. You helped me with a case at Madame Moiselle's, remember?"

Maybe waved her champagne bottle. "I ain't seen Franki in months."

I wished there was a swing or patio furniture around because the case was draining, and it wasn't because of the blood-swilling vampires. "I'm Franki, so you have seen me."

"Okay." She moved to close the door.

I kept it open with the butt of my hand. "What are you doing at a frat house? Dancing?"

"I quit the strippin' business." She straightened, but then swayed on her high-heeled slippers. "I got tired of being objected by men."

If she didn't want to be "objected" by men, she'd picked the wrong outfit—in both senses of the word. "What are you doing now?"

"I'm a mom."

That statement shook me more than the stench. "A mother? Really?"

"Uh-huh. I got twenty sons." She took a swig from her bottle, and rightfully so after that revelation.

"Wait." A light went on in my brain, which was more than I could say for Maybe's. "You're the frat housemother?"

"The pay is great, and I get to lay around all day."

I had no doubt about that, or about the fact that the frat was going to stay suspended. "Listen, I'm investigating a case, and I need to talk to the person who reported Mr. Charalambous missing."

She tried to put a hand to her cheek but missed. "Someone stole our scotch? I'd better call the cops."

"Uh, one of your sons already did." I didn't correct her on the scotch issue because Charalambous did sound similar to Chivas. "Can you ask one of the guys inside who made the call?"

"Wait here. I can't let you inside on account o' I have to protect my boys." She slammed the door, and I closed my eyes and nose to shield myself from the odor onslaught.

A car passed with music blaring, and I turned and surveyed the multi-million-dollar homes glowing in the golden streetlight of St. Charles Avenue. I was no expert in architecture, but even I could spot several styles, Spanish, Italianate, Gothic, which raised two questions. *Was Phil right that the killer had matched the style of the tomb to his victim? And if so, why?*

I leaned against a twenty-five-foot-plus column, and another question popped into my head. *How was it possible that a bunch of college students lived in an estate in the Garden District, while I lived in a rundown fourplex near the university?*

The door opened.

A bored-looking frat boy appeared with a joystick. He wore the standard "frattire," a backwards baseball cap, pink polo shirt with a turned-up collar, belted khaki shorts, and boat shoes. "Yeah?"

"Are you the individual who reported Gregg Charalambous missing?"

"No."

Great. The talkative type. "And your name is?"

His lids lowered. "Craig."

Clearly, I wasn't going to get an invite inside, but from the way it smelled, that was fine. "Can you please tell me who contacted the police about Gregg?"

He turned his head. "Yo, Dom. Door."

A dark-haired male in a New England Patriots T-shirt and jeans strutted over with a bag of Cheetos and a set of chopsticks.

Craig gave Dom a hard stare. "What are you doing?"

He shrugged. "I didn't want to get my hands dirty."

If this guy was a neat freak, he'd picked the wrong kind of organization to associate with.

Craig widened his eyes at his finicky frat brother. "This investigator wants to know why you called the cops about Gregg."

"Oh, uh..." Dom gazed at the manicured lawn rather than at me. "On Saturday night, Craig and I went with him on one of those French Quarter walking tours to get ideas for our Halloween party, and he never made it home."

I pulled a pen and notepad from my bag. "Do you happen to know Gregg's address?"

"On the couch by the stairs." Dom gestured behind him.

"He lived here?" I tried to see inside, but neither one of them moved aside. And I wondered what they were trying to hide.

Craig tightened his grip on the door handle. "Moved in his senior year."

If Gregg had been the age of most seniors when he moved in, that would've been eighteen years before. "But you have to be in school to live in a frat house."

Dom gave an I-know nod. "He was."

I would never again feel guilty for taking five years to graduate. "What made you think he was missing and not at a friend's house?"

"He didn't show up on Sunday to make the mold for the ice luge, and he knew how important that was to the frat."

"What for?"

Craig's head retracted to emphasize his smirk. "Uh, for the party?"

And I'd thought jack-o'-lanterns were the Halloween must-have. "What can you tell me about Gregg?"

Their faces were as blank as uncarved pumpkins.

I stifled a sigh. "You know, personality, likes, dislikes?"

Dom's face tightened in concentration. "He played the kazoo."

In my opinion, that alone was enough to get the guy offed. "Did he have enemies?"

Craig burped. "Every woman he ever dated."

"Could you give me their names?"

Dom scratched his head. "I don't even think Gregg knew them."

The more I heard about the guy, the more I questioned whether he *had* been murdered by a vampire. From the sound of things, the killer could've been an ex out for blood. "Did he have any family?"

"Delta Upsilon Delta." Craig's tone signaled the end of the discussion.

They didn't know much about Gregg. Or, that was what they wanted me to believe. "Just a few more questions. Does the phrase Campari Crimson mean anything to you?"

Dom squinted. "Sounds like a drink."

Of course a frat boy would think that. "When was the last time you saw him?"

Craig squared his stance. "At Molly's on Decatur. The tour we were on stops there for a drink break."

"What company did you use?"

He adjusted his cap. "Where Dat Tours."

I jotted down the name. "Which one? Ghosts and Goblins?"

Dom frowned as though he regretted what he was about to say. "Vampires and Victims."

"You're being ridiculous, Franki," I said as I peered at Thibodeaux's from the rearview mirror of my Mustang in my driveway. It was hard to see through the thick rain, but I could make out a few people inside. After all, it was only ten p.m.

And yet my gut told me to stay in the car.

I looked again at Veronica and Glenda's apartments.

Darkness.

No signs of life.

I glared at myself in the mirror. "Okay, that was melodramatic even for you. They're just out somewhere. Now get out yourself and let Napoleon out."

I threw open the car door and dashed from the driveway to the porch, wishing I'd turned on the outside light.

As I fumbled to get my key into the lock, water dribbled down my neck, reminding me of blood.

And vampires.

And victims.

I spun around and surveyed the cemetery. After seeing the gruesome photos of the crime scene, the caped figure weighed on my mind, as did Phil's meat cleaver. And salami.

Thunder boomed, startling me from my thoughts.

I turned back to the door.

Lightning lit up the sky.

And the Bride of Frankenstein in my doorway.

I screamed like the bride when she'd met the monster in Dr. Frankenstein's lab, and I launched my bag into the air.

A clunk echoed in the night followed by the groan of metal.

Water doused my head with the intensity of a fire hose.

"That's a fine way to welcome your family." My mother's shrill voice sliced into my brain like a dissection kit. "And you broke Glenda's gutter."

I sputtered and pulled a cluster of slimy leaves from my eyes.

My mom stood before me wearing a face full of cold cream, a hairnet over her bouffant brown bob, and a 1970s chiffon nightie that could've doubled for Lily Munster's shroud.

One day I would listen to my gut.

I collected my bag from the wet grass and glanced at the driveway, longing to escape and looking for the Ford Taurus. "I didn't know you were here because I didn't see your car."

"Anthony took it."

"Where?" I brushed past her and entered the apartment. "You just got to town." I wanted to add, *And remarkably quick.*

She closed the door. "He said he wanted to go to the French Quarter to start looking for work."

That explanation was as thin as a sheet of my nonna's seven-yolk ravioli dough and every bit as rich. Still, the news that he was out alone made me uneasy in light of Chandra's prediction and what had happened to Gregg. The truth was, I was worried about my brother, which is why I took Josh Santo's case despite my suspicions about the guy. But I knew better than to tell any of that to my mom. Otherwise, she would never leave.

I tossed my purse on the floor and kicked off my shoes.

Napoleon lay on his back on the bearskin rug with his paws twitching like he was running in a dream.

I felt betrayed that he'd slept through my scream. "I hope you're at least running to my rescue in your sleep."

The twitching stopped.

"Apparently not," my mother said.

Scowling, I set off for the bath. I entered my bedroom, and a bolt of lightning illuminated the room.

I went rigid as though I'd been struck.

Because I saw a sight more terrifying than the Bride of Frankenstein standing in my doorway—a Bride of Dracula sleeping in my bed.

I stomped into the living room to confront my mother, who was rummaging in her purse on the velvet zebra-print chaise lounge. "You brought Nonna?"

"I had to, Francesca." She pulled out a tissue and wiped off the cold cream. "Your father needs me at the deli, so I can't make Anthony's meals."

I rested my head in my hands. Sending a surrogate to cook for your thirty-two-year-old slacker son was not conducive to helping him start a new life—or to getting him out of my apartment.

"The good news is that she'll cook for you too." My mother adopted the forced cheerful tone she used every time she opened a gift from my father. "And you'll hardly notice they're here because you're never home."

And I was going to make it a point to be home even less. "They've got one month," I growled. "No more, no less."

I stormed to the bathroom, grateful that I didn't have any straight razors, and switched on the light. I looked like Sissy Spacek in *Carrie* but without the pig's blood.

Blood.

Why did I have to go there?

I stripped off my wet clothes. Things were tough enough in my personal life, so I couldn't get carried away about vampires in my work. Bloodsucking zombies did not exist, and I had to stop worrying that they did.

My ringtone sounded from my purse in the entryway, but I needed a soak—and a shot—before I could face my mom again. The call was probably from Bradley, and it would serve him right to wait.

"Detective Sullivan! It's Brenda Amato. We met in March?"

I bristled at the realization that my mother had rifled through my purse—and that she'd assumed the breathy voice she reserved for attractive men. I threw on my robe and rushed into the entryway.

"Why, yes, Detective." She fiddled with her hairnet in full-on flirtatious mode. "Franki *does* sound like me."

I did *not* sound like my mother, especially not when she was imitating Marilyn Monroe. Outraged, I did an impersonation of my own—Jack Nicholson's psychotic stare in *The Shining*—and grabbed the phone. "Franki here."

"Brenda adores me." His normally smug tone smacked of extra smugness. "Like mother, like daughter."

I sputtered again—without the gutter water.

"I see you're still overcome by my embrace, but we'll have to table our relationship talk for another time." He paused to let the insinuations stew. "I imagine Phil showed you the family photo album?"

"Mm-hm," was all I managed. My mother was studying me for any signs of emotion, so I couldn't allow my cool façade to crack.

"Then you understand that we need to keep the puncture wounds between us—and the so-called 'residents and guests' of St. Cecilia cemetery."

I wanted to tell him to drop the cemetery sarcasm, but my mom's eyes were trained on me like Napoleon's were when I had human food or a dog treat. "Not a problem."

"Meanwhile, I suggest you brush up on local legends about vampires."

"Vampires?" My façade cracked like an old coffin. "Surely you don't believe in them?"

"Not the undead kind." He'd gone from smug to spookily serious. "But there are real, live people who drink human blood. And we've got a homicidal one on our hands."

6

"The *Times-Picayune* mentions the puncture wounds?" I stood before Veronica's desk holding the Baileys Chocolatini creamer I'd planned to pour into my morning espresso.

"That's what it says." She looked at the article. "Someone must've leaked it to the press, and you know what that means."

"Yeah, it could compromise the investigation, and Sullivan's going to blame me."

She folded the paper. "No, it's going to bring all the crazies out."

I gaped at her. "Who do you think we've been dealing with up until now?"

"I know the detective's got you spooked about this case." She reclined in her fuchsia chair. "But I can guarantee that you won't be killed by a vampire."

"Only because my family's going to kill me first." I shook the creamer in lieu of my fist. "I barely slept last night after the shock of my mother and the gutter. And she cleared out at three a.m. when Anthony blew in. Then I kept getting woken up by thunder."

"I didn't hear any thunder."

"That's because it was only in my apartment, i.e., Napoleon and Anthony's snoring and Nonna in the bathroom."

She grinned and rose to her feet. "Why'd your mom leave so early?"

"Her official line was that she had to get to the deli by eight," I said, following her to the kitchenette. "But she really wanted to clear out before Anthony or Nonna had time to decide to go back to Houston with her."

"Ah." She poured some French Press. "What about Bradley? Have you talked to him?"

"Not since the phone call fiasco at the cemetery." I leaned against the doorjamb. "But that's probably a good thing. You know how worried he gets about my homicide investigations, and I don't relish the idea of telling him that this one involves a vampire. And Chandra."

"Not to mention frat boys." She swallowed a sip of coffee. "Which reminds me, since Glenda and Carnie know Maybe Baby, we should have them ask her about Delta Upsilon Delta."

"Don't mess with me when I'm on edge, Veronica." I blocked the doorway, prepared to do battle. "Glenda and Carnie suck the lifeblood out of me, and given the nature of this case, I don't have any to spare." I punched the double option on our new espresso machine for emphasis. "Besides, I told you about Maybe. Do you really think she's going to be able to tell anyone what those boys are up to?"

"Valid argument, the latter not the former." She took a seat at the table. "So what do you suggest?"

"David and the vassal are in a frat, even if it is for computer science, so we have them find out what the DUDs are hiding."

"That could get complicated, and we don't actually know that they're hiding anything. Maybe they didn't invite you inside because they're being cautious after getting suspended."

"Hiring a stripper house mom seems cautious to you?"

Veronica cocked her head, conceding defeat. "Then you think they're behind Gregg's death?"

I opted not to rehash my reservations about Josh. "It's too early to say." I pulled my Whole Lotta Latte mug from the machine. "First I need to interview the other people on the Vampires and Victims tour. And I need to figure out what Campari Crimson means."

"Any ideas besides a mixed drink?"

"Not so far. But why would a guy who's dying write the name of a drink?"

She lowered her mug. "To tip off the police that it was drugged?"

"But that wouldn't tell them much in terms of solving the crime, unless the drink is specific to a particular bar. Even then, why not write something more incriminating like the killer's name?"

"Maybe he didn't know it."

"Based on what his fellow DUDs said about him and women, that's probably the case. But he could've been out-of-his-mind drunk too." I grabbed a teaspoon and stirred in a half-cup of creamer. "Not to stereotype, but to stereotype, he was a frat boy, and he was last seen at a bar."

"I guess we'll never know. The coroner's office can't very well test his blood-alcohol level, can they?"

I dropped the spoon into the sink. "That really could've been left unsaid."

The door buzzer sounded.

Veronica looked at her watch. "Are you expecting a client?"

"No, but I'll go. Maybe it's someone with a normal case." I picked up my mug and headed down the hall, but when I entered the lobby my hopes of normalcy waned.

Chandra sat on one of the couches in a short yellow-orange dress with a wide silver belt that resembled a Hula Hoop encircling the waist, and her big bob had gone totally blonde. Except for her Moon Boots, she looked like Saturn.

"If you came to remind me about Lou's cooking class tonight, I'm on it."

"I wish that was the only reason I've come." Her moon pie face turned maudlin. "The spirit told me they found his body at Saint Cecilia Cemetery. He popped in yesterday while I was getting my highlights done, and my stylist was so spooked she spilled the bleach."

That explained the hair. "Actually, I was contracted by a suspect in his death."

She gasped and pressed her paddles to her mouth.

My gaze dropped to her charm bracelet, which I willed not to jangle. "If you want to see Lou in that gumbo pot come Mardi Gras, don't channel the spirit."

"But he'll want to talk to you if you're working his case."

Ignoring her, I took a sip of my Chocolatini latte and grimaced, not because of what she'd said but because the creamer made the coffee taste like Count Chocula, which wasn't the flavor I'd been going for.

"Aren't you going to ask what he said?"

I walked to the reception desk and pretended to check the calendar. "Not even if you pay me quintuple my fee."

Her head rotated like a planet in the solar system. "But he could help you solve the case. And save your brother."

In light of my living situation, saving Anthony wasn't a selling point for the spirit. On the other hand, he'd been my protector since we were kids, and I felt the same protective instinct toward him. "All right, but this had better be worth my time."

"Oh, it is. And you need to listen anyway because a blood moon is coming."

I'd about had it with the sanguine scares. Nevertheless, it was good to be prepared. "Could you elaborate?"

"It's a red eclipse that causes blood moon fever in vampires."

I went to the couch and lay down. "I'm going to need you to tell me what that is first."

"It coincides with the eclipse, so it lasts up to three days and increases vampires' lust for blood." She lowered her brow and scrunched her face, like a killer Kewpie doll. "They'll hunt you with a ferocious intensity, and if you try to escape, they'll become enraged and plunge their fangs into your veins and suck you drier than a mummy."

On second thought, it wouldn't hurt to hear Gregg out. "What did the spirit say, exactly?"

Chandra crossed her legs and bounced a boot. "Well, he's beside himself, as you can imagine, so I didn't get every word. But there was one thing he said over and over again."

I waited, but apparently Gregg's message had fallen into a void in space. "And that is?"

Her eyes grew as big as Jupiter. "Bros before hos."

My lips curled, and I considered pulling the saturnine belt from her waist and strangling her with it. The phrase was something a frat guy would say, but it also smacked of someone jerking my crucifix chain. "Why are the spirits you talk to always so vague about the details of their deaths? I mean, how come Gregg didn't just tell you who killed him instead of stringing us along?"

"He's trying to protect his fraternity brothers." She fluffed her hair in a huff. "There's a real vampire out there who could seek revenge on them."

"Drop the supernatural shmatter, okay?" I sat up, annoyed. "Even you know vampires aren't real."

"That's what they call themselves, 'real vampires,' as in flesh and blood."

That left a bad taste in my mouth. "Yeah, theirs and other people's."

She pointed at me, producing an ominous jingle. "You joke, but there's a huge community in New Orleans. And in Buffalo."

Hollywood, sure. But Buffalo?

"And they're very active."

I cringed. "You say that like they're community-oriented or something."

"They are." She pulled a phone from her Chanel bag. "If you don't believe me, look up the New Orleans Vampire Association. They do lots of charity work, like feeding the homeless."

That sounded all kinds of wrong. But Anthony was kind of a charity case, so it was possible that this crowd would latch on to him —with their teeth.

"And they have annual vampire balls during Halloween," she

said, "similar to the one Anne Rice's Vampire Lestat Fan Club puts on."

Certainly not my scene, but a gathering of vampires could be useful for identifying suspects. "Do you know any of the names?"

"Endless Night is a big one, and there's the Blood Lust Vampire Ball."

After learning about blood moon fever, I planned to pass on the latter.

"Oh, and...what's it called?" Chandra did a search on her phone and held up the display. "Here you go. The Crimson Cotillion."

The *crimson* hit me like a meteor.

Was there a connection between the cotillion and Gregg's dying message?

"SURE YOU DON'T WANT the vampire experience?" The sixty-something owner of Where Dat Tours pushed a brochure through the slot beneath the ticket booth window. "You can spend twenty-four hours living like one of the bloodsuckers, including sleeping in a real coffin."

From my position on the river walk, I saw a steamboat sailing up the Mississippi, and I was tempted to dive into the water and swim after it. "Just the names and addresses of the people who took the Saturday night tour."

"Your loss." He took a bite of a chicken parmesan po' boy glistening with grease, like his skin, and tossed it onto the wrapper. "Our intensive tour might help you solve your case."

His comment reminded me of Sullivan's recommendation that I study local vampire legends—and of how important it was not to talk with your mouth full. "What time does the next Vampires and Victims group leave?"

"At midnight." He sucked tomato sauce from his thumb.

"I'll take a ticket." I pulled a couple of twenties from my wallet. "But that's awfully late."

He took the bills and pocketed one of them for the information
I'd requested. "We have to wait till the vampires come out."

Normally, I would've smirked at the line, but evidently it was true
for New Orleans. And Buffalo.

"Give me a minute to get you those names." He passed me a ticket.
"In the meantime, meet your tour guide." He cast a leery look over
my shoulder. "And keep her outta my hair."

That would be easy since he hardly had any. I looked behind me
and did a double take. The head hippie from the sit-in, Pam, was
strolling up the river walk with her dachshund, Benny. She wore a
macramé halter-top, striped hip-huggers, and daisy sunglasses, while
Benny sported Pam's peace-sign shades—and a rainbow headband.

I turned to the owner. "You *do* have me down for the vampire tour,
right?"

He gave a tired nod. "Looks like a bad flashback to Haight-
Ashbury, don't she? But she ain't from San Francisco. More like
Mars."

Pam cut in front of me and put Benny and an old pair of loafers
on the counter. "You got my scratch, Marv? I need to get my Earth
shoes resoled."

I assumed scratch was money, but I was confused about the Earth
shoes. They looked like they should've been buried, not given new
life.

"You gotta get in line. I'm helping this PI." He jerked a thumb in
my direction. "She's investigating that guy from your tour who got his
blood drained."

Pam lowered her daisies. "A brunch eater, crawdad killer, *and* PI?
Karma's gonna sock it to you."

"It just did." I locked my eyes on her like a laser pointer. "Anyway,
I came to ask you a few questions."

"I talked to the fuzz last night." She leaned against the counter.
"And I was working when the stiff took my tour, so you'll have to talk
to Benny about what went down."

My gaze dropped to the dog and back to her. "Come again?"

She patted Benny's head-banded head. "This boy doesn't miss a beat. Problem is, he only speaks Bulgarian."

Marv was right about the Mars thing. This woman was far out, as in spacey. "That's okay. I prefer the human perspective, anyway."

"Whatever bakes your brownies." She pushed up her daisies.

"Here's your list, lady," a Scooby Doo voice said.

I jumped and stared at Benny, whose paw rested on a sauce-stained sheet of paper.

Marv rose from below the counter with a grin. "Like how I did that?"

I replied with a side-eye and then scanned the names. Besides Gregg, Craig, and Domenic, I didn't recognize any of them. "What can you tell me about the victim and his two frat brothers?"

Pam picked up Benny and sat sit-in style on the grass. "They were crooked."

So she'd noticed something suspicious too. "How so?"

"They couldn't stand up straight."

I cocked my head and scrutinized her face. Either this chick was way-out or I was way-off. "Why's that?"

"Because they were crooked." She waved her arms like she was doing the Hippy Hippy Shake. "You know, stoned? Blitzed? Drunk?"

I joined her on the ground. Our rap sessions were exhausting. "What about the others?"

She took the list. "Drea and Dale Bacigalupi spent the whole time hassling with their kids. And this Raven Smith chick came alone. So did Thomas Van Scyoc, but the dude was a total loner. Every time I looked at him, he was checking out my neck."

That got my attention. "Were you wearing a necklace?"

"My *Why-be-rude-when-you-can-be-nude* charm. It's battery operated, so it blinks."

Nothing eye-catching about that. "Who else took the tour?"

"The only other one was Linda West. I really dug her. She's a manager at Pharmanew, but she's got a groovy plan to take it in a holistic, anti-aging direction."

I knew the company. It was a leader in the pharmaceutical industry in the central business district downtown.

"Anyway, a girlfriend canceled on her, but Linda was rip city."

I imagined teeth tearing into flesh. "What do you mean by rip?"

She gave a sad headshake. "I mean she's a gas, man. Like 'Jumpin' Jack Flash'?"

I sighed. If I questioned Pam again, I was going to need an interpreter fluent in hippie. Or Bulgarian. "Let's go back to Mr. Van Scyoc. Anything else you can tell me about him?"

She handed me the list. "When he introduced himself, he mentioned that he runs Belleville House, the old fogies' home on Royal."

"Good to know." Bayou Cuisine was on the same street, so I could stop by before cooking class. "Hey, does the phrase Campari Crimson mean anything to you?"

"Reminds me of Mellow Yellow or Kozmic Blue."

I was pretty sure those shades hadn't made the color wheel. "Great. Well, I'm coming on your midnight tour, so if you remember anything else, you can tell me tonight." I stretched out my legs. "Oh, and before I forget, do you cover the story of the Compte de Saint Germain?"

Pam leaned back on her hands. "All the way to 1983."

"Do you mean 1903? When he showed up in New Orleans?"

"I'm talking about the count's last-known alias, Richard Chanfray. He supposedly committed suicide in St. Tropez in 1983."

Josh hadn't mentioned that part of the de Saint Germain story. "But if he died, then obviously he was a mere mortal and not a centuries-old vampire."

"Who said he croaked? They never found his body, just a suicide note." She plucked a wildflower and slipped it into her hair. "I figure the count pulled another one of his disappearing acts and is still out there doing his blood-sucking thing, maybe even here in New Orleans."

I gave her a get-real look.

"If you don't believe me, look Chanfray up." Pam stood and

brushed off her hip-huggers, and Benny stood and shook. "I gotta bug out."

You already have.

After she'd split, so to speak, I crossed the train tracks that ran along the river and entered the French Quarter. As I made my way to Royal Street, I googled the counterfeit count. A 1970s photograph of Chanfray popped up juxtaposed with a painting of the real count from the court of Versailles.

And my blood ran as cold as the waters of the Mississippi.

Chanfray was the Compte de Saint Germain's doppelgänger.

But he was also a dead ringer for Josh Santo.

A PETITE MIDDLE-AGED nurse entered the lobby of Belleville House in a uniform eerily similar to Nurse Ratched's in *One Flew Over the Cuckoo's Nest.* "Mr. Van Scyoc is ready for you."

The "ready for you" was unsettling, especially considering that the name Belleville and its sterile, rundown atmosphere evoked New York's infamous Bellevue psych ward. Nevertheless, I suppressed my lobotomy fears and followed her down a hallway. Both the wallpaper and the laminate floor were yellow—not mellow, but medicinal. And the nostril-stinging odor of ammonia didn't help the ambience.

The nurse opened an unmarked door that made an ominous creak. She gestured for me to enter. "Ms. Amato."

"Thank you, Sylvia." The thirty-something male behind the desk spoke in a subdued, lugubrious tone as though we were in a funeral home rather than a retirement home. Adding to the macabre mood, he was thin and deathly pale. "Come in. And close the door."

I hesitated because it seemed like a setup. The walls were bare, and the only thing on the desk was a large computer monitor, making the office seem staged.

Reluctantly, I shut the door, and it creaked a final warning. I took a seat in a folding metal chair, but I kept my feet planted firmly on the dingy tile floor in case I needed to bolt. "As we discussed on the phone, I'm here to ask you about the vampire tour you took on Saturday night. But first, I was wondering whether the police have questioned you about the death of Mr. Charalambous?"

He flipped his dishwater-blond bangs to one side and folded his hands on the desk. "Yes."

I waited for him to continue, but he appeared to be waiting for me. "Well, could you tell me if you noticed anything unusual about anyone on the tour, including Mr. Charalambous?"

"I did."

Had working with the elderly slowed this guy down? I scooted my chair closer to his desk, trying to instill a little life into him. "How about I run through the list of attendees, and you give me your impressions?"

"No need. We had name tags." He fixed his slanted blue eyes on me and sat motionless, so much so that he didn't blink.

Irritation invaded my chest. *Why couldn't I catch a break on just one of these interrogations?* "What can you tell me about the victim and his fraternity brothers?"

His smile was cordial, like I'd inquired about his relatives or friends. "They were fine."

"And the Bacigalupi family from Utah?"

He smacked his lips and nodded. "Them too."

An alarm went off on his watch.

He reached into a desk drawer and produced a plastic container. "Would you like half a peanut butter sandwich or some mashed potatoes?"

"Oh, I already ate." I was ravenous, but I'd have sooner taken meds from the man than eat his peanut butter and potatoes.

Thomas pulled out his sandwich. "Can I ask you something?"

"That would be terrific," I gushed, overexcited about the prospect of a two-sided conversation.

"If Gregg had his blood drained through holes on his wrist, why are you questioning me and not that woman with the Mardi Gras boa he was talking to?"

How he'd made the connection between blood loss and a feather boa I did not know. "I plan to meet with everyone from the tour. But are you talking about Linda or Raven?"

"Raven." He popped a piece of bread crust into his mouth.

"What about her?"

He chewed and studied his sandwich. "She had white-blue eyes with pinpoint pupils. And fangs."

I stared at him, thinking I hadn't heard correctly. "Like, prominent canine teeth?"

"No, I have those." His gaze rose to meet mine. "What I mean is, why is everyone asking *me* what happened to Gregg when you guys could ask the *vampire*?"

I felt faint, like I'd been drained of blood, and questions hung over me like dark shadows.

How many vampires were involved in the case?

And would someone else die during the blood moon?

If so, was it Anthony?

Or, despite Veronica's guarantee, could it be me?

7

"But I taught-a you how to cook-a." The outrage in my nonna's voice threatened to reach through the phone and shake some sense into me. "Why you wanna take a class-a?"

Since I was standing in the kitchen classroom at Bayou Cuisine with Lou and two female students, I couldn't tell her I was on a case. "I thought I'd learn how to make something besides Italian."

Silence. Like the calm before the sirocco that scorched Sicily in summer.

The receiver struck a hard surface.

She'd either dropped it in dismay or thrown it in disgust. To Italian grandmothers, eating other ethnic foods was the culinary equivalent of attending a non-Catholic service, and that was a sin more serious than blasphemy. "Everything okay, Nonna?"

"I smack-a the phone because I can't-a smack-a you. You're throwing your life in-a the trash."

I grimaced and glanced at the salvaged ingredients next to my mini stovetop. She didn't know how right she was.

A middle-aged male entered in a *toque blanche* and white double-breasted jacket. He took his place at the kitchen counter facing the class and checked his utensils.

"The chef's here. I've gotta go."

"I save-a some *arancini* for you. You're gonna need-a real food."

She was right about that too. I might've been throwing my life in the trash, but that didn't mean I had to eat it. "Don't bother. You should invite Santina over because I won't be home until after midnight."

"No! *You* got a date-a?"

I didn't appreciate the implication that I would cheat on Bradley, much less her shock at the idea that someone might have asked me out. "Obviously, I meant work."

"All work and-a no play make-a Franki a *zitella*." She spewed sarcasm like water from a spaghetti strainer.

And her use of the Italian word for old maid rubbed me raw like a parmesan cheese grater. "Um, *zitella* is not part of the expression. You're supposed to say I'm 'a dull girl.'"

"That goes without-a sayin'."

A lot of things went without-a sayin', but that had never stopped the woman before. "See you tomorrow, Nonna."

I ended the call and shoved the phone into my bib apron pocket. The talk about work reminded me that I had to do some, i.e., size up the sabotage suspects. I'd positioned myself between Lou and Michele Guffey, a short brunette with blue Manga-girl-sized eyes. Next to Michele was Sara Pizzochero, who was blonde, blue-eyed, and lean, not like a bimbo but a black belt. *The competitive type.*

"*Bonsoir*, new student." The chef approached my station and took a long, loud slurp from a CC's Coffee go-cup. "I'm Chef Guenat, but everyone calls me Chef Mel." He flashed an LA smile—Los Angeles, not Louisiana—to match his accent. "I've been here for twenty years, except for a brief layoff, so it would be silly to call me by my last name. And Mel is swell."

Great. Instead of the Crazy Cajun, I get the Kooky Californian. "Uh, yeah."

He returned to the front of the room. "Tonight the menu is red beans and rice and cornbread with honey. By the way, Mel is like *miel*,

which is French for honey, so it's like you're adding me to the recipe."
He gave a happy laugh.

No one laughed with him.

"Now let's get cooking." He chuckled, pleased with the pun.
"Speaking of cooking, it's a science, and precision is key to flavor."

So is fresh food.

"Start by *dicing* the vegetables. Don't chop or mince. And be
careful with the knife." His brow shot to the brim of his chef's hat.
"Cooking is a dicey business."

I hacked into an onion, unsure how much longer I could hack his
puns.

My phone buzzed, and I thought it might be Bradley. I didn't dare
look at the display for fear of being sliced and diced by Sara and
Michele. They'd been eyeing me like they wanted to eat me, which
was a possibility in a waste-cooking class.

Truth be told, I was hungry too, so much so that I almost regretted
not eating Thomas's peanut butter and potatoes.

My gaze strayed to some seasoned almonds.

"Lou, are those for us?" I pointed to the dish.

"Yeah, Chef Mel always brings snacks. The guy spoils us rotten."

An apropos phrase considering our dumpster-dived grub. But if
the snacks had come from outside the school, they were more than
likely from a store. I popped one into my mouth as a tester. It was
spicy and extra crunchy. "Wow. Those almonds are intense."

"Oh, they're not almonds." Michele spoke like Cinderella.
"They're Creole cockroaches."

My stomach reared like a devil's horse, the only bug more horri-
fying than a cockroach. I stuck out my tongue and slapped it several
times to knock off any remnants of shell or guts.

Chef Mel practically tee-heed. "My special spice mix tickled your
tongue, eh?"

Sara snickered. "It was probably the little feet."

I gagged and gave her a glare. Despite her cute Italian accent, the
black belt was my bet for Lou's saboteur. All I had to do was catch her
in the act.

Chef Mel tapped a tablespoon on the counter to get our attention. "Next, chop the Andouille and sauté it with the vegetables over a low heat."

I didn't see the sausage, so I removed the lid from one of two covered bowls. It contained the red beans.

With...legs?

I leapt as high as a graveyard grasshopper. "Those aren't beans, they're *June bugs!*"

"All right, I confess." Chef Mel held up his hands in surrender. "They're out of season, so they were frozen."

Bile crept up my esophagus. At least, I hoped it was bile. "What the hell is the rice? Maggots?"

His head bobbed up and down. "That's a great idea for a future class."

One I had no plan to attend.

I put the lid on the bowl, and my stomach growled, not because I was starving but because it was warning the bugs to keep out.

I leaned in to Lou. "He should've called this red bugs and rice. I mean, trash is one thing, but bugs are a whole other deal. And where does anyone get frozen June bugs, anyway?"

"He caught 'em." Lou placed a skillet on the gas stove. "In the spring they swarm the streetlights in front of the school all the way down to Belleville House, that retirement home."

"I know the place."

"Yeah, I redid their pipes last spring." He pulled up his chef's pants. "Completely clogged with calcium deposits. Put in all new PVC."

I removed the Andouille from the second bowl and started chopping. "That must've been lucrative."

"Nah, I barely recouped my costs." He added oil to the skillet and turned on the burner. "They ran outta funds when they paid off a family after a wrongful death."

My gut tingled, and I had to reassure myself that the cockroach couldn't have survived my molars. "Do you know how the person died?"

"Not specifics, but you hear a lot working underneath floors." Lou threw a handful of sausage into the pan. "And somebody's grandpa had lost a lot of blood."

I stopped chopping. "From an accident? Or abuse?"

"Couldn't tell ya, but it sounded odd." He wiped his hands on his apron, smearing Andouille juice across the bib. "The family said his blood was missing."

"I MEAN IT, VERONICA." I shielded my mouth and phone from view of the pedestrians outside Molly's at the Market. "There was something serial killerish about that Thomas guy. I wouldn't be surprised if he bled the grandpa dry."

"A nurse or another staff member is a more likely culprit." Her voice was hushed despite the background noise at Galatoire's restaurant. "And the man could've died from an undiagnosed medical condition, for all we know."

"An autopsy would've determined that."

"Not necessarily. But I'll find out whether a court case was filed in the morning. Dirk and I are about to be seated, and then he's taking me to the French 75 Bar."

Envy pierced my chest like a poisoned Cupid's arrow. "Bradley took me there once—when I was more important than his job."

She sighed. "You just said that you missed a call from him when you were in class. Why don't you call him back?"

I leaned against the wall of the Irish pub. "Because I don't want to."

"Normally, you'd be desperate to contact him." Her tone had softened. "What's going on with you?"

An elegantly dressed couple passed by, arm in arm, and another arrow stabbed the open wound.

"I guess I don't know what to say to him."

"How about—I miss you, and I can't wait until you're home?"

I sniffed. "I haven't decided if I do miss him. Besides, with

Anthony and Nonna around, it might be better for him if he stays gone."

"Oh, Franki. You know he adores your family."

I'm glad one of us does.

"Hang on a sec," Veronica whispered to someone, presumably her boyfriend. "Why don't you go unwind at my apartment until Dirk and I get there?"

The offer was tempting, but a couple of French Quarter Task Force cars rolled by, reminding me that I had work to do. "I told you, I've got that tour at midnight. And I'm already at the pub. Someone here could remember seeing Gregg on Saturday night."

"Are you going to interview Raven tonight too?"

"Don't say 'interview' in reference to a vampire, okay?" I flashed back to the vampiress at the Krewe of BOO! parade. "And you can't seriously expect me to talk to her in the middle of the night."

"You'll have to," she said gravely.

"Why's that?"

"Because she can't come out of her coffin during the day or she'll burn up and blow away." Veronica giggled, and I heard Dirk yuk it up too.

"I know someone who's burning up." My tone was as dry as vampire dust. "And she's coming in late tomorrow." I ended the call and entered Molly's.

It was nine o'clock, which was early by New Orleans standards, so I had my choice of seats. I climbed onto a stool at the far end of the bar. The pub was a hangout for local notables, particularly politicians and journalists, so I needed to question the staff away from interested ears. I also wanted to avoid the center of the bar because there was a coffin hanging overhead and because the late owner, Jim Monaghan, Jr., sat on top of the cash register—in an urn.

A young male bartender with black hair, glasses, and a "Marco Arroyo" nametag tossed a Guinness coaster in front of me. "What can I getcha to drink?"

I jerked backward and slid halfway off my barstool.

He had a full set of vampire teeth.

"Sorry." He spit out the offending eyeteeth. "We host an annual Halloween parade, and I've been getting into the spirit."

I wanted nothing to do with the spirit—his, Chandra's, or anyone else's.

He turned on a faucet and scrubbed his hands. "Drink's on the house."

Molly's famous frozen Irish coffee enticed me, but caffeine was a bad idea before a creepy tour. On a whim I asked, "How about a Campari Crimson?"

"What's in it?"

That answered my question. "Never mind. What do you have on tap?"

"Abita Amber, Chafunkta Voo Ka Ray—"

"Are you okay?" I interrupted.

His brown eyes got big. "Are *you*?"

"Oh. I thought you were choking."

He gave a sympathetic smile and pointed at the label on the tap. "It's an Imperial IPA. The Voo Ka Ray is a play on *Vieux Carré*, as in French Quarter."

"Got it. I'll take one of those." I slid a twenty across the bar. "Listen, Marco. I'm a PI, and I'd like to ask you some questions about a tour group that came in Saturday night."

"Now I get why you jumped when you saw my teeth." He filled a frosted mug. "You want to know about Gregg."

"Why would you make that association?"

He placed the beer in front of me and put the bill in a tip jar. "Because everyone's talking about how he died, especially after the blood bank break-ins."

"Don't tell me you believe a vampire killed him?"

"Either that or it was one of his ex-girlfriends." His demeanor was nonchalant, as though either option was equally possible.

"Is he a friend of yours?"

"He was kind of a regular and a local legend."

"Why?" I asked in a what-in-the-hell-for way.

"He's the oldest student and frat boy in the city of New Orleans, if not the entire state." He grabbed some dirty mugs from the bar and placed them in the sink. "You've got to admire that kind of devotion."

If you could call it that. "Let's go back to his girlfriends. Do you know any of them?"

"Fortunately, no. But it was clear he had a type. Crazy."

Although I was willing to entertain the possibility that an angry ex had killed Gregg, especially since Craig had also mentioned his exes, I couldn't imagine a woman, even a wack job, single-handedly stringing him up. "You were here on Saturday, right?"

"I served his whole group. We take care of them pretty quick since they only have about fifteen minutes."

"Does anything stand out about his behavior? Or who he was with?"

"We were slammed, so I didn't notice much." He rested his forearms on the counter. "But I did see him talking to a dark-haired lady with a boa."

She could've been the vampire Thomas mentioned, but the description fit a lot of women in the quarter on any given day of the week. "Did she have glowing eyes and vampire teeth?"

His mouth twisted in an apology. "I went through a rough divorce, so as far as I'm concerned all women do."

I took that as a no, but I planned to follow up with the vampire herself. During daylight. "Anything else you can tell me about the group?"

"Yeah, one of the guys has been in here before with a cocktail club. He has dirty blonde hair, pale skin. Seems like a loner."

That sounded like Thomas Van Scyoc. "Did he talk to Gregg?"

"Apart from ordering a drink, I've never seen him talk to anyone. He just stands around and watches."

Definitely Thomas. "What's the name of this cocktail club?"

"OBIT."

I frowned. "Reminds me of obituary."

"It's supposed to. Their full name is the Grande and Secret Order of the Obituary Cocktail, but don't be put off by that. They're good people."

I was sure they were, but I had my doubts about Thomas. And the creepy cocktail club only reinforced my suspicions given the Campari Crimson clue.

WHILE THE VICTIMS and Vampires tour members assembled in front of the tall white wall surrounding the old Ursuline Convent, I pulled Pam aside. "So, I ask you about a murder involving a guy drained of blood, and you don't mention the vampire on his tour?"

She pointed to her necklace. "Like the locket says, live and let live."

I gave her a you-should-know-better glare. "You came of age with the Beatles. It's 'Live and Let Die.'"

"I don't have time for your hang ups, dig? I've got a tour to do." She yanked up her hip huggers and led Benny to the head of the group.

"All right, people." Pam raised her arms like she was communing at a be-in. "I'm going to lay a righteous and frighteous story on you about this convent and NOLA's founding mothers. Locals consider it a point of pride to be a descendent of one of these first mamas. They call 'em the Casket Girls."

That explains a lot about this town.

"In the 1700s, King Louis XV sent ships with prospective wives for the colonists. The French skirts brought these freaky hope chests they called *cassettes*, but everyone in the colony called them *casquettes* because they looked like caskets."

Benny groan-growled—either that or it was Bulgarian for "bummer."

"The girls stayed at the convent until their weddings went down. But after they made the scene, the death rate doubled, and a rumor circulated like a doobie at a drum circle that they'd smuggled vampires in those casquettes."

Talk about a tale from the crypt.

"Now, life in a swamp colony was like a bad trip, so some of the girls cut out and left their hope chests. The nuns stored them in the attic, which is the only pad in the Quarter with shuttered windows."

I studied the gray and black shutters, which looked coffin-like on the white, stuccoed convent.

"That's because the nuns had opened the chests, and they were empty. They told the Archbishop, who was hip to the vampire rumor, so he had the windows shuttered and the chests sealed with nails and screws blessed by the head preacher man, Pope Clement. Yet passersby have seen the windows open in the wee hours—when the vampires come out of the *casquettes*."

My gaze darted back to the shutters, just to check.

"In 1978 two reporters asked to see the infamous *casquettes*, but the Archbishop told them to split. They said, 'Hell no, we won't go,' and that night they climbed the wall and set up video cameras. The next morning, their equipment was scattered across the grounds, and they were dead on the steps." Pam held out her hands. "And this is the trippy part. The dudes were almost decapitated, and eighty percent of their blood had been drained."

A cold hand brushed the back of my neck, and I let out a scream from beyond the casket.

Detective Sullivan laughed low in his throat. "I'm beginning to think I make you nervous, Amato."

Pam grimaced like she'd done a hit of acid. "No, baby. That chick was already flipping out." She picked up Benny's leash. "Okay, gang. Let's head around the corner to Royal Street."

The group followed Pam, but I turned on Sullivan. "Real adult of you to go for my jugular during a vampire story."

He pulled his shoulders back, accentuating the breadth of his chest in his cable knit sweater. "You had a moth in your hair. What was I supposed to do?"

"Leave it." My tone was as tense as my limbs as I stalked after the group. I'd had it with him. And with bugs. "What are you doing on this tour, anyway?"

"I thought I'd take my own advice and brush up on vampire lore. Plus, I got a little carried away at dinner, so I wanted to walk it off."

Sullivan grabbed his six-pack gut and gave me a sidelong look. "Italian is heavy, but I can't resist it."

My stomach fluttered like it was full of moths. *He* was *talking about food, wasn't he?*

I stole a glance at him.

He ogled me like I was a leg of prosciutto.

The fluttering intensified, as did my pace.

It was unfathomable, but I felt like I did when my Catholic school went from all girls to coed—like a young Eve being introduced to an apple. Except that this one was rotten. With a worm. "I took you for an Irish stew guy."

"I won't turn down a plate of meat and potatoes. But I've developed a weakness for arancini."

"Arancini?" The coincidence caught me off guard.

"You know, those Sicilian rice balls? They've got a crispy fried outside, and then you bite into one." His pitch was low and verging on lustful. "And you taste that soft, saucy center."

I re-upped my speed, and so did my pulse. Sullivan was trying to seduce me, but that was no longer the source of my nerves. It was his reference to arancini *al sugo*.

"Now that we're all here." Pam shot me an incensed stare as we rejoined the group. She pointed to a brick mansion with a wrought-iron balcony at the corner of Royal and Ursuline. "This is the former home of Compte Jacques de Saint Germain."

And the present house of Josh Santo.

Pam launched into the legend of the count, but my mind returned to those rice balls.

I side-stepped to Sullivan. "Hey, so, most restaurants around here don't make the arancini with sauce," I whispered. "Where'd you get them?"

He leaned so close his breath tickled my ear. "Your nonna."

The scream that erupted from my throat could've awakened the undead in their *casquettes*.

Pam squeezed her live-and-let-live locket like she wanted to make war, not love. "Could you wait till I get to the hairy part, man?"

What I'd heard was more "hairy" than any vampire legend. I'd told Nonna to invite Santina, not Sullivan. But I shouldn't have planted the idea in her head. The woman didn't make a move that wasn't motivated by meddling, and this one was straight from her manual. What puzzled me was the devious detective's motive for accepting.

Was his interest in me purely personal? Or did it have something to do with the case?

"Look." Sullivan put a hand on my back and pointed.

I shivered, but I told myself it wasn't his touch. It was the sight of Josh exiting the front door on Royal Street in a top hat and cape.

"It's been heavy, Amato." Sullivan's lips grazed my hair. "But I just got a new walking partner."

I watched both men disappear into the darkness, and my heart was as jittery as my head. But my thoughts had nothing to do with Sullivan or Josh or even Bradley. I was fixated on Marv at Where Dat Tours.

Was he serious when he'd said vampires went out after midnight? If so, was Josh one of them? And could he be the count?

Pam gestured to the second-floor balcony. "You'll notice that one of the windows has been bricked over. Locals believe that when evil goes outside, you need to brick it up so it can't come back in."

She was referring to the woman who'd jumped from the window to escape the count's killer bite. *But* was *evil still inside?*

I had to find out.

While the group focused on Pam, I slipped down Ursuline Street to the side of the house and tried the windows.

One opened.

After a quick look around, I climbed inside.

And I stiffened like a corpse.

I stood in a red living room with a high ceiling, a grand staircase, and a gorgeous chandelier that reflected the streetlight streaming through the windows. But there was no furniture, like when the count had lived in the house. And a foul odor hung in the air.

Trancelike, I moved from room to room.

All empty.

Then I entered the kitchen and opened the fridge.

Wine bottles.

Were they filled with human blood?

Using a sheet from my notepad, I took one and placed it in my bag.

Fighting back fear and nausea from the smell, I returned to the living room and climbed the stairs.

All of the bedrooms were empty, except for the master.

And what I saw there curdled my blood.

A coffin and a reddish-purple stain on the hardwood floor.

8

A door slammed.

My eyes opened.

It was as dark as a black hole, and I was supine on a hard surface.

I reached beside me, and my fingers touched something flat and smooth, like a wall. Of wood.

My lungs stopped breathing.

Was I in Josh's coffin?

A cork popped from a bottle.

My heart stopped beating.

Josh was about to drain my blood and bottle it.

I bolted upright.

The covers fell to my lap.

Bewildered, I glanced around. I wasn't in the coffin. I was in the space between my bed and the wall. "I've got to stop waking up like this."

I kicked off the covers and rose to my feet.

And I almost fell to the floor.

Nonna lay on the bed with her arms crossed on her chest.

Like a body in a casket.

Lungs panting, heart pounding, I leaned over to make sure she was alive. Her breast rose and fell, to my relief. In one hand she clutched her rosary, and in the other a piece of paper.

Curious, I worked the paper from her grasp and then opened a curtain and held it to the moonlight.

Sullivan's business card?

My lips tightened along with my fists, and for a second I thought about strangling her. Instead, I shredded the card.

A cabinet slammed.

Anthony must've come home.

Or...was it Josh?

I opened the door and peered out.

A figure in dark clothing was at the kitchen counter where I'd left my purse.

Fear gripped my torso.

Had Josh come for his wine?

"Yo, sis!"

My skeleton nearly jumped from my skin.

Anthony strutted up in a black velvet tracksuit. "I know it's excitin' seein' your big bruthuh, but be cool." He bobbed his head, his blowout immobile. "Now that I'm in The Big Easy, you get ta see me all the time."

The reminder did nothing to calm my skittish skeleton.

His Neanderthal brow lowered, and his gaze swept over my gown. "Did you get that tent from Ma or sumpthin'?"

I didn't know what irked me more—the pajama jab or the permanent Jersey accent he'd acquired from watching *The Sopranos*. "You're not planning on coming home this late every night, are you?"

"Chill, awright? I had a meetin' on Bourbon Street."

I smirked. "Job hunting until four a.m.?"

"It's a jungle out theuh." He let out a wet-sounding burp and pulled a jar of Nutella from the pantry.

My stomach seized, and I snatched the jar.

"Oooh!" he shouted like a goomba at a garden party. "Whatsa mattuh wit you?"

"My apartment doesn't come with free food."

"Nice hospitality. What's a guy s'ppose ta eat?"

With no cash and no culinary skills, Anthony should've been taking the waste-cooking class, not me. "How about Nonna's arancini?"

He opened the refrigerator and grabbed a package of prosciutto and a brick of mozzarella. Then he shoulder-shut the door. "Your boyfriend ate 'em all."

I shook the Nutella at him. "Wesley Sullivan is not my boyfriend."

"That ain't what Nonna says." He went into the living room, and I followed. With napkins.

"She doesn't get a say in this."

"Maybe she should." He flopped onto the chaise lounge and kicked his Adidas onto the coffee table.

Napoleon, whose ears were fine-tuned to the sound of food packaging, emerged from beneath the armchair and assumed the begging position at my brother's feet.

"So you're anti-Bradley too?"

"It ain't dat." He broke off a piece of mozzarella and tossed it to Napoleon. "I'm sick o' da constant meddlin'."

I was tempted to shove the cheese brick down his throat. As a male in an Italian family, the only thing expected of him was that he love his mother, whereas I had to get married, have kids, and keep house, all while holding down a job. "How is that possible when the meddling is about me?"

"'Cause I'm always havin' to hear about it."

"Pardon me for indirectly imposing." I sunk onto the chaise lounge and opened the Nutella.

Napoleon moved to sit at my feet—not out of love or loyalty but an intense passion for anything I ate.

Anthony grabbed a wine bottle from the end table and took a swig. "You know, that detective dude might be Irish, but he's practically a *paesan*."

"That detective dude put me in jail last year and then harassed me the whole time I was working a case."

"Cut the guy some slack, will ya? His old lady walked out on 'im."

Sullivan lived and breathed police work, so his personal life came as a shock. "He was married?"

"Until his lady dumped him for a rich guy."

"That's terrible." His wife's betrayal didn't excuse his behavior, but it could've explained his surly attitude. And the change I'd noticed in him. Maybe he was over his ex.

Anthony rolled a slice of prosciutto. "He also told Nonna he felt bad for treatin' you like crap."

"Well, he should." My tone was hard, but my resolve to dislike the detective was softening. I licked Nutella from my finger. "What did she say?"

"That he couldn't have treated you as bad as Bradley does."

The chocolate-hazelnut soured in my mouth. Sullivan knew too much about my relationship as it was. He didn't need any more ammunition.

"And dat ain't the woist of it." Anthony jolted me with his elbow. "She laid the lemon tradition on him."

"Oh, God." I reached for his wine to wash down the bitterness and paused. "Where did you get that bottle?"

"On the counter."

Unless Nonna had brought wine, then I didn't have any in the house except for...I swallowed hard. "On the counter in my purse?"

His smile was sheepish. He'd been caught red-lipped.

"Don't freak out." I held out my hands to calm him even though I was on edge. "That wine is evidence in a case, and it might've been mixed with human blood."

"The label says Chianti!" He launched the wine.

Red liquid rocketed across the room, and the bottle landed on the bearskin rug in front of the fireplace with a splash.

On my face.

This Anthony thing isn't working out.

He put his head between his legs and heaved.

I dabbed my face with the napkins. "Try not to throw up on my floor, okay? In fact, why don't you go to the bathroom while I google what to do?"

He stumbled to my bedroom, and I rushed into the kitchen for my phone.

Sullivan had called at two a.m. and sent a text.

SANTO GAVE *me the slip at St. Louis Cemetery No. 1. He went to an area where Anne Rice fans hang out and disappeared like a puff of smoke.*

OR LIKE A VAMPIRE BAT. I didn't believe Josh could turn into an animal, but there were things about him that defied human explanation. And if I was going to continue to represent him, I had to clear him as the killer.

It was time to get information about the underworld he inhabited. And I knew where to get it.

"DAVID, STOP WITH THE LEG BOUNCING." I glanced at Raven Smith's kitchen to make sure she was still brewing tea. "You're shaking me off the couch."

"Dude, why is everything in her apartment yellow?"

I followed his gaze to a poster of a fanged smiley face. "Well, she is fairly young." I figured she was maybe late twenties. "But it is disturbingly sunny for a vampire."

"And it's freaking me out." His leg practically pogoed. "Why couldn't I take the wine to the police station?"

"Because that's the vassal's job. You're a PI now, so man up." I neglected to mention that I'd brought him along because I was as freaked out as him. And because he was young blood.

Raven returned to the living room and set a tea tray on the coffee table with a clatter. "I'm sorry, but I'm so over being a suspect in these kinds of crimes." She flipped her hair, which was as black as the bird she shared a name with. "Like I told that detective, it's profiling."

She should have thought of that before having her canines enhanced. And before buying the luminescent contacts. "No offense, but you *are* an obvious suspect."

The look she laid on me was as pointed as her teeth. "I'm not a sanguinarian, okay? I'm a psychic feeder."

I pulled a notepad from my bag. "How does that work?"

She sat cross-legged on a sun-shaped cushion. She was fit but so thin that the black fabric of her yoga pants sagged. "Instead of human or animal blood, I feed off people's energy and emotions."

Oh, like Chandra.

David swallowed. "Are those the only ways to, uh, feed?"

"There are also vampires who use tendrils from their minds to drain energy from a person's aura."

Doom darkened David's brow. "Like a Star Trek creature."

And my mother.

Raven poured red liquid into a floral porcelain cup. "Would either of you like some hibiscus tea and raspberry shortbread cookies?"

After what had happened to Anthony with the wine, I wasn't willing to gamble on anything blood colored, especially considering the source. "We had coffee before we came."

"And beignets." David bobbed his head in time with his leg.

I gave him a look that said *give it a rest.* "Going back to sanguinarians, is it safe to drink blood?"

"It depends on whether it's diseased and, if so, the type. That's why they vet their donors."

"Donors?" David gave me a scared side-eye.

She tucked a long lock behind her ear. Her neck was smooth, sans bite marks. "There are people who want to be in relationships with vampires, to love and nurture them."

For the life of me, I couldn't fathom why.

"And it violates our code of ethics to feed from unwilling donors, so I didn't kill Gregg. I'm not the blood bank thief, either."

"Vampires have ethics?" That seemed like an oxymoron.

"Those of us who belong to a house or coven do." She spooned sugar into her cup. "But if the killer is a role-player or a Ronin, then no."

The culture reminded me of Dungeons and Dragons. "Could you define those terms?"

"Roleplayers are usually Goths who dress like stereotypical vampires and sleep in coffins, but they don't feed. Ronins are real vampires who don't belong to a house. In a sense, they're rogue."

I jotted down the descriptions, wondering which one fit Josh. "Are you affiliated with the New Orleans Vampire Association?"

"I'm with NOVO, the New Orleans Vampire *Organization*. We split with NOVA after a disagreement over charity sponsorship."

I looked up from my pad. "About feeding the homeless?"

"It's a good cause, but it doesn't fit with our mission." She smiled, uncovering her cuspids. "We sponsor a blood drive."

David plastered himself against the couch, and I was tempted to follow suit. I didn't know about their Buffalo brethren, but The Big Easy vampires needed a publicity agent. "Which house are you with?"

"I'm the head of the House of Lestat, after the Anne Rice character."

"So, can you tell me why her fans hang out at St. Louis Cemetery No. 1?"

"That's where Lestat's lover, Louis, is buried. It's fiction, of course. And like most of the depictions of us in books and movies, the story is exaggerated. We're really just regular people."

There was nothing regular about feeding on human blood. "Then why is your house named after a fictional vampire?"

She sipped her tea, pinky extended. "Because Rice's novels are partially responsible for the emergence of our culture. Thanks to her we organized, which is why New Orleans has the largest community in the nation. It's also why we have the best bars, like The Dungeon, and the best balls."

"Have you been to the Crimson Cotillion?" I asked.

"That's our event." Her cheeks turned pinkish. "It's this Saturday. You guys can come as my guests."

"Uhhhh." David was stuck.

I unstuck him with a knee knock. "We'd love to. Is there a theme?"

"Eighteenth-century French Court or anything in basic black. And there'll be music, dancing, and drinking."

The drinking caught my attention. "Is Campari served?"

Her iceberg eyes chilled me to the bone. "I don't know what Campari Crimson means. But yes, we serve most red liqueurs, wine, sodas." She smirked. "No blood."

She broke a cookie in half and licked raspberry jam from her finger.

At least, I hoped it was raspberry jam and not the blood clot spread from Boutique du Vampyre. "I'm curious. Why would you go on the Vampires and Victims tour?"

"As head of my house, I receive a salary from NOVO. One of my duties is to keep the organization informed about how we're being represented in the community. We have a reputation to protect, you know?"

I didn't, but I nodded.

She picked up her teacup. "Anyway, I left after the bar break at Molly's. The tour guide seemed sensitive to my people, but she told the same tired legends. And I don't like hearing us described that way."

"As bloodthirsty killers?"

Her eyes flashed, as did her fangs. "As I said, we feed only from willing donors. And we leave them alive."

David's leg had jumpstarted into action, so I switched to a non-sanguine subject. "About the bar, a witness said Gregg spoke to a woman with dark hair and a Mardi Gras boa. Was that you?"

"I was wearing a boa to try to blend in with the Quarter crowd, but it made my neck itch, so I took it off before we got to the bar. And I didn't talk to him."

Thomas Van Scyoc had said otherwise, so someone was lying. "Maybe the witness confused you with another woman on the tour, like Linda West?"

Raven's cup wobbled. "I don't know her." She paused. "What I meant was, I don't look like her."

Based on her bout of nerves, I had a feeling she did know Linda. And that she'd talked to Gregg.

The question was, had she lied about not feeding on blood too?

MY RINGTONE SOUNDED, and my eyelids flew open.

Linda West's office was so spa-like that I'd drifted off. If Private Chicks were half as inviting as Pharmanew, I would've moved in and left Nonna and Anthony to fend for themselves.

Actually, who was I kidding? I would've moved into Private Chicks that day if I could've gotten Veronica's permission. As it stood, I was almost ready to sleep in one of Chef Mel's dumpsters.

I yawned and pulled my cell from my purse. The number on the display was unfamiliar, but it could've been Sullivan calling about the wine. "Hello?"

"Miss Franki?"

I stared at the device, dumbstruck. Glenda had never called me. In fact, I'd never seen her use a phone. "Hey, I'm about to interview someone for a case. Can I call you in an hour?"

She blew a burst of what had to be cigarette smoke into the receiver. "No, child. This is urgent. The Lilliputians are back, and they're powwowing in your apartment."

I breathed in the sandalwood scent of the lit candles and mentally uttered an "om." "Yeah, my nonna's visiting. She must've invited her friends over."

"Well, every time those little people come around, they try to tie me up."

I mind-uttered another om. My nonna and her nonna friends, aka the *nonne*, had used their aprons and tablecloths to cover her nudity. But, like Gulliver during his travels, Glenda lacked self-awareness and couldn't see that her nakedness would be offensive to female octogenarians from Roman Catholic Sicily. "Just stay away from them, and they'll leave you alone."

"I'm not worried about myself, sugar. It's Miss Carnie. She came over to debut her costume for the Lucky Pierre's Halloween show, and they called in a priest."

Gesù. I grabbed the miniature rake from a Japanese Zen garden on Linda's desk and dragged it through the sand, trying to recapture my shattered serenity. "That doesn't make sense. They've met Carnie. What's the costume?"

"Countess Dragula. She got the idea from that Dracula float at the Krewe of BOO! parade."

Cristo. The *nonne* were planning an exorcism. "Don't open the door. I'll get there as soon as I can."

"There's no time." Her drawl verged on desperate. "Miss Carnie's got to go rehearse."

Rehearse? She was born for the role, especially if the countess was an energy-draining feeder. "Then what do you want me to do?"

"Meet me and Miss Ronnie for happy hour at Thibodeaux's. We need to have a powwow of our own."

The line went dead, and I nestled into the fluffy white chair. Even if a Native American Indian shaman led our powwow, he couldn't heal us from the damage Nonna would inflict.

The door opened, and a petite brunette in her early fifties glided into the office. She was pretty, possibly of Japanese origin, and well put together. Her skirt and blouse matched the cherry blossom paintings and green walls.

"Sorry for the delay. We had an issue with a shipment." She rested her hand on my shoulder. "Could I get you some mineral water or a protein shake?"

After dropping David by the office, I'd had a late breakfast—and an early lunch. "Thanks, but I overdid it on the Bywater Bakery's Halloween king cake."

"Then you need some nutrients." She tapped her smooth cheek. "They help the skin stay young." She pressed a button on her phone. "A green juice, please."

Linda didn't take no for an answer.

She folded her hands on her desk. Even her rings matched the office decor. "Isn't it terrible what happened to Gregg? Before we went to Molly's for a cocktail break, I told him he should find a nice girl and settle down. And then he started talking to that vampire."

"You saw him talk to Raven?"

Her face drooped from disappointment. "The whole time we were at the bar."

"Was she wearing a Mardi Gras boa, by chance?"

She nodded. "A man was selling them in front of the Ursuline convent, where our tour met. My girlfriend Belinda thought it was weird that a vampire would wear one."

"Belinda?" Pam said that Linda's friend had canceled. "Could I get her full name and contact information?"

"Sure, but she left before the tour started." Linda wrote Belinda Baca and a phone number on a pink Post-It. "This was her first trip to the city, and when she saw that convent in the moonlight, she chickened out and went back to her hotel."

I couldn't blame the woman. Convents were scary enough during the day, never mind at night in New Orleans. "Were you or anyone else on the tour or in the bar wearing a boa?"

"Not that I saw." She touched her blouse. "I never wear the cheap ones because they shed."

Raven must have been the woman Thomas identified. But even though she'd lied about talking to Gregg, I wasn't ready to convict her of his killing. She could've been too frightened to confess to the conversation.

A blonde with big blue eyes entered and handed me a glass.

"Thank you, Christine." Linda looked pleased.

To be polite, I took a sip. The juice tasted like dirt and iron. "Mm."

Christine left the room, and I ditched the glass on the desk. "So, I was wondering whether Campari Crimson means anything to you?"

Linda toyed with her necklace and stared at the Zen garden. "I told Detective Sullivan that it must be a mixed drink. What else could it be?"

I shrugged. "I wish I knew."

The corners of her mouth sagged. "If Gregg had listened to my advice, he'd still be alive. Instead, he went for the bad girl and got himself killed."

"You think Raven did it?"

Her almond eyes widened. "Since his blood was drained, it had to be her."

"What makes you so sure?"

"Well, I don't know her personally, but I know of her. She worked at a retirement home called Belleville House."

The revelation hit my stomach with a thud. Or maybe it was the fiber in the green juice. "That's odd, because their director was on the tour, and he didn't mention that when I interviewed him."

Linda didn't appear surprised. "Maybe he had professional reasons. But until about six months ago, she worked there as a nurse."

Another thud. And another oxymoron. *Raven hadn't mentioned a healthcare career. And how would a vampire get a nursing job, anyway?* "How do you know she worked there?"

"We market our products to a few doctors who have patients at Belleville, and their staff told me about her. Doctors' offices can be gossipy, but when three different sets of employees tell the same story, I listen."

I wanted to listen too, but she wouldn't get to the point. "What is the story?"

"Raven was fired. And rumors started going around." Linda leaned forward, and I saw concern in her eyes. "Blood bags were missing. And they were the same type that was stolen in Metairie, B Positive."

I was breathless, as though my blood had stopped carrying

oxygen. It looked like Raven had also lied about being a psychic feeder, unless she'd stolen the blood for someone else.

But either way, if she'd stolen bags of blood, then she could have stolen it from the elderly gentleman who'd died at Belleville—and from Gregg too. Which meant that I needed to find out their blood types—and fast.

Because a vampire would need to feed again.

9

The young officer's gaze swept me like a bug detector from behind the counter. "You're that PI lady who stripped."

My lips flattened. I should've expected to be ID'ed for my striptease. I *was* at the Criminal Investigations Division. "Good memory."

"Oh, I wasn't at Madame Moiselle's that night. But everyone at the station still talks about how Detective Sullivan tipped you a fiver for doing a crab walk."

If only I had pinchers. "Is he around?"

"Behind you, Amato." Sullivan's drawl crawled up my back and caressed the nape of my neck.

Without thinking, I leaned backward. Then a police siren yelped in my head. *Why had I reacted like that?* I turned, hoping he hadn't noticed my body's betrayal.

Sullivan's eyes were alight with laughter. "Couldn't stay away?"

Apparently, he *had* noticed. I tightened my grip on my bag, hoping to get a better grip on myself. "Don't get excited. I came to talk to you about the case."

"Let's go to my office. I was about to have a late lunch."

I followed him down a hallway, and he ushered me inside a stark white room. A diploma from Notre Dame and numerous awards adorned the walls, but no family or friend photos. Six months before I would've blamed the professional décor on his all-work-no-play personality, but after Anthony's revelation, I blamed it on his divorce. Because, as I'd been finding out, the detective was definitely the type to mix business with pleasure.

"Have a seat." He pulled out a chair.

I sat quickly, way too aware of his powerful presence behind me.

He settled in at his desk and shot a rapid-fire glance in my direction.

An air-raid siren wailed. *Wesley Sullivan was nervous. Danger was imminent.*

"Care to join me?" He removed the lid from a jumbo Tupperware container. "There's enough here for the whole Homicide Section."

A garlic-and-wine aroma beckoned to my DNA, but breaking bread with Sullivan seemed like cheating on Bradley, especially in light of the arancini affair. "I've eaten, thanks. Did my assistant drop off the wine bottle?"

"It's already at the lab." He chuckled and pulled a paper plate from a desk drawer. "Carmela told me what happened with Anthony."

I overlooked his first-name basis with my nonna in favor of a more pressing problem. "You talked to her today?"

"When she dropped this off." He spooned food onto the plate.

Spaghetti and chicken breasts. *Al limone.*

My mouth puckered. Nonna was planting lemon tradition seeds in hopes that they would sprout—into a proposal from Wesley, not Bradley.

"Anyway, my contact at the lab is putting a rush on the tests, so I should have the results in a few days." Sullivan filled his fork with noodles. "But she said it didn't appear to contain blood."

Anthony would be relieved, which was why I planned to wait to give him the news. "So, Josh was just hoarding wine like his vampire count crush?"

He swallowed and smirked. "The kid *is* twenty-six. But he's still on my suspect list."

He was still on mine too. "What about Raven and her firing from Belleville?"

"She denies stealing any blood. And before you ask, I know about the old man, and she denies that as well." He lowered his fork. "You know, this meal is exquisite. Would you like a bite?"

"Uh, I've had it." My tone was as sour as the sliced lemon on the chicken, which I wanted to knock from his desk. But I didn't want to jeopardize the new spirit of cooperation between us. Sullivan's insight and information could help me solve the case. "And you believe Raven?"

"She doesn't strike me as a liar, but we're digging around in her background. The problem is that no police reports were filed on either incident, so it's going to take time."

I wasn't surprised the crimes hadn't been reported. Corruption seemed rampant at the retirement home. "I'd be willing to believe Mr. Van Scyoc had something to do with the missing blood."

"Yeah, there's something not right about that guy. But he doesn't have a record, and he had a business incentive to keep the offenses quiet."

True, but I didn't think Belleville's income was his sole incentive. "Were you able to verify the blood types in either incident?"

"Both B Positive. But Mr. Charalambous had O Positive."

My B Positive blood began to race. "O Positive can donate to B Positive. So there could be a link to the blood bank break-ins."

Sullivan stared at me interrogator style. "You're a good investigator. You know that?"

I flushed at the compliment. Another betrayal by my traitorous body.

He smiled and refilled his fork. "Now I insist you try this spaghetti."

I opened my mouth to refuse, and he shoved a forkful inside. Olive oil dribbled down my chin.

He wiped away the oil with his napkin.

Our eyes met, and I froze with spaghetti dangling from my lips.

His gaze was sincere, soft, sexy.

Sexy? A tornado siren sounded as a twister churned in my chest.

I pulled away.

Hurt flickered across his brow. Then he reclined in his chair and laid a lazy grin on me. "I was just telling Bradley that I could see why he's so into you."

"When—" I choked on the spaghetti.

"Easy, Amato. You'll ruin your digestion." He patted my back. "Your roaming Romeo called when I was at your place for dinner."

I ignored the jab at my boyfriend and mentally jabbed myself. I was sure Bradley had tried me at home because I hadn't returned his call to my cell. And I didn't want him calling the house with Nonna on the prowl. And Sullivan too. "What were you doing answering my phone?"

"What your nonna told me to do." He stabbed a piece of chicken with his fork. "She was busy in the kitchen, and she'd sent Anthony to the bathroom to fix his hair."

An advanced tactical maneuver from her meddling manual. Distract dim-witted grandson so targeted suitor can do your wedding bidding.

"Look, Wesley...we need to talk."

His face darkened, and I was sure he anticipated my impending rejection.

The door opened with such force that it blew my hair.

A ginger-haired officer aimed eyes as intense as gun barrels at the detective. "We've got to go. ASAP."

The Charalambous case? My gaze sought Sullivan's.

But he wouldn't look at me.

He rose and strode from the room.

OUTSIDE THIBODEAUX'S, I turned my back to the cemetery and dialed Bradley's number. Maybe it was me but discussing a wounded relationship while staring at a graveyard seemed like a bad omen.

The phone picked up, and so did my stomach.

This is Bradley Hartmann.

My stomach dropped. Voicemail. Again.

I'm away on business until the 9th, but please leave a message and I'll return your call promptly.

The tone beeped, and I tapped *End*, another less-than-positive sign.

Bradley might've been returning other people's calls promptly, but not mine. I'd left him three messages in as many hours.

With a sigh, I went back inside the tavern and headed for the bar.

Creedence Clearwater Revival's "Bad Moon Rising" blared on the stereo. I'd forgotten about the blood moon, and I didn't appreciate the reminder. *Foreboding omen number three.*

"He's still not answering." I sat on the stool next to Veronica.

"I ordered you a Candy Corn in honor of Halloween." She slid the Galliano and Arancello cocktail in front of me. "It's only six o'clock in New York, so he's probably still working. But before he calls, you need to contact Wesley and tell him you're not interested."

My body tensed like I'd been found out. *Why had it done that?* Sullivan was attractive, but that didn't mean I was interested. *Did it?* No, I was just tired from lack of sleep. And from the energy-draining vampires in my life.

"Franki?" Veronica's gaze bore into my brain. Like a tendril. "You're *not* interested, are you?"

"How could you ask me that?" sprung from my mouth, which had skillfully avoided her question.

"Well, he is really handsome." She glanced at the celebrity gossip show on the TV above the bar. "Anyway, I suggest you be firm when you talk to him, because he doesn't strike me as the type to accept defeat."

Didn't I know it. Sullivan was a fighting Irishman, and he had the Notre Dame diploma to prove it. "Let's talk about something else."

"Okay, then." Her voice was as bright and bubbly as her pink Prosecco. "How's it going at home?"

I gave her a voodoo-stickpin stare.

"Let's try work. Where are you with the case?"

"I've interviewed everyone except that family from Utah and Linda's friend. But right now I'm focusing on Thomas and Raven. Neither mentioned knowing the other or the incidents at Belleville."

Veronica's mouth twisted to the side. "My guess is that there's a settlement preventing them from talking. But I couldn't find any record of one at the courthouse."

I sucked down some Candy Corn. "They didn't involve the police, so maybe they cut out the attorneys too."

"It's not uncommon." She straightened the bow on her blouse. "Can you imagine how damaging it would've been if the man's death had gone public? I'm sure Belleville paid out quite a sum to keep it quiet."

"That's what Lou said." I chewed my drink straw. "I just wonder if the real culprit was identified. Raven denied any involvement to Sullivan, and I have my suspicions about Thomas."

"In the Charalambous case as well?"

"Definitely. But I also suspect anyone else who had the strength to overpower and hang Gregg—like his frat brothers and Josh."

Her eyebrows twerked. "What about Raven? Or Linda?"

"Linda's only about five foot one, and Raven's not much taller, so I don't see how either of them could have done it. Unless the stereotype about vampires having superhuman strength is true—in which case, I'd have to go with Raven."

"Don't underestimate the power of a woman, Miss Franki," Glenda drawled at my back. "I've met some who can work a pole one-handed."

I thought of Raven's yoga pants. If she was a practicing yogini, then she might've been strong enough to put Gregg on that hook.

"Oh my gosh, Glenda." Veronica squealed with delight. "You look so Victorian Vixen."

Despite my better judgment, I spun on my stool. Glenda wore a tiny corset on each breast, a G-string, and thigh-high stockings that laced up the back with red ribbon. "Mm, it's more Victorian Vampire...Stripper."

Phillip the bartender delivered a plate of eggplant fries to Veronica and tossed a coaster in front of Glenda. "My friend Lisa's a vampire."

Every time he spoke, I imagined Jeff Spicoli in *Fast Times at Ridgemont High* falling from a van in a cloud of pot smoke. "You say that like it's normal."

Glenda rested her corsets on the counter. "Vampires are people too. And as long as they're not hurting anyone, I don't have a problem with it."

"Call me crazy," I said, "but isn't biting someone and draining their blood the definition of hurting them?"

Phillip shook dishwater-blond bangs from his cheeks. "Lisa's not doing it to be mean, man. It helps with her fibromyalgia."

"I'm sorry, what?"

"She says a lot of vampires have it." He placed a flute of champagne in front of Glenda. "Vampirism is an affliction. Their bodies don't produce enough energy. Drinking blood makes them feel energized."

I suffered from low energy too, but I preferred coffee. Nevertheless, I was intrigued by the news. Raven hadn't mentioned a medical component to vampirism, and I hadn't thought to look for one.

Glenda raised her glass. "Let's move to a table for our powwow, shall we?"

I grimaced and rose from my stool. I'd already been dreading the meeting, but after seeing her corsets I had a feeling she was going to hold court.

We settled into a booth overlooking the street.

"Now let's get down and dirty." Glenda shot me a regal stare. "When we first met I told you The Visitor Policy—female tenants aren't allowed to have more than two male friends spend the night at one time—"

"Because you've got a reputation to protect, and you don't want people thinking you rent to whores," I parroted.

"If the Lilliputians try to tie me up again, I'm going to have to amend that policy. Miss Ronnie will confirm that it's within my legal rights as your landlady."

Veronica nodded. "She put a proviso in the rental agreement."

"I've got nothing against little people, sugar, but those Sicilians are sneaky suckers. I can take one or two, but any more than that and they get my hands behind me. And frankly, I have to question their moral character."

My head tipped forward. "You're talking about the elderly Catholic women who hang out with clergy?"

Glenda sipped champagne. "The Bible says *Thou shalt not take the name of the Lord thy God in vain*, and yet the *nonne* drop *Oddio*'s and *Dio mio*'s like Dulcolax."

I couldn't argue with her there, except that my nonna was an aficionada of the enema.

"And don't forget, *Thou shalt not covet*."

I blinked. "What are they coveting?"

She caressed her corsets. "Not everyone can wear costumes like this, Miss Franki."

My jaw loosened, like the screw in her head.

Veronica flipped her hair and leaned forward. "I think they object to your nudity, Glenda. They feel it's indecent."

"Showing what the good Lord gave me?" She arched her back to emphasize what he'd given her. "Sounds to me like they need to get their minds out of the proverbial gutter. And by the way, I think one of them broke mine."

"That wasn't the *nonne*. It was me."

She relaxed her corsets. "Why didn't you let me know?"

"Um, I've had other things to worry about? Anyway, I'll have Anthony fix it for you. He needs something to do."

Glenda pursed her lined lips. "Carlos could use a barback at Madame Moiselle's."

Veronica shook her head. "Franki's mother would not like that."

"Yeah, she'd haul ass here and drag him home to…" I stopped to grab ahold of the lifeline she'd lowered. "What do I need to do to make that happen? A résumé? References?"

"I'll talk to Carlos today, sugar. Tell Anthony to be at the club tomorrow at five."

"I will personally escort him." And because I was eager to stay in Glenda's good graces, at least until my slacker brother got the job, I added, "I'll talk to my nonna about the gatherings."

"Speak of the she-devil." Glenda gestured to the window. "You can talk to her now."

Nonna trotted toward the tavern in her black mourning dress and matching apron, holding a red pasta fork.

I scooted from the booth. When I got outside, Nonna was at the door.

She pointed her pitchfork at me. "It's-a time for dinner."

"Veronica and I are discussing a case." *A mental one.* "And I was going to grab a bite with her and Glenda."

She cast a wary glance at the tavern. Like a typical Italian grandmother, she viewed food from any kitchen other than hers as suspect, and tavern fare was essentially waste cooking. "But I make-a *caponata.*"

"I'm surprised you had time to make anything for your family after all that cooking you've been doing for Detective Sullivan."

Nonna's gaze dropped to her apron. "I am a woman of-a many talents."

Tactics was a more appropriate term. "Uh-huh. And why did you have a priest come to the house today? Was it because of Carnie's Countess Dragula costume?"

"You think I haven't seen a man dressed like a woman vampire? Look at-a the family photos of-a your *nonnu's* mamma."

It hadn't occurred to me before, but my great grandmother did bear a strong resemblance to George Hamilton in *Love at First Bite.*

Her eyes narrowed to slits the size of noodle molds. "I need-a counsel, so I called Father John."

"Who's he?"

"He help-a you with-a that *Limoncello Yellow* murder. You know, that handsome, young-a priest from Our Lady of Guadalupe Catholic Church?"

My mind went to the gutter—not in the sense of impure thoughts about Father John but in the sense of finding the broken piece and hitting myself over the head with it. "A policeman is one thing, but a priest? Do you have no boundaries at all?"

"*Madonna mia, che sacrilegio!*" She put her hands to her bosom. "You need-a to go to confession."

I ignored the confession comment. Nonna and I both knew that she would talk the father into leaving the Church if it meant finding me a husband. "If you weren't trying to fix me up, then why did you call him?"

"Because-a Wesley tell-a me about your case."

If *Wesley* didn't watch out, he was going to find my nonna's pasta pitchfork in his posterior. It was hard enough having Nonna meddle in my personal life, so I didn't need her in my professional one. I summoned my best Robert-De-Niro-in-*Taxi-Driver* voice. "You stay out of my case and stay away from Sullivan, *capito*?"

She jutted out her chin, Mussolini style. "But you need-a protection from-a the *vampiri*. And Father John gave-a me some tips."

I hadn't thought about using the Church as a resource on vampirism, but it wasn't a bad idea. "What I need is protection from your meddling."

"One of these-a days, you'll thank-a me." She shuffled across the street.

Resisting the urge to shout, *I'll thank-a you when you leave me be*, I stormed inside the tavern.

Veronica and Glenda were back at the bar, staring at the TV.

"What's going on?" I asked.

Veronica's blue eyes were cloudy. "There's been another blood-bank incident. We're waiting for the news conference to start."

I glanced at the screen as Sullivan took the podium. "So that's why the officer dragged him from his office today."

"I'd like to drag the detective from his office"—Glenda raised her cigarette holder to her lips—"to my boudoir. Just look at the way he's gripping that podium. If he put that vice grip on me—"

"Sh." I shushed her with a surly stare, irritated that I was irritated. I trained my gaze on Sullivan's face, careful to avoid his hands.

He grabbed the microphone and forced it toward him.

I swallowed and resolved to try harder to focus on his face.

Sullivan glanced to his left at the superintendent, who nodded. "It is with great regret that we inform you of a break-in at The Blood Bank on Governor Nicholls Street at approximately three a.m. this morning."

"Three a.m.?" I echoed.

Veronica touched my arm. "What is it?"

"That's right around the time Josh Santo gave Sullivan the slip." I looked at the TV.

"The blood stores were untouched. However..." The detective fell silent and clenched his jaw. "An employee of the establishment was found deceased at the scene."

10

The door to the Compte Jacques de Saint Germain's former home opened with a creak. Josh appeared and shielded his eyes from the morning sun.

My eyebrows arched like bat wings. "Batman pajamas? Really?"

He looked at his attire. "What's wrong with them?"

"Individuals under investigation for living as vampires should probably avoid anything with bats, particularly after a killing involving blood."

"I hadn't thought about that." He stroked his furry face. "Would you like to come in?"

With the daytime pedestrian traffic, the count's house didn't seem as creepy. But Josh still did. "Only if we keep the door open."

He gestured for me to pass.

I shot a wary stare at his hand. "You go on ahead. Then I'll come in."

"That's cool." He stifled a yawn and headed inside. "I'm going to get some coffee. Want some?"

"I'll pass." The wine weighed heavily on my mind.

I stepped into the entryway and entered the living room. Sunlight streamed from the windows, giving the bright red space an inviting feel that had been absent the night before.

Emboldened by the warm vibe, I followed Josh into the kitchen. But I didn't close the front door. "I'm amazed you're not in jail."

"I was at the police station until a few hours ago." He poured himself a cup of coffee. "Money buys good attorneys."

"It must, because you're doing everything you can to make yourself the prime suspect in these murders."

He sipped from his mug. "How do you figure?"

"Your behavior, your clothes, your house." I leaned my forearms on the far end of the island. "And somehow you even look like de Saint Germain, and Richard Chanfray."

He smirked. "Well, I did study abroad in France."

The look I gave him was lethal.

"That was a joke. Gah. Do I look three hundred years old?"

"No, but a witch I met during my last case didn't look three hundred either."

"Whoa. You know a witch?"

"That's not the point, okay? I don't believe anyone can be that old, but something is off about you. And if I'm going to work for you, you have to stop the nighttime prowling."

He pulled himself onto the black granite countertop and cradled his coffee. "That was impressed upon me by my attorney."

"Good. Because there's an actual vampire suspect in this case, and you act more suspicious than she does." I pulled my black sweater over my waistband. "Now get some furniture, would you? You're not helping yourself or me by living like the compte."

"I know, but furniture is hard." He spoke in a whine. "I get overwhelmed when I have too many options. And I can't decide who to hire to help me decorate."

"I'll simplify it for you. Don't hire a mortician."

He recoiled and curled his lip. "Why would I do that?"

I straightened, preparing to tackle some tough topics and, if the conversation took a wrong turn, him. "I came in here last night, okay? I know about the coffin."

He looked offended rather than outraged. "You broke into my house?"

"A window was open." I skipped the minor detail of me opening it. "And it's not like you have anything to steal."

"Uh, my action figure collection?"

Was this kid for real? "What is a coffin doing in your bedroom?"

"It came with the house."

My eyelids lowered to *likely story* mode. "Did the big red floor stain come with the house too?"

Josh banged the back of his head against the cabinet. "Ugh. So I spilled some wine." He pointed at me. "I might be careless, but you have trust issues."

I shot him a look that said the next red spill would be his blood. "I'm sorry, but I'm not going to trust anyone who impersonates a homicidal vampire. Now, I have to ask you this. Did you kill that man at The Blood Bank?"

"His name was Todd Plank."

My eyes grew as big as the floor stain. "You knew him?"

He held up his hand. "I didn't say that. Detective Sullivan told me his name during questioning. And I didn't kill him."

"Then why did you ditch Sullivan last night?"

"I was hiding. He was in plain clothes, so I didn't know who he was."

Any normal person would hide from a French Quarter stalker in the middle of the night, but not in a cemetery. In The Big Easy, those places were disturbing, and dangerous, as Gregg's murder attested. "He said you vanished right in front of him, like an apparition."

"I slipped inside a tomb."

My stomach rose up as though it wanted to escape from my mouth and run screaming. "*Inside?*"

Josh's eyes gave a not-again roll. "An empty tomb, all right? Then I watched him and figured out who he was. I stayed hidden, though. That guy's built like Robocop."

Despite the circumstances, I was glad he'd noticed Sullivan's physique too. It was further proof that I wasn't interested in the detective, just observant. "And this tomb happened to be where Anne Rice buried her fictional vampire, Louis?"

He exhaled and met my gaze. "I'm not gonna lie. I idolize Louis. I mean, Brad Pitt played him in the movie. But I went there because it was the closest place I could think of to hide."

I scrutinized his face. Despite his facial hair, he had a genuine innocence about him, which made me think Veronica might have been right when she'd called him a harmless young man. "What else did the police tell you about the victim?"

Josh was silent.

And his hesitation gave me pause.

"He was hung upside down like Gregg, and his blood was drained the same way."

My stomach nose-dived into my body cavity. The news confirmed what I'd suspected. The blood bank crimes were linked to Gregg's death. Were they linked to the ones at Belleville House too?

He placed his mug on the counter. "I know this is going to sound crazy, but I told the detective that the killer could've been a woman I saw at the intersection of Bourbon and Governor Nicholls."

"Oh, great." I threw my head back and then jerked it forward again. Even though I was inclined to believe Josh, I wasn't ready to bare my naked neck to him. "So you *were* near The Blood Bank last night."

"I was hanging out on Bourbon, I swear. But check this out." He slid to the floor. "I saw her around two thirty. And she was wearing *a cape.*"

My body tensed, ready for fight *and* flight, with him on the ground. "Two people wearing a cape in the same area? Come on."

"I'm not lying." His whine had returned. "She looked like Little Red Riding Hood. You know, with her head covered?"

Although I was skeptical, I had to consider the lead since there were female suspects in the case. "Did you notice anything else about her?"

"I only got a good look at her when she passed by a street lamp.

But she was small, around 5'3" or 5'4". And she was wearing tights. Or maybe yoga pants."

My stomach did a downward dog.

Raven?

~

"Tales from the Crisp?" I pulled David's cereal box from the office kitchen cabinet and contemplated the coffin-shaped contents. Based on the ingredients, I was going to have to follow it up with a bowl of Fiber the 13th.

Veronica appeared in a black-and-white pantsuit that matched the newspaper in her hand. "*You* are going to eat *cemetery-themed food*?"

I dumped some mini coffins into a bowl. "After the Creole Cockroaches at Bayou Cuisine, I figure I can digest anything. And I didn't eat breakfast before going to Josh's, so I'm as hungry as a wolf. Make that a werewolf."

"Your funeral."

I gave her a death stare.

She opened the paper with a snap. "I came to tell you that Todd Plank wasn't just any employee at The Blood Bank. He was the CFO."

"What would a big-time manager be doing at the office at two-thirty in the morning? Those people don't work."

"Maybe he was killed earlier. *The Times-Picayune* doesn't give a time of death."

"Then why would Josh or Raven be in the area that late? Returning to the scene of the crime?"

"Or coincidence." She scanned the article. "It describes him as a family man, an active church member, and an avid runner. He was also a Virginia Tech grad. Shame, isn't it?"

"I'll say. Can you imagine having the HokieBird as a mascot? I mean, it's a goofy turkey on steroids." I poured milk over the coffins and watched them float. "And why would educated people pick burnt orange and maroon for their school colors? The entire state of Texas knows those shades don't mix."

I turned to leave the kitchen with my Tales from the Crisp and found Veronica staring at me like I'd risen from the crypt.

"Honestly, Franki. I was talking about the man's murder, not his alma mater."

"Sorry. I'm a little worked up." I headed to my office with her on my heels. "I've been researching medical conditions for vampirism, and in the process I've learned something truly bloodcurdling." I paused to heighten the drama of my discovery. "Vampire serial killers are a thing."

"What makes them serial killers? She asked the question like we were discussing the vampire breast lift fad rather than a ferocious murderer.

"They feed from people to kill them." I sat at my chair, cradling my bowl. "There was one in Germany, one in Japan, and three in the U.S. And, in at least two of the cases, the men claimed to be centuries-old vampires."

She tossed the newspaper on my desk and leaned against the doorframe. "So you think we have a vampire serial killer in New Orleans?"

"Now that there's been a second murder, yes." I scooped a couple of coffins. "And get this. One from Massachusetts, who was called 'The Schizophrenic Vampire,' drank his own grandmother's blood, which is eerily reminiscent of that grandfather at Belleville House."

"Is that what psychologists attribute this to? Schizophrenia?"

"That or paraphilia, which is sexual perversion." I shot her a squeamish look. "I haven't found any condition that causes a physical need to consume blood, but I did find something called Clinical Vampirism, or Renfield's Syndrome, which is an obsession with drinking blood."

Veronica stuck out her tongue and crossed her arms. "So what's your next move?"

"Well, tonight I have the waste-cooking class and before that Anthony's interview. In the meantime, Sullivan isn't returning my calls about the Plank murder, and I need to figure out if Todd knew anyone on the Vampires and Victims tour." I chewed the skin on my thumbnail. "If he didn't, the killer could be someone from the community at large."

"I don't know. My instincts tell me it was someone from the tour. Have you talked to the Utah family or Linda's friend?"

I crunched the coffins. "I've left messages for them. Somehow I need to verify whether Josh really saw Raven near The Blood Bank. But she's not likely to admit to that, so I'm thinking about tailing her after the cotillion."

"Make sure David goes with you." Her eyes narrowed into an or-else stare. "If there is a serial killer, I don't want you investigating alone."

"Trust me, I don't want that either."

She moved to leave and stopped. "By the way, it's probably for the best that Sullivan isn't returning your calls."

"Except that I no longer have his input on the case."

She shrugged. "You've solved murder cases without him. You'll do it again."

I smiled on the outside while my inside wrestled with an uncomfortable reality—I was disappointed that Sullivan hadn't called. And I didn't know if it was because I was going to miss having a big, burly sidekick on a skincrawler of a case, or because I was going to miss him.

The lobby buzzer sounded.

"Yo, sis!"

I knew one guy I wasn't going to miss—that is, if I could ever get him out of my house. "Why, Veronica? Seriously, just why?"

Her eyes crinkled, and she exhaled a laugh. "I'll pop out and say hello."

I followed her into the lobby, carrying my bowl and wondering whether the sugary coffins had cast a pall on my day.

Anthony had wasted no time in making himself comfortable. He reclined on the couch in the wife beater, red track pants, and Italian-flag socks he'd left the house wearing the night before.

"Eyyy, Ronnieee." He gave her a bloodshot wink. "Lookin' good, girl."

The odor of Bourbon Street wafted from his mouth.

"Nice to see you too." Veronica wrinkled her nose. "I'll leave you two to chat."

I waited until she'd disappeared and then turned on him like bad wine. "Why are you here? Your interview isn't until five, which is seven hours from now."

"The *nonne* are watchin' Netflix, so I'm jus' gonna crash heuh till then."

That statement was packed with problems, so I decided to pick it apart in order of utterance. "How many *nonne*?"

"I dunno. Eight, nine. They all look the same."

I'd told my nonna not to have more than a couple of friends over. So something was up, and whatever it was would turn my life upside down. "What are they watching?"

He nestled his head into a cushion and closed his eyes. "*Dracula.* Nonna said they was doin' research. Prolly lookin' for ideas to accessorize their death dresses."

Mannaggia. It wasn't mourning fashion they were researching, but how to meddle in my case. "Since you've got the whole day free, I need you to do two things. First, go home and talk to Glenda about fixing a broken gutter. And then, so you don't blow the interview, get some sleep."

"That's what I'm tryin' ta do, if you'd stop wit' the naggin'."

I approached the couch and balled my fist, and not to fist pump. "I didn't mean here. This is a business, and we have a serious case to solve."

An eye opened, and he grabbed my bowl. "Yo, gimme a bite o' that."

"That's it. I'm calling Mom." I marched to my office.

"Yeah, go tattle," he taunted. "Real adult."

I might've been behaving childishly, but I sure as heck wasn't going to take adulting lessons from him.

Intent on telling my parents what I thought of the Anthony

arrangement, I reached for my desk phone. It was ten a.m., so I dialed their work number.

"Amato's Deli. Larry speakin'."

The New York accent and name belonged to a seventy-something regular who worked in Houston's Rice Village, where our family business was located. So it didn't make sense for him to be answering the phone. "Larry from the Drycleaner's?"

"Now it's Larry from the Deli."

I imagined him serving customers in his gray flat cap, gray clothes, and gray frown. "This is Franki. Can I speak to my mother, please?"

"She ain't here."

"Okay, then put my dad on."

"He ain't here either."

I almost keeled over. At least one member of my family was in that deli at all times during working hours. "Where are they?"

"At home gettin' the place ready for a party."

My parents hadn't had a party since I was ten. And the only preparation they'd done was put out chips and dip, mix martinis, and set out Yahtzee scorecards. "On a Thursday night? What's going on?"

"Life, baby. Life."

The phone slammed into the cradle.

I stared at my cell. I didn't know what was more disconcerting—the notion of my mom and dad actually enjoying their lives or the discovery that they'd replaced my brother with the likes of Larry.

And then the confusion cleared. My parents didn't care who worked at the deli as long as it wasn't Anthony. And now that they'd stuck him with me, they were living it up.

The cover popped off my phone from the sheer force of my squeeze.

I didn't begrudge my mom and dad a good time, quite the contrary. But I wasn't going to pay for their parenting mistakes. One way or another, Anthony was returning to the nest. And he was taking Nonna with him.

A buzz came from the lobby, followed by a door slam.

I said a silent prayer that Anthony had left. And wandered into oncoming traffic.

Then I asked forgiveness for that last part and threw in a couple of Hail Marys as an added precaution. After all, he was probably in danger, and I had to keep him safe.

With my conscience clear, I reentered the lobby and found my brother still supine, showing David and the vassal the *Forza, Itala!* tattoo on his bicep.

"If it means *Go, Italy!*," the vassal said, "shouldn't there be another 'i' for *Italia*?"

"Yeh, but this ways it's an Italian chick's name, Itala." Anthony gave a sly sneer. "Know what I'm sayin'?"

A round of knuckle-bumps ensued.

"Sorry to interrupt the bonding, but we have work to do." I looked at Anthony even though I was talking to the boys. "I'm sure you two heard about the Todd Plank murder?"

David gave a clinched-jaw nod in contrast with the vassal's version.

I looked at David, apologetic. "Per Veronica, you're going to have to be my date to the Crimson Cotillion."

Anthony's low brow lowered. "My brutha, you can do bettuh."

The boys snickered, and I wanted to knuckle-bump *my brutha*'s thick skull. Instead, I opted for more subtle revenge. "Vassal, I need you to stay on Detective Sullivan for the lab results on that wine. There's a good chance it contained *diseased* human blood."

Anthony shuddered and rubbed his biceps, and I smiled inside.

David cleared his throat. "So, we have a contact at Delta Upsilon Delta. He's a freshman pledge named Andrew Maloney."

Given recent developments, I'd almost forgotten my suspicions about the frat. "That's great. How do you guys know him?"

The vassal stepped forward, hands clasped behind his back. "He's in our coding course. As it turns out, he wanted to pledge our fraternity. But his brother was a DUD, so he's a legacy."

And what a legacy it was.

"When we saw him in class this morning, he told us their Halloween party is tonight."

I thought of my parents. "Why is everyone having Thursday parties when Halloween is on Saturday?"

"Uh, part of the DUD credo is to maximize their party potential," David said. "They have theirs tonight so they don't miss the Friday and Saturday sorority parties."

Anthony's church face reflected his somber respect. "Dem boys is smart."

Said the guy with the bad grammar and the misspelled tattoo. "Can you guys get an invite?"

"We already received one." The vassal glanced up at me. "You can be my date."

"Thanks, but the frat would be less than thrilled if I showed up."

"Damn straight," Anthony exclaimed. "She'd kill the party."

The spikes in his hair had nothing on my stare. "Keep it up, and I'll kill you."

The vassal, who had turned as red as my brother's track pants, closed his mouth to swallow. "You would make an enjoyable guest, but that's not why I invited you." He glanced at David. "Andrew said there's a room at the fraternity house that is off limits. With you there, we have a better chance of finding it and gaining access."

I pushed my brother's feet off the arm of the couch and took a seat. "It's probably their pledge initiation room."

David scratched the back of his ear. "Uh, in the frat world it's known as a hazement, as in hazing and basement, and Andrew said he and the other pledges have been in there. Only Craig Rourke and Domenic LaVecchio have a key to the room I'm talking about. The freaky thing is that he heard Craig call it The Dungeon."

That *was* freaky. And frightening. Because The Dungeon was also the name of the local vampire bar.

The one Raven had mentioned.

~

ANTHONY STRAIGHTENED his oversized gold chains and raised the
collar of his tracksuit jacket. "I look good, right?"

He was nervous about the interview, so I searched for a tactful but
truthful reply. "You look like you were born to work at Madame
Moiselle's."

"Got any advice before I go in?"

Because he was applying at a strip club, it was the one time I
could safely say, "Just be yourself."

"Cool." He gave me a high five.

"Oh, and did you talk to Glenda about that gutter?"

"I'm on it, awright?"

Something told me he wasn't, but I kept my mouth shut. "Make
sure you're not just on it, but all over it, okay? I've got to get over to my
cooking class."

He nodded. Then he pounded his chest and strutted inside, and I
headed back to the office.

No one doubted my brother's employability more than I did, but
after that display, I felt he might've finally found his career path.

To avoid the tourists and the local happy hour crowd, I turned off
Bourbon. I'd only walked a few hundred feet when I sensed I was
being followed. At the Royal Street stop sign, I casually glanced
around while waiting for traffic to pass. No one looked suspect—in
terms of stalking, anyway.

I forged ahead, attributing my unease to Anthony and the case.
And to the evening's menu at Bayou Cuisine.

At the next intersection, I spotted a group of twenty or so people
standing outside Harry's Corner, a popular dive bar.

A silver-haired gentleman in an expensive button-down shirt and
slacks smiled as I approached.

"Is there a special going on, or something?"

His green eyes narrowed in mock conspiracy. "It's a meeting of the
Grande and Secret Order of the Obituary Cocktail. You should
join us."

I flinched. According to the bartender at Molly's, Thomas Van
Scyoc was a member.

"Nothing to be afraid of." The man patted my arm. "It's a spin on the gin martini, not a death warrant."

Not the drink, maybe, but Thomas might be. "A stiff drink is exactly what I need. No pun intended."

"None understood." He bowed and gestured for me to enter.

The bar was musty and dark, like a proper hole in the wall. I squinted until my eyes adjusted. Then shock dawned on me like an atom bomb.

Thomas sat at a lone two-top in the back.

And with him sat Craig Rourke.

11

"Tonight's recipe is courtesy of deadfood.com." Chef Mel beamed from behind the classroom computer. "Alligator Chili, Cajun comfort food."

Somehow, I failed to find comfort in the dish or the website.

"Where'd you get gator meat?" Lou asked.

"Out on I-10."

Under normal circumstances, I would've assumed he was talking about a grocery store or butcher shop located along the highway. But given the class, I knew he meant on the actual road, as in roadkill.

Mel looked over his shoulder at the blank projector screen. "Uh-oh. We have a technical issue. While I work on getting the recipe up, go ahead and start on the alligator. And remember, this is a no-fry zone. Get it? No fry?"

Unfortunately, we did.

I poured oil into a sauté pan. While I waited for it to heat, I opened three cans of expired tomato sauce. And I thought about blood.

And Thomas and Craig.

I couldn't imagine why the two men would've met unless it had to do with the murders. And yet, based on the evidence I'd gathered, Raven and Josh were the most likely suspects.

There was no way around it. My best shot at identifying the killer was to decode Campari Crimson, and I wasn't convinced it was a drink. The only other ideas that came to mind were a title or some kind of symbol, maybe related to voodoo. If that were so, it wouldn't hurt to consult Father John. Catholicism and voodoo were inextricably linked in New Orleans, so local priests were well versed in the subject.

Mel placed a stepladder beneath the ceiling projector. "Once you've got the alligator going, turn to the four special ingredients at each of your stations. And say, Seasoning's greetings!"

I wanted to greet him—with a cloud of the Slap Ya Mama seasoning.

"For today's cook-off, choose one of the four to flavor your chili."

Sara looked at Michele. "I only have three."

"I've got four." Michele looked at me.

Sara approached my station and tripped, knocking my bottle of Peychaud's Bitters to the floor with a crash. "Sorry." She knelt to pick up the glass. "I'm such a klutz."

Was she? The athlete? I narrowed my eyes like Eastwood. "That was going to be my special ingredient."

Michele glanced at Chef Mel, who was jiggling the projector's power cord. "We're not supposed to share since this is a competition," she whispered, "but I could give you some of mine."

"Thanks." I crouched to help Sara, and Michele poured Peychaud's into my pan.

"Hey," I whisper-scolded. "I was supposed to do that."

"Well, I had to do it while Chef Mel wasn't looking, otherwise you would've been disqualified." She batted her big eyes. "I only put a couple of drops."

I wasn't so sure about that. The fishy-rot odor of the alligator had taken on a tutti-frutti licorice scent.

After Sara and I cleaned the mess, I decided to engage Michele in a conversation about the contest to try to gauge her competitiveness.

To keep it casual, I diced a bell pepper. "Did the chef say anything about the school's Mardi Gras float during the first week of class?"

She sized me up with a sidelong glance. "It's a gumbo pot. And the winner gets to dress up like a piece of okra."

Chandra hadn't mentioned the costume. "Sara, you'd look good in that."

Michele halved a jalapeño with a thwack. "I would too. I've been a princess every Halloween since I was born."

"What does that have to do with okra?"

"Cinderella and the pumpkin? Snow White and the apple? Tiana and the beignet?" She raised the knife. "Shall I go on?"

"No, no." I took a step back. "I see the correlation."

"I'm glad you came around." She dropped the knife and clasped her hands, and I half-expected her to break into song. "Can you imagine how wonderful it would be? A princess in a parade?"

I imagined a stalk of okra in a tiara and a sparkly green dress. "I guess?"

"I'd be the prettiest piece of okra you ever saw." She grabbed the ends of her apron and twirled like Cinderella in her ball gown. But instead of a dreaminess to her tone, there was a determination that was decidedly Disney villain.

Perhaps both women had been sabotaging Lou.

"Okay, recipe's on the screen." Mel climbed from the stepladder. "I had to switch out a cable." He wiped his hands on his chef's pants. "I used to sell car parts, so I know all about that."

I wasn't sure what cars had to do with projectors, and I didn't ask. He was likely to explain it. In painstaking detail.

Sara tasted her chili. "You know what would be good in this? Cynar."

Lou's head popped up from his pan. "What's that?"

"Artichoke liqueur," she replied. "But it's actually made with a lot of herbs and plants. Like bitters, or Aperol and Campari."

Chef Mel strolled to her station. "Campari is made with sixty-eight herbs, fruits, roots, and spices. The recipe is secret, but I've got it mostly figured out because I trained to be a sommelier."

"Mel the sommelier." Lou chuckled and bounced to his tiptoes in his toe shoes. "Fun to say."

The chef's face lit up like the projector screen. "That's right! So-Mel-YAY. It's like 'so Mel' with a cheer."

Except that none of us were cheering.

Mel settled onto Sara's stovetop with a one-arm lean. "I have a super sensitive nose and palate. I've identified sixty-one of Campari's ingredients. There's carminic acid, which gives it the red color, from the cochineal bug."

A bug? No wonder he knew about the liqueur.

"And bitter orange, cherry, grapefruit, quinine, bay leaf, thyme, clove..."

My stress level grew with the list.

"...vanilla, rhubarb, cascarilla, ginseng..."

And I wasn't just tense because the chef was going to name all sixty-one of the ingredients he'd identified, although that was a huge part of it. There was something about the secret recipe that stressed me out. It was as though my body sensed something my brain wasn't ready to grasp. *But what?*

Did the secret ingredients hold the key to the case?

"Buffy the Vampire Slayer?" I stood before Veronica's bedroom mirror, scrutinizing my reflection in the black sleeveless shirt and red pleather pants. "You had fun with this, didn't you?"

She collapsed over the back of her vanity chair and vibrated in a silent giggle fit. After what was practically the length of a Buffy episode, she stood and wiped a tear from her eye. "I really did. But the case aside, it's the perfect costume for the frat party. You look like a sorority girl in that blonde wig."

"Except that I'm six foot one in these boots, which is at least half a foot over the standard sorority girl size." I turned away from the mirror. "Also, my biceps are disturbingly reminiscent of Anthony's, and there's a good chance a drunk frat boy will mistake my thighs for giant cocktail wieners."

Veronica's Pomeranian, Hercules, licked his lips, confirming my fear.

"That outfit is great on you. And they'll all be so drunk they won't notice what you look like." She patted the back of the chair. "Now come sit down so I can do your makeup."

"Okay, but I'm starting to think that I would've been better off going to Glenda for a costume."

Our eyes met in the mirror, and we laughed so hard my pleather almost split. After a thorough check of the seams, I tossed my phone on the vanity and took a seat.

Veronica sponged foundation on my face. "Have you thought any more about that secret recipe?"

"I did some research on Campari. Apparently, only one man in the world knows the full list of ingredients. And he has some of the herbs delivered to the factory in unmarked paper bags, so the employees can't figure out what they are."

"Wow. What about how it's made?"

"They steep the dry ingredients in vats of water for a couple of weeks before adding a sweetening syrup and the red bug juice."

She grimaced and reached for an eyeliner pencil. "You're not going to like this, but it reminds me of a voodoo potion."

I shook my wig, wigging out. "I've already gone there, and I don't want to go again. A voodoo vampire investigation is too over the top, even for New Orleans."

Hercules stood and shook his cream-colored fur.

"See? Even Hercules says it's too much."

Veronica shook her head and draped a silver chain around my neck that had a cross and some sort of ornate tube.

I looked down. "What's this round thing?"

"A vampire whistle."

"I had no idea there was such a thing. But then again, I didn't know that real vampires existed, either."

My ringtone sounded, and I reached for the phone. "Maybe it's Sullivan."

Her eyebrow went on the offensive. "What about Bradley?"

The question rattled my brain, and my bones. *Why had I thought about Sullivan first?* "It's Linda West's friend. I need to get this." I answered on speaker, avoiding her eyes. And her energy-sucking tendril. "Hey, Belinda. Thanks for returning my call."

"Sorry I'm just getting back to you." Her voice had a warm, close-friend quality. "I've been doing double duty at my job answering phones, so I can barely bring myself to call anyone when I get home."

"I understand, so I'll make this quick." I gestured for Veronica to continue with the makeup. "Linda mentioned that you decided not to go on the tour because you got scared. Was that because of the theme, or was it one of the other guests?"

"Honestly, I was just tired, but I didn't tell Linda that. She dragged me all over the city that day, and then she made me work out with her on her cable machine before the tour."

Despite the size of my thighs, I gave Veronica a don't-get-any-ideas glare as she lined my eyes.

"When we got to the convent, we had to wait for the other people to show up. And by the time they did, I was falling asleep on my feet."

"Did you interact with any of them?"

"No, but I could smell alcohol on the breath of that poor guy who died, and I was standing two feet away from him."

So Gregg had been drinking. "Did you notice anything unusual about him or anyone else?"

"Uh, besides that vampire chick?" She laughed. "If anything was unusual, it was that she acted completely normal, while another guy on the tour stared at my neck. Or maybe it was my boa. I don't know, and I don't want to."

Veronica straightened, and we shared a look.

"Did this guy have dirty blonde hair and pale skin?"

"That's the one. I tell you, it's hard to tell the crazy people from the sane ones anymore."

Especially in The Crescent City on the eve of a blood moon.

"Other than that, there's really nothing I can tell you except be careful out there."

"Thanks, Belinda. You do the same." I hung up and absentmindedly tapped the phone on my leg.

Veronica opened a tube of mascara. "What are you thinking?"

"Thomas keeps coming up, doesn't he?"

"I've noticed that too. We need to send an undercover PI inside the retirement home, but it has to be someone he wouldn't recognize. David's too inexperienced, so I'll start thinking about who we could hire."

I gripped the cross. Instead of being relieved that I didn't have to go back to Belleville, I was apprehensive. Veronica was right. We had to send someone inside. But somehow I knew I would live to regret that plan in ways I couldn't yet fathom.

"THE IDEA WAS to turn the Frat Castle into Dracula's Castle." Andrew Maloney's voice boomed above the strains of fratmusic.com as he plowed through the partiers in his Pittsburgh Pirates uniform. "We wanted a totally frightening fratmosphere."

The castle was frightening but not for the reason the DUDs had intended. Apart from The Munster Mansion–type candelabras and cobwebs, the interior of the Garden District estate was a dilapidated version of the ramshackle fraternity in *Animal House*. Even more terrifying, it stunk of stale beer, dirty socks, and, thanks to the sorority girls in attendance, Viva La Juicy perfume.

"Drinks are here." Andrew stopped at a table with more bottles of booze than a French Quarter bar. "And check out the ice chest I made." He shot me a proud smile and pointed to a coffin full of oversized syringes filled with red Jell-O shots.

"Fratastic," I said in keeping with the Greek speak. I gestured to a fountain of blood-colored queso. "Did you do that too?"

"Queso is Craig's thing. He eats it at every meal."

That explained a lot about his disposition. "Where is he, anyway?"

"Something came up, and he had to go see his grandma. I don't think he's back yet."

Since I'd seen him at Harry's Corner, I wondered whether he'd fabricated the grandma story to cover his meeting with Thomas. "What about Dom?"

He swung his baseball bat toward the ice luge. "He's the luchador."

Domenic sported a mint-green mask with a matching Mohawk. But from the way his head hung, he was in no shape to wrestle.

A fratdaddy swaddled in a toga marched up to Andrew. "Yo, NIB. We're here to party, not practice our swing. We need frat water on the fratio, stat."

"Sorry about that, man." Andrew removed his cap and rubbed his shaved scalp as he turned to me. "I've got to restock the beer." He put his cap back on and pulled the bill low. "The room you're looking for," he said from the side of his mouth, "is at the end of that hall by Gregg's couch."

"On it." I spun around and started.

The vassal stood beside me in a black leather jacket reminiscent of James Dean's bad-boy look. Perhaps more rebellious, he wasn't wearing his glasses.

"So, uh..." I pursed to block a smile. "What's a NIB?"

"A Newly Initiated Brother, or Bro, depending upon your preferences."

"Ah." I looked at his motorcycle boots. "Who are you supposed to be, anyway?"

"I'm Angel." His eyes grew to their lens-enhanced size. "Buffy the Vampire Slayer's lover."

I cocked my wig in alarm. Apparently, the vassal hadn't invited me to the party solely for business purposes. "Well, I've got to get to work, so you and I need to split up." I let the double entendre sink in. "Find David and tell him to keep an eye out for Craig. And you stick close to Dom. Text if you have any problems."

Without waiting for his reply, I battened down my blonde wig and headed for the hallway. As I passed the ice luge, a frat boy in a sorority girl costume poured red liquid down the chute and into the mouth of a waiting Baywatch babe.

She spat the liquor onto the floor. "Hey! That wasn't Fireball."

"Because it was Campari."

I stopped so abruptly I feared my wig would keep walking. "Why'd you pick that?"

He looked me up but not down. "It looks like blood. Why else?"

"Do you guys drink Campari often?"

"For Halloween." His close-set eyes narrowed to a semi-cross. "What's it to ya?"

Domenic's head popped up Chucky style. "Watch the frattitude, bro." He engaged the gaze of his fellow fratter in a staredown. "She's no ordinary sorostitute."

I didn't appreciate the backhanded compliment. Since becoming a fake blonde, I'd bonded with my sorority non-sisters. Also, I wasn't sure whether Domenic had defended me because he knew who I was or because he'd taken a liking to me. Either way, I didn't wait to find out. I fled to the entryway, and when I was certain I hadn't been followed, I speed-walked past Gregg's couch to the end of the hall.

There were two doors, so I picked one and peeked inside.

At the head of the room stood an altar, but it wasn't the church variety. The Delta Upsilon Delta seal hung on the wall, and below it was a formidable paddle.

The hazement.

Marveling at the brazenness of the suspended DUDs, I pulled the door closed and practically jumped from my wig.

None other than my brother strutted up with a Madonna in tow —not the Virgin Mary, but the singer of the "Like a Virgin" era. Although, based on the bump on the woman's belly, she was decidedly unlike a virgin.

"What are you doing here?" I huffed.

"Celebratin'. I got the job." He pulled the Madonna close. "This fine filly is Crystal. She's a cocktail waitress at Madame Moiselle's."

Well, she certainly couldn't strip in her condition. Then again, this was New Orleans, so she could. "Anthony, you have to leave. You know I'm not here to party."

"Not dressed like that you ain't." He yukked and angled a glance at his date, who was tucking a boob into her bustier. Taking advantage of her distraction, he leaned in. "Yo, you think your pants'd fit me?"

If I could have pulled a Buffy and slayed him, I would have. My mom was going to hear from me in the morning, that is, if she could work me into her social calendar.

"I'm bored, Ant'ny," Crystal Madonna whined. "Let's find another room."

As if she needed one.

"Later, sis." He winked. "You and Nonna don't wait up."

"When I get home, that gutter had better be hung up."

He raised his free hand and waved goodbye, without turning around.

Clenching my teeth, I grabbed the other door handle and yanked. It was locked.

The Dungeon.

I removed a bobby pin from my wig and took out my fraternal frustrations on the lock. Within a few minutes, the handle turned, and I slipped inside. Rather than turn on the light, I used the one on my phone.

The room had no windows, and three of the walls were black. The fourth was covered in a rough substance similar to volcanic rock.

My chest constricted at the sight of a coffin, but I told myself it was probably a party decoration that hadn't been put to use. Beside it was a blue tarp draped over an object that was maybe six feet wide and five feet high.

Slowly, I removed the cover.

And my eyes went vassal wide.

Before me were two hospital beds complete with IV stands. And plastic packages that appeared to contain blood bags.

I tapped my phone's video feature to record the discovery for the police.

The wood floor creaked.

And I was glued to it.

A hand gripped my mouth, and another twisted my arm. My phone fell to the floor as my shoulder wrenched, sending a searing sensation through my body that was part pain and part fear. I thrashed from side to side desperate to save myself from a fate involving those blood bags. And that coffin.

But I couldn't break free.

I kicked behind me.

My attacker shoved me face first into the coffin, seizing upon my unbalanced stance.

"Help." My cry came out a statement, stifled by a gasp as I crashed into the pinewood.

The coffin slammed shut.

And my world went as black as the walls.

12

Fear penetrated my skin like a poison.

And squeezed oxygen from my lungs.

Breathe. I needed to breathe.

I flipped onto my back and rammed the coffin lid with my shoulder.

Locked.

Had I been the target of a fraternity prank? Or the victim of a more frightening plot?

Domenic had probably recognized me and followed me into The Dungeon. Or Craig might have come back and caught me in the room. Thomas too. He could have been at the party in costume, stalking me the entire time. And when I gave him an opportunity, he shoved me into the coffin.

But why?

Was the plan to leave me to suffocate? Or siphon my blood on one of those beds?

Fear paralyzed my muscles.

I had to think. React.

David and the vassal knew where I was. They would look for me if I didn't turn up.

But when?

I had one-to-two hours of air, and then I was out. In more ways than one.

Fear permeated my veins.

Waiting to be rescued wasn't an option. I had to free myself.

But how?

Yelling would consume too much oxygen, and I wouldn't be able to out-shout the music. I couldn't out-wait it either. It was only around ten p.m., which meant the frat party was just getting going.

Fear pierced my heart.

Stay calm, Franki.

I inhaled.

Pine. I smelled pine. *A soft wood with some give.*

Using my hands, I pushed the lid. The wood yielded, which meant there was a chance it would crack. I pumped until my arms were too weak and switched to my knees. And when my knees began to throb, I switched to my feet. But there wasn't enough space to get my heels on the lid, so I kicked with my toes.

If I made it out of the coffin alive, I would kiss Veronica for making me wear the Buffy boots. After that I would kick the last breath out of whoever had locked me inside.

Seconds ticked away.

Minutes.

An hour?

My limbs had given out, but the lid hadn't. I lay soaked in sweat. The air was stifling, and I wasn't sure how much of it was left.

The ringtone of my phone sounded, and I could tell it was right outside the coffin where it had fallen when I was attacked. I was sure it was Bradley calling.

His face materialized.

And an ache ate at my gut. *Was this the last time I would see him? As a mirage in my final resting place?*

The Cake song "Never There" blasted on the stereo, and the beat shook the coffin, mocking me and my relationship in my final moments.

The ache turned to anger. I loved Bradley, but a relationship was hard when one of us was always at work. And if the New York trip had taught me anything, it was that he loved his career more than me.

I shook my head, and Sullivan appeared.

My anger dissipated. And my gut filled with regret. The detective had feelings for me, and I felt something for him as well. He'd been around when Bradley hadn't, and I'd come to depend on that.

Hang on.

Sullivan. He would stop by the frat party as part of his investigation, and as soon as he spotted David and the vassal, he would ask where I was. Unless he avoided them because I'd rebuffed him in his office.

My hope faded, and so did the detective.

The coffin returned to black.

And my panic escalated to terror.

No one was going to save me.

Phil popped in with a huge grin.

Wait. The creepy cemetery caretaker?

Horror dawned on me like a zombie apocalypse. Phil had come to put me in the crypt that was for sale. And probably to gloat because I didn't have a coffin bell.

What had he said about that thing? It was the origin of the phrase dead ringer.

And saved by the bell.

My hand went to my neck.

The vampire whistle.

I put the tube into my mouth and blew. The noise was so shrill it shook me from my semi-shock.

And reminded me of my mother.

I blew until my ears rung. But my lungs were winding down, and so was my oxygen.

Was this it? My end?

A door slammed, and I jumped.

Heels clicked across the hardwood floor. But they stopped and started. Or maybe serpentined.

I spit out the whistle and kicked and pounded and yelled. I didn't give a damn if Domenic or Craig or Thomas had come to bleed me dry.

I wanted out.

I wanted air.

I wanted life.

A metal latch clanked. The coffin lid creaked open.

Cool air blanketed my body and lined my lungs.

I shot to a sitting position, fists raised.

Maybe Baby squinted at me with one eye and slurped from a straw in a half-empty hurricane glass. "What's all the racket about?"

I stared at her while I caught up on my breath. I knew she wasn't the brightest sequin on the stripper costume, but that was dull even for her. And even for drunk her. "Uh, I needed to get out of the coffin?"

"You don't have to be snippy about it, sister."

Operating on the assumption that the "sister" was a sorority sister, I removed my blonde hair. "Maybe, it's me. Franki. The PI?"

She hiccupped. "Why are you wearing a wig?"

"It's a Halloween party?"

She hiccupped. "That's for the boys."

"Then why are you dressed like a French maid?"

She hiccupped. "I'm not. I'm a nurse." Her head lolled to one side. "Hey, so I can cure myself of these hives."

Florence Nightingale she was not. Nor was she Noam Chomsky.

After another hiccup, Maybe pinched her nose and drained her hurricane. "You'd better get up 'cause we've gotta beat it. I need another drink, and this place is off limits."

"Why? What's it for?" I stepped from the coffin on loose legs and scooped up my phone.

"Well, it ain't finished, but it's a play room for Craig and Dom."

She was taking the house mom job too far. "These guys are not little boys. For example, I've never seen a play room with..."

My voice trailed off as I gestured at the far wall.

The hospital beds and IV stands were gone.

ALCOHOL WAS DEADLY, but a double shot of honey bourbon at Thibodeaux's brought me back to life. Basking in the warmth of the buzz, I threw a twenty on the counter and exited the bar. Before crossing the street, I checked both ways. Not for cars, but for cape-wearing vampires and blood-draining frat boys.

When I got to my lawn, I turned to the cemetery and pointed my index and pinky fingers downward in a *scongiuri* gesture to ward off bad luck—specifically, a return to a coffin while I was still alive.

Next, I flashed a *scongiuri* at the fourplex, where a FIAT was parked, because it was a telltale sign there were *nonne* inside. And a midnight gathering of *nonne* could only mean misfortune.

The necessary precautions taken, I sprinted to my porch. A new length of gutter that Anthony hadn't bothered to hang lay on the welcome mat .

Gritting my teeth, I gripped the door handle and hesitated. The *nonne* thought unescorted women who stayed out after dark were *buttane*, the Sicilian word for whores. So I had to forget about my brother and prepare for all inferno to break loose when I entered the house—and in high-heeled boots and red pleather pants.

Bracing myself for the *buttana* backlash, I opened the door. But the only blast was from the odor of garlic bread.

Nonna and her friends Santina and Mary sat in black mourning dress on the chaise lounge clutching rosaries, transfixed by the TV.

Napoleon, belly up on Santina's wide lap, rolled his eyes into their sockets and back into his head.

So much for greeting his owner, returned from the near dead. "Why are you ladies up so late?"

The *nonne* started.

"Oh, Franki." Nonna looked like she'd been caught stealing from the communion plate. "We're...watching-a midnight-a mass."

Santina and Mary nodded with eyes as big as Hosts.

I removed my coat and hung it on the rack. "On a Thursday in October?"

Nonna angled a glance at her friends. "It's a rerun."

I might've been a lapsed Catholic, but I could still sniff out a sin. I walked in front of the screen and saw a scene with Lestat and Louis in *Interview with a Vampire*, which explained the garlic bread. "Gosh, Nonna. I never knew Tom Cruise and Brad Pitt were priests."

"It's a movie about-a midnight-a mass."

I turned and shot her the eagle eye. "Led by vampire clergymen?"

The *nonne* bowed their heads, but not in prayer.

"I know you guys want to help with my case, but I've got it under control." That wasn't entirely true given the coffin mishap, but I wasn't holding a rosary like they were. "So please, leave the investigating to me."

"You got it all-a wrong-a." Nonna smoothed her skirt. "We're-a watching this-a movie for the local history."

I picked up a copy of *The Vampire Combat Manual: A Guide to Fighting the Bloodthirsty Undead*. "Is this part of your local history study too?"

"All-a right, all-a right. We're-a trying to help."

"Well, don't. PI work is dangerous."

"So are vampires." Mary reached for a piece of garlic bread. "We've been doing research to figure out how you can fight them."

Santina worked a rosary bead. "*Hai bisogno di un esorcista.*"

"I don't see how an exorcist can help." Unless he could evict the meddling demon from Italian grandmothers and their friends.

Nonna clasped her hands. "Talk-a to Father John. *Ti prego.*"

Defeated, I dropped the book on the table. I couldn't say no when she begged. "I'll go tomorrow if you promise you won't interfere in the case again."

Her face went flat. "I..."

Santina, Mary, and I tilted our heads.

"...promise," Nonna said.

Of course, her word was suspect after the hesitation—and after she'd tried to pass off Cruise and Pitt as priests—but I had to go with it. "Did Bradley happen to call?"

She snorted. "You'd-a be more likely to get a call-a from Tom or-a Brad."

Even more upsetting than the comment was my suspicion that she was right.

With a sigh, I went to the kitchen to drown my coffin and relationship sorrows in food. I reached into the fridge and pulled out a bowl of *bucatini alla siciliana*, thick spaghetti, eggplant, mozzarella, and parmigiano in a garlic-basil tomato sauce.

As I prepared a plate, I heard Lestat ask to be put in his coffin and my stomach slammed shut.

"*Madonna mia!*"

"*Madre santa!*"

"*Maria dolcissima!*"

Three invocations of the Virgin signaled a Catholic crisis. I looked in the living room and saw the *nonne* crossing themselves as though the devil had come to watch the movie with them. My gaze darted to the TV.

Blood gushed from Lestat's throat, and that creepy Claudia kid held a knife.

I told Veronica that vampiress was evil.

Nonna pressed pause on the remote. "Franki, Lestat drink-a the bad-a blood."

Santina's face was as white as her hair. "*Sangue morta.*"

"Dead blood?" I looked at Mary.

"It's a scene where Claudia tricks Lestat into drinking blood from dead twins," she said.

"Remember that for your case, eh?" Nonna shook her rosary at me. "Blood from-a the dead kill-a the vampires."

As though I kept a vial of that lying around.

"Blood is life," Mary said. "And it's good for you. Have you ever eaten blood pasta?"

I looked at my bucatini and dumped it in the trash. "I'm sorry, what?"

"*Sì, pasta al sangue.*" Santina gave a curt nod of approval. "*È buona.*"

Mary grabbed another slice of garlic bread. "In Trentino-Alto Adige, they make pork blood tagliatelle called *blutnudeln.*"

The Northern Italian region bordered Austria and Switzerland, one of which had to be responsible for the deathly dish.

"It's made with rye and wheat flour, eggs, and lots of blood." She bit into the bread with gusto and covered her mouth. "Pig's blood is so rich in vitamins and minerals that it's considered a superfood."

I'd sooner eat slop from a trough. "I'll stick to supplements, thanks."

Nonna pressed the play button, and Lestat resumed bleeding out.

I headed for the bathroom to get ready for bed. But I wasn't thinking about Lestat, the coffin, or the blood. Instead, that pasta recipe had gotten me thinking about Campari again.

There was something about the ingredients, something I'd overlooked or couldn't grasp.

I scrutinized my reflection in the mirror. My skin was sallow. Lifeless. If anyone needed a superfood it was me. But not pig's blood or any other sanguine concoction.

And then a thought hit me so hard I sat on the side of the tub.

Was Campari Crimson a drink made with blood?

WITH EYES IN ADHD MODE, I lay rigor mortis–like on the pallet between my bed and the wall. It was one a.m., and sleep was nowhere in sight. The narrow space again evoked a coffin, and thanks to my recent burial, it seemed especially closed in. But there was no way I'd bunk with Nonna given her Bride of Dracula gown. And nowhere outside my bedroom was safe with my brother in town.

"*Dio mio!*"

I jumped even though the cry had come from Santina in the living room. And I wished the *nonne's* Netflix binge-watchathon would end. After *Interview with a Vampire*, they'd started the sequel,

Queen of the Damned. Between their wailing and everything that had happened, from Bradley and Sullivan to the case and the coffin, I related to the title.

Where was Bradley, and what was he doing besides not calling me? Granted, I hadn't phoned him back, but I expected him to fight a little harder for my affections. It seemed the least a man in love would do.

I was disappointed in Sullivan as well. I'd left him a message about my stint in the coffin, and no matter how hurt his feelings were about my rebuff, I expected him to contact me. But so far, my near death hadn't warranted so much as a text.

As I ran through my missing persons list, I couldn't help but think of Craig. Although I hadn't seen him at the party, I suspected him of trying to do me in. After all, his absence would give him an alibi. He could tell the police he was at his grandma's instead of putting me in my grave.

Regardless of whether the coffin-closer was Craig or even Domenic, one of them hadn't wanted me to live to talk about those hospital beds in The Dungeon. Or those IV and blood bags. *But what were they doing with the stuff? Were they drinking it with Campari? Or was I way off base?*

One thing I was sure about, the coffin incident had convinced me that I'd been followed when I left Anthony at Madame Moiselle's. And if Craig was the culprit, he could target David or the vassal at the frat house.

I pulled my phone from the nightstand to check on the boys. It rang in my hand. *Pam? At this hour?*

I tapped *Answer* and heard the noise of a crowd. "What's happening?"

"The retirement home dude is here."

"Thomas?" I sat up. "Where?"

"On my Vampires and Victims tour, man. Where else?"

"Why would he take the same tour again?"

"How should I know, man? Maybe bloodsuckers are his bag."

The conversation reminded me of a Cheech and Chong skit I'd seen on YouTube, but without the Maui Wowie. "Reveling in tales of people getting the life drained out of them is a strange bag to have, especially since he was on the tour with Gregg."

"Yeah, at first I thought the cat was just square, but he's hippy dippy looney tunes."

There was so much I could say to that it was almost unfair. "Why? What did he do?"

"We're on the bar break at Molly's, and he's staring at me like a wacked-out weirdo while he sips his red drink."

The color caught my attention. In New Orleans, "red drink" usually meant Barq's Red Crème Soda, but I had to be sure. "He's not drinking Campari, is he?"

"Nah, the bartender poured him a soda."

Not as alarming, but suspect nevertheless. "Is that frat boy Craig with him by chance?"

"No, he's solo. Same as last time."

Thomas could be the one to fear instead of Craig, unless...

Were the two in cahoots? That would explain how the killer had hung Gregg from the hook.

"Pam, do you have someone to walk you to your car?"

"My old man's with me, and our ride is our feet." Her pitch was in protest mode. "Cars are for capitalists, dig?"

I sighed. Everything was political these days. "Listen, besides the incidents at the Ursuline Convent, are there any other local legends or incidents about drinking blood that could explain the phrase Campari Crimson?"

"Well, back in the 1930s John Carter and his brother Wayne liked to unwind from their day laborer jobs with human blood."

My throat squeezed shut. "From a glass?"

"Negative. Straight from the source. A chick who escaped from their pad in the Quarter told the fuzz they'd been sucking blood from her wrists. The fuzz went to investigate and found four others they'd been feeding from tied to chairs and fourteen bodies drained of blood."

I lay back and pulled the covers to my neck. "They sound like the real vampires here in New Orleans, except for the dead people part."

She stoner-laughed. "It took eight cops to cuff them. And after they were executed for the crimes, people reported seeing them around. A year later, when one of their relatives died, an undertaker discovered that John and Wayne had split from the family vault."

"*O, Signore!*"

Nonna's shout sent a shock through my system. If the Catholic caterwauling didn't stop soon, I'd go to my grave for good.

"Hey, the bar break's over. I'll rap at you later." Pam hung up before I could get a word in.

For all her emphasis on peace and love, that hippie was kind of rude.

I tapped David's number.

"Yo," he answered. "I was about to text you."

Thomas Dolby's "She Blinded Me with Science" played in the background. Songs with academics in the title didn't strike me as the DUDs' type of music. "You back at your dorm?"

"In the car." His voice was charged with excitement. "Sullivan just showed up at the frat house with five cops and shut the party down."

I rose to my feet. "Did something else happen?"

"He knew about the coffin thing, and he was raging. The dude burst in like Schwarzenegger and ripped off Domenic's mask. He didn't confess, but Sullivan knew it was him."

My brain told my body not to react, but my heart fluttered nevertheless. I swallowed and shook it off. "Did Craig ever show up?"

"Not that I saw. But that's when the cops cleared us out, so I can't say for sure."

I peered through the curtains. Until I knew where Craig was, I planned to stay on heightened alert. "So, change of plans about the Crimson Cotillion. I need you to keep an eye on the frat boys as they party hop the next couple of nights. See if your friend Andrew can help you with that."

"But you need someone to go with you. The vassal would do it."

I smiled at the memory of my Buffy boyfriend. "I'd rather have the two of you helping me find out what the DUDs are doing with those hospital beds."

David was silent for a moment. "Do you think they're, like, involved in the murders?"

"This case is so confusing, I have no idea. But based on what happened to me tonight, it would be a grave mistake to put it past them, pun intended." I sat on the side of the bed and pulled aside a curtain for another check.

And I dropped the phone on the bed.

A figure crept past my window, but all I could see was the top of a dark-haired head.

Craig?

13

"**D**avid, I've got to go." I pulled my purple Ruger from the nightstand drawer. "There's a man outside."

"Uh, you should call the cops. I'll try to contact Sullivan."

"No, don't." My tone came out too terse, but given the detective's feelings for me, I couldn't let him come to my rescue. "I can handle this. And don't forget that I've got three Sicilian grandma's here, and when they're mad, they've each got the strength of Samson and ten vampires. I'll text you when I know more."

I closed the call and looked at my gun. I was in my nightgown, so I stuck it under my arm to hide it from the *nonne*. I wanted to break the prowler situation to them gently to avoid total chaos.

Calmly, I entered the living room.

"*Santo cielo!*" Santina gesticulated at my side. "*Una pistola!*"

I don't know why I thought I could get anything past a nonna. They were akin to drill sergeants, and all grandchildren in their vicinity were on permanent uniform inspection.

Nonna clambered from the chaise lounge. "Franki, what're you up-a to?"

"Don't get all agitated," I said, already knowing the command was futile. "I saw someone outside and—"

"It's-a the vampire!" Nonna shuffle-ran to the kitchen.

Santina and Mary scrambled to their feet. The former held out her rosary cross, the latter a loaf of garlic bread.

Nonna returned waving her rolling pin. "I club-a him with-a this, and-a we tie him up-a with an apron."

For the first time, Glenda's Lilliputian story made sense.

The *nonne* fell in line behind me with their weaponry. In my white gown and their black dresses, we resembled a nun rebellion.

I pulled out my Ruger and peered through the peephole. "Stay back until I make sure he's not hiding on either side of the porch." I turned and pointed to my gun. "I don't want any of you getting shot, okay?"

The *nonne* crossed themselves.

I opened the door and crept onto the porch.

A clatter ensued, and I went airborne.

Then I face-planted in the yard.

"Now's not the time to mess with that gutter, sugar," Glenda chided from the stairs above. "The police just arrested a man on our side street."

I spit out a patch of grass, but I was so mad at my slacker brother that I could have spit blood. I kicked the gutter from beneath my feet. Then I pulled myself up and put my gun on safety. I looked at Glenda, who stood at the second-floor railing in nothing but a see-through robe. "Did you get a look at the guy?"

"No, but I think he was a peeping Tom." She pulled the sheer fabric around her nude body, as though that would help.

"Well, I'm glad you reported him."

"Oh, I didn't call the cops, Miss Franki. I thought you did." She gasped and her eyes grew wide, and she strut-scuttled into her apartment and slammed the door.

Convinced a vampire serial killer was behind me, I spun with my Ruger aimed.

It was Nonna, apron in hand.

I lowered the pistol, but my pulse stayed raised. "You can't sneak up on me like that. I've got this gun, remember?"

"And I've got-a this." She lifted the rolling pin.

I didn't argue because that kitchen utensil could probably stop a bullet. She'd brought it from Italy, where it had been passed down for so many generations that the wood was almost petrified.

A squad car turned in front of Thibodeaux's and pulled into our driveway. Two officers got out. One was a kind of Shaquille O'Neal on steroids, and the other was a tiny blonde with a bun.

"I'm a PI, and I'm carrying a firearm." I crossed the lawn, followed by the *nonne*. "I just had a creeper outside my bedroom window."

The male officer gestured to the back of the car. "We've got him, along with his sidekick."

Craig and Domenic?

"I'm Officer Honoré," he said, "and this is Officer Gentilly. We found the two of them in the alley, casing the place."

I looked in the rear passenger window, and it was a good thing the authorities were present or there would have been a shooting spree. "That's my brother." My brow had dropped as low as my growl. "And his date."

"*Antonio mio?*" Nonna stabbed the sky with the rolling pin and threw open the car door. "Get in-a the house."

He shrunk into the seat. "I'd rather go to jail."

"You ain't talkin for me," Crystal shouted. "Can I get out now?"

Nonna eyed her Madonna getup, lingering on her bustier and then her baby bulge. "Take her to the hoose-a-gow."

I leaned inside the car. "Anthony, what were you doing lurking outside my window?"

"Not lookin', that's fo sho. I thought you were at the frat party."

"So?"

He shrugged despite the handcuffs. "I didn't think you'd mind."

And then I got it. He'd planned to sneak Crystal into my room. With the *nonne* in the house.

I slammed the door. "Nonna, will you please take the ladies inside? I need a word with the officers."

She screwed her mouth into a scowl and shook the rolling pin at her grandson. Then she and the other *nonne* headed into the house.

"I'm sorry you had to come out for a false alarm, Officers." I lanced my brother with a cutting glare. "It won't happen again."

Honoré tugged at his belt. "Actually, ma'am, we weren't responding to a call. We came by because Detective Wesley Sullivan sent us."

His words hit me like a blow. *Had someone else been killed?* "What happened? I'm Franki Amato, a friend of the detective's."

The pair exchanged a lascivious look that said they not only knew my name, but also my infamous striptease.

I felt as naked as Glenda, and I crossed my arms against my night-gown. "What's going on?"

Gentilly gave a flat smile. "We can't go into specifics, but this evening Sullivan came by some disturbing information."

"While he was at the frat house?"

"That's privileged," Honoré said, "being that it's part of an investigation."

I had a bad feeling about where this was going. "Can you at least tell me why the information is disturbing? I'm assuming it's about the same case I'm working."

He glanced at his partner. "The detective believes you could be the next victim."

Fear punched my heart, knocking it to my gut.

A BELL RANG, and my eyelids fluttered open.

There was a high ceiling above me, so I wasn't in my bedroom.

A priest collar came into my line of vision.

My fingers grasped at cold, slick wood, and fear pierced my soul. *Was I in a coffin receiving last rites?*

The collar lowered, and Father John's face appeared.

"You're in Our Lady of Guadalupe Church," he replied as though he were omniscient. "It's seven thirty Saturday morning. You fell asleep in a pew."

"Bless me father for I have sinned." I blurted the line whenever I saw a priest, normally over guilt for lapsed attendance at church. But in this case I said it because the father was so devilishly sexy that I felt unclean.

His sensuous lips spread into a smile. "Your nonna told me you'd be coming by, but I would've recognized you from that spontaneous confession."

Embarrassed, I looked down and caught sight of my phone. The bell I'd heard was a text from Chandra, demanding I drop by with a class update. Before I left the church, I planned to pray she went away.

He slid into the pew. "So, how long has it been since you were last here?"

Guilt inflamed my skin like a bad rash. "Uh, not that long, really." I sat up and scratched my neck. "I was working a case that involved voodoo. This time I came to ask you about vampires."

His blue eyes twinkled. "Usually people come to ask me about God. But I love a good vampire flick."

He also loved James Bond and could have played the Pierce Brosnan version in a film. I mentally crossed myself for that last thought and cleared my throat. "I'm sure my nonna told you all about my investigation."

"She did, and the whole city is on alert after the murders. But how can I help?"

"I was wondering if you knew of an offering or potion made with human blood?"

"Not personally, but I'd be willing to bet there is one. I'm sure you've heard the story of Madame LaLaurie, the local nineteenth-century socialite who was so obsessed with staying young that she bathed in human blood to get the proper nutrients for her skin."

I had, and I'd hoped I wouldn't hear it again. "Yeah, but this involves drinking blood, not bathing in it. And it's urgent because we're in a blood moon, and I think the killer is still hunting victims." I stopped short of mentioning that I was on the kill list. "If you can think of anything that might point me in a direction, I would be grateful."

"Well, vampires play no official part in Catholic dogma or doctrine, but I'm sure you've seen Van Helsing in *Dracula* hold up a cross to invoke God's protection."

"Last night, in fact." I shot a pleading look at the Virgin above the altar, imploring her to stop the *nonne's* research. "But this isn't about the supernatural vampires from books or movies. It's about real ones here in the city."

"Ah. The *Twilight* phenomenon."

"What's that?"

"A couple of years ago the Vatican warned of a surge in demonic possession and blood consumption because of the *Twilight* movies and *True Blood*, the TV show filmed here. The vampires have been glamorized, and the ones in *Twilight* sparkle."

I thought it was Anne Rice's doing, but now that he mentioned it, sparkly vampires were preferable to creepy Claudia. "What's the Vatican's stance on this?"

"That the Church's role depends on the cause of the vampirism. If an evil spirit has possessed the body, an exorcism is performed. But the Church gives precedence to medicine because it's often a sign of mental illness."

Or fibromyalgia.

"But whatever its cause, we must heed the words of Matthew 7:1."

"Always."

"Shall we recite the verse together?"

My face burned like a votive candle. "How about a word or two to get me started?"

His brow lowered. "Judge not, that you be not judged?"

"Father," I said with the patience of Job, "if you saw the people in my life, you'd know I'm the living embodiment of that concept."

"Good, good. As members of the Lord's flock, we must have mercy on those who have fallen and raise them up."

"Definitely." *But if someone tries to drain my blood, that sucker's going down.*

I heard a noise and looked over my shoulder.

Near the entrance, a woman placed an offering of cake below a statue of a Roman centurion holding a cross and stepping on a crow. Locally, he was known as Saint Expedite, but the Church didn't recognize him because he represented the commingling of voodoo and Catholicism.

The unofficial saint reminded me of Cecilia, the patron of music, and the cemetery where Gregg had been killed. And I got an idea. "Father, are any saints associated with vampires?"

"There's Saint Marcellus of Paris, the patron saint of Vampire Hunters. In the fifth century he destroyed a vampire in a cemetery outside the city. His feast day is coming up on November first, All Saints' Day."

Also The Day of the Dead. "I'm surprised the Church recognizes an incident like that. Do you think people lived as vampires back then?"

"Possibly. But my guess is that it was one of those cases of a sick person coming back from death's door."

"I don't understand."

"In those days, little was known about medicine and disease was rampant. There were cases of people being presumed dead who were probably in a coma. When they woke up, the assumption was that they'd died and turned into vampires. That's why the tradition began of holding vigil over the dead until they were buried. We saw it in the 1800s when yellow fever struck the city. I'm not sure whether you know this, but Our Lady of Guadalupe was built as a mortuary chapel for the victims."

I did, and it was one of the reasons I'd been reluctant to come. "Any others?"

"Yes, the Polish invoked Rocha against vampire attacks. We know him as Saint Roch, the patron saint of miraculous cures."

I dropped to the kneeler attached to the pew. St. Roch was the name of a neighborhood near the French Quarter.

It was also a cemetery.

And somehow in that moment, I knew it would be relevant.

WHEN I TURNED my Mustang onto Frenchmen Street at eight a.m., I spotted Chandra and Lou's yellow neon sign glowing on a shotgun-style building.

"Crescent City Plumbing & Palmistry." I shook my head. "What a concept."

I parked, shut off the engine, and reached for my bag. I noticed a group practicing Tai Chi in Washington Square Park and envied them, not because they were exercising, naturally, but because they got to be outside instead of trapped in a psychic plumbing house.

I turned to exit the car and let out a scream.

Chandra stared killer-Kewpie-doll style in my window, and in the morning sun her accidental bleach job radiated yellow like her sign.

She yanked open my door. "I sent Lou to pick up breakfast, so you don't have much time to catch me up on his case."

I climbed from the driver's seat and surveyed her outfit from feet to torso, red platform heels, a black leather miniskirt, and a white T-shirt with a red barbell and the phrase *Training To Survive The Blood Moon*. But I was too tired to worry about the ominous implication. "I see he let you keep the crescent theme for your joint venture."

"Well, my brand is the Crescent City Medium, and he uses a crescent wrench in his work. So it makes perfect sense."

It didn't, but I stayed silent as I followed her up the porch steps.

"We don't open for business until nine, so let's enjoy the parlor." She led me to a room at the front of the house that looked like a hotrod showroom version of a plumbing supply store. There were bathroom fixtures tricked out in florescent paint and chrome, and along the wall was a row of toilets with wings and flames on the sides. And somehow, the place had a new car smell.

Chandra beamed like the moon. "Lou specializes in custom commodes."

It seemed appropriate for a man who ate garbage. "But you're only doing palmistry now?"

"Oh, I still read tarot and the crystal ball, but the palm-reading gets clients in the door."

I'd already guessed that it wasn't the dragster toilets.

She flopped onto a loveseat made from the back of an old Chevy and toilet pedestals and patted the space beside her, causing her charm bracelet to jingle.

I took a seat next to her, wondering if we were going on a car date or a girls' bathroom trip. Either way, I hoped a spirit didn't tag along.

Her upper lip twitched. "Lou tells me your alligator chili had quite a bite. Apparently, that roadkill gator wasn't dead."

"I was sabotaged by a wannabe Disney princess named Michele." My tone was as bitter as the Peychaud's she'd used.

"Did she sabotage your red beans and rice too? Because Lou said he had a bite of your bugs, and they started crawling in his belly."

I turned and laid a look on her. "Um, I'm not in the competition, remember? I'm there to find out who's sabotaging your husband?"

"And you're not doing your job, are you? Because Lou told me someone named Sara won best roadkill recipe on Thursday night."

"She's from Italy, okay? Italians can make anything taste good."

"Then what happened to you?"

I gasped at the attack. "Have you considered that Sara and Michele might be sabotaging me too?"

"Sounds like someone's got a bug up their butt." She giggled and pressed red-lacquered paddles to her lips. "Or in their gut."

I channeled the Tai Chi group to keep cool. "I'm going to find out who's sabotaging Lou. I'm leaning towards Michele, but I need more time."

"And some sleep. You look like death warmed over."

Under the circumstances her analogy, while clever, wasn't cute. "Thanks to the frat boy case and my family, I haven't been getting much sleep."

She fluffed her voluminous bob. "Neither have I. Between those murders and the blood moon, I've been working overtime, and I'm ready to stop. I mean, I haven't had a minute to get my hair re-dyed brown."

Given that a vampire serial killer was after me and she'd taken potshots at my cooking, I had a hard time sympathizing. "I can't help you with the blood moon, but I'm working on solving the murders."

"Are you close?"

I didn't want to talk shop with Chandra because I ran the risk of a spirit showing up. "Let's just say that I have a number of suspects, but the picture's fuzzy."

"Maybe I can help you clear it up." She scooted from the loveseat and pulled me to a long yellow hallway.

"Where are we going?"

"To my office. You said the picture was fuzzy, so I'm going to look in my crystal ball." She opened the door to a blue room with plastic stars on the walls and a card table with folding chairs.

Apparently, they'd spent all their money on Lou's plumbing parlor. "This really isn't necessary."

"It is too. My hair's not going to dye itself, and I need a polish change on these nails." She spritzed Chanel No. 5 in the air, took a seat, and folded her hands in her lap.

After a minute, I glanced from the crystal ball to her. "Are you warming up or something?"

"I'm waiting for you to pay me."

"What? This was your idea."

"This is your investigation. You're being paid, so why shouldn't I?"

If a vampire didn't bleed me dry first, Chandra definitely would. I sighed and reached into my bag. "It's twenty, right?"

"Thirty. My fee went up when we bought this space."

I pulled out three tens and slammed them on the table. "For that amount, you'd better ID the killer."

"Please." She grabbed the cash. "I'm not an FBI profiler."

I almost said *you're not a psychic, either.* But I was so desperate for a break in the case that I wanted to hear her out.

She shoved the bills into her bra, which was her cash register, and waved circles above the crystal ball.

"You see anything?" I asked, eyeing her charm bracelet.

"Boat shoes."

My brow shot up. Frat boys wore boat shoes. In fact, Craig had been wearing a pair the day I met him. "Are they in a closet or on a person?"

Chandra gazed at the ball. "Someone's wearing them, but I can only see from the ankles down. And it's weird because the shoes aren't touching the floor."

"So, they have their feet up?"

"Wait, the picture flipped." She tilted her head to the side, but her bob didn't budge. "The shoes are upside down now."

"Huh?"

"Whoa. It just zoomed out, but it's really blurry." She studied the ball. Then her red nails flew to her mouth, and her eyes assumed the shape of a full moon. "A young man with dark hair is hanging by his feet."

I jerked forward. Craig had dark hair. "Where is he?"

She squinted. "In a tiny concrete room."

My mind went blank. I couldn't imagine a room like that in a house, not even a garage. Then I remembered the nickname for New Orleans cemeteries, cities of the dead.

And I remembered something else that made my stomach freefall.

Gregg had been hanging by his feet too.

In his tomb.

14

Glancing over my shoulder, I climbed the stairs to Private Chicks. Then I tapped the number of the Utah family that had gone on Gregg's ill-fated vampire tour. Even though I was alone in the stairwell, I couldn't shake a bad sensation that had followed me from Chandra's, but that was probably because of her foreboding crystal ball vision. And those flaming toilets.

"You've reached the residence of Dale and Drea Bacigalupi," the woman on the answering machine said. "Please leave a message."

Frustrated, I tapped *End* and shoved the phone into my back jeans pocket. I'd already left several messages. And it was nine a.m. on a Saturday, so I had hoped to finally catch them at home. Either they were still on vacation, or they were avoiding my calls.

I reached the third floor and took one more look behind me before inserting the key into the lock.

The door opened.

But I hadn't turned the handle.

Tensing, I crept inside.

And I discovered the cause of my bad sensation.

Anthony lay on his belly on a couch in a wife beater, boxers, and socks. His head was turned to one side and semi-hanging off the seat, and a dark substance rimmed his open mouth. His arm hung lifeless to the floor. Next to his hand, a spoon.

My heart beat so hard it throbbed in my head. *Was this some kind of drug thing? And was that blood around his mouth?*

I rushed to him and stumbled on a small object.

My office Nutella jar.

And it was empty.

He's not dead. He's in a chocolate hazelnut–induced coma.

"REDRUM," I growled like that kid in *The Shining*. And it was a good thing I didn't have his knife.

"Franki, what's happening?" Veronica stared at me from the hallway with her hand on her heart.

"What's Sleeping Ugly doing in the office?" I asked, not unlike Jack Nicholson when he said, "Heeere's Johnny!"

Her eyes popped, and she took a step back. "He was asleep outside the door, and I invited him in. He told me what happened with the police last night and said he was afraid to go home because your nonna was waiting for him with her rolling pin."

I whipped out my phone. "I should've let those cops cart him to jail."

"You're not calling the police, are you?"

"My parents." I tapped their number.

"What for?"

"I'm going to tell on him." I turned away from her grimace and listened to the phone ring.

"Joe Amato." My father always answered as though all callers would be looking for him.

"Dad."

"Franki! How's my girl?"

There was a lightness to his tone that I hadn't heard in…ever. It was probably from all the partying he'd been doing since my mom had unloaded my brother. "I'd say not great, but it's more like despondent. I'm calling to talk to you about Anthony."

"That's your mother's department." The lightness had turned leaden. "Brenda!"

I rolled my eyes. For my Italian-American father, childrearing was the wife's responsibility, especially when said rearing had failed.

"Hello?" My mother answered in a voice reminiscent of Edith Bunker when she was in a cheerful mood.

"You have to do something about your son," I barked à la Archie Bunker.

The line went dead.

"Ugh. The call dropped." I tapped the number again.

The phone rang once.

"Francesca?" my mom answered.

"Yes—"

The line went dead again.

"What the hell?" I punched the number.

Someone picked up the receiver and put it back in the cradle.

I gasped and looked at Veronica. "My mother is hanging up on me. She's not going to do anything about him."

"Can you blame her?"

I contemplated my brother. "Uh-huh. Absolutely."

Anthony flipped onto his back, splayed his legs, and snored like a drunk with severe allergies and sleep apnea.

Another "REDRUM" escaped my lips. A blood bath was about to go down, vampire-serial-killer style. I shoved the phone into my pocket and prepared to string my brother by the heels just as Chandra's spirit friend had predicted outside Boutique du Vampyre.

"You need to go cool off." Veronica spun me around and pushed me into the hall. "And we need to talk about your case."

I broke free and made a play for my brother, but she latched onto my arm and dug in her high heels.

"Let me kill him," I wheezed. "Everything will be so much better. The dark cloud might even lift off the city."

"You agreed to host him for a month. So, technically, you can't kill him for another three weeks."

I relaxed, and she seized the opportunity to pull me to an armchair in her office.

As she adjusted her ponytail, which had been knocked off kilter in the kerfuffle, I heard a second snorer and looked for the source.

Hercules was on his back on a dog bed in the corner with his legs splayed wide like my brother's. Men were the same, regardless of the species.

Veronica took a seat behind her desk. "Now that you're settled, I wanted to talk to you about a call I got from Detective Sullivan this morning. First, he told me about the coffin, and I was horrified." Her tone was soothing. "Are you all right?"

Self-pity welled up within me and threatened to spill from my eyes. "I haven't had a chance to think about it."

"Why don't you take some time off? You could go to New York and see Bradley."

"And do what? Watch him work?" I crossed my arms. And my legs. "Besides, we're not talking."

"Which is another good reason to go." She leaned forward. "After the trauma you've experienced, you need to see him and clear the air."

"People are dying, Veronica. On a case I'm working. So, I'm going to the Crimson Cotillion tonight to try to find out who's doing the blood draining."

She rubbed her forehead. "I'm glad you brought up the cotillion. After I talked to the detective, I called David to make sure he was still going with you. But he said you reassigned him to watch the fraternity brothers?"

"Because they had blood bags and IV stands in their Dungeon room. Not only that, Craig met with Thomas Van Scyoc before the frat party, and he's been MIA ever since." I held back the news that Craig could be dead per Chandra's crystal ball. If I'd shared that, Veronica would have had me admitted to Belleville House.

"I wish you would've told me this on Thursday night. I could've hired a PI to help out."

My self-pity turned stoic. I didn't want any interference in my job. There was already enough of that in my home life and relationship. "You don't need to hire anyone. I've got this."

"I'm not so sure. And I can't go to the cotillion because I'm in the middle of an asset search for a trial on Monday, so..."

I didn't like the way her voice trailed off.

Or the way she gripped the arms of her chair.

"So...?"

Her gaze dropped to her desk. "I've hired Glenda to go in my place, and she's bringing Carnie for reinforcement."

When I'd had that bad sensation, not even in my darkest moment could I have imagined investigating a vampire ball with the likes of Glenda and Carnie. Instead of "REDRUM," a song came to me that captured my mood exactly, "It's My Party" by Leslie Gore.

Veronica flopped against the back of her chair. "I tried to get someone else, but no one was available on such short notice. Detective Sullivan said he'll be there, but given his recent advances, I didn't think you'd want to hang around with him."

"Are you kidding?" I laugh-snapped. "At this point, I'd even go with the vampire serial killer. As his date."

"Be serious."

"I am. And I'll handle this on my own, thank you."

"You're my best friend, so I don't want to pull rank. But if you insist on going alone, I'll have to play the boss card."

I exhaled and frowned at Hercules, who'd awakened and was doing the unspeakable thing that only males of certain species could do.

Veronica waved to get my attention. "Hey. You know there's safety in numbers, and I want you to go armed."

Given recent events in the case, I had to agree. But just about bringing my gun. Because if a vampire did attack me, the only things I could count on Glenda and Carnie to do were shimmy and insult him. "Okay, but I don't see why you're so dead set on this."

She winced.

And it was right after I said dead. "Why did you make that face?"

"Because I haven't told you about the rest of my conversation with the detective. As your employer, he wanted me to know you're in danger."

"Oh, David already told me that," I said, relieved Sullivan hadn't dropped some other bad news bombshell.

"Well, David wouldn't have known the reason."

I had a feeling in my blood that I was going to wish I didn't know it either.

"The New Orleans PD have determined that Thomas Van Scyoc used a computer at Belleville House to google you." She paused and looked into my eyes. "And he specifically looked up your home address."

FROM THE DRIVER'S seat of my Mustang, I caught sight of the small Saint Anthony statue in the garden behind the Saint Louis Cathedral. His outstretched arms beckoned to me in the waning daylight, but I averted my eyes to the Bourbon Orleans Hotel where the Crimson Cotillion was underway. As the patron saint of lost things, Anthony was a double reminder of my brother, who I wanted to forget.

A Goth Marie Antoinette passed in front of my car in a bloodied pearl choker and black French *pannier* gown—the kind with the doublewide hip span—decorated with red satin rosettes. She turned and stared at me through a black handheld mask of a face. Then she entered the lobby.

That was disturbing. And the mask was a reminder of someone else I wanted to forget. I glared at Carnie in the rearview mirror.

She was in the backseat drawing the eyebrows on her Countess Dragula look, which had turned out to be a vampire version of Cher in her infamous academy awards outfit—the one with the black feather headdress that looked like a murder of crows.

"Are you done painting? It's seven o'clock, and we got here at six forty."

She lowered her purple garage doors—drag for single-shadowed eyelids—and pursed her *I Love Lucy* lips at Glenda, who was beside me in the passenger seat. "Look who's ungrateful after we worked so hard to make her presentable."

"Hard?" I snort-laughed. "I look like a cross between Amy Winehouse and Elvira. And this ratty wig weighs like ten pounds."

"Gurrrl, that beehive cost me three hundred dollars at Fifi Mahony's, and it's an improvement over that limp brown blanket you call hair."

I kicked open my door, wishing it was her derriere.

"Don't get out yet, Miss Franki. I have to put on my costume." Glenda stuck a pair of plastic fangs in her mouth. "Ready."

"That's it?" I gave her the once-over. "Teeth, pasties, and a thong?"

"This is what they wear at Casa Diablo in Portland, and it's a vampire-themed vegan strip club."

Because everyone knows that blood is vegan, not to mention the female flesh they're selling.

A young man in a Bourbon Orleans uniform approached the car. "Are you ready for valet service?"

"Please." I handed him the keys. "And don't bother putting up the top." I shot a loaded look at Carnie. "Otherwise, my hair won't fit."

She slammed the car door. "Don't blame the wig. It's your big head."

"Can we just go inside?"

She extended her handbag arm. "Purse first, ladies. And Franki."

Sighing, I entered the marble-columned lobby. Femininity digs from a drag queen were exhausting.

We stepped into the elevator, and I pressed the button for the second floor. "To review, while I keep an eye on the vampire, Raven Smith, you guys collect drink samples, especially the ones with Campari."

"Carnie's going to handle that, sugar. Miss Ronnie gave her the vials and said I was to stick to you like a pasty."

Somehow I knew that wasn't Veronica's analogy. "Uh, don't stick that close. It's a square room, so you'll be able to see me from anywhere."

The elevator doors opened, and a huge, hooded executioner stood before us against a soundtrack of harpsichord music. "Your tickets." His voice was deep with a hint of Caribbean or West African French. "Or your heads."

My hand moved to my too-exposed throat. The Elvira dress was cut low, and the sword-wielder had noticed. "We're guests of Raven Smith."

His black eyes bore into mine through slits in the leather. "*Carpe noctem.*"

"Seize the night?" Glenda translated. "I'd be happy to do that, Mr. Handsome Hangman." She tapped just above his nostril holes. "With your assistance."

Taking that as my cue to run for my life, I entered the Orleans ballroom. The hotel alleged that it was haunted by a Confederate soldier and nuns and orphans from the Holy Family Sisters' Convent that had been on the site in the early 1800s. I didn't believe in ghosts, but the way the yellowed damask drapes hung from the windows like giant phantoms was vaguely unsettling.

And the décor for the Crimson Cotillion only enhanced the eerie setting. The chandeliers had been covered in red fabric to give the room a bloody pall, and a guillotine towered in a corner. Beside it was a bucket of human heads that had been strategically placed next to a buffet of steak tartare to give them that raw meat smell. The *pièces de résistance*, however, were the guests' prosthetic teeth and blood-stained eighteenth-century clothing.

"Looks like the Vampire French Revolution," Carnie said.

For once I agreed with her.

A young man in a top hat and Regency shirt approached and passed out his business card. "Jay Owens, *mademoiselles.*"

Carnie raised a painted arch. "Why should I care?"

"Because I'm the top-selling fangsmith at vampires.com. Normally, a good set of fangs runs you two-to-five grand. But you've got a healthy set of chompers, so I could do yours for the discount rate of only fifteen hundred." He stretched back his lips to reveal considerable canines.

"Flash those fangs at me again," she said, "and these chompers will be all over you."

Jay backed away, and I didn't blame him. A three-hundred-fifty-pound Dracula Cher was truly terrifying.

"Complimentary Vampire Cocktails." A courtesan with bottom fangs handed Glenda and Carnie yellow drinks from a serving tray.

I declined with a wave. Then I realized that what I'd thought was a straw was actually a syringe—filled with a red substance. "What is that?"

"Raspberry puree," the waitress replied. "You inject it into the drink."

I nudged Carnie. "Definitely get a sample."

Glenda squirted the puree and took a sip. "It's just punch, Miss Franki. But it's too rich for my blood."

"Put a stake in it, will ya? There are vampires in the room." I looked around to make sure no one had overheard. And I got quite a shock.

Josh Santo stood near the guillotine in his Compte de Saint Germain getup.

I strode over to my client and eyed his red wine. "What's a guy who claims that his only interest in vampires is the count doing at the Crimson Cotillion?"

"The count became famous in the court of Versailles. For all we know, he's with us tonight."

Even though I knew that was absurd, I did a side-eye sweep of the room. "So this is book research?"

"Not entirely. I'm on a date." He flashed his Donny Osmonds. "With Raven Smith."

"You're kidding, right?"

He winced and wrinkled his lips. "What? I'm not a ladies man, but I do all right."

"With a suspect in your case?" I wanted to roll my eyes, but my wig would have tipped me flat on my back. "For such a smart guy, you're totally clueless."

"I resent that."

"I don't care."

"And you're not making much progress, so I decided to do some investigating." He swirled the sanguine liquid in his glass. "Because I'm pretty sure she's the one I saw outside the blood bank the night Todd Plank was killed."

The drink reminded me of the count's love of wine mixed with blood. And of those bottles in Josh's refrigerator. And I wondered whether he and Raven were involved in the murders together. "How did you find Raven, anyway?"

"You're not the only PI I've got working this investigation. I hired a backup in case you suck."

I was about to thank him for the vote of no confidence, but I didn't trust him either. "Has it occurred to you how bad this will look to the police?"

"It's hard to see how I could look any worse."

"Especially after a stunt like this." I shook my head, and the beehive wobbled, almost knocking me off my feet. Clutching it with both hands, I scanned the crowd. "Which one is Raven?"

"She's in one of those Marie Antoinette dresses. But hers is all black."

She must've been the woman who walked by my car because I hadn't seen any other Goth doublewides. "Huh. I saw her earlier, but she didn't say hello even though I'm her guest tonight."

"Don't take it personally. She's pretty stressed out."

That detail got my attention. He was either covering for her avoidance of me or something else was eating at her. Maybe guilt. "Do you know why?"

"Planning a party." He gave me a pointed look. "Being a suspect in some murders."

"*Touché.*"

Josh cleared his throat and looked at his glass.

I turned expecting to find Raven listening to our conversation. Instead, it was Detective Sullivan dressed as Barnabas Collins.

"Can I have a word with the Mistress of the Dark?" he asked.

My stomach fluttered, but I wrote it off to the horror of his ruffled collar and not the unexpected sexiness of his cloak. "You want to talk now? Because I've been trying to reach you for a couple of days, and you haven't responded."

"I'll explain outside."

I followed him onto the balcony. He walked to the rail overlooking Orleans Avenue, and I glanced at the sky and repressed a gasp.

Night had fallen, and the blood moon glowed as red as the covered chandeliers. It was frightening and strangely fascinating, but I had to look down. My big beehive threatened to snap my head from my neck. "Well?"

He turned to face me. "I've been swamped—"

"But you found time to call my boss? Next time I'm in danger, I'd appreciate a personal call." I regretted the *personal* comment because a corner of his mouth lifted like a ray of hope.

"Fair enough."

I took a step back. There was something about his half smile and *Dark Shadows* costume that was mesmerizing, like Dracula's gaze. "Anyway, what have you found out about Thomas Van Scyoc?"

"He seems awfully interested in you, for one thing."

"And what about Craig? Has he turned up?"

"Negative. And zero activity on his credit cards and bank account."

I thought about Chandra's crystal ball, but I kept my mouth shut. Sullivan would have either laughed me off the balcony or had my PI license stripped if I'd confessed to consulting with a psychic. "What happens next?"

"We check out Craig's grandmother. She stayed at Belleville House while Van Scyoc was there."

I couldn't have been more gobsmacked if a bat had flown into my beehive. "Where is she now?"

He rubbed his jaw. "In an apartment in Metairie."

"Where the blood bank was broken into." *And robbed of my B Positive blood type.*

"We've ruled out her connection to that."

"But you suspect Craig, right?"

"Not exactly."

"Why not?"

"That's getting into territory I can't discuss." He made up the step I'd put between us. "And I didn't ask you out here to talk about work."

Alarmed, I jerked my head up to look at him, and my beehive propelled me backwards.

He caught me and pulled me to his chest. "Forgive me, but I can't resist all that neck you're showing."

His lips locked onto mine, and I responded as though in a trance.

The kiss was soft, and then it deepened until I feared he would suck the blood from my body. I knew it was wrong to be with him, but there was a sensuality to his mouth that was intoxicating. The same way Dracula's female victims described his bite.

"Franki?"

The intoxication turned toxic. It was a male voice, but it didn't belong to the detective because our lips, among other things, were still entwined.

I pulled away and spun around.

Bradley stood in the doorway holding a yellow rose. His face was grim, or maybe Grim Reaper. He stood as still as a statue, like Anthony, the patron saint of lost things.

And I couldn't help but wonder if the saint had foreshadowed the loss of our relationship.

We locked eyes, perhaps thinking the same thing.

He walked toward me, handed me the rose, and then turned and made his way through the crowd.

"Bradley, don't leave." I went after him and got caught between two French doublewides.

By the time I broke free and exited the ballroom, he was nowhere in sight. I took the stairs to the lobby and hurried to the street, which was oddly empty for a Saturday night.

Bradley was gone as he had been for so much of the time we'd been together. I knew I should feel sad, but all I felt was numb. Probably because I was so used to his absence.

Nevertheless, I leveled a silent accusation at Saint Anthony.

Thanks to a spotlight at the base of his statue, he cast a looming shadow on the white wall of the cathedral. But in the red light of the blood moon, he no longer seemed to beckon to his flock. Rather, he looked like a man about to be crucified.

My hand throbbed, and I looked down. I was gripping the rose, and its thorns had pierced and bloodied my palm.

I backed toward the hotel entrance.

Because I sensed that my relationship with Bradley wasn't the only thing that would die that Halloween night.

I just hoped it wasn't my brother.

15

"Franki, get out of that glass."

Veronica's tone was insistent, but I was in no mood to be pushed. I'd spent the night in Glenda's giant champagne glass in her all white living room. The glass wasn't the traditional flute shape, more like a martini. Either way, it had become my sanctuary in dark times. And it was a great place to reflect over drinks. "Go away. It's Sunday. A day of rest?"

"This is important." She tugged my arm, which dangled from the rim. "Would you wake up?"

I opened my eyes expecting to see the ceiling, but a black blanket covered my face.

Wait. That was no blanket. It was...*some kind of animal*?

"Get it off!" I kicked and flailed, but it was wrapped around my hung-over head. "What the hell is it? A land octopus?"

"Calm down, okay? I think it's a wig."

Anger surged through my veins. *Dracula Cher strikes again.* I gripped the longhaired hive and heaved it across the room.

It hit the wall with a thud.

"Good thing there's no furniture in here," Veronica said. "That thing could break something."

"You don't have to tell me." I massaged my trapezius muscles. "That wig took out my relationship with Bradley, not to mention my neck."

She sighed, stalwart. "When Glenda let me in, she told me what happened with Detective Sullivan. I asked her to leave us alone for a few minutes so I could tell you how sorry I am."

I was sorry too, but I didn't want to dwell. Otherwise, the tears would start, and the only thing I wanted to see pouring was another drink. "I'm going to drop by his apartment today to talk to him."

"Tell me something."

I sat up from my reclining position, and an empty Prosecco bottle rolled off my belly. Even worse, I was still in the Elvira dress. "What?"

"How did you feel about that kiss?"

I slithered down the side of the glass, so she wouldn't spot the lie I was about to tell. "I don't know."

"Did you enjoy it?" Her tone told me that she could see through the glass—and through me as well.

I sunk to the bottom. "Um, it was all right, I guess."

"You sound undecided," she said, completely convinced. "So if I were you, I would figure out exactly how I felt about Sullivan before I went to Bradley's."

Veronica wasn't going to let this go, and I was getting annoyed. But I was more irritated with me than I was with her. Because the truth was that kiss was amazing, and I was coming around to the notion that Sullivan might be pretty great too. We had things in common, like our snarky sarcasm and our careers in solving crime. Ever since Anthony had told me about his ex-wife, I'd started to see him as a human—more importantly, as a man. And if I compared him to Bradley, one thing stood out. Sullivan was around when Bradley couldn't find the time. And even though I loved him, I wasn't going to wait anymore.

A random thought emerged from the depths of my brain like a bubble from a glass of champagne. *Was Sullivan the suitor who would eventually propose to me per the lemon tradition?*

I pressed my temples. The lemon legend was the invention of

desperate *nonne*, like mine. *So what was I thinking? Did I get brain damage from that heavy wig?*

"What's going on in there?" Veronica asked.

"Oh, just wrestling with my Elvira dress." I adjusted the cleavage area for effect and peered over the rim. "What time is it, anyway?"

"Eight thirty. By the way, I knocked on your door earlier, and no one answered. Is your nonna at church?"

"Probably. But I sent her to Santina's for the night because I didn't want her home alone if the lunatic vampire showed up. God only knows where my brother is."

"Why don't you come down?" Veronica extended a hand.

It finally hit me that she was still in her nightgown. And she never left the apartment until she was put together. My gut lurched, but not from the booze. "Is Anthony okay?"

Her head moved backward. "As far as I know."

"Then until you tell me what this is about, I'm thinking I'm safer up here."

She crossed her arms. "This morning I got a call from the detective—"

"I told him to call *me* next time." My affection for Sullivan turned to anger.

"He tried, but you didn't answer. You were asleep?"

"Whatever he said, I don't want to hear it." I hung my torso over the side and pointed the empty Prosecco bottle at her. "Did Glenda tell you that when I went back inside after Bradley left, he actually tried to kiss me again?"

"Look, he didn't call about you, okay?" she huffed. "It's about Raven."

I retreated back to the bottom. *She didn't have to say it like I was being selfish, or anything.* "What about her?"

"Sullivan went to her apartment this morning to ask what she was doing with Josh at the cotillion. She wasn't there, but her front door was wide open, and the bedroom and living room had been turned inside out."

My gut contracted. *Was this what I'd sensed when I saw Saint Antho-*

ny's shadow? *The looming specter of Raven's death?* "No, that's ridiculous."

"It's not ridiculous. It's real."

"Sorry, I'm not all awake," I said, embarrassed that I'd chastised myself out loud. "Did Sullivan go to Josh's? Maybe she slept at his place."

"I thought you said he didn't have any furniture?"

"He has a coffin. And she's a vampire?"

Veronica's lips curled. "Well, Josh wasn't home, and apparently he's not answering his calls. Sullivan thinks that either someone ransacked her apartment while she was out somewhere, or she was there and attempted to fight the person off." She bit her lip. "And lost."

"Let me guess, he thinks that someone is Josh."

"He was the last person seen with Raven. But I can't believe that nice young man is the killer." She gasped and touched the glass. "What if both of them are in danger?"

"If so, that leaves Thomas Van Scyoc. And maybe Craig. Just because he's missing doesn't mean he's lost."

"I was thinking that too."

Something vibrated beneath my bottom, like Glenda's glass bed had Magic Fingers. I reached below me and pulled out my cell.

The display showed an unmarked number.

I flashed the phone at Veronica and tapped *Answer.* "Hello?"

"It's Josh." The statement wasn't a greeting—it was an act of force. "Don't put me on speaker. Be quiet and listen."

The glass lost its safe-haven quality, and I felt exposed.

Was Josh Santo about to confess?

"Here's your mimosa, sugar." Glenda placed a flute of champagne before me on her glass-top kitchen table. "It'll soothe your nerves and kick that hangover to neutral ground."

Neutral ground was New Orleanian for the median, and in the

case of a hangover, the expression was more fitting than *the curb*. "Thanks, but I don't see the orange juice."

She dragged off her cigarette holder. "I refuse to sully my bubbly with fruit."

"Just take a gulp," Veronica prodded from a pink fuzzy dining chair. "And then tell us what Josh said."

I drained half the glass and coughed, but it wasn't because the bubbles had tickled my nose.

The executioner had entered the kitchen still wearing his hood.

Glenda pressed a hand to the bosom of her red string negligee. "Miss Ronnie, this is Hermann, our hangman friend. I asked him to drop by after his shift. With that vampire after Miss Franki, we needed a bodyguard in the house."

He bowed as though happy to be of service, but I was sure that serving me hadn't been on his mind when he'd spent the night.

"No hoods at the table, Hermann honey." Glenda blew a stream of smoke at his package, where her gaze was directed. "It's rude."

The name fit him. At six-foot-five or so, the guy was a monster.

"I must go, Miss Glenda," he said in his French accent. "But first I will keep my promise."

I glanced at Veronica. "Uh, what promise is that?"

"It's the strangest thing." Glenda felt him up as she spoke. "Hermann saw Josh put Raven in a cab at the end of the evening."

"That confirms what he told me on the phone a few minutes ago. But what's so strange about it?"

"They were on a date, sugar. Why didn't they go home together?"

I rolled my eyes. In her world, a date meant a sleepover. Going out and getting to know one another weren't included in the deal. "Maybe fangs aren't his thing." I turned to Hermann. "How do you know it was them?"

"Miss Glenda asked if I had seen a guy in a top hat and cape with one of the Marie Antoinettes. I saw them when I was leaving at around three a.m."

"Out of curiosity, how many Marie Antoinettes were there?" Veronica asked.

He rubbed his hood. "Maybe two?"

Since it was a French Revolution party, I was surprised there hadn't been more. "You've been very helpful, Hang—... uh...Hermann."

He bowed again.

"I'll just show him out." Glenda took him by the bicep, but from the way she'd been checking out his behind, she would have rather grabbed a glute.

"It's great that he was able to corroborate Josh's story," Veronica said.

"Not all of it." I looked over my shoulder to make sure Glenda and her hangman were gone. "Josh took breakfast to Raven's apartment this morning and saw that the place had been trashed. He was sitting in his car contemplating calling the police when Sullivan pulled up."

"What? The detective didn't mention that when he called me this morning."

"Because Josh spotted him first. Then he drove home, dropped off his phone, and took off."

Veronica put her face in her hands.

"I know he's young, but he's not the sharpest canine in the vampire mouth, is he?"

She placed her palms on the table. "It looks bad, but I still don't think he's the killer."

"Actually, I think you're right."

Her eyes widened in mock shock, and she tossed back her drink.

"You're hilarious," I said, but I wasn't laughing. "I'll tell you what changed my mind. Not only did he hire us, he contracted at least one other PI and then started doing some investigative work of his own." I paused. "And it's looking like Raven didn't have anything to do with the murders, either. I just hope she hasn't become one of the victims."

We fell silent, like an execution had gone down.

"What about the drink samples?" Veronica asked. "Did Carnie get them?"

"You mean Count Drunkula?"

"I thought she was Countess Dragula."

"She was until she finished off every drink she took a sample from."

She lowered her eyelids, unamused. "Please tell me she got the vials?"

"They're in my bag in the living room."

"Good. I'm going to have them tested at a private lab, along with a sample of Campari. If we can get an ingredient list, things might start to make sense."

I swirled the liquid in my flute, glad it wasn't red. "We should also look into the details of Raven's firing from Belleville House. Since she's disappeared, it's the next logical step."

"I agree. But I'm a little confused about Thomas's role." Veronica leaned onto her elbows. "I know you're suspicious of him for not telling you that Raven was a nurse at the retirement home. But according to Linda at Pharmanew, he's the one who fired her for stealing the blood bags. Why would he do that if he was involved in the killings?"

"Because he needed a scapegoat when the family of that blood-drained grandpa hired an attorney. And maybe he killed her last night to stop her from turning him in." I tipped my flute at her. "Remember, I saw him meeting with Craig right before I found those blood bags at Delta Upsilon Delta. So Raven, Thomas, and Craig could all be connected."

"This is scary."

"I'll say." I flashed back to the coffin. "So who do we send inside?"

"I've got a woman to play the part of an elder relative."

I drained my champagne. "What about the PI?"

Glenda sashayed into the kitchen, and based on the lopsidedness of her lingerie, she'd shown Hermann more than the door. "Miss Ronnie and I talked about that before she woke you. Instead of a PI, you need an actor-actress type to question that Thomas character."

For a moment I'd thought she was referring to herself, but the last part threw me. "Like who?"

"Isn't it obvious, sugar? Miss Carnie. She's perfect to go undercover."

Those champagne bubbles had clearly gone to my brain. "Did you say perfect?"

She struck a pose with her cigarette holder. "Look at what a good job she did collecting those drink samples."

"If sobriety was any indicator, I'd say she failed."

Veronica leaned in. "This assignment doesn't involve alcohol, Franki. And we need someone in the retirement home who's tough and smart, on the off chance something goes wrong."

I pressed into the pink fuzzy chair back and crossed my arms. "Well, I'm done working with her. That queen is damn difficult."

"You won't deal with her directly. We'll set up a spy app on her smartphone so we can listen in."

Carnie would find a way to make the assignment backfire on me, that much I knew. But I had no proof, so I resorted to the only thing I had left. I poured another so-called mimosa and chugged the whole thing.

Then I stood and headed for the door.

"Where are you going, Miss Franki?"

"To find that executioner. I need him to chop off my head."

"*Aiutami Dio.*" I closed the front door behind me and hoped God had heard my appeal for assistance. Because two FIATs had pulled into my driveway, and I didn't want to be stalled out. After a shower and a change of clothes, it was ten thirty, and I had to get to Bradley's before he went anywhere.

The FIAT doors opened, and nine *nonne* piled out. In their black mourning dresses and matching veils, they looked like someone had died.

I tensed for a split second in light of my premonition from the previous night, but I reminded myself that they always looked funereal. "Did you ladies go to mass?"

Nonna gripped her purse. "We had-a more serious matters to address-a."

Words escaped me, and so did my calm. *What could a group of Italian Catholic women take more seriously than a sermon?*

A possible answer came to me that could have spelled my doom. The grave air they had about them probably meant they'd caught wind of the demise of my relationship. "So, what have you been doing?"

"We come from-a the archbishop."

Mary stepped forward. "He's got the pope's ear."

Holy crap. Were they trying to convene the Third Vatican Council to stage a marriage intervention?

Nonna produced a black velvet bag from the depths of her purse. "Open. And-a tell-a me what you see."

I held my breath and peered inside. "Um, a miniature Bible, a rosary, a compact, and"—I looked at my nonna—"a toy gun?"

"It's-a full of holy water."

"O-kay. But why?"

Mary nodded. "One squirt of that will lay a vampire out flat."

My sigh of relief was so deep it was almost my last breath. They had consulted with the archbishop to make me some sort of vampire protection kit. "What's the compact for?"

Nonna's eyes assumed a sly slant. "To make-a sure the suspect has a reflection."

A woman I didn't know stepped forward and pressed two garlic bulbs into my hand. They had been made into earrings that would have gone great with my Amy Winehouse–inspired Elvira costume. "*Grazie.* I'll, uh, wear them when I'm investigating."

My nonna wagged her finger. "You keep-a the bag-a with you too, *eh*?"

"I'll take it everywhere." And it was true too. I could use that holy water for all kinds of situations.

A familiar black BMW rounded the corner, and the sight of it made me feel like a hit-and-run victim.

"It's-a Bradley." Nonna vice-gripped my forearm. "Get-a the holy gun."

I wrested my arm free. "He's not a vampire."

"*No, eh?* Then why he suck-a the life outta you?"

I stared at her, stunned. She was so desperate to get me married that I had never listened to her criticism of my boyfriends. But where Bradley was concerned, she'd just hit the coffin nail on the head. As of late, our relationship had left me drained.

Nausea set in. *Was this really the end?* "Nonna, I need to speak to him alone."

She patted the black bag in my hand and motioned for the *nonne* to follow her inside—to spy from the window.

I zombie-walked to the end of the yard.

Bradley exited the car. And the style of his suit told me everything I needed to know.

He was going back to work.

I clenched my teeth and exhaled my contempt.

"I don't have long." His tone was dead. "I'm on my way to the airport."

"From The Big Easy to The Big Apple so fast?" I quipped.

His eyes went from brown to black, and he shoved fists into his pants pockets. "I just want to know why."

"Detective Sullivan and I weren't on the balcony to make out, Bradley. That kiss was a complete surprise."

"Not to him it wasn't." His tone had come back to life, and it had a bite. "That bastard had it planned."

"Even if he did, he's not the problem."

"And I am?"

I looked at the grass. "You're always at work."

"I'm trying to build a future for us."

"Meanwhile, I'm living in the present. And you're not in it."

He pulled back as though he'd been punched. "Is that what you want? Me out of your life?"

Outrage swelled my chest. "I didn't say that."

"But it's what you meant." He turned and got into his car.

"Oh, this is just *perfect*." I marched in front of the hood. "You're leaving. Like you always do."

He started the engine, backed up, and sped away.

I watched his car disappear, maybe for the last time. I wanted to cry, but I was too incensed that he'd driven away.

The sound of an engine made my heart accelerate.

Had Bradley come back?

A taxi pulled up with my brother in the back.

In a way, I was relieved. I didn't have anything left to say to Bradley. I'd told him the problem. It was up to him to respond, if he wanted to, of course. And I wasn't sure he did.

After paying the driver, Anthony exited the cab in a tight T-shirt and my Buffy the Vampire Slayer pants, which was fitting given that red was the only color I saw in that moment.

"This is when you come home?" My pitch was shrill like my mother's, and suddenly I understood her quite well. "Eleven a.m.?"

"Eyyy, tone down the mom. I got a new lady, and I stayed at her place." He strutted up the driveway toward the house.

Anthony was the second man to blow me off in less than two minutes, and I was so done with that. "Don't walk away from me. We need to talk."

"Yo, I ain't got time. I've gotta crash before my shift tonight."

"I thought you stayed at a woman's house?"

"I did, but I wasn't there to sleep, if you know what I'm sayin'." He stepped onto the porch and kicked the piece of gutter he was supposed to have hung.

If only the vampire protection kit contained a stake. "You need to hang that thing *right now*."

"I'll get to it later, awright?"

"It's *all right*, not *awright*," I shouted. "And no, it's not all right."

He slammed the door.

I strode to the gutter and, imagining it was both Anthony and Bradley, stomped it flat. Then I hurled it across the yard. And it hit the windshield of a black SUV that slammed on the brakes.

Horrified, I rushed to the street to apologize and check for damage.

The car was an unmarked police vehicle, and Sullivan was behind the wheel.

He leaned across the passenger seat and pushed open the door.

"Hey, I'm sorry—"

"Get in."

There was a hard edge to his voice that matched his gaze. And I knew we weren't going down lovers' lane but on a highway to hell.

I opened the door and climbed in.

16

Sullivan lowered his metallic shades. "Where's your boy?"

My behind had barely touched the passenger seat, so I wasn't prepared for the question. "Bradley?"

"I know he's not around," he drawled. "I was talking about your client, Josh Santo."

The comment struck me like a police baton, not only because Sullivan was spot on about Bradley's absence, but also because I felt protective of him, regardless of our dating status. "Actually, you just missed him."

"Josh, right?"

He exuded smugness, and I was determined not to let him win, even though I'd lost. "Wrong. Bradley."

"Well, from the way you launched that chunk of metal into the street, I'd say the two of you didn't make up. Now what about your client?"

Anger radiated from me like a heater, but I refused to give him the satisfaction of knowing that his kiss had been the breaking point in my relationship. "Josh called me an hour and a half ago, but he didn't tell me where he was."

"So that was after he left his cell phone at home to evade arrest."

"You're wrong about him. He didn't do anything to Raven."

He removed his sunglasses. "Leave that to the police to decide."

I met his gaze. "Are you implying that I'm not smart enough to eliminate him as a suspect?"

"I'm implying that we have information you don't."

That wasn't what I'd wanted to hear. "Can you clue me in on what it is?"

"No, but I'll clue you in on this. If I find out you're hiding him, I'll throw you in jail."

Despite the seductive scent of his cologne, the spell from the Bourbon Orleans balcony was broken, and so was my tolerance for his behavior. "Is this what you do after you make a pass at a woman? Pound your chest like a big ape?"

"Exciting, isn't it?"

"Honestly, it's appalling." That was a partial lie. A certain amount of chest pounding could be appealing, especially if the chest being pounded was as ripped as the detective's.

"That's because you've been ruined by that metrosexual boyfriend of yours."

"Bradley is not metrosexual." I wished my high pitch didn't make an interest in fashion sound negative. "He's just...a bank manager."

He laughed through his nose. "Same thing. What you need is a touch of the Irish."

"Italian and Irish don't mix."

"Sure we do." He leaned close. "Like fire and fire."

I pressed myself against the door to escape his body heat. "You proved my point. That's a combustive combination."

"It's better than fire and water, which is what you've got now."

The analogy caught me off guard. I would have never admitted it to Sullivan, but that's what Bradley had been lately—a splash of water, and a cold one. "Did you really come here to pry into my personal business when Craig and Raven are missing?"

"That's the difference between me and your boyfriend. No matter what's going on in my professional life, I make time for the important things."

The implication that I was unimportant to Bradley hurt, and a veil of tears blurred my vision. I looked out the passenger window, and the veil began to lift.

Because my nonna was on the porch, and she appeared to be aiming something at the car.

I squinted. *A tennis ball?*

Then I straightened and opened my eyes wide. That lunatic Sicilian was holding a lemon.

The tears dried up, and so did my patience—for Nonna's meddling, Bradley's working, and Sullivan's interfering. Oh, and my brother's shirking. "Can I go now?"

"You may not."

Stunned, I turned in my seat. "I must have misunderstood the stupid thing you just said."

"Nothing stupid about it. It's called police work." His stare was hard like his tone. "You're going to stick with me until your boy calls again. And, obviously, I mean Josh."

I looked around, incredulous. "What if he doesn't call? You expect me to sit in this car all day?"

"Nah, we've got to drop by St. Cecilia Cemetery to see Phil Redman."

"The caretaker? Uh-uh, no." I shook my head hard. "That dude is weird."

"Maybe so. But the killer left us a message with the Greek Orthodox tomb, and we need to explore that further."

"What's to explore?" I threw up my hands. "Gregg was Greek too. There's your answer."

"We have to understand how it applies to the entire case."

"What we have to understand is the message with Todd Plank. Why was he left at the blood bank and not in a tomb?"

"He could've been killed because he was in the wrong place at the wrong time."

I tapped my fingers on my lips. "Or maybe there was bad blood between that vampire and Todd."

He gripped the steering wheel. "Is that supposed to be a joke?"

"Not at all. I just don't understand why the killer would knock off Todd when there were pints of blood waiting for the taking."

He shrugged. "Probably because Todd tried to stop the theft."

"Or it was a revenge killing."

"We're looking into connections between the suspects and Todd, but so far we haven't had any luck."

His phone rang, and he grabbed it as though it was a call from the Commissioner of Gotham City. "Sullivan."

I glanced at the porch.

Nonna tossed the lemon into the air and caught it. And her smile told me there was some kind of Sicilian voodoo going down.

I made a slicing motion, but not in reference to the citrus fruit.

Then I looked across the street at Thibodeaux's Tavern and longed to go in for a drink. And a charcuterie board with a cheese plank on the side.

"That was the station." Sullivan tossed the phone onto the console. "Raven hasn't used her credit or ATM cards."

"She hasn't been gone that long. Maybe she hasn't spent any money. Or she used cash."

He slung me the side-eye. "With her purse and keys inside a ransacked apartment?"

I didn't respond. We both knew my hypothesis wouldn't pan out.

"Buckle up, Amato." He slipped on his sunglasses and put the car in drive. "You and I have got a body to find."

"Phil's around somewhere." Sullivan stood hands on hips scanning the grounds of Saint Cecilia Cemetery. "Let's check the back."

I followed him through the graves, and bits of rock and crumbling concrete crunched beneath my boots. But I refused to look down. I was too afraid those bits might be bones like the ones I'd seen the last time.

I didn't look up, either, because the giant tomb-top skeleton would be beckoning. Instead, I kept my eyes on Sullivan's back and focused on not noticing how broad it was.

And muscular.

We snaked our way around a walk-in crypt, and I stopped, statue-like.

Phil sat cross-legged with his back against the mausoleum wall, munching a turkey leg.

And a shriveled mummy in a rotten suit stood next to him.

"Got a lunch guest, Phil?" Sullivan asked.

Phil patted the mummy, whose lack of lips made it appear that he was smiling from ear to ear. "Every so often one of our guests comes out and pays us a visit. Lying on one's back for an eternity gets old, I would imagine. Perhaps that's why Lionel Batiste, the jazz musician, asked to stand at his own wake."

I pulled the holy water gun from my purse and squeezed the trigger against my temple. To bless myself.

"Detective, your friend looks a little peaked."

His *friend?* I thought. *What about* yours?

"You all right, Amato?"

"Mm-hm." It wasn't true, but I had to keep my mouth closed. The scent of decay was everywhere, and I didn't want to swallow any dead guy spores.

Sullivan flashed me a smile as wide as Phil's lipless companion. Then he turned to our host. "We've got another missing person who might've met the same end as Gregg Charalambous."

Phil chewed a piece of turkey skin. "Unfortunate, that. But since his body was discovered, it's been kind of dead around here."

I didn't roll my eyes. I was too freaked out.

"The name is Raven Smith." Sullivan crossed his arms. "What does that tell you in terms of a tomb?"

"Raven is from the Old English Hræfn," Phil said, sounding like he was clearing his throat. "And of course Smith is also Old English. It comes from smitan, or smite, and refers to one who works in metal, such as a blacksmith. But I'm afraid we don't have any Old English–style tombs in New Orleans."

Sullivan rubbed his chin. "I don't have any information on her ethnic background, but I could get that for you."

Phil opened the mausoleum door next to him. Inside was a carboy for brewing beer that contained an ominous brown liquid. "Could I interest either of you in a pumpkin porter? I brewed it for the Halloween season."

Sullivan held up his hands. "On duty."

I shook my head, but it was to shake off the repressed scream that threatened to strangle me.

"Shame you're always working, Detective. Pardon the cliché, but you should live a little."

"I lived a little last night, in fact." Sullivan cast me a knowing look.

My face grew hot, and I avoided the mummy's eye sockets. It wasn't that I thought he was judging me, because he was way past deceased. I just thought the live a little comment was inconsiderate given the surroundings.

Phil placed the turkey leg on his thigh and poured himself a beer. "Did Ms. Smith perhaps belong to any professional, religious, or social organizations? They have their own tombs all over the city. For instance, St. Louis Cemetery No. 1 has The Italian Benevolent Society tomb and the Orleans Battalion of Artillery Tomb, but I don't suppose either of those would fit."

I covered my mouth, still intent on not inhaling any dead guy. "She belongs to the New Orleans Vampire Organization where she works, but she used to be a nurse."

"You could try the Charity Hospital Cemetery, which now holds the Hurricane Katrina Memorial. But it was never intended for medical professionals, only for paupers and unclaimed bodies."

"That could be the place." Sullivan turned to me. "Raven was an orphan."

Maybe that was why she'd joined NOVO. It had houses, which functioned like family.

"There's the Protestant Orphan's Society tomb in Lafayette Cemetery No. 2, but that's for boys." Phil pressed a finger to his glistening beard. "You might try the Poydras Tomb at Lafayette Cemetery No. 1. It was for girls."

Sullivan nodded. "We'll check it out."

Phil wiped his palm on his shorts and rose for a handshake, and I realized that he had a tattoo of bees on his knees to go with the cat in pajamas on his arm. It was beyond me how a crypt keeper could be so happy. Or a mummy, for that matter.

"Let's roll, Amato."

"Wait. What about Craig? Aren't you going to ask about a tomb for him?"

"Never mind that." Sullivan pushed me toward the exit.

"Drop by when you're off duty, Detective," Phil called. "I'm working on a French Morbier cheese that will go marvelously with this porter. It's ash-ripened. Made with two batches of milk."

Ash-ripened? I picked up my pace. I had to escape the hellish cemetery deli before I got sick.

A ring tone sounded, and Sullivan stopped behind me.

I turned to wait. It was a different phone than the one he'd left on his console.

"Excuse me a sec." He stepped behind a mausoleum.

I wasn't sure whether it was his ex or another cop, but I wanted to find out. I crept to the grave and listened.

"Rourke." Sullivan's voice was low, but Craig's last name resounded in my ears.

I walked around the side to confront him. "Why were you talking about Craig?"

"I wasn't." He slipped the phone into his pocket.

"You said Rourke."

"O'Rourke. He's a colleague, and we're throwing him a retirement party."

I was dismayed by how easily he lied. "I'm not leaving until you tell me what's going on with Craig."

"We're not looking for him, remember? We're looking for Raven on the off chance there's still time to save her. Now come on." He walked past me.

I stayed behind. "I meant what I said. I'm not going anywhere until you tell me where Craig is."

"You're acting like a spoiled brat." He moved toward me.

I leapt backward into a crypt and jumped like I'd been scorched. It was one of those pizza-oven types Phil had told me about.

Sullivan scooped me into his arms. "Gotcha."

I struggled. "If you want to live, you'll put me down."

"I will when I put you in the car."

He strode through the cemetery as though my 170 or so pounds were a bag of raked leaves.

His strength was surprising. And I stopped resisting. I'd been lonely, and a little human contact was nice at a cemetery, especially when it came from a strong manly chest.

We arrived at the entrance, and he kicked the gate open.

The squeaky slasher soundtrack sound shook me from the spell.

Once again I was reminded of Dracula's ability to seduce and enthrall his victims. *Was Sullivan doing that intentionally to keep me from asking any more Craig questions?*

And is that what the killer had done? Seduce and enthrall the victims?

TACHYCARDIA WREAKED havoc on my heart as I passed beneath the arched Lafayette Cemetery No. 1 sign. I'd been there for a previous case, and I didn't relish being back to look for a vampire victim. "Do you know where this tomb is?"

Sullivan closed the wrought-iron gate. "No idea. You want to split up?"

"Leave me alone in this place, and I'll bury you in it."

He chuckled, but I didn't laugh. I was busy scouring the grounds. Although the cemetery was in the posh Garden District, it was no less eerie or unsafe than its poorer counterparts. Among its creepy credentials, Anne Rice had chosen it for Lestat and Louis's roaming grounds, and she'd staged her own glass-coffined funeral there to publicize a book. Even more disturbing, it was the site of music videos by LeAnn Rimes and New Kids on the Block.

A chilly wind whipped dirt and debris into a frenzy.

Sullivan took off his sunglasses. "Cold front's coming in."

Let's hope. Based on the setting, I wouldn't have ruled out a poltergeist warning us to leave.

Under the watchful eyes of concrete angels, gargoyles, and human likenesses, we walked through the crypts. Many of them were multi-chambered and bore the names of bygone organizations and old fraternal orders, like the New Orleans Home for Incurables and The Independent Order of Odd Fellows. Others were individual tombs representing the ethnic diversity of the city's early settlers.

All the graves had begun the process of returning to the earth from whence they came, like their departed inhabitants. And I willed those inhabitants to stay where they were instead of coming out to pay us a visit.

"Here's the Society for the Relief of Destitute Orphan Boys." Sullivan patted a structure with four slots.

I was surprised Phil hadn't mentioned the tomb. "That's not it. We need the one for girls."

Sullivan scanned the area and gestured to a broken glass candle at the entrance to a crypt. "A voodoo working. Lafayette's popular with that crowd."

I shivered and wished I had a coat or a blanket, but I wasn't cold. I just wanted to pull it around me, so I could hide.

"Don't be scared, Francesca." He slid his arms around my waist as easily as my given name had slipped from his lips. "I'll keep you safe."

A Bateson's Belfry rang in my brain. Bradley and I had split only hours before, so I wasn't exactly on the market for another man, especially not the one who'd broken us up. And even if I were looking for a new guy, I'd be damned if I would do it in a cemetery. "What are you doing right now?"

"Making time for the important things." He reeled me in.

My tachycardia went atrial fibrillation. "We're looking for a body, remember?"

"And I found one." He pressed hard against me, leaving no doubt whose body he meant.

"I was talking about Raven?" I pushed against his chest and broke free.

Hurrying out of range of his arms, I went toward a corner of the cemetery. I passed a crumbling mausoleum with weeds protruding from the brick seals—and something that was either a root or a finger.

I stopped and looked casually over my shoulder, trying not to seem desperate for Sullivan to catch up.

He pointed past me. "That's it up ahead."

A crypt marked Poydras Orphans' Rest loomed before us. It consisted of three walk-in tombs in a cruciform shape. Books and movies had trained me to think that vampires shrunk away from crucifixes, but I had no idea if the same was true of real vampires, and particularly vampire serial killers.

Sullivan ran his hand over a door. "It's been stuccoed recently."

My heart resumed its arrhythmia. "As in, last night or today?"

"No, not the seals. I meant the whole tomb. Let's check the other doors." He worked his way around the cross, and I followed behind.

But not too close.

"I don't see any signs of tampering." He slammed his hand on the side of the tomb. "Damn it. Where could she be?"

I glanced at the ground.

Something red lay nestled among the leaves. Probably a plastic flower from a nearby grave. I kicked the pile and gasped.

"What is it?"

"A red satin rosette."

Sullivan must have seen Raven's dress at the cotillion because he began kicking leaves around the tomb.

I worked the opposite side. Within less than a minute, I'd uncovered a metal handle that I knew would lead to an underground vault.

"Wesley." His given name was the logical choice. The discovery of a murder victim's grave was an intimate moment.

He rushed to the site. Our eyes met in grim acceptance, and he bent over and threw open the door.

The hole was as black as I'd envisioned the entrance to the netherworld.

He switched on his cell phone light and looked inside. "There's a ladder." He pulled a pistol from the back of his waistband. "Wait here."

I swallowed and watched him descend. My stomach sunk further with his every step. He disappeared, and I heard a splash, presumably his feet on the floor since the vault was below the water table.

Silence.

He swore.

My stomach splashed down. "Is she there?"

Nothing.

My stomach rose until I thought it would surface and spring from my throat. "Are you all right?"

"Fine." His tone was anything but. "Don't come down."

I exhaled.

Then I turned on my phone light and stepped onto the ladder.

And descended into hell.

Before reaching the bottom rung, I held on with one hand and shined my light on the ground. Water pooled around rotting coffin planks, old bones, and clumps of something that I wanted to believe was dirt and dead weeds, not decomposing flesh and hair.

My stomach had steadied, but bile threatened to escape.

Slowly, I raised the light to dangling bare feet, a black French pannier dress with red satin rosettes, and a face the same ghostly hue as the pouf wig.

I moved the light upward along a cable that had been tied from the back of the French dress to a ceiling beam.

Then I lowered the light again.

Raven's canines were bared, but in fear not fight. And her dark eyes bulged as though she'd seen the devil. The thick tree roots around her head were so gnarled and twisted that, had it not been for the wig, she would have resembled Medusa more than Marie Antoinette.

Around her neck was the choker of four strands of pearls that had been covered in fake blood for the cotillion. And yet, apart from the red that rimmed the slits at her ankles, there was no blood anywhere else.

Not even in her body.

I lowered the light to search for her shoes. They were in a corner above the water next to a semi-rounded piece of rubber a few inches in length.

Sullivan slipped an arm around my waist, but I didn't push him away. I let go of the ladder and clung to him.

With all the life I had left.

17

T hunder cracked, and lightning flashed outside Private Chicks. The effect was not unlike a glinting guillotine blade crashing down and lopping off heads.

I huddled in a corner of the lobby couch, grateful that I was in the office and that it was morning.

Veronica took a seat across from me with a mug and her laptop. Her face was as gray as Raven's. "I'll never look at a picture of Marie Antoinette again without thinking of that poor woman. I just can't imagine the crime scene."

My latte tasted bitter despite a half cup of frothed Baileys Amaretto creamer. I could imagine the crime scene. In fact, I'd spent the entire night trying to unimagine it. And it had been impossible with the Bride of Dracula and the Creature of the Night staying at my house.

"And I'm amazed that crypt keeper knew exactly where to look for Raven," Veronica said. "Are you sure he isn't the killer?"

"I asked Sullivan the same thing. But there must be some other psycho cemetery buff out there because Phil has alibis for Gregg's and Raven's murders."

"Where was he?"

"At a Do-It-Yourself taxidermy workshop and a Renaissance Fair."
I shuddered. "That alone should get him arrested."

"The taxidermy?"

I gave her a you-should-know-me-better-than-that look. I'd
always been clear that I didn't do renaissance or medieval. "Obviously, the Ren Fair. He's the king, which warrants a beheading."

She smirked and opened her computer on the coffee table
between us. "By the way, I took those drink samples from the cotillion
to the lab. It's going to take a couple of weeks to get the results."

That was too long, but the samples no longer seemed relevant.
"Now that we know Raven wasn't the killer, I don't expect the lab to
find any blood in them. It's time to focus on Thomas. I'd give
anything to know if he was at the cotillion Saturday night."

"Wouldn't you have seen him?"

"Not if he was wearing a full face mask like Raven's." I sat up and
put my feet on the floor. "Wait. I didn't see hers in the burial vault."

Veronica sipped her coffee. "It's probably in her apartment. She
wouldn't grab her mask when she was being abducted."

"Unless the killer made her bring it with her for some twisted
reason. I'll ask Sullivan if they found it in the water." I sat my mug on
the coffee table and shot him a text.

Her brow arched until it almost formed a question mark. "You
two have been working pretty closely."

"What? No." My defensively dismissive tone belied the lie.

"You were rivals on the *Amaretto Amber* case. Now you're texting
like old friends, or..."

I resented the unstated implication. "We had to team up, Veronica. A vampire serial killer is hunting victims, and my brother and I
are potentially among them."

Thunder boomed, and we both started.

Unnerved, I pulled my feet up and clutched a couch cushion to
my chest.

She set down her mug. "I wouldn't blame you if you wanted to
back out of your contract with Josh and let the police take it from
here."

The case had gotten under my skin. But it was also in my blood. "I'm too close to solving it. And even if I did back out, I'd still be on that maniac's kill list."

Footsteps pounded up the stairs.

Our eyes met.

The lobby buzzer went off, and David entered.

Nevertheless, I jumped.

"Uh, sorry to scare you." He tossed a soaked umbrella by the door. "It's like a hurricane out there."

And in my head. "What's the word on Delta Upsilon Delta?"

He dropped his backpack at his desk, and the thud reminded me of the guillotine.

"Pretty much what you'd expect." He flopped onto the couch next to Veronica. "Parties, kegs, and girls."

That was predictable. "Any news on Craig?"

"Uh-uh. But Andrew said some of the guys asked Domenic about him the other night, and he totally shut them down."

Veronica shot me a side-eye. "Sounds like Domenic knows something."

I tossed the cushion aside. "I think Sullivan does too. Any time I bring up Craig, he changes the subject."

David leaned forward, elbows on knees. "Maybe he's trying to keep your mind off him. Because if he's the killer..."

I was glad he hadn't completed the thought.

Veronica opened a file on her laptop. "Well, that's why I had you come in before class, David. Carnie was able to book a six p.m. tour of Belleville House tonight, so maybe we'll get some answers about Thomas's involvement in the murders."

"And whether Craig and Raven were in on them," I added.

David's leg began to bounce. "Do you think that Thomas dude is a real vampire?"

"He's pale enough to be one." Thomas's peanut butter and potato dinner reared its unappetizing head in my brain. "And his diet is certainly suspect."

"Uh, did you need me and the vassal to help?"

Veronica glanced at his leg and smiled. "Only with testing the mic. Franki and I will be listening to Carnie and her grandmother from my car outside."

I bolted upright. "You got Carnie's grandmother?"

"Relax. It's not her real grandmother."

With Carnie in the mix, I was going to stay on edge. "Well, who is she, then?"

Red marks appeared on Veronica's face like multiple scarlet letters, and I knew I wasn't going to like whomever she'd hired.

"Before you get mad, Franki, *she* approached *me*."

My mental Rolodex spun into action. Glenda was older than Carnie, but she'd sooner play a nun than someone's grandmother. The Rolodex spun to the next card. Blank. We didn't know anyone else who was old enough for the assignment.

Except...

I Mount Vesuviused from the couch. "My nonna?"

Horror flickered across David's face, and he fled to his desk.

Veronica stood and held out her hands. "She refused to let me say no."

Too angry to pace, I stalked instead. "The woman could wear down a Mafia boss, Veronica. You have to work around her. You know that."

"I do. And I understand your concern, but—"

"Concern doesn't describe it." I stopped right in front of her. "You know how Italians use the English word for privacy because they don't have a word for it?"

She nodded.

"That's my nonna with subtle. The word is not part of her culture. So she'll blow into Belleville and go all organized crime on Thomas. And then what happens?"

Veronica licked her lips. "She's not going to do that because you're her granddaughter, and she knows what's at stake."

"At stake? Is that supposed to be a vampire pun?"

"Of course not. I'm taking this very seriously."

"Then prove it by hiring professionals."

She touched her face as though I'd slapped her.

Thunder rumbled.

I scowled at the ceiling. I felt terrible about the hiring comment. I didn't need nature to rub it in. "I'm sorry I said that. But—"

The vassal burst in, glasses askew and his checked shirt untucked on one side.

"Bro!" David rushed to his side. "What happened?"

Thinking he'd been attacked, I tabled the nonna tantrum. "Is someone chasing you?"

His usual mouth breathing had escalated to mouth wheezing. "I saw Josh Santo being arrested."

A cell door slammed shut in my mind. "Where?"

He removed his glasses. "Boutique du Vampyre."

My gut slammed shut too. The location wasn't good news.

"Sullivan's in with the chief." The blonde officer gestured to an office down a hallway. Then she grimaced. "And if I were you, I'd leave him there."

She walked away, leaving me confused. That was an odd thing to say to someone she didn't know. But then again, my reputation preceded me around the police station. Either way, she obviously had issues with the detective, and I could relate. He probably hadn't shown his colleagues his new softer side.

I took a seat outside the chief's office and hoped I didn't have to wait long. I had to convince Sullivan that arresting Josh had been a mistake. Otherwise, the consequences would be grave. Literally.

"This is a huge win for the department, Wesley," a male voice boomed. "New Orleans can rest easy again, and you'll be a local hero after the press conference."

Until the vampire serial killer resumes the blood drainings.

"I appreciate that, Chief. And I am relieved, not for myself but for the citizens of this great city."

My gaze darted to the door. I'd never heard Sullivan be smarmy.

"Admirable sentiment, Detective. Now how're you gonna celebrate?"

"I've got me a date."

I felt the tiniest pin prick in my belly, and my hand flew to my abdomen. *What was that about? Was I jealous?*

Of Sullivan?

"You always were a lady killer." The chief laughed, enjoying his murder pun. "Is she anyone I know?"

"Franki Amato."

My head recoiled. He was awfully confident considering he hadn't even asked me out.

"Isn't she that PI?"

"The one and only."

The chief laughed and pounded the desk.

Offended, I rose from the chair. I didn't see what was so funny about going out with me, even though the detective definitely wasn't.

"I still wish I'd been at Madame Moiselle's to see that crabwalk she did onstage." The chief stopped to guffaw. "Your reenactment at that meeting will go down in police history."

The prick turned into a pierce. Right in my gut.

Sullivan chuckled. "Yeah, I can't vouch for her dance moves. But I do like those curves."

"Didn't you say she had a boyfriend?"

"You used the word 'history,' and that's what he is."

I moved toward the office tempted to burst in. *How was Sullivan so sure about Bradley and me? Unless he'd talked to him...*

The pierce became a stab.

No, he wouldn't have.

Would he?

The door opened, and the detective strutted out. He took one look at me, and his conquering-hero smile faltered.

"Can I speak to you privately?" My words formed a question, but my tone left no room for a no.

What remained of his smile fled the battlefield. He ushered me into his office and held out a chair. "Please. Have a seat."

"Drop the gentleman routine. We both know it's an act."

Sullivan pursed his lips and ambled behind his desk. Slowly, he sunk into his seat. "Surely you can't begrudge a man a little locker room talk after a big victory?"

I found myself thinking of that hangman from the cotillion. "It's interesting that you would use a sports analogy. Because it didn't seem like I was a trophy as much as a soccer ball you were kicking around."

"I'm sorry you took it that way. Sometimes we men get carried away, but I want you to know I respect you."

"Is that why you reenacted my striptease? Because you respect me so much?"

"Come on, Amato. Where's your sense of humor? You and I both know that was funny."

"This is my business, Sullivan. I can't have you making me the butt of your meeting jokes. It's unprofessional, not to mention damaging to my reputation."

"Message received." His fingers formed a steeple in front of his chest. "Now what did you come to talk to me about?"

"Josh Santo. He didn't kill Raven."

The concern left Sullivan's eyes, and competition replaced it. "Then what was he doing at Boutique du Vampyre?"

"It's a hub for the local vampire community, so he was probably looking for information about the killer."

Sullivan leaned back in his chair and moved his hands behind his head. "If you believe that, then I have some swampland to sell you."

"And if you close the investigation, someone else will die. Maybe even someone in my family. Or me."

"That's not going to happen. I saw to that when I threw that creepy client of yours behind bars." He leaned forward, his face earnest. "And one of the reasons I did it was to protect you, Franki. Can't you see that?"

My anger would have softened, but it was too upset at his arrogance. "Uh, I don't need your protection. But even if I did, how could you protect me when you've got the wrong guy?"

He put his head down for a moment. Then he looked at me interrogation style. "You got any evidence to back that up?"

"I'm working on it."

"Like you said, this is business." He spread his arms. "And if you
haven't got a product, you lose the sale."

"I wouldn't gloat if I were you. Your evidence is circumstantial,
and Josh has unlimited funds. So even if you get lucky and no one
else dies, when this goes to trial your case will fall apart." I paused to
smirk at the accolades on his office walls. "You'll go from local hero to
enemy number one."

His brow lowered. He picked up a designer pen and stared at the
enamel. "I was going to ask you to dinner—"

"So I heard. But I don't mix business with pleasure."

He half-laughed. "Good one."

Ignoring his virtual pat on my back, I resumed my investigation.
"I sent you a text about Raven's cotillion mask. Did you find it at her
apartment or in the vault?"

"No we did not."

"You should find it." I grabbed the door handle but kept my eyes
on him. "Because the killer has it."

"Well, I say Josh disposed of it."

"It's Serial Killers 101, Sullivan. They love keepsakes. Vampires
would be no different." I pulled open the door.

"End your investigation, Amato. Or I'll have to get in your way."

His words struck my back like bullets, and I turned to scrutinize
his face. The softer side was gone, and I wondered if it had really
existed. "You're not my employer, and I'm going to honor the contract
with my client."

"And how are you planning to do that?"

"Not that I owe you any explanations, but I'm going to the frat
house to get some answers about Craig."

"He's not the killer. Thomas either. You're the one who's mistaken
here."

"Given the wrongful arrest of Josh, I can't take your word for that."
I exited and slammed the door.

Thunder blasted the sky, shaking the station.

Nature's timing couldn't have been worse. It served as an unsettling reminder that, in terms of the law, I was alone in my convictions about the killer. And without Sullivan to back me, the case had gotten a whole lot more dangerous.

Possibly deadly.

"HALLOWEEN IS OVER." I surveyed Maybe Baby's French maid costume as she leaned in the doorway of Delta Upsilon Delta. "Why are you still wearing that?"

She pulled up a fishnet thigh high. "'Cause I got nursing duty till noon."

"What is this nursing—"

The hospital beds.

I tossed my wet umbrella on the porch and pushed past her. And I ran down the hallway to The Dungeon.

"Hey!" she squeak-shouted. "You can't go in there. My patient has a right to congeniality."

I pulled my Ruger from my bag and twisted the doorknob.

It turned.

The Fatal Funnel.

It was a police expression for a doorway that had a potential adversary lying in wait on the other side, and it weighed on my mind like a guillotine. Or a coffin with a lock.

Was Craig inside?

Or Domenic?

I took a breath and kicked open the door. Jerked my gun to the nearest corner.

"Holy shit!" a man yelled. "Don't shoot!"

I pivoted and aimed at a Jim Morrison lookalike in aviator glasses who sat upright on a hospital bed with hands in the air. An IV in his arm was attached to a bag of clear liquid.

I did a quick check of the rest of the gray room. The coffin was gone, replaced by a plastic nightstand.

"You don't have to worry about me, man. I mean, lady," he fumbled. "I won't take another shot for at least a year."

Shot? Was he talking about his IV drip? I pointed my gun at the bag. "What is that stuff?"

"Saline and vitamins."

I lowered my gun. "Huh?"

"You know." Maybe peeked at me with one eye. Her lace French maid hat had fallen over the other. "Like at the Remedy Room?"

I glanced at Jim Morrison for a translation.

He removed his hair but left his sunglasses. "Oh, she means the hydration therapy place on St. Charles." He'd gone from fearful to jovial in a split second. "Our frat isn't supposed to be drinking because of a suspension, so the saline flushes out the toxins. I feel a lot better, but I *am* freaked out about the damage I did to my liver. I've probably cut my life short by a decade."

Because of this case, I'd probably cut my life short too. "Is that what you and your frat brothers do in here? Get saline infusions to cure your hangovers?"

He nodded. "For now, yeah. We're making it a gaming room, though. Like the Batcave. That's why we did the rock treatment on the walls."

Josh Santo had a Batman thing too. *What was it about guys and men dressed like bats?* "What about blood bags? I thought I saw some in this room during the Halloween party."

"Nooo." He waved me off with a grin. "Blood's not our bag."

I smacked my Ruger against my palm to let him know I wasn't joking, but I should have smacked *him* for that pun.

"If you don't believe me, check in the nightstand."

I opened the top drawer. It was filled with packages marked IV Solution Bags, and a Ziploc full of orange pills. "What are these?"

He removed his shades. "Some kind of pain killer?"

"Easter egg dye?" Maybe guessed.

I snorted. The DUDs hunted chicks, not eggs.

I hung on to the pills and searched the other drawers. Nothing. I was willing to believe I'd been wrong about the blood bags, but there was still the question of Craig's involvement with Thomas. And his whereabouts.

"Those are supplements," a male voice said.

I spun around and raised my Ruger.

"Whoa. Be cool, all right?" Domenic stood in the doorway in a gray sweat suit. He had headphones around his neck.

I wasn't ready to trust him. "Hands up. Get over by the bed."

He complied. "I just came to see what was going on."

"Me too." I leveled the gun at his forehead. "So why don't you tell me where your sidekick is?"

"Craig? None of us have seen him since the day of the party."

"I was here that night, and your freshman pledge Andrew told me he'd gone to see his grandmother. Is that true?"

"As far as I know." He looked at his soccer slides. "But she's not answering her phone. Neither is he."

I looked at Maybe and bald Jim Morrison for confirmation, and they nodded. "What about his parents? Did you call them?"

"He doesn't have any," Domenic said. "He lived with his grandma."

"You reported him missing, right?"

"He's my friend." His tone had gone from nervous to irritated. "I called the cops and talked to the detective who busted up our party."

Maybe squeezed her arms against her breasts. "He means the dreamy one that was just on TV. Did you know he caught a vampire?"

Disappointment rumbled in me like the thunder outside. Sullivan had gone ahead with the press conference despite my warning. "And have you heard back from the detective?"

"Just that the police are working on finding him. Nothing else."

I scrutinized Domenic's face, but I couldn't tell if he was lying because he always looked the same. I raised the bag of pills. "I'm taking these with me for testing."

He bowed his head, which told me he'd lied about them. They weren't supplements—they were drugs.

I kept my gun trained on him. "I need Craig's grandmother's name and number."

"He's got it." Domenic pointed to his brother in the bed.

My gaze shifted, but not my aim. "What's your name?"

"Jeremy Nickel."

"Why do you have her number?"

"Because our grandmas are friends. They stayed at the same retirement home until Craig's grandma moved out about six months ago."

My chest tightened and so did my grip on my gun. "Belleville House in the Quarter?"

Jeremy's eyes and mouth went wide. "Dude. Are you psychic?"

"Never mind that. Why'd she leave?"

"Something about an accident with a blood transfusion."

A chill ran through my veins like a rush of saline solution. It sounded like Craig's grandmother had experienced the same mistreatment as the dead grandfather Lou had told me about. If so, the nurse who'd taken their blood must have been Raven Smith. And that could only mean one thing.

When Craig met Thomas at Harry's Bar, it wasn't to talk about some evil blood plot. It was probably to discuss a settlement, which I was sure Belleville House wouldn't have wanted to pay.

Had Craig made himself the next target?

A vision of a body hanging by boat shoes flashed like a lightning bolt in my head.

Or was he already dead?

Instinctively, I reached for my phone to call Sullivan. Then I changed my mind. Every time he'd brushed off my questions about Craig, I had assumed it was because he was convinced of Josh's guilt. But the DUDs had reported Craig missing, and the detective had never mentioned that.

Rain pounded the frat house, and the light in the gray room turned a shade blacker.

Sullivan was hiding something. And I didn't have much time to figure out what.

18

Linda West examined the bag of orange pills I'd placed on her desk at Pharmanew. "The three and the zero tell me they're thirty milligrams, but there's a mark on the other side I don't recognize." She twisted her seashell necklace. "I used to be able to ID common meds on sight, but since I became a manager, I've lost track of what they look like."

I leaned forward, hating to leave the fluffy white chair cocoon. "It's really important that I find out what they are."

"This doesn't have anything to do with Gregg and Raven's murders, does it?" Her almond eyes grew round, and she pressed her palm to her pink cashmere sweater. "The police held a press conference this morning and said they'd arrested the killer."

"Don't worry." I had to play it vague to avoid contradicting the information the New Orleans PD had made public. "I can't say anymore, though, because it's confidential."

"I understand. You know, I feel so much better knowing that a vampire is off the streets. But, not to speak ill of the dead, I was shocked it wasn't Raven since she stole that blood from Belleville House."

I avoided comment and looked pointedly at the pills.

"Who is the man they arrested?"

"Josh Santo." I glanced up. "He was my client."

She gasped, and her brow furrowed. "Why would he hire you if he killed those people? To spy on the investigation?"

"In a way," I hedged.

"Well, thank goodness it's all over and you're safe."

"Yep. Onto the next case." I concentrated on the bag, hoping she'd get my drift.

Her gaze returned to the pills. "We have several Pharmacy PhDs in our lab, but they don't deal with oral meds. Your best bet is a pharmacy. They'll have pill ID software."

"I'd rather not go that route because they're probably illegal."

She glanced at the clock. "I suppose I could try running them by our lab techs. Let me see if anyone's back from lunch." She rose and smoothed her pink skirt. "In the meantime, I'll have my assistant, Christine, whip you up a protein shake. You need to nourish your skin and organs after the stress of that investigation."

I smiled and wondered if some of the ten or so Hershey's Kisses I'd taken from the reception candy dish were smeared across my teeth. As much as I wanted to avoid another green juice concoction, I was so hungry that my stomach acid was staging a coup. I'd skipped more than a few meals thanks to the case, not to mention my moocher brother. Even though he couldn't seem to make it home to hang Glenda's gutter, he managed to be in my kitchen every time Nonna pulled a dish from the oven.

She glided from the room, and I leaned back in the soft chair and inhaled the scent of the sandalwood candles. Like Glenda's giant champagne glass, Linda's office was a retreat from the harsh reality raging outside.

Within seconds, my eyes had closed.

Thunder crashed.

My lids flew open. Danger was lurking. I sensed it in my DNA.

I had to get up. Stay alert.

I went into the lobby to look for Linda. I had to get back to Private Chicks to prepare for the undercover operation at Belleville House, things like testing the equipment and stress-eating about my nonna being involved.

Christine sat at her desk, oblivious to my presence. Apparently, she hadn't gotten the order to make the shake. Either that or she couldn't pry her eyes from the Panda Cam livestreaming on her computer.

I grabbed a handful of Kisses from the dish. "So, what's it like working for Pharmanew?"

"Oh, it's easy," she said, still staring at the screen. "And Linda's super nice—like Girl-Scout-troop-leader level. She bought a cable machine for the office so we can work out. And for birthdays she decorates our desks with glitter, balloons, and chocolate. She even gets us a cake and a bottle of wine."

"What?" I munched a Kiss. I needed to tell Veronica to up her boss game.

"Yeah. Christmas too. But the best part for me is that she was born in Paris, which is cool because I studied French in college, and I married a guy from France." Christine tied her blonde locks into a knot. "Don't tell her I said this, but I don't want her to get promoted to CEO."

I peeled the wrapper from a Kiss. "She's up for a promotion?"

"Yeessss," she whined. "And I would miss her as my manager."

If she gave me booze, chocolate, and cake, I'd miss her too.

The sound of high heels clicked in the hallway, and Linda entered with the pills and a shake. "No luck. Only one of our lab techs is in the office, and she didn't recognize the meds." She tossed the pills on Christine's desk and handed me the glass. "Drink this."

I immediately took a sip. Linda might be tiny, but she had the presence of a drill sergeant.

Christine picked up the bag and turned it over in her hand. "These look like generic Adderall."

I approached the desk. "The ADD drug?"

She nodded. "When I was in college, it was literally all over campus. Adderall helps you focus whether you have ADD or not.

There was a guy in my dorm who exploited his diagnosis, so he could sell his pills to students before exams."

"That's terrible." Linda scowled and turned to me. "My daughter's in college, and I wouldn't want her taking that. It's dangerous to take meds you don't need."

"I'm sure you have nothing to worry about with your daughter." But the DUDs, on the other hand, did. Because I planned to turn the generic Adderall over to the police.

"Did I show you a picture of her?" Linda's scowl had spread into the smile of a proud mother.

"No, but..." Before I could come up with an escape strategy, she'd strong-armed me to a break room behind the reception area. There was a refrigerator covered with pictures, presumably employee family members.

"That's Jessica there." Linda pointed to a photo of herself and a young woman posing in front of a party banner that said *Happy Mardi Gras*. "Isn't she cute?"

"Adorable," I replied. But I wasn't looking at her daughter. My gaze was fixed on the boas the two women wore. They were the same five-dollar brand sold in French Quarter tourist shops that Raven had been wearing the night Gregg died.

But Linda had insisted that she never wore cheap boas because they shed on her clothes. Maybe there was a simple explanation, but it appeared as though she'd lied.

Why wouldn't she be honest about such a mundane thing?

THE SKY outside my office window was so dark that I feared it would open up and unload hell on earth, and it was only four thirty in the afternoon. Decatur Street was no less concerning. Rainwater ran in the gutters and threatened to rise, and the sidewalks were unusually tourist-free even for a storm. It was as though nature and New Orleans knew evil was imminent despite Josh Santo's arrest.

Veronica entered and held up two wire surveillance kits. "Carnie is worried that Thomas might suspect she's recording him with her phone, so we're going to spy the old-fashioned way."

I turned back to the window.

She sighed, and I heard the kits hit my desk.

"I know you're nervous about your nonna going undercover, but I can't imagine anything going wrong."

"It's not just that." I began to pace. "Something's not right with the case. I'm missing a detail or evidence, and I can't figure out what."

"Well, I've been thinking about the picture you saw of Linda and her daughter in the boas, and I'm not sure it's relevant. That Mardi Gras party could've been where she learned those feathers shed and decided never to wear one again."

"I don't know." I sunk into my rolling chair. "Because Linda told me Raven was the only one who wore a boa, but Belinda specifically mentioned wearing one."

"I'll bet she meant that Raven was the only one who wore a boa on the Vampires and Victims tour. Belinda went back to the hotel before it started."

I chewed my thumbnail. "Could be."

She sat on the edge of the armchair. "You don't think Linda had something to do with the murders, do you? She did disclose Raven's past at Belleville House."

Bracing my feet on the floor, I rolled my chair from side to side. "Yeah, but she was just repeating doctor's office gossip, so I'd be hard-pressed to come up with her motive. And as pink and petite as she is, she hardly seems like the blood-drinking type."

"What about that Utah family? Did you ever get a hold of them?"

I pushed from the chair, too anxious to stay seated. "No. And if this undercover sting doesn't produce anything incriminating on Thomas, it might be worth a trip to Utah to track down the Bacigalupis."

"Personally, I think your efforts would be best spent on finding Craig. If what that frat boy Jeremy told you about the blood transfusion is true, then he and his grandma could be in hiding."

"You mean under police protection, right? Because that would explain why Sullivan didn't tell me Craig had been reported missing."

She studied her French manicure. "But it's also possible that they went into hiding on their own, and Sullivan just didn't share the news of the report. I could see Craig not wanting to invite unnecessary scrutiny on himself because of those Adderall pills you found at the frat house."

"If those pills were even his, he could've easily gotten rid of them." I twisted my hair and stared unseeing at the floor. "What I'm afraid of is that one or both of them is dead."

The lights flickered, and the room went dark.

I returned to the window, worried that the power outage was a darker omen than the storm.

Veronica stood. "I'll get the candles from the kitchen."

"I'll go. I need to move around." I turned and collided with an ape-like figure towering in the doorway.

My scream was primal. *Was it a Vampire Bigfoot?*

"Franki, really." Veronica pressed a hand to her heart. "It's Carnie."

I exhaled. *I was half right, anyway.*

Carnie removed her rain poncho. "I'm not surprised you'd be terrified since I'm disguised as you."

Even in the dim light I could see that her costume was no mirror image. Her wig was the color and consistency of the bearskin rug on my living room floor. And she'd accessorized Mom jeans, a shapeless sweater, and worn boots with a cloth version of my leather hobo bag that looked like a sack a Depression-era freight hopper would've carried.

I unclenched my lips. "Not that I'm admitting you look like me, but didn't you get the memo that we don't want the director of Belleville House to know I'm involved in this sting?"

"Oh, he's not going to recognize you." She tossed her wet poncho on my desk. "You're too forgettable."

My fists clenched. I wanted to go ape on her.

The lights flickered on, and the lobby door slammed.

"Yo, sis. If you're in heuh, come out *subito*."

I threw my head back. Carnie and Anthony at the same time were more than a bad sign. They were a curse.

My brother macho-walked into the room in a white Italia-embla-zoned tracksuit followed by my nonna in a mourning veil. "What's this about you usin' Nonna as vampire bait?"

I met his chest with mine. "She knows I don't want her to go in that retirement home. But it's not like we can count on you to help, can we?"

"*Smettetela,*" Nonna ordered.

We did what she said. It wasn't the Italian *Stop it* that shut us down, but the black handbag she'd raised. She'd never actually hit us with it, but we'd had occasion to see it in action. And the damage it had inflicted was worse than a baseball bat made of lead.

Nonna raised her veil. "I'm-a *siciliana*. I can track a man like a blood-a-hound."

No one knew that as well as I did. She'd been on the trail of my future husband for almost fifteen years. "Still, I wish you wouldn't do this, Nonna. I would never live it down if something happened to you."

She put a hand on my cheek. And gave me a smack. "Toughen up-a, *nipote mia*. There's a vampire after you, and we gotta get him-a first."

I rubbed my face. If I didn't know better, I would've sworn she'd been in the mob.

Veronica turned to Carnie. "Now that we've settled that, however unconventionally, let's get this mic on you."

She pulled up her sweater, revealing her boobie-bib.

"Eyyy!" Anthony stroked his stubble and gave a nod. "Sweet bullet-proof vest."

He'd obviously never seen the drag queen undergarment, and I wasn't about to explain it to him. *But what did he think the latex breasts were, bullet stoppers?*

"Hey, sis." He snickered and backhanded my bicep. "Does she look like you, or what?"

If Nonna hadn't been beside me with her bag, I would've ripped off a bullet stopper and beaten him with it.

Veronica clipped the mic to Carnie's bib and tucked the earpiece wire under her wig. "Since both you and Carmela will be wearing a wire, we'll have to turn off one of your receivers when we're listening from my car. Franki, can you go into the lobby for a test?"

"Glad to." I picked up the receiver and fled the room. I parked on a couch and listened to the chatter in my office via the tiny device.

"Will I be able to wear my rain poncho?" Carnie asked. "Or will it dislodge the mic when I take it off?"

"It shouldn't," Veronica said. "Since it drapes over you like a cape."

Josh came to mind. And so did the other caped figures associated with the case—the one on the video of The Blood Bank break-in prior to Gregg's murder, the one in the cemetery by my house, and the one Josh had seen at The Blood Center the night Todd died. *Were the caped creepers the same person? Or had Josh been right when he said that the one he saw was a woman?*

"Come in, Franki 2," Carnie cooed into the mic in her falsetto.

I refused to respond since I was clearly Franki 1.

"Oh, how silly of me. You probably didn't recognize me since I didn't imitate your voice." Carnie cleared her throat. "Come in out there now," she boomed in a crass male baritone.

I squeezed the receiver and visualized her head. I was tall for a woman, but I'd never been mistaken for a man.

A shock ran through me, but it wasn't from the device.

I had the distinct sensation I'd been doing that very thing.

Mistaking the killer for a man.

RAIN PUMMELED the roof of Veronica's white Audi. Even though I was safe and dry inside the car, I felt like I was drowning. Nonna and Carnie had been inside Belleville House for a mere minute, and I'd been unable to breathe for every one of those sixty seconds. We'd parked only thirty yards away, but given my fears about the situation, the retirement home might as well have been located on the moon.

Veronica patted my arm. "Inhale. Everything's fine."

So she thought. But it seemed like I'd sent my nonna inside the Colosseum to face hungry lions. Nevertheless, I switched off her receiver since Carnie would be doing most of the talking.

"I'll take you to Mr. Van Scyoc's office now." The nurse's voice came in clear through Carnie's receiver. "But keep in mind that we'd like to go home sometime tonight."

I turned in the passenger seat. "That's surly Nurse Ratched, a.k.a. Sylvia. I swear she had something to do with this."

"Rudeness doesn't make a murderer, Franki."

"No, but Josh saw a petite woman in a cape near the blood bank on the night Todd died, and this nurse is petite. At the time, I suspected Raven. But now that she's dead, I think it could've been someone working with Thomas."

"You have nothing linking this nurse to the crimes. And for all we know, the woman Josh saw was an innocent passerby."

"When are two people wearing capes at the same event?"

"A vampire ball?"

She had me there. "Okay, but randomly on the street? Capes aren't that common. And think about it. If some kind of blood business is going on in Belleville House, it's likely that a nurse is in on it."

"It's more likely that Raven took blood from those patients, got fired, and that was the end of it."

The creak of a door hinge made me stiffen.

"Mr. Van Scyoc? Francine Clamato and her grandmother, Carmen Miranda are here for their appointment."

I turned squarely in my seat and glared at Veronica. "That's how she disguises Franki Amato and Carmela Montalbano?"

Veronica looked out her window. "That wasn't part of the plan."

I grabbed the fast-food bag at my feet. We'd stopped by Willie's Chicken Shack so I could stress-eat Cajun tenders. But after hearing those names I regretted not getting one of Willie's 190 daiquiris with Everclear.

"Welcome to Belleville House." Thomas sounded almost sincere. "We're thrilled that you would visit. I'm the executive director."

"You got a wife-a?" Nonna asked.

I smacked the Willie's bag. "Is she actually trying to fix me up with a vampire serial killer?"

"Shh." Veronica slapped my thigh. "Between you and the rain, I can't hear what he's saying."

I shoved a Cajun tender in my mouth to plug it up.

"I'm sorry about that, Mr. Van Scyoc." Carnie's tone was terse. "Grandmama *does* like to meddle."

"It's-a Nonna. Do I look-a British?"

Veronica pressed a hand to her temple. "This isn't going well."

"You think?" I loaded another tender.

Thomas chuckled. "We have quite a few matchmakers here, so I'm used to it. But tell me, which care service were you interested in? We offer independent and assisted living, as well as memory care."

"Independent, definitely," Carnie drolled.

"You got-a that right, buster."

I sunk into my seat and wished the rain would carry me away. If Nonna didn't be quiet, she'd blow Carnie's cover.

"Well, we have a lovely facility with a lot of recreational activities. Are there any in particular you're interested in, Mrs. Miranda?"

"The bath-a-rooms."

Thomas gave a breathy laugh. "We have private baths in every room, and in every hallway in the building."

Veronica turned toward me. "He's really chatty. I thought you said talking to him was like trying to get blood from a stone?"

"Nice analogy," I snarked. "I'm sure you're proud of yourself."

She smiled as though she was.

"I told you, Thomas is weird. So he probably likes Carnie."

A creak sounded.

I reached for a tender. "I think he just shut the door."

Veronica raised the receiver.

"Actually," Carnie said, "we have a medical need I'd like to talk to you about. And it's *urgent*."

The way she'd stressed *urgent* had me concerned. That wasn't part of the script as far as I knew. But neither was the Francine Clamato and Carmen Miranda bit.

"Whatever it is, I'm sure we can accommodate it. We have round-the-clock nursing care headed by Sylvia Blaylock, the RN who brought you to my office."

I tapped Veronica. "Hear that? She's the head nurse, so she had to be aware of the blood incidents."

"That's comforting, Mr. Van Scyoc, because my grandmother has aplastic anemia."

"Wow." Thomas's surprise was genuine. "I would've never guessed. She looks so vibrant."

"It's her Mediterranean diet."

"We have a dietician on staff and meal plans that would support her condition."

"Mm hm." Carnie didn't sound convinced. "What we need is a doctor who can perform frequent blood transfusions."

The room was silent, and Veronica and I both sat taller.

"I see," Thomas said. "Our nursing staff can perform transfusions as needed."

"Yes, well." Carnie paused. "This is rather delicate, but I've heard some rumors about Belleville House."

"That problem has been addressed." The lukewarmth had left his words. "I have a brochure that vouches for the quality and integrity of our medical staff. Let me find that for you."

Wood scraped as though a drawer had opened, and papers shuffled.

"That's odd," he said. "I seem to be out of them. Let me run and get one for you."

The door creaked.

"Can you hear me, Franki 2?" Carnie whispered into the mic.

"I'm Franki 1, Francine."

"More like Franki 1000, but we'll discuss that later. We've got a problem. Carmela slipped out, and I'm betting Thomas went to find her."

The Cajun tenders Zydeco-danced up my throat. That was why she'd stressed the word "urgent."

I grabbed my nonna's receiver and flipped the *On* switch. "Where are you, Nonna? Come in."

And then I waited, my whole body tense.

"Her mic is silent, Carnie," Veronica said. "Can you check the nearest ladies room?"

Lightning flashed, and I felt like I'd been struck. I didn't hear Carnie's reply because I'd already exited the car.

I ran down Royal Street with Nonna's receiver pressed to my ear. But all I heard were the sounds of traffic and my feet splashing in puddles.

Had my Nonna gone to the bathroom and turned off her mic out of modesty?

Or had someone turned it off for her, like that Nurse Ratched, Sylvia?

19

"Carmela, is that you?"

The elderly man's words stopped me in the street, despite the hard rain pelting me like rocks.

"Luigi Pescatore." Nonna's tone was a mix of wonder and affection. "I haven't seen-a you since-a 1973."

"Those were fun times, eh? Back when you still had your produce business in the Quarter with Giuseppe."

"God rest-a his soul." Her tone had turned wistful after the mention of my grandfather.

Veronica pulled up, and I opened the passenger door.

"Carnie's looking for her," she said as I climbed inside the Audi. "But I'll go in with you."

"Not yet." I pulled the door closed. "I hear her. She's talking to some man who knew her and my *nonnu*."

Veronica reached into the back seat and handed me a towel.

I put the receiver on the console and dried my face and hands.

"So, how did you know I was here?" Luigi asked.

"I saw you walk-a through the lobby and come-a to this-a room."

He gave a raspy laugh. "I talked my way into this apartment after a guy died because it's near the action. Speaking of action, you look good in black, *signora*."

I recoiled so hard the back of my head hit the window. "What kind of man flirts with a woman in a mourning dress?"

"An Italian."

I had to give Veronica that.

"What are you doing in New Orleans?" Luigi asked. "I thought you moved away."

"I'm-a still living in-a Houston with-a my son, Joe. But I'm visiting my *nipote*, Franki."

I tensed and reached for the Cajun tenders. "What if Thomas or Sylvia is listening outside the door?"

"You'll go in and get her," Veronica said, "and I'll call the police."

"Franki's a private investigator." Nonna's pride was audible. "And she's-a talented."

I appreciated the vote of confidence, but not at that time or in that place. Because I wanted her to stop saying my name and leave.

"Is she as pretty as her nonna?" Luigi flirted.

"*Lusingatore.*"

"Flatterer, indeed." My emotions roller-coastered from a high of fear for her safety to a low of outrage at his advances. "What if he's one of those sweetheart swindlers who prey on old women for their money?"

Veronica tilted her head like I was unbalanced.

I popped a tender into my mouth and resolved to eat my emotions rather than express them, as I'd been brought up to do.

"What brings you to Belleville House?" Luigi asked. "Did you come to see Mario Lupone? He's down the hall, you know."

"I didn't know he was-a here. I came-a to check-a the place out. But with-a so many handsome men-a, it's-a good-a place to retire."

My mouth dropped open. Forget Luigi. What was my mourning-dress-wearing nonna doing flirting with a man?

Luigi's laugh became a cough. "It's in the French Quarter, so it's a great place to live. But…"

My stomach clenched. I didn't like the way his voice trailed off.

"But-a what?"

"You're not hard of hearing are you?" His pitch had lowered, and my heart rate had followed suit.

"*Nossignore*. My ears work-a fine."

"Good. Because I can't say this too loud."

Veronica and I exchanged an arched-brow look and leaned closer to the receiver.

"It's fine for me to live here," he whispered, "because I've got a blood disorder."

I reached across the console and grabbed my best friend's hand.

"But if you're healthy, go somewhere else. Because sooner or later, they'll put something in your food to knock you out. And while you're unconscious, they'll steal your blood."

Veronica and I were no longer holding hands because we were gripping our faces.

"Who told-a you this?" Nonna asked.

"It's a retirement home. We all talk, in our rooms, the cafeteria, the recreation center, you name it. And we look out for each other, which is how I know what's going on."

There was a knocking sound.

"They found her." I grabbed the passenger door handle, and Veronica grabbed my forearm.

"Who is it?" Luigi called.

A click followed. "There you are." Carnie's tone was calm, so I relaxed a little. "You had me worried, Nonna."

"That's your granddaughter?" Luigi's shock blasted through the receiver like a bullhorn. "She's big for an Italian."

Despite the scary situation, my lips spread into a grin.

Carnie harrumphed. "Big is an ironic choice of words from such a small man."

"Mind-a your manners, *nipote mia*. And close that-a door."

Another click.

"Nonna, we don't have much time." Carnie singsonged the warning. "The staff is looking for you."

"So I ran into an old-a friend," she scoffed. "Big-a deal. Now Luigi, who's-a taking the blood?"

Carnie gasped. "He knows about that?"

"We all do," Luigi replied. "The head nurse, Sylvia, is behind it. A man died after she took too much blood, and she pinned it on a young nurse named Raven and got her fired."

"That's right." Carnie was angry. "And then Raven was murdered."

"I saw that on the news," he said. "We all thought Sylvia killed her, until that young man got arrested."

Like all New Orleanians, Luigi thought the police had gotten their man. But his words convinced me that the killer was most likely a woman.

"Gigi"—Nonna used the Italian nickname for Luigi—"why does this-a Sylvia take-a the blood?"

"Rumor is, she's selling it."

"Come again, G?" Carnie boomed.

"There's serious dough in blood," he said, accepting his money nickname. "I did some research on this, and it's a multi-billion-dollar industry. The Red Cross and the American Association of Blood Banks sell donated blood to hospitals for as much as a hundred and fifty bucks a pint."

My gaze darted to Veronica. "We've got to go to the police."

She took a deep breath and pressed her lips together.

Luigi coughed and took a loud sip of something. "We don't think Sylvia's stolen anyone's blood since Raven got fired, probably because she hasn't figured out a way to do it without the director catching on. He's an odd one, but he's an upstanding man."

"Thomas is innocent?" I said, dumbfounded.

Veronica shrugged. "It *is* possible."

"Also," he said, "a lot of residents moved out, and now the director and the staff are bending over backwards to keep the rest of us from going. My guess is, Sylvia's lying low."

My laugh was not amused. "Except for potentially killing off people who could've turned her in."

Veronica gripped the steering wheel. "She certainly had a motive to kill Raven. And she could've had some illicit arrangement with a blood bank CEO like Todd."

"But Gregg? What was her connection to him?"

She exhaled and shook her head.

"Uh, Nonna. We really should be on our way." Carnie's voice cracked.

And that got my attention. *Had she heard someone coming?*

"*Va bene.*"

The fabric of Nonna's dress whooshed, and I imagined that she'd stood.

"One-a more thing," she said.

I slammed my head against the seat and held my breath to keep myself from screaming, *Getoutnowwhileyoustillcan.*

"Did-a you know that-a man who was-a killed?"

"Everyone at Belleville knows each other, Carmela." Luigi's tone had turned foreboding. "His name was Craig Rourke."

"You interrupted my dinner for this?" Detective Sullivan spoke into the phone, but he sounded like Detective Callahan, a.k.a., Dirty Harry.

I glanced across the Audi console at Veronica and then at the fourplex, glad Nonna and Carnie had exited the car. "Uh, I've got you on speaker, FYI. And we've notified the police, but I thought you'd appreciate a heads-up."

"What I'd appreciate is you staying the hell out of my investigations, but no matter how many times I tell you that, you don't listen." His breathing had elevated to raging-bull level. "I should bring you up on charges for going inside Belleville House."

Veronica opened her mouth, but I held up my hand to stop her.

"We didn't go inside. My nonna went to visit a friend, and he told her about Sylvia." I Grinch grinned, because what I'd said was technically true. "And now that we know Craig Rourke's grandfather died while having his blood siphoned off, I suggest you release Josh Santo."

"First of all," he said, audibly seething, "Raven was fired for the Rourke death, which was settled by attorneys. So until someone at Belleville files a report of a new incident, we have no case to investigate." He paused to refill his lungs with the air he'd fumed out. "Second, we interviewed Van Scyoc on two separate occasions, and we're satisfied that he and his staff are not involved in the murders."

I decided to bait him. "Then why are Craig and his grandmother still in hiding?"

He hesitated. "I don't know what you're talking about."

Veronica and I exchanged a gotcha look. Sullivan's feigned surprise told us he was lying.

I chuckled the way he did before he patronized me. "Craig and his grandmother are hiding out because they're afraid of the killer. And if they thought Josh was the guy, they'd be home now."

"Who says they're not?"

"As of this morning, no one had seen or heard from Craig at Delta Upsilon Delta, where, by the way, they're buying or selling Adderall."

"You went—"

"I told you in your office that I was going to the frat house, so let me finish." Summoning my De Niro-style Dirty Harry I added, "Because I'm. Not. Done."

Sullivan was silent, and Veronica raised her eyebrows, then her thumbs.

"So you and your colleagues need to reopen the investigation both for the victims of this case and the residents of Belleville. And you can start by arresting that nurse, Sylvia." I gave a satisfied nod, and Veronica nodded too.

"Here's the puzzle piece you're missing. Sylvia has alibis for each murder. Josh doesn't."

My bravado deflated somewhat, but I had to keep up the show. "What alibis are those, exactly?"

"She was with her companion."

"Oh, well," I said, pulling out my best sarcasm. "We all know a companion wouldn't lie."

"We got the right man, Amato." His words erupted like bullets from a machine gun. "Deal with it."

"Wesley," a female purred into the receiver. "Our food is getting cold."

That explained why he was mad about the dinner interruption. What it didn't explain was the pang in my gut.

Muted conversation followed between Sullivan and his date.

Meanwhile, I tried to figure out what the pang was about. *Did I care about Wesley? Or was I missing Bradley?* I hadn't had a moment to decide how I felt about either man. But Wesley's restaurant date reminded me of the brunch I'd missed with Bradley.

And I got mad all over again.

"I'll tell you what, Amato," Sullivan semi-shouted into the receiver. "Since I'm celebrating another successful case in the company of a beautiful woman, I'll grant you a final warning. Drop your investigation *pronto*, or you'll be sharing a cell with your client."

"In Italian, *pronto* means *ready*, not *immediately*," I yelled.

But my cell phone screen had already gone blank.

Sullivan had hung up.

"He sounded serious." Veronica's tone was worried. "Are you going to listen to him?"

"Not if my life depended on it." I did a secret *scongiuri* before opening the door to ward off the bad luck I'd just cast on myself.

Veronica climbed from the car. "Why don't you crash at my place? Dirk's out of town."

The reference to her boyfriend reopened the Bradley wound. "Thanks, but I'll shack up with the Bride of Dracula."

I shut the car door and dashed through the rain. The banged-up piece of gutter I'd thrown at Sullivan's SUV was on the porch, and I was happy to see it. Because if that devil detective showed up at my house again, I planned to flog him with it.

Hoping Nonna had gone to bed, I crept inside.

Anthony was on his back on the chaise lounge. Mouth open, legs splayed. And snoring.

I hung up my jacket and noticed Napoleon was at my feet. He looked at the chaise lounge and back at me. Apparently, even he was sick of my brother.

I slammed the door.

Anthony sat up. "I'm up, Ma. Jeez."

"Mom's not here." I kicked off my wet boots. "You're living off your sister, remember?"

He muttered something and settled back onto the chaise lounge.

I squatted to scratch Napoleon's fluffy face. "Uh, shouldn't you be at Madame Moiselle's?"

"I got someone to cover my shift."

"Again? Have you been working at all?"

"I've been working out at my lady's home gym." Eyes still closed, he raised an arm. "Check out these guns."

"Obviously, I meant your job, not your body."

His eyelids flipped open. "I had to take some time off and get some rest, all right?"

I went into the kitchen for a much-needed drink, and Napoleon trotted behind. "What for?"

"To be in shape to take her out. She's not like Crystal. She's classy."

It wasn't hard to be classier than a pregnant woman who wore a Madonna bullet bra around town.

"She wants to go to St. Roch Tavern tomorrow night."

I paused. When Father John had told me that Saint Roch was invoked against vampires, I'd been certain that information would become relevant to the case. But Anthony was just talking about a bar, so surely it was a coincidence. And I was probably overreacting. "How are you going to take her out if you don't have any money?"

"I've got my tips."

"I could use some of those too, you know." I popped a cork from a Chianti bottle for emphasis.

"Women. Always after our dough." He rolled over and put a cushion on his head.

I considered throwing the cork at him, but I poured myself a glass of wine, instead. And I sat at the kitchen table to think about that women and dough remark.

Dough was the word Luigi had used to describe the booming blood industry. And Sylvia selling stolen blood. I didn't buy her alibis, but I would need hard evidence to convince Sullivan and the police that she was a murderer—and, if I was honest, myself.

Stealing blood from unconscious individuals was a horrific crime, but it didn't make Sylvia a vampire serial killer. And all I had to go on were the suppositions of an old man and his retirement home neighbors.

The next step would be to follow Veronica's advice and find Craig. I could recruit David and the vassal's help in tracking him, but that would take time. And I didn't have it.

Because the killer would strike again. And if it was Sylvia, odds were she was already on to me.

I looked at the kitchen clock.

Nine p.m.

The perfect time to go back to the source of this sick nightmare.

I stood and slugged from my wine. Then I grabbed my bag and headed for the door, hoping it was safe to go outside.

"Aw, man." Pam jerked her body at the sight of me like she was letting it all hang out at Woodstock. "You're getting to be a drag."

She tugged Benny's leash in my direction, and I rose from the bench across the street from the Ursuline Convent where I'd been waiting for two hours. The storm had let up, so I brought Napoleon along to give him a break from the trauma of my family, but Benny paralyzed him with fear. He didn't know what to make of a Dachshund in a paisley vest and flower-power pants, much less one that spoke Bulgarian.

"This won't take long. I need to ask you a couple of questions about the case."

"Why? The fuzz solved that."

"A man's freedom is on the line. I want to be sure they got the right one."

She cocked her head and narrowed an eye. "I didn't have you pegged for an ego trip. I thought you were a square." Her gaze dropped to Napoleon. "Like your dog."

Pam was one to judge in her granny square-crocheted threads. "Napoleon's not as fashion backward as Benny. He prefers to go natural."

"Right on." Her head bounced. "So what did you want? My midnight tour starts in ten minutes."

"I'm pretty sure Campari Crimson is a blood drink, maybe with some sort of special ingredients. Can you think of a crime that involves anything like that?"

"On my tour, I talk about a 2003 murder involving a group of Goths, but they denied the part about the blood drink."

"That's fine. Even if it's a local legend it could've inspired a copycat."

"Well, a guy we call Kevin, for his family's sake, came here for a convention and met a chick in a bloody wedding dress, who called herself Never. She was with her old man, Worry, and a couple of their friends."

The names Never and Worry would have been enough to make me run screaming. "Where'd they meet?"

"Here in the Quarter, at The Dungeon."

The vampire bar.

"Anyway, this Kevin had laid out some bread for a suite with a hot tub, so he invited them to party at his hotel pad." She flipped her hair. "Back at his suite, they killed him with a champagne bottle and drained his blood. Then they sat in the hot tub and drank it from Dixie Cups, maybe mixed with some of that champagne."

I swallowed a bitter taste. I would never understand how human beings could commit such a heinous act. "Were they arrested?"

"Yeah, they're in the pen."

At least there was that. But drinking bubbly blood from Dixie Cups wasn't the cocktail I was looking for.

I feared I was at a dead end.

I glanced at Napoleon, who stood as stiff as a Westminster show dog while Benny gave him the sniff over. "I'd give anything to know how the killer sniffed out the fact that there were people on the tour with a B Positive blood type."

"Oh, I can tell you that. Someone asked if there was a type of blood that was more appealing to vampires, and they all started talking about what blood type they had."

My blood began to boil. "And you didn't think to mention this?"

"I told the fuzz, man." She flailed her arms. "What more do you want?"

"I want you to tell *me*, Pam. *Me*." I pounded my chest. "The private investigator who's questioned you three times."

She jumped back. "You're beyond ego trip. You're just plain gone."

Napoleon poked Benny with his nose, and Pam yanked the leash. "And your dog's a head case too."

I crammed my fingers in my hair and squeezed. The characters I had to deal with for my job might kill me before the vampire serial killer did. "Who asked the question about the blood type?"

"That was over a week ago, man. I can't be expected to remember that."

And yet she remembered the 60s so clearly.

Pam looked at the tourists gathered in front of the convent. "Like, I need to split."

I also wanted to split—her. "I'll make this quick. I never heard from the Utah family. Is there anything you might've forgotten to tell me about them?"

She jutted out her jaw. And her hip. "The dad was some kind of tech dude."

"What about the mom? Was she petite, by any chance?"

"Nah, around my height."

Pam was about 5'6", so the Utah mom wasn't the caped woman

Josh saw the night Todd Plank was killed. She was a long-shot suspect, but I had to rule her out.

"Oh, I get it." Pam bobbed her head. "You think that Josh dude had a chick helping him."

"Not exactly."

"Don't tell me you think some petite chick killed those people by herself. She couldn't have lifted them. Not without a rope or a pulley."

My knees gave out, and I fell onto the bench. *Why hadn't I thought of that?*

"Are you tripping? Because that would explain a lot."

I stared into the distance, still processing my thoughts. "No, you just helped me figure something out."

"Righteous." She held up two fingers. "Peace, love, and granola, baby." She tightened Benny's leash and headed across the street.

I reached into my bag and pulled out the rounded piece of rubber I'd found beneath Raven in the burial vault.

It was part of a pulley wheel.

Like the ones used in traction suspension systems of hospital beds.

20

"**W**hat's gotten into this city?" I leapt from my desk and stormed into Veronica's office. "Did you see this morning's paper?"

She looked up from a filing cabinet. "I haven't. Why?"

I poked the front-page. "According to *The Times-Picayune*, the police are giving Sullivan a medal of commendation for his work on the case."

She pulled a file and slammed the drawer. "For a second I thought you were going to tell me that someone else had died."

"Fortunately, no. But if he gets a medal for pinning the murders on the wrong guy, I'm going to be just as devastated."

Veronica tossed the file on her desk and took a seat. "Because you don't want to see Josh Santo's life ruined? Or because you have unresolved feelings for the detective, like he does for you?"

"The former. Obviously." I sunk into the armchair. "I was starting to think Sullivan was a good guy, but I was dead wrong on that one."

She opened the file and scanned the contents. "Has it occurred to you that he might really believe Josh is guilty?"

"I've given him reasons to think otherwise, and a good cop would investigate those leads instead of accepting a medal." I took out my frustration on the newspaper, wadding it into a ball. "And I didn't tell you this, but when I was at the police station yesterday, I got the feeling he'd said something to Bradley."

She tipped her head in a he-might-have move. "Well, he is competitive. Why don't you call Bradley and ask him?"

I threw the paper into her trash bin. "Because he was too complacent about not seeing me for our brunch date. And for the whole two weeks of his trip."

"How does flying home to surprise you qualify as complacent?"

I looked away. That *was* a gallant gesture.

"He loves you, Franki. And deep down you know it."

I pulled my knees to my chin. "Love isn't always enough. I don't want to be with a workaholic who puts his job before me."

"So tell him that."

"Why? He's the president of an important bank, and it's not like he's going to give that up for my sake."

"Maybe he can delegate some of his responsibilities. He *is* in charge."

I picked a thread from my corduroy pants. "If he can do that, then he should've done it by now."

She closed the file. "Why don't you come to lunch with Glenda and me? We're going to the Royal House Oyster Bar for Bloody Marys." Her smile went askew. "Or Prosecco."

The drink reminded me that I had work to do. And eating oysters with Glenda and her oversexed libido was never an appetizing idea. "Can't. I've got a pulley wheel to identify." I slid from the chair. "But bring me a double order of their oyster tacos, and I'll pay you back."

"You want two?"

"I've got that cooking class at Bayou Cuisine at six. And the last time I went hungry, I ate a cockroach."

She gave a grossed-out giggle. "Two it is. But be careful tonight. Another storm is moving in, and this one is supposed to be severe."

More foreboding. Why not?

I headed for the lobby.

The vassal had pulled his chair up to David's desk, and both boys stared at the computer.

I walked up behind them and studied the traction suspension system pictured on the screen. "Have you found anything?"

The vassal twisted in his seat. "There's no serial number or identifying mark on the rubber, so we won't be able to trace it."

Disappointment sucked the air from my lungs. "There has to be some way to nail the killer. We've got to keep digging."

David spun his chair. "At this point, our only option is to try to find Craig Rourke and his grandma.

The lobby buzzer went off as Glenda sashayed in. The temperature had dropped, and she'd dressed for the occasion. Sort of. She wore a white fur hood with matching wrist and ankle warmers, but the rest of her snowsuit was missing. And so were her clothes.

She lowered her hood. "Y'all looking at porn?"

Smirking, I stepped aside to reveal the screen. "It's one of those traction systems they use in hospitals to lift the limbs of a patient."

"Close enough." She gave a slow and sultry wink. "I've got one in my bedroom."

David turned and fixed his gaze on the computer.

But the vassal gave Glenda a slack-jawed once-over. "You don't look like you have any physical issues."

She struck a pose that was at odds with her virgin white fur. "You've got that right, young man. All my parts work, and I can prove it, if you like."

The vassal's already magnified eyes popped, and a faint sheen of perspiration coated his glasses.

Directing the conversation back to the case I said, "David, what else are pulleys used for?"

"Lots of things." He talked to the screen to avoid turning around. "Curtains, garage doors, any kind of lift."

The vassal rubbed his lenses with the tail of his shirt. "And they're used in industries besides medicine. Construction and shipping, for example."

I wrinkled my lips. "What you're saying is, I can't link that wheel to a nurse."

"I knew you suspected Raven, Miss Franki. But do you still think a woman did this?"

"I can't rule it out." I flopped onto a couch. "But I can't prove it either."

"It reminds me of that old detective fiction cliché, *cherchez le femme*." She wriggled her hips to emphasize the gender. "And since you're looking for a woman, don't forget that pulleys are used in contortionist equipment."

I rolled my eyes and stretched out onto my back. "I don't know what that is, and I'm not sure I want to."

"Child, is your mind always in the gutter? And, by the by, Anthony still hasn't fixed mine."

I pulled a cushion over my face and considered suffocating myself with it. Then I had a coffin flashback and moved it from my mouth. But I kept my eyes covered.

"What I'm talking about, Miss Franki, are all those torture devices women use to tone their muscles and lose weight."

She was referring to exercise equipment, which was an appropriate description in my book. "Men work out too, you know."

"And thank God they do, sugar. But if you're trying to connect a pulley to a woman, then a gym is the place to start."

Under the cover of the cushion, I tried to think, but not about Glenda's suggestion. Most weight machines didn't utilize pulleys, and if they did, it wasn't like they were detachable for use in raising a dead body.

I snorted. The idea was laughable, really. Because the only exercise equipment with detachable pulleys were cable machines.

I threw off the cushion and shot up.

Linda West?

No. Surely not.

∽

"CAN I tempt you with a piece of my sourdough?" Chef Mel approached my kitchen station with a basket. "I made it from Sorrel. She'll be eight years old on January tenth."

My eyelids pulled back in alarm. Given the way the guy scavenged for ingredients, a statement like that was inflammatory.

"Sorrel is his sourdough starter." Sara spoke with a laugh in her voice.

Mel beamed like a proud father. "The flour came from the dumpster behind the Poeyfarre Market, so there might be a weevil or two. But they enhance the flavor of the wild yeasts and bacteria in the sourdough."

Lou's brow Groucho-Marxed. "And give it an extra bite."

I'll bet they do. To be polite, I took a slice of the bug bread and put it on my counter, intending to toss it at the first opportunity. My stomach already ached, but it wasn't because of the four fried oyster tacos I'd eaten before I came. It was the conviction that something awful was going to happen that night, and I knew what it was.

Another blood-draining death.

The killer had been silent too long, and I didn't need science or Chandra's psychic nonsense to know that a vampire serial killer would need fresh blood.

It made me sick.

And also concerned.

I was on the killer's list, so the blood-draining death could be my own. Or my brother's.

But there was nothing I could do that I hadn't already done. Sullivan and his medal ceremony were clear signals the case was closed. And I couldn't tail the killer because I was no longer sure who it was. Nurse Sylvia seemed the obvious suspect, but I couldn't stop thinking about Linda and her cable machine.

Thunder rumbled outside.

The storm was about to start.

"Hey." Michele put a hand on my arm. "Are you okay?"

"Huh?"

"You seem kind of out of it," she whispered.

Michele was right. And I had to stay alert to catch her or Sara because I wanted to be done with the filthy food class. "I'm allergic to mold, and it makes me groggy."

She gave a satisfied smile that she tried to disguise as sympathy.

My eyes darted to Sara. She pretended to examine her cooking utensils, but she was smug too, like a cat that had eaten a parrot.

They were closing in on me. I could feel it.

"Okay, waste-cookers." Chef Mel slurped from a coffee cup at the head of the room. "It's time to get started on the main course now that you've all had a sourdough starter." He laughed. "Get it? I said starter instead of snack? For the bread?"

"Uh, yeah." I scratched my arm. "We got it."

He tee-heed. "Tonight we're making an Emeril Lagasse dish made famous by Jazz Fest, Crawfish Monica. It's Cajun-style mac and cheese, only it has crawfish in it." He paused. "And Monica."

Crickets. But thankfully not on the menu.

I opened the container at my station. The crawfish looked like they hadn't swum since the summer.

Chef Mel raised a stainless steel shaker. "To save time, I pre-mixed Emeril's Bayou Blast seasoning, so you each have one of these at your stations. For the special ingredient, you'll choose which of these white wines to use in your recipe." He gestured to four bottles on a table in front of his station.

"I'm a beer man, myself," Lou commented randomly.

The chef flashed a California smile. "What about you, newest student?"

Michele and Sara hit me with hostile gazes.

"I'm all about wine," I replied in a teacher's-pet tone.

Lou approached the table to ponder his selection, and Michele and Sara shifted their eyes to his unattended sauté pan.

Were both *of them sabotaging him?* Before they caught me staring, I turned to my own pan. And started.

Chef Mel stood in front of my station with his coffee mug.

"If you like wine, you should try Cocchi Americano." He leaned on my counter. "It's an aperitif wine laced with quinine, which is used to treat malaria."

Not a ringing endorsement.

"You might've had it in a Corpse Reviver #2."

I pulled a head from a crawdad. "You sure know a lot about alcohol."

"Besides studying to be a sommelier, I also study cocktails. I have a full bar in my house. Vodka, rum, bourbon…"

He lost me with the list—just long enough to see Michele dump half of her Bayou Blast into Lou's pot and then join him at the wine table.

That princess is going down.

"…gin, tequila, brandy…"

Sara entered my peripheral vision as she tiptoed behind me to Lou's pot and tossed in more Bayou Blast.

I'm taking down the athlete too.

Finally, I was free of this case.

"…whiskey, sake, grappa…"

And of Chef Mel's lists.

But his knowledge of alcohol gave me an idea. "Chef," I interrupted, "have you ever heard of a drink made with blood?"

"I made one just the other night called Reign in Blood."

He had my full attention for a change. "What kind does that call for? Animal or human?"

"Ha ha, very funny." He tapped my arm. "A butcher friend gave me some day-old pig's blood."

As if fresh pig's blood wasn't gross enough.

"You use it to coat the inside of a chilled chalice, and then you strain in the other ingredients."

I held my breath, hoping I could crack the mystery of Gregg's Campari Crimson message. "What are they?"

He put down his mug to tick off the ingredients on his fingers. "Scotch, crème de cacao, cherry liqueur, Averna, coffee, and blood orange juice."

The blood orange juice and the Averna were intriguing, especially since the latter was an amaro produced by Campari. "Can I ask you a personal question?"

"I'm an open book." He chuckled. "And I tell a pretty good story."

"Uh-huh. So, why would you want to drink something like that? You're not a vampire, are you?"

"No, but I'm a blood brother." His mouth widened into a grin. "Just kidding. But there are people who drink human blood."

"I know. Real vampires."

He grabbed his mug and slurped. "Them too."

I cocked my head to the side. "There are others?"

"Yeah, a startup called Ambrosia does infusions of plasma and blood from eighteen-year-olds that supposedly keeps you young."

The victims in the case were too old to fit that demographic. Especially Gregg Charalambous. But if there were non-vampire segments of society who sought out unnecessary blood infusions, I needed to know who they were. "Who's Ambrosia's target market?"

"Rich people. It costs eight thousand dollars a pop, and you've got to do quarterly infusions, so you're looking at thirty-two grand a year." He shielded his mouth from the others. "Their biggest clients are Silicon Valley CEOs."

Christine said that Linda was up for promotion as CEO of Pharmanew, but that was too much of a long shot. Sylvia, on the other hand, could've been selling the blood she stole to a company like Ambrosia, albeit one that purchased the blood of older individuals or lied about the ages of its sources.

"The theory is that if you have young blood injections, you can prolong your life indefinitely. It seems like science fiction, but proponents argue that it works because of specific blood nutrients."

Nutrients.

The word sent a burst of energy through my system like I'd had an infusion myself.

It all made sense.

Campari Crimson was a cocktail of blood and other ingredients that the killer was using in a creepy quest for eternal youth.

And during my investigation I'd discussed that very subject with two people. One was Father John, who'd told me that the psycho nineteenth-century socialite Madame LaLaurie relied on the nutrients from bathing in human blood to stay young.

The other was Linda West, who'd been preoccupied with me getting nutrients for my skin. And who Pam had said was taking Pharmanew in a holistic, anti-aging direction.

"YOU'RE TOTALLY FINE, FRANKI," I said to myself on the drive home from Bayou Cuisine. "You're in your car, and Nonna's got dinner waiting in the oven that wasn't scavenged from a trash can."

But I wasn't convinced about the fine part.

The sense of safety I'd had in the waste-cooking class—aside from the threats of student sabotage and food poisoning—had dissolved on the walk to my car. No one had followed me as far as I knew, but there was a presence or a force that loomed.

And it was dark. I could feel it in my blood.

I pulled up to a stoplight and checked the locks for the third time. Then I switched on the windshield wipers. A light rain had begun to fall.

The proverbial calm before the storm.

"Why did you just think that?" I asked myself aloud.

"Because the case is getting to you," I replied.

"Okay, enough with the split personality stuff, you two," I said.

Oh my God, do I have one?

I gripped the steering wheel and tried to get a grip on my head. Maybe it would help if I ran through the suspects out loud.

"Let's start with Thomas. Seems like a serial killer, looks pale, and has a poor diet, so he could use some blood nutrition."

"Linda. Works for a pharmaceutical company, is into nutrition, and is over fifty, so she could be concerned about staying young."

"Sylvia. Also over fifty, a nurse who would know about nutrition, stole and sold patients' blood."

I threw up my hands. "It has to be Sylvia, right?"

The light turned green, and my phone rang. Startled, I pressed too hard on the gas. My tires spun, and the car fishtailed to the right and came to a stop.

I exhaled hard, grateful that another car hadn't been in the lane beside me. Then I grabbed the phone from the passenger seat and looked at the display. *Bacigalupi family.*

The Utah mom.

I answered and put the call on speaker. "Hello?"

"This is Drea Bacigalupi." Her voice was soft, feminine. "I apologize for taking so long to call you back, but we've been on vacation."

The rain had picked up, so I kept my eyes on the road and my ears on the phone. "Thanks for getting back to me."

"No problem. Dale and I were shocked to hear what happened after that tour we took, but we're relieved the case has been solved."

"Yes, well, I represent the individual who was arrested, and if you don't mind, I'd like to ask you a few questions about the bar stop."

She hesitated, possibly conflicted about helping me with the case of an accused killer. "I guess that would be all right."

"Do you happen to remember if anyone was wearing a Mardi Gras boa?"

"Yes, because my daughters wanted one, so we went all over the Quarter looking for them."

"And what did this person look like?"

"Mm...She was petite and had dark, longish hair."

Raven or Linda. "The woman with the vampire teeth and white-blue contacts?"

"No, there was another one. She looked like she might be Asian?"

Linda.

"Anything else you remember about her?"

"Well, she was flirting with—"

The phone cut out.

"Hello?" I shouted because the rain had intensified, and it was getting harder to hear. "Can you hear me?"

"Yes, I'm here," Drea said.

"Could you repeat that last part?"

"I said that she was flirting with the fraternity boy, or man, who died. And then Dale and I saw them together after the tour. They were on Bourbon Street, and he looked pretty drunk. He was stumbling, and he had one of those drinks that comes in a long green cup."

The drink was a hand grenade, and the information she'd provided to me had the same explosive effect. "Thank you, you've been very helpful."

"No problem. I hope everything works out."

Me too. I tapped *End* and dropped the phone in my lap.

And I got angry. Angry that Linda had lied to me, angry that I'd been tricked, angry that Sullivan had been so stubborn.

Rain washed over my windshield. The storm was getting intense. I turned up the windshield wipers and pulled a U-turn.

For the police station.

My phone rang again, and I jumped.

It was my mom. Under normal circumstances, I wouldn't have answered. But regardless of what was happening with the case, I wanted to get rid of my brother. "Hello?"

"Francesca, this is your mother."

"It can't be. My mother abandoned her kids."

"You're in a mood."

"Woman," I paused, overcome by the enormity of everything I faced in that moment, "you have no idea."

She sniffed. "Now I see what Anthony's talking about."

"Oh, so you've been talking to him and not me?"

"Well, no." Her tone was laced with guilt, and a pending excuse. "But only because I've been so busy at the deli."

That's not what Larry said.

"But he just texted and let me know that you're mistreating him."

My overcome feeling morphed into outrage.

"And no matter how mad you are at *me*, Francesca," she droned, "you have no right to take it out on your brother."

I smacked the steering wheel, wishing it was him. This was probably about the gutter I'd asked him to hang, and I didn't have time for this *merda*. "Just tell me what the text said, all right?"

"'HELP ME, MAMMA' in all capital letters."

My blood stood still. That didn't sound like my brother. I mean, it did, but it was alarming that he hadn't added a request for money or food onto the message. "Mom, did he say anything else?"

"He didn't, even though I replied and demanded an explanation about what was going on between you two. Now, you agreed to let him stay for a month, so I want you to settle down and honor your commitment."

"Okay. I will."

"I understand that he can be a tad trying, but he *is* your brother."

I didn't argue about that "tad" because I wasn't mad at him anymore. All I wanted to do was find him.

Alive.

"Mom, I'm driving, and the weather is getting bad. Anthony and I will call you tomorrow, I promise. Love you."

Without waiting for a reply, I hung up and hoped I could make good on that promise.

Rain assailed the car.

The calm before the storm was over. I was in its eye.

Was Anthony in its eye too?

I tapped his number.

While it rang, I tried to figure out where he would be. It was eight thirty, so he should have been at work at Madame Moiselle's. But as the namesake of the patron saint of lost things, I doubted he was where he should have been.

"Come on, brother. Where are you?"

Then I remembered. He had a date at St. Roch Tavern. With a new woman. Who was classy.

Fear boiled in my gut.

No.

That would be too crazy, even for a serial killer.

His phone went to voicemail.

Full.

The spirit that Chandra had supposedly channeled outside Boutique du Vampyre infiltrated my brain. The young man, theoretically Gregg, had warned that Anthony would meet his same horrible fate.

I screeched to a halt on the side of the road and searched for the tavern's address. Google Maps showed that St. Roch Tavern was on St. Roch Avenue in the St. Roch neighborhood.

Near the cemetery named St. Roch's Campo Santo, which was Italian for holy ground.

The fear erupted from my gut and shot through my limbs. It was like the anti-vampire saint was trying to tell me it was time for me to fight a vampire too. Or maybe it was the killer sending me a message that it was time to put my brother and me to rest in the Italian cemetery.

Hands trembling, I texted Anthony and asked him to drop everything and call me. To make sure he did, I added that we'd just inherited money from a relative in Sicily.

Rounding up my resolve, I pulled onto the road and hit the gas.

Anthony drove me insane, but he was my brother. And among Italian-Americans, family was everything. Nothing and no one could change the fact that we were related.

By blood.

21

F rom the doorway of St. Roch Tavern, I scanned the dingy, stale-smelling room. The only people in sight were a couple of hipsters playing pool and a group of gutterpunks crowded around two pinball machines.

It was eight forty-five, so I had no idea if Anthony had already been at the bar, or if he was en route. But the rhythmic dripping of water from my trench coat reminded me that precious seconds were ticking away. And the cobweb decorations left over from Halloween did nothing to ease my anxiety.

I approached the brick bar, and a young bartender with a scruffy blond beard and mustache emerged from a side door with a bowl of lemons. The fruit reminded me of the day Anthony told me that Nonna had enlightened Sullivan about the lemon tradition. That was also the day he'd convinced me that the detective was a good guy. But Sullivan had fooled us both.

And so had Linda West.

The bartender placed a lemon on the wooden countertop and cut it in half with a thwack. "Pabst Blue Ribbon pitchers are six dollars tonight."

A voodoo doll on the wall behind him caught my attention. It had

"Bad Tippers" written on it and a pin had been shoved through a red heart on its chest. "I'm not here to drink."

"Then what can I do for you?" He sliced the lemon, and the sound of the knife cutting through the thick, fibrous peel was unnerving.

I held up my phone display with Anthony's Facebook profile picture. "I'm looking for this guy. Has he been in here tonight?"

He raised his eyes from the lemon. They were ice blue, almost as white as Raven's, and they moved from my phone to me. "Who's asking?"

"His sister, Franki Amato."

"Stephen Hart. Pleased to meet you." He resumed slicing. "I wish I could say the same about your brother. He left maybe twenty minutes ago. I had to cut him off after he got loaded on Negroni Sbagliatos."

I stiffened. Negronis were made with Campari, and the word *sbagliato* hit me like an accusation. It was Italian for *mistaken* or *wrong*. And I had been so wrong when I'd ignored Anthony's announcement that he was coming to a tavern named after Saint Roch. "Was he with a petite woman?"

"Yeah. Pretty. Asian eyes." He resumed slicing. "She had to help him out."

My heart sunk at the news he was drunk. "St. Roch's cemetery is up the street, right?"

"Before the old Fountain of Youth Bar." *Slice.*

I gripped the edge of the bar. I hadn't been sure that Linda had taken Anthony to the cemetery until I heard that. It seemed that the area was symbolic to her on a number of levels.

"It closed at four, though. I used to give tours of the place, so I know the schedule." *Slice.*

And the cemetery layout. "Are there many Italian tombs?"

He looked up and caught my gaze. "Lots of them. It was originally for Germans, but in the 1900s Italian and Sicilian families were buried there, like the DeMajos and the Lupos, who started Central Grocery. They had an altar built for the cemetery that was blessed by the pope before it was shipped from Italy."

I was dumbstruck. My father had gotten his start in the deli business at Central Grocery. *Did Anthony tell Linda that?*

"But now the only thing St. Roch's is known for are the body parts." *Slice.*

My parts tensed like they were about to be sliced. "What do you mean?"

"Braces with old shoes attached, glass eyes, hands, feet, you name it. They're all in a building in the back by the chapel. People used to leave them as votive offerings to Saint Roch for healing." He gave an uneasy smile. "One of these days you should check it out."

"I'll do that." *One of these days is now.*

I turned and exited the tavern.

Rain came down like bullets, and I hurried to my Mustang. I pulled my gun from the glove compartment and shoved it into the waistband of my jeans.

Thunder cracked, shattering my calm.

And I broke into a run.

Lightning struck repeatedly, lighting my way to the cemetery.

And I prayed to Anthony, the patron saint of lost things, that I would find my brother.

With his blood still intact.

THE ARCHED WROUGHT-IRON sign said *St. Roch's Campo Santo*, but it should've cited the quote above The Gate of Hell in Dante's *Inferno*, "*Lasciate ogni speranza voi ch'entrate.*" Abandon all hope ye who enter.

Because the entrance was an awesome and terrible sight.

Two angels with hands clasped in prayer topped seven-foot pedestals on either side of the scrolled wrought-iron gate. And the sign perfectly framed the three-story Gothic Revival chapel in the back. Through the gate was a wide avenue that led to the chapel, and at the midpoint a giant crucifix and a statue of a sleeping girl at its base.

The appearance was so austere and foreboding that terror washed over me in tsunami-type waves, as did the torrential rain.

But I had to go inside.

I had to save my brother.

I reached for the gate. Padlocked. And apart from a six-foot-wide piece of fence on either side of the pedestals, the cemetery was surrounded by a mausoleum wall too high to climb.

How did Linda get in?

Or was she even at the cemetery?

As much as I wanted to turn around and run to the safety of my car, I couldn't yield to doubt. Too much was at stake.

My brother's life.

There wasn't enough space for me to fit between the sign and the gate, so my only option for entry was to climb the fence on either side of the pedestals. It was topped with spikes to keep people out.

But before starting my ascent, I had to get the attention of the police. I pulled my phone from my trench coat pocket. Then I did the *scongiuri* gesture for good measure. Because I planned to report a murder, but I didn't want to curse my brother. Or myself.

I tapped the phone icon on the display.

Nothing.

I tapped again.

Frozen.

I shut down the device.

And waited.

While seconds ticked away.

I pressed the power button.

The screen remained black.

Water damage.

I wiped rain from my eyes and glanced at the businesses across from the cemetery.

But the street was as dead as St. Roch's residents.

I'm on my own in this godforsaken place.

My stomach was heavy, like I'd consumed a tombstone. Nevertheless, I grabbed the wrought-iron fence, found a foothold, and climbed. The cold metal bit into the palm of my hands, but I banished the pain from my mind.

After a couple of slips, I reached the top of the fence and came face-to-face with one of the angels. "Pray for me."

She stared straight ahead, unmoved.

Positioning my hands between spikes, I hoisted myself and swung my leg over the fence. I lost my grip on the wet metal and came down on a spike that sliced into my thigh. I winced and bit my lip as those lemons from the tavern flashed before my eyes. Then I glared at the angel and jumped.

My boots hit the wet concrete, and I fell to my knees. The pain was intense, and a cry escaped my lips. All I could do was hope that the heavy rain had drowned out the sound.

Rising to my feet, I touched my throbbing thigh. When I pulled my hand away, there were dark splotches.

Of blood.

I considered making a tourniquet from my sweater, but I was afraid to waste any more time.

Crouching low, I pressed my fingers to the wound to stem the blood loss and limped through the rows of graves as fast as my legs would allow. My soles made scraping sounds, threatening to give me away.

Even though the storm obscured the moon, the tombs radiated an eerie light, and so did the statues of the fourteen stations of the cross set in alcoves along the mausoleum wall. The cemetery was small, which made it easy to survey the tombs. Most were too low for a person to enter, much less hang a man in, so I limped to the larger crypts, checking the seals on the doors for breaks.

Within minutes that seemed like hours, I'd checked the likely graves. I stopped and wiped rain from my eyes and looked over my shoulder. Only two buildings were left, the chapel and the one that probably held the offerings to Saint Roch.

My thigh and knee hurt so badly that my limp had progressed to a drag, and I was losing time and hope of finding Anthony alive. I removed my hand from the wound and used both hands to drag my leg to the offering room.

The door was locked, so I rushed to a side window. Despite the darkness, I didn't need my phone light to see the disturbing offerings the tavern bartender had mentioned. Among a stand of votive candles and plastic flowers, hung rusted leg braces, various limbs, hearts, a liver, even a brain. The floor was paved with bricks that said *Thanks* and *Merci*. And dangling from the same hook as a foot was a purple rosary that I wished I could get. Then I thought of the one in The Vampire Protection Kit and wished I had it.

Because there was only one building left to search.

The chapel directly behind me.

I turned and got vertigo, or maybe I was lightheaded. I told myself it was because of the cold and wet, not the blood oozing from my leg. Or the fear of finding my brother dead inside.

As I dragged my body toward the chapel, I read the message above the entrance. *The National Shrine of Saint Roch Patron Saint of Miraculous Cures.* And I prayed that if anything had happened to Anthony, Saint Roch would perform a miracle and cure him.

And that Saint Marcellus of Paris would help me fight the vampire.

I reached the door and released my leg. With a bloodied hand, I pulled the handle.

It opened.

In a scene straight from a horror film, I saw my brother suspended upside down from a cable that had been strung in front of the altar.

His hands were tied behind his back, and he was as stiff as his gelled hair.

And his brand new boat shoes.

A scream tore from my abdomen.

Chandra's crystal ball vision had come true.

AT THE SOUND of my scream, Anthony flopped like a fish on a hook before the Gothic altar.

"Oh thank God." I dragged my leg to the isle between the two rows of pews, but my strength was waning.

"You stay away from me." He thrashed with his eyes squeezed shut.

"Anthony. It's me, Franki."

"Let me go, and I'll clear outta town," he shouted, unwilling or unable to hear me. "I swear on the Bible."

The cable bounced from his weight but held firm. It stretched across the chapel from the frosted windows, well below the vaulted ceiling. I would've had to climb the altar to reach it, but I couldn't in my condition.

A petite woman entered my peripheral vision.

"Don't move." I spun and reached for my gun.

It wasn't there.

Luckily, the woman was a wooden statue next to the altar.

I exhaled and hung my head. "It's okay, Anthony. False alarm."

He was limp, passed out.

I glanced around the white marble floor for my gun. But I knew I'd lost it running in the rain or jumping from the fence.

What are you going to do now?

As I made my way to my brother, I looked at the main altar. In front of dark wooden panels, there were painted statues of Saint Roch and a dog atop a marble tomb with a glass façade.

Christ was inside.

And I focused on his likeness until I reached my brother.

His eyes flipped open. "Mamma?"

I slapped his face. "It's Franki. Get a hold of yourself."

"Sis." He seemed unfazed by the slap. "My date is the vampire killer."

Given the situation, I'd figured that out. "Where is she?"

"She went to get balloons and a cake, like this was some kinda party."

Christine had said that Linda liked to celebrate, but to use Anthony's language, the lady was a freakin' nut job.

A sob wracked his body. "She's gonna drain my blood."

"Try to stay calm." I steadied his swaying frame, but in truth I was swaying too. His head was level with my chest. "Lower your arms as much as you can. I'll untie your hands."

"She's comin' back." Another sob. "To get me." His breath reeked like a bayou.

"Don't worry. She's not here now." I checked over my shoulder, just in case. Then I rose on tiptoes, wincing at the pain in my knee, to reach his zip-tied hands. I knew how to break a zip tie, but it involved slamming the bound wrists against one's behind, and that required a standing position.

After only a few seconds of pulling the tie, my fingers and hands tingled, and the lightheadedness had intensified. I looked down at the floor.

Blood pooled beside my boot.

Mine. From my thigh.

My gaze went to Christ in his tomb, and I thought of how he must've bled on the cross.

My brain screamed, *Make a tourniquet*, but seconds were ticking away. I shook my head, and the movement made the room spin. I wrapped my arms around Anthony's torso to stay upright.

"This ain't no time for a hug." His tone was more level, relaxed.

"I'm trying to steady you," I lied. He hadn't seen my injured leg, and I didn't want to alarm him. "Just watch the door."

"Oh, I am. That woman is a maniac."

And yet she'd seemed so nice. I should've suspected her for that reason alone. I pulled my car key from my pocket and tried to pry the tie from the release. In the meantime, I had to talk to stay alert. And ease the fear. "Where did you meet her?"

"Madame Moiselle's. She asked me out."

"You never work. When were you there?"

"The night I got hired."

The same day I'd gone with Anthony to the interview and suspected that I was being followed. "Did she pump you for information about me?"

"No, but I told her about the family. And you."

I wanted to choke him with the zip tie, but I couldn't get it off. My fingers were useless, slipping. And I was slipping too. "Why would you do that?"

"Because I'm proud of you. You've made sumpthin' of yourself." He paused. "I haven't."

A cocktail of shame and affection infused my system. But it wasn't the time to get choked up because that could prove fatal for both of us. I had to keep talking, stay alert. "Why are you dressed like a frat boy?"

"I thought Linda was classy, so I had to dress right."

If I hadn't been so dizzy and tired, I would've rolled my eyes. Classy wasn't a word I would've used for frat boys or their frattire.

The key slipped from my fingers.

I bent to retrieve it, and the chapel tilted. I collapsed onto the cold floor.

Make a tourniquet.

"What're ya doin'?"

"I need a minute." I had a T-shirt under my sweater, so I removed my trench coat. The effort was exhausting.

"You're not givin' up on me, are ya, sis?" Panic had returned to his voice.

"No, never." And I meant it. I would do anything to help him. He was my brother, and I loved him. But I would need a miracle cure to get us out of there.

I looked at Saint Roch and prayed for healing.

Then I lowered my gaze to my thigh.

A red silk rosette lay on the white marble between my legs.

I tried to pick it up, but it smeared.

It was liquid.

Blood.

Anthony's scream sliced through my skin, my bone.

And bashed my brain.

I crumpled and rolled to my back.

The last thing I saw was a Mardi Gras boa and a black handheld face mask.

22

"I'm so glad you could come to our party, Franki."

The black mask came into focus, and a couple of balloons.

Upside down?

My gaze dropped to the floor, but I saw the vaulted ceiling of the chapel. I turned my head.

Anthony was beside me, eyes closed, breathing ragged.

I was hanging.

For a blood draining.

"What did you hit me with? A karate chop?"

A hiss came from behind the mask. "That's stereotyping."

I couldn't afford to upset her, not in my position. "I just meant that I don't see a weapon."

She pointed to a black Michael Kors bag on a pew. "I used my purse."

As the granddaughter of a black-bag nonna, I should have thought of that.

Linda giggled and tickled my nose with the boa. She took a step back to survey the macabre scene she'd created. In place of her usual pinks and greens, she wore black and red, her Goth Marie Antoinette colors.

My skull throbbed. Inexplicably, I felt better, probably because of the fear-induced adrenaline and the blood gathered at my head.

Blood.

I looked up at my leg. She'd knotted a scarf around my thigh. "Why did you tie off my wound?"

"Because I'd rather bleed you dry from your throat."

I tensed my neck and wished I'd left my trench coat on. "Either you're insane, or you're high on your blood transfusions."

She pulled off her mask. "Let's not be rude."

"Why not get a vampire facelift like Kim Kardashian instead of stealing blood?"

"I don't know what you're talking about."

"You're mixing transfusions of stolen blood and herbs. Campari Crimson?"

"That sounds like a fun drink."

I ignored her odd enthusiasm. "Is the youth elixir for you? Or is it a prototype for a Pharmanew product?"

She pulled a compact from her purse and checked her makeup. "A woman doesn't share her beauty secrets."

I shouldn't have been surprised by that statement. Linda was the epitome of femininity, except for her killer instinct. "You make real vampires look bad, you know that?"

"Impossible." She snapped the compact shut. "I work hard on my appearance."

She was too vain to grasp what I'd meant. "Fine. Don't tell me anything. I've figured most of it out. You were getting blood from Sylvia Blaylock at Belleville House until a man died. Then you went to the blood banks, but the police were all over that. So, you had to prey on private citizens, some random like Gregg, and some you wanted to do away with, like Raven."

A round of dizziness and nausea hit. I was talking too much. I had to slow down, think of an escape. And distract her while I tried to free my wrists. "The only thing I don't understand is how Todd Plank factored into this."

"Ugh. That man." She tossed her purse with the compact on a pew. "And they call *me* a Pollyanna."

I'd touched a nerve.

Her eyelids lowered, and she twisted an end of her boa. "He thought he was going to waltz in from the outside and get the CEO position at Pharmanew, after the years of blood, sweat, and tears I've put into that company."

Interesting analogy.

"I'm the one who convinced the good old boys on the board that the future was in pharmaceutical blood products. Then they went behind my back and recruited Todd, and it wasn't just because of his work at The Blood Center. They had the gall to imply that I was too old to be the face of the business. So they picked a man with a shaved head and a soul patch. Can you imagine?"

I wasn't a fan of facial hair, so I really couldn't.

"And the insulting part is that Todd looked great. He was only a few years younger than me, but it might as well have been twenty." She ripped a handful of feathers from the boa. "Men always age better."

Except for diehard frat daddies like Gregg.

"And then Todd came in for an interview. I eavesdropped, and you won't believe what I heard." She shot me a complicit look, as though I would share her outrage.

"He wanted to introduce critical debate and other corporate BS into our office culture." Her tone was a mix of indignation and incredulity. "But we do things *my* way at Pharmanew."

I'd seen that side of Linda at her office. But I couldn't have known how dead set she was in her ways. Literally.

"I was in the lobby when he came out of the interview, and he was wearing a Virginia Tech scarf and backpack. Orange and maroon." She shuddered and pulled her boa tight. "They would've ruined my office color scheme."

Linda might've been psychotic, but when it came to school colors she knew the score. "Yeah, they're a tragedy together."

Her face brightened. "I knew you'd agree. Let's celebrate, shall we?" She pulled a bucket of ice with a bottle of Prosecco from beneath a pew. "It's just as well that your brother passed out. I want us to have a private toast."

The woman was determined to have a party. "What's the occasion?"

She broke into a cheerleader-style smile. "I got the CEO position."

I would've been open-mouthed, but gravity and nausea held my jaw down. "This was all about staying young to get a job?"

"I'm a single mom, and you know the pressure on working women to maintain their looks. Isn't that why you quit the police force and became a private investigator?"

There were shades of Carnie in that comment, and I wriggled my wrists harder. But the zip tie held firm, and my skin stung to the bone.

She removed the foil from the Prosecco bottle and popped the cork.

Anthony jerked awake. "I lied," he shouted. "We're not B Positive, we're type O."

My side-eye could have cut him. "You told her our blood type? Isn't that a little personal for a first date?"

"He did." Linda poured herself some bubbly. "And I'd been planning to use him for info about your investigation until then." She raised the plastic flute. "Cheers."

She took a sip, and I tasted blood.

I told myself it would be hers, not ours.

Linda looked around the chapel satisfied with the party she'd put together and put the flute on the floor. And she pulled a cake knife from her purse that could've made quick work of Phil's cemetery salami. "I'm sorry about this, Franki. But the police have their killer, so I need to destroy the remaining evidence." She ran her fingers over the blade. "It's just a bonus that you two have my blood type."

"We're not teenagers." I struggled against the zip tie, swaying slightly. "Their blood is better."

She shrugged. "That's okay. You're both still pretty young. And my ex-husband is Italian, so I guess you could say I have a taste for you."

My nausea threatened to spill. I swung and caught sight of the dog beside Saint Roch. I had to get home to Napoleon, see my Nonna, hang with Veronica and sometimes Glenda, avoid Carnie. Talk to Bradley. "You'll eventually get caught. I guarantee it."

"I doubt that." She smiled sweetly and flipped her hair. "No one ever suspects nice women like me."

She had a point. Two, actually, because she'd pressed the tip of the knife to my neck.

"Get your hands off my baby sistuh." Anthony swung and grabbed a handful of Linda's hair.

He'd freed his hands. That passed out thing was an act.

"Never touch my hairdo." She ran to her compact and straightened her bangs. Then she raised the knife and moved toward my brother, scowling.

He held out his hands, and she slashed his palm.

At the sight of his own blood, he crumbled like Linda's party cake.

My protective instinct took over. "Swing, Anthony. Move your body!"

Arching as best I could, I raised my arms behind me and slammed my wrists against my backside.

The zip tie broke in a single try.

Linda screamed, but I didn't waste one precious second finding out why. Propelled by blind terror, I used my abdomen and hands to climb my legs to the horizontal cable above my feet.

"I told you not to touch my hair," she shouted.

"Move and I'll rip it out." Anthony was angry. And sober. "Hurry, sis."

Gripping the cable with my left hand, I used my right hand to unbuckle my boots. Then I moved it to the cable, slipped my feet from my shoes, and dropped to the floor.

Pain jolted from my knees to my hips, but I stayed upright. Our lives depended on it.

I spun to face Linda.

Incredibly, she stood as still as the statue of the petite woman beside the altar as Anthony two-fisted the hair on her scalp.

I yanked the knife from her grasp. "Are you really so vain that you would rather be caught than lose your hair?"

Her brown eyes darted upward to her forehead. "I don't want to be bald like Todd."

A somber silence filled the chapel.

I tied her wrists and ankles with the ribbons from the balloons. For the first time, I read their message.

Congratulations!

"LINDA WEST HAD us all fooled, Amato." Detective Sullivan sat slumped at his desk. And he was so pale that I half-wondered whether Linda had drained his blood during her interrogation.

But I did nothing to ease his embarrassment. It was eleven a.m., and I'd spent a sleepless night in the hospital getting my thigh stitched. I was beyond exhausted, like I still had one injured leg in the grave, and I couldn't muster any sympathy for Wesley Sullivan and his wounded ego.

He gazed at me from beneath his eyelashes. "She paraded around in a cape, made puncture wounds on her victims, and leaked the news of the fake bite marks on Gregg Charalambous to the paper to make sure everyone thought the killer was from the local vampire community." He pointed a finger at me. "And Mr. Santo's behavior didn't help him seem innocent."

I didn't bother to argue that I'd given him plenty of reasons to consider suspects other than Josh. All I wanted was to see him released from jail and get answers to my questions.

As though reading my mind, Sullivan glanced at the clock. "We got the court order to release your boy's, I mean, your client's bond a few hours ago, so he should be out shortly."

My stare was half-lidded. "Did you ask Linda about that Campari Crimson message on the crypt wall?"

His lips protruded. "She apologized to Gregg before she killed him and made the mistake of explaining why she was doing it. After she left, he somehow managed to get down and survive long enough to write it on the wall, despite the blood loss."

Maybe a healthy dose of Adderall was behind that. "So what happens to Sylvia Blaylock, the nurse?"

"She'll remain in custody. We've opened an investigation at Belleville House in light of her alleged involvement."

I was relieved to know she could no longer harm the residents. "And Thomas Van Scyoc? Has Linda clarified his role?"

"According to Ms. West, he didn't know anything illicit was going on until Craig Rourke's grandfather died. Sylvia accused Raven, the obvious target, and said she was selling the blood to Linda. He confronted Linda, who convinced him the best solution for everyone was to fire Raven and settle privately with the Rourke family."

I shook my head. "That explains why he lied about seeing Raven talking to Gregg at the bar."

"It also explains why he was on that vampire tour to begin with. Linda heard that Raven was taking the tour from some friend of hers at a doctor's office, and she convinced Thomas to go."

"To show Raven that they were keeping tabs on her?"

He nodded. "And to remind her that she shouldn't go to the police about the blood business at the retirement home."

If only Raven had confided in me. "Pam said Thomas went on the tour a second time. Do you know why?"

"Linda was furious about that. Apparently, he wanted to go back to hear the vampire stories because he was too busy watching Raven to listen to them the first time around."

I still think that guy has serial killer tendencies. "And Craig Rourke? Why was he on the tour?"

"That was the only coincidence. He was telling the truth about being there with Mr. Charalambous and Mr. LaVecchio to get ideas for their Halloween party. But he figured out who Thomas was and told him they needed to meet up to talk about what had happened to his grandfather. Craig wasn't happy with the settlement his grandmother had agreed to. He thought people should've gotten prison time for his grandfather's death."

He was right about that. Because if they had, the other murders wouldn't have happened. Settling a homicide via attorneys should've been against the law.

Sullivan sat back, and his lips thinned. "There is one surprise that came from Ms. West's interrogation."

My gut tensed. "What's that?"

"Turns out she's a descendent of one of those Casket Girls that the hippie tour guide talked about."

I almost slid from the folding chair. "Her assistant told me she was born in Paris, but I never would've guessed her French roots went that deep."

"Her heritage was the inspiration for the blood cocktail."

"Then why name it after an Italian liqueur?"

"I asked her that. She said the final product looked like Campari, and it was made through a similar process. And, she just liked the crimson color."

I did too. It was far superior to maroon.

"Any other questions?" Sullivan sounded hopeful, like we were on the mend.

I wanted him to know there was no chance of reconciliation, at least, not that day. "Did Linda do anything to directly frame Josh Santo for the crimes?"

He looked at his hands, folded on the desk. "No, that was police error."

I remained silent, encouraging him to continue.

His eyes met mine, and they verged on pleading. "My error, to be specific, and I can't apologize enough."

I rubbed the knot on my head to keep from feeling sorry for him. I wasn't ready to accept his apology after my brother and I had come so close to being a blood fountain of youth. "Any idea what was in that purse she nailed me with?"

"A jade Buddha."

I gasped. "Oh, and asking her if she did karate was a stereotype?"

Sullivan laughed, and the smile slowly slipped from his face. "I always appreciated your sense of humor, Amato. Now that this is over, I'd like to take you out to dinner. If you'll let me."

Just like that, as though all was forgiven because he'd apologized. "I'm not interested in a personal relationship with you."

"Relationship?" He held up his hands in a slow-down gesture. "Hell, I've already got that."

My head retracted. "Your dinner date from the other night?"

"My wife."

The dizziness returned like I'd been hung upside down all over again. "I thought you were divorced."

"That was my first marriage. But this second one isn't going too well either."

I sat still as I processed the revelation that he'd been married the entire time he'd been coming on to me. I felt bad that I'd kissed him back, but only for his wife. Because I didn't actually care about him. It was the attention I'd responded to, not the man. I reached for the crutch I'd received at the hospital.

Sullivan stood. "Let me get the door."

"I don't need your help. I proved that when I solved your case." I met his stunned gaze as I rose to my feet. "Oh, I almost forgot. Since you referred me to Josh Santo, I owe you a favor." Resting on my crutch, I pulled the bag of Adderall pills from my purse and tossed it on his desk.

He shot me a questioning look.

"Courtesy of Delta Upsilon Delta. They'll help you focus on your work. And your wife." I turned and, with a grin as wide as the state of Texas, exited into the hallway and closed the door behind me.

Veronica stood outside with Josh Santo, who wore the tails, top hat, and cape he'd been arrested in.

He flashed a mouthful of ivories in the midst of his facial fur. "I was just telling your boss to expect a substantial bonus. If it weren't for you, I'd be in prison for life."

I smiled but kept quiet. It wasn't modesty so much as the size of his teeth.

"Franki's a fighter." Veronica gave me a one-armed squeeze. "That's why I had to have her at Private Chicks."

"So, what's next for you?" I asked.

Josh stroked his beard. "I'll finish my book about Compte de Saint Germain, but not here in New Orleans. I've decided to sell the house and move to Transylvania."

I faltered despite my crutch. Either that kid was a vampire, or he made some really bad choices. "Can I ask you a personal question?"

"I suppose." He sounded suspicious.

"Your resemblance to the count is uncanny. Did you have plastic surgery to look more like him?"

He smiled, but with his mouth closed. "I didn't want to mention this during the investigation, but I'm related to Richard Chanfray."

Veronica pulled her purse over her shoulder. "Wasn't he the man in St. Tropez who claimed to be the count?"

I gave her an uneasy stare. "Yeah, the one who supposedly committed suicide in '83, and his body was never found." I cast a wary eye on Josh. "But obviously it's a freak coincidence that you and your missing relative are both carbon copies of an eighteenth-century vampire."

"I guess. But we'll never know, will we?" He spun, flaring his cape.

I blinked and watched him head for the exit. I wanted to like the guy, but there was something odd about him.

He stopped and turned around. "Before I go, I need to get something off my conscience."

I shifted on my crutch, steeling myself for something shocking.

Josh pressed a finger to his bottom lip. "That guy who gave you the yellow rose at the Crimson Cotillion, is he your boyfriend?"

"It's complicated. Why do you ask?"

"Before you got there, Detective Sullivan was talking to him."

I stood upright at the news, and my crutch clattered to the floor. "Did you hear what they said?"

"It was too loud in that ballroom." He smoothed his mustache.

"But after talking to Sullivan, your boyfriend put a ring box back in his pocket."

Veronica slipped her arm through mine and held on with all of her weight.

If she hadn't, I would've gotten life without parole for draining the blood of a detective.

23

"What are you doing here?" Veronica asked as I hobbled into Private Chicks the next morning. "I told you to take the rest of the week off."

I went to a couch to lie down. It was only nine a.m., but after hop-walking three flights of stairs I was done for the day. "Every nonna in New Orleans is at my apartment right now, so I had to escape."

Her eyes went wide. "What about Glenda's visitor policy? She told you no more than two."

"Yeah, they tied her up. And they threatened to feed her actual food if she complained."

A crooked smile appeared on her face. "Are they trying to take care of you? Or did something happen to the pope?"

"It's way worse than all of that. Last night I told Nonna about Sullivan thwarting Bradley's proposal, and she sent out an emergency *nonne* summons."

Veronica put both hands to her mouth, and her face looked like mine probably had when I saw Anthony hanging.

"Before you call me a fool, I wanted her to know what kind of person Sullivan was so she'd stop campaigning for him to be the savior of the lemon tradition."

"I get that, but you know there's going to be fallout."

I shrugged. "She'll pray, meddle, plan some Sicilian vendetta, but she'd do those things even if I hadn't lost a proposal. The good news is, she'll be doing them in Houston because she and Anthony are going home this weekend."

"Your brother is leaving?"

"After his encounter with Linda, he decided that living in The Big Easy is hard. And get this, he says he wanted to quit the strip club anyway because there's no future in it."

"I'm not sure what to say to that."

"Oh, I am. Bye-bye, brother," I said with a wave.

"How did your mom take it?"

"She's not happy, but I repeated her words back to her. 'It won't be for long. Just until he gets on his feet.'"

Veronica shot me a warning look. "Don't mock your mom. She could send him back."

"Nah, I told her the next time he shows up at my door, I'll make sure his blood is actually spilled." I glanced around the lobby. "Hey, where are David and the vassal?"

"At the electronics store. Josh wired payment to our bank, and he was nice enough to include bonuses for them too. Speaking of which, I'll go write your check."

Veronica left, and I closed my eyes, grateful to be in a no-nonna zone.

The lobby buzzer went off, and I crossed my fingers that it wasn't a client with a homicide case.

"Sleeping on the job?"

The accent wasn't Carnie's, but the comment was. I opened my eyes.

Chandra stood before me looking like a space oddity in a purple and silver jumpsuit that said Mercury Made Me Do It and red Ziggy Stardust boots.

"I'm resting."

She fluffed her bob, which was already as big as the sun. "I suppose you're allowed after catching that killer."

I sat up and adjusted my leg. "So how's Lou?"

Her tiny mouth was almost swallowed by a scowl. "He's got third-degree burns on his tongue from all the Bayou Blast in his Crawfish Monica. If I ever see those conniving classmates of his, I'll give them a Bayou Blast." She clenched a fist. "Boston style."

That sounded like a powerful punch. "They got what they deserved when Chef Mel disqualified them from the competition. And when I Bayou Blasted their dishes." I couldn't see my smile, but I knew it was sly. "Just be glad Lou's getting to ride in that gumbo pot next Mardi Gras."

"Oh, I am, and Lou is too. He's hard at work putting flames on the side of his okra costume."

Lou had to be a descendent of the caveman who discovered fire. "How's that going to work?"

"He wants to be chargrilled okra, not boiled. By the way, I told him that I'd hired you to go undercover at Bayou Cuisine, and he's so grateful for what you've done that we decided to give you a bonus."

She beamed and handed me a check.

"Fifty dollars," I said, trying to sound psyched.

"And that's not all." Her tone held the promise of more cash and prizes. "Lou said to stop by the showroom and pick out a custom commode."

My apartment looked like a whorehouse, and he wanted to pimp my toilet. "I'd love to take him up on the offer, but my lease forbids me from making changes to the fixtures."

"That's too bad." She tugged at an earring. "But Lou could make you dinner now that he's a chef."

Given his taste in food, I would've rather had the tricked-out toilet.

"Anyhoo, I need to get back to the office. Now that Halloween is over, I'm slammed."

"Why's that?"

"The holidays are around the corner."

"What does that have to do with the psychic business?"

"You know." She flicked her wrist, and her charm bracelet jingled. "The Christmas spirit?"

I wasn't following her, but I nodded. If there was an actual spirit associated with the season, I didn't want Chandra to channel it.

"I'll call you about that dinner." She winked and pulled the door closed behind her.

Veronica returned to the lobby. "Did I hear Chandra?"

"She paid me." I held up the check. "There's an extra fifty bucks in it. And if I didn't rent from Glenda, I could've gotten a free flaming commode."

"Gosh, I don't know if Josh's bonus can compete with that."

"A kid who made fifty million from the sale of his company can't do better than a john?" I shook my head. "Anyway, I wanted to apologize for getting so mad about you hiring Nonna."

She sat on the arm of the couch. "You were being a good granddaughter. I can't blame you for that."

"But it turned out to be the best decision you could've made. If we'd sent someone else inside Belleville, they wouldn't have known Luigi Pescatore. And his information helped solve this case." I hesitated because what I had to say next was going to hurt. "Carnie did a decent job too."

"You should tell her that."

"Not even if Linda escaped from jail and held another cake knife to my throat."

Veronica's hand went to her neck. "Speaking of the case, every station in town wants an interview with you."

"I know we could use the free publicity, but I don't feel up to it yet."

She pulled a lock of my hair from my eyes. "Why don't you call Bradley, Franki? Whatever Sullivan said to him was obviously a lie."

I cradled a cushion against my chest. "Until he caught us kissing on the Bourbon Orleans balcony."

"Even if it doesn't change things, you should at least set the record straight."

I dropped my chin onto the cushion. "I'll think about it."

"That's a solid start." She handed me a check. "Now, go spend some of your hard-earned bonus on something fun."

I glanced at the amount and saw a five and zeroes. "Another fifty dollars. You're right. I should save part of this."

Her brow crinkled. "You're tired. Look again."

I'd never been a numbers person, so I read the spelled-out version. I bolted up on my bad leg.

"Fifty. Thousand. Dollars?"

Veronica squealed and clapped.

And I was out like I'd been whacked with Linda's Buddha bag.

WHEN I ENTERED MY APARTMENT, *nonne* were wailing, rosaries were clicking, teeth were gnashing, but I didn't care. I'd just deposited a check for fifty thousand dollars in an otherwise empty bank account, and the sun was finally shining in New Orleans. I was so jazzed I'd even ditched the crutch.

Anthony sat at the kitchen table, half awake, in front of a double espresso. There was a mark on his cheek in the shape of my hand from the slap I'd given him at St. Roch's. It was fairly satisfying.

He looked up. "What're you smiling about?"

I mentally crossed my fingers. "I just found out there was no blood in that Chianti you drank."

His head dropped, and he exhaled a breath. "I'll drink to that. We got any more wine in the house?"

My head dropped, and I exhaled too. Then I handed him a check. "This is for you."

His face turned white, except for the bruised area. *"Five. Thousand. Dollars?"*

We were as different as olive oil and balsamic vinegar but definitely related.

"Yo, is this the dough we inherited from that old Sicilian dude?"

I started to tell him the truth about that text I'd sent him but thought better of it. If he knew I'd gotten fifty thousand dollars from Josh, he might come back for another check. And I wanted him to stay gone. "Yeah, I wanted you to have all of it. But I made the check out to Mom."

His brow went gorilla. "Is this like some 'o the money I owe her, or sumpthin'?"

"It's to get you started at a trade school. When you pick one, mom will pay the tuition."

"Whoa." He stood and gave me a hug. "I've been thinking of what you did. You know, going into the police academy?"

I pictured him crying in the chapel. "I'm not sure that's right for you. Why don't you research all the programs out there before you make a decision?"

"I love you, sis. You know that, don't you?"

"I do, and I love you back." I pulled Nutella from the pantry, relieved to find it untouched. "But if you love me so much, why did you text Mom when you were in trouble?"

"I dunno." He returned to his seat. "I guess I always go to Ma when there's a problem."

"Precisely. You're a *mammone*, a mamma's boy, and you need to kick that habit." I pointed the jar at him and regretted using the phrase while holding my one true addiction.

"I'll think about it."

"That's a solid start," I said, mimicking what Veronica had said to me about Bradley. And I regretted that too because it reminded me that I should call him. But I didn't know what to say.

There was a banging sound outside the house, possibly on the roof.

The *nonne's* heads rose from their rosaries.

"I'll go see what it is." I returned the Nutella to the pantry so as not to tempt Anthony unnecessarily and went outside.

A fire truck was parked in front of the fourplex, and a firefighter stood on a ladder nailing the gutter to the roof while Glenda looked on in red studded stripper heels and an Italian-flag-adorned chef's apron with the words *How you lika my new apron?*

I knew her answer to that question. "I'm so sorry Anthony never fixed that for you."

She took a long, slow drag off her cigarette holder as she admired the fireman's posterior. "It worked out better this way, Miss Franki."

I had to agree. "How'd you get the fire department to come out for this?"

She loosened her apron strings to give me a peek at the pasties underneath. "I might be retired from dancing, sugar, but I've still got pull in the community."

I was sure she did. "Anyway, I haven't forgotten about The Visitor Policy, so I'll have the *nonne* out within the hour. They came to help me with a personal issue."

"Miss Ronnie told me about you and Bradley." She exhaled a puff of smoke, and I couldn't help but think it was symbolic of our relationship. "I can only take men in small doses, but that banker beau of yours is a keeper. That's why I called him."

"You—" I got a mouthful of her smoke and choked.

"Someone's got to talk some sense into you two, and I'm the logical person to do it."

I kept my mouth shut, both because I didn't want to inhale any more smoke and because I thought it best not to respond to that comment.

A male cleared his throat behind me, and I knew it wasn't the fire chief.

I turned to see Bradley. In place of his usual suit, a fisherman's sweater and jeans. He looked so handsome I had to resist the urge to touch him. "Shouldn't you be in New York?"

"I never boarded the return flight."

I hadn't expected that.

"I'm glad to see you're okay. I heard the news, and I was so proud of you for sticking to the case and catching the killer. You're a hero in this community, and you deserve the credit you're getting."

My mouth opened, but I couldn't speak. I was embarrassed by the praise, not to mention caught off guard. Bradley wasn't a fan of my profession, and yet his tone was positively pleased.

"Anyway." He reached into his back pocket and pulled out a jewelry box.

It was too big to hold a ring, and I was relieved. The way things stood, I would've had to refuse his proposal.

"I wanted to give you this." He handed me the box.

Glenda kicked my bad leg with her studded shoe. "Open it, Miss Franki."

I gave her a scram stare.

Her brows raised, she slipped her cigarette holder into her mouth and resumed watching the fireman's backside.

Too curious to resist, I opened the box and stifled a gasp. It was a pair of ruby and diamond earrings to go with a necklace Bradley had given me for my birthday. "These are gorgeous. But...you can't buy my affection."

He shoved his hands into his pockets. "That's not what this is about. I'd planned to give them to you for Christmas. But in case we don't make it, I wanted you to have them now."

I snapped the box shut. "It used to be that I didn't trust you, but the situation is reversed. So how could we possibly make it?"

"I don't have the answer. But I can promise I'll have more time for you, so we can try to work things out."

I wasn't ready to believe him. "You always say that."

"I resigned from Pontchartrain Bank."

I was so floored the vertigo returned for a few seconds. "But you loved your job."

"I love you more." His tone was decisive, firm.

My heart swooned, and my leg threatened to give out. But I didn't move. I was still processing the news. "What are you going to do for money?"

"I've got plenty put away for a while. I'll eventually look for something less demanding, but as of this week I'm taking a year off."

I looked at the box. "To do what?"

"Focus on us, if you'll let me."

I wanted to say yes, but I was still unsure about everything.

Instead, I came up with a compromise. "Well, I'm between cases, and you're between jobs. So why don't we start with dinner?"

His gaze never left mine. "I'd like that."

The fifty thousand dollars was burning a hole in my bank account. "Okay, but I'm buying."

His smile spread to his eyes. He extended an uncertain hand, but I went in for a hug.

"*Carmela*," Santina shouted. "*È un miracolo!*"

I turned to see *nonne* high-fiving in the doorway. Then I looked at Bradley. His expression was neutral, but I saw hope in his eyes.

And I'm sure he saw it reflected in mine.

"Excuse me for a sec." I went to the porch, and the black dresses parted like the Red Sea to reveal my nonna, holding a lemon and a paper sack.

I leaned in close, so Bradley wouldn't hear. "Don't read anything into this, Nonna. It's a date, not an engagement."

"*Eh*, there's still-a six months for the tradition to work." She tossed the lemon and caught it in the sack. "I got-a this in-a the bag."

COCKTAILS

Here are two of my favorite drinks from *Campari Crimson*. If you like cocktails, wait until you find out what the title refers to!

NEGRONI SBAGLIATO

When I finish a Franki Amato mystery, I toast with a drink made of the liqueur featured in the title. I also reference a drink in each book as a clue to the next title in my series (hint for the next Franki Amato mystery—it's a yellow liqueur, but not Limoncello). Anyway, my celebratory drink was a Negroni Sbagliato, which means *wrong* or *mistaken* Negroni, because the drink plays a role in the climax of *Campari Crimson*.

Ingredients
   1 ounce Campari
   1 ounce sweet vermouth
   1 or 2 ounces Prosecco
   orange wedge

Fill an old-fashioned glass with ice. Add Campari and vermouth and stir. Top with Prosecco and stir again. You can also serve this drink without ice in a champagne flute. Garnish with an orange wedge.

VAMPIRE COCKTAIL

I make this drink on Halloween with friends because it's served with syringes filled with raspberry puree to look like blood, of course. It's not easy to find large syringes, so I need to thank my dermatologist for providing them (lucky I had an appointment that morning). The drink is deliciously decadent, so I included it in a scene at a vampire ball.

Raspberry puree
    2 cups raspberries
    1/4 cup sugar

Ingredients for the cocktail
    4 ounces vodka
    2 ounces amaretto
    2 ounces orange juice
    6 ounces club soda
    4 large plastic syringes

Puree the raspberries in a blender or food processor. Strain the puree to separate the pulp from the seeds. Discard the seeds.

Combine the pulp with the sugar in a small saucepan over medium-high heat. Stir frequently, and cook until the mixture darkens, about ten minutes. Chill and then fill the syringes with the puree.

Fill four old-fashioned glasses with ice. In a shaker, mix the vodka, amaretto, orange juice, and club soda. Pour into the glasses and add a puree-filled syringe. Before drinking, squeeze the puree into the glass. The end result resembles a bloody tequila sunrise.

CALL TO ACTION

Dear reader,

Thank you so much for reading *Campari Crimson*! The writing business gets harder every day, so I appreciate your support. We authors would simply not exist without you.

To that end, there are other things you can do to help:

1. Write a review of *Campari Crimson* on Amazon, Barnes and Noble, Goodreads, BookBub, and any other place your heart desires.

2. Sign up for my newsletter at traciandrighetti.com. I'll send you "Fragolino Fuchsia" for FREE!

3. Follow me on Facebook, Twitter, Instagram, BookBub, Amazon, and Goodreads. The links are provided in the About the Author section.

4. Email me at traci@traciandrighetti.com. Your greetings, comments, and suggestions often get me through the writing day!

5. Next, read "Cannellino Caramel," the bonus story included only in the hardcover version of *Campari Crimson*. It's a wild NOLA time!

A presto,
    Traci

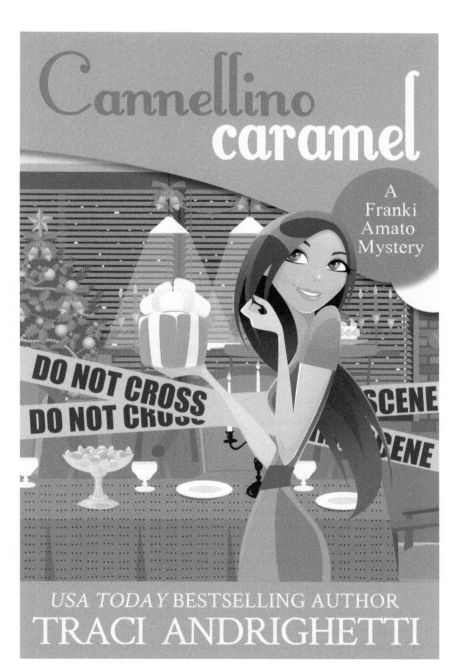

Cannellino caramel

A Franki Amato Mystery

USA TODAY BESTSELLING AUTHOR

TRACI ANDRIGHETTI

CANNELLINO CARAMEL

by

TRACI ANDRIGHETTI

***

STORY BACKSTORY

Thank you in advance for reading Cannellino Caramel! I hope you get a kick out of Franki's family Christmas in New Orleans. Things are never normal for the Amatos, and I like to think that makes for a fun story.

Cannellino Caramel was inspired by a minor detail in *Kitchen Confidential*, the book that made Anthony Bourdain famous, and by a scene in the 2016 *Parts Unknown* episode set in Houston. Although my family and I lived in Houston for years, Bourdain managed to show me new things about my ex-city. I will miss his ability to surprise, amuse, and enlighten me more than I can express.

While we're on the subject of Houston, Kevin Kwan, the author of *Crazy Rich Asians*, went to my high school (Go Falcons!). And I went to see the movie while I was writing Cannellino Caramel. Why is this relevant? Because I thought it would be fun for you to know that the ring mentioned in this story is a much more modest version of Michelle Yeoh's fabulous emerald featured in the film. After all, rings are important, especially during the holidays.

And speaking of holidays, may yours be full of family, food, and delicious drinks.

Cin cin (Cheers)!
Traci

1

"Why isn't that Santa wearing a shirt? And what's that sign on his crotch?" I rose from the rococo chaise lounge in my living room to inspect the tree ornament, and what I read soured the sugarplums dancing in my head. "Don't open until Christmas?"

Veronica Maggio, my best friend and boss at Private Chicks, Inc., the PI firm where I worked in New Orleans, went as still as the gold fringe on the lilac velour armchair where she sat stringing popcorn.

Appalled, I snatched the offending ornament from the branch and gasped at the one behind it. "She baked an anatomically correct Gingerbread Man?"

"You know Glenda has different taste, Franki."

Calling our landlady's taste 'different' was like calling a strip club a restaurant. The analogy was pertinent because Glenda O'Brien, the owner and upstairs resident of the fourplex where I rented a sketchy furnished apartment next door to Veronica, was an ex-stripper and something of a local celebrity. And at well over sixty, she dressed like she still worked the bawdy Bourbon Street strip scene.

Veronica reached for her cocoa. "And don't forget that you told her your tree was bare."

"I *said* that I needed a few more ornaments. You know I never use the word 'bare' around Glenda because I don't want to encourage her." I plucked a randy reindeer from a branch. "And obviously I was trying to make this place look less French Quarter brothel and more family Christmas party."

"Well, I'm sure Glenda thought your family would like the decorations. After all, they *have met* her, and they seem fine with her idiosyncrasies."

"She hasn't met my dad, and I can assure you that he wouldn't be fine with this." I held up an ornament of Mrs. Claus with an elf—and they weren't making toys.

Her cornflower-blue eyes widened and dropped to the popcorn strand in her lap. "Speaking of your family, a storm is on its way, and meteorologists are predicting dangerously high winds."

"I know, which is why I told them not to come." The storm wasn't the only reason, but that was the excuse I was going with. I loved my family, but spending extended periods of time with them left me feeling like a hit-and-run victim.

"What time are they due to arrive?"

"They left Houston at one, and it's six now. So, any minute. But they can be a little late because our reservation isn't until eight."

"What are you going to wear?"

"My new green silk dress."

She flipped her blonde locks. "Well, I hope Bradley can make it back from Boston in time for the dinner, because that green is gorgeous with your brown hair and eyes."

I ignored the compliment and focused on the Bradley issue. If my boyfriend was a no-show, my matchmaker Sicilian nonna would ruin the meal by trying to recruit his replacement from the restaurant staff. "I haven't heard from him since his flight got rerouted to Jackson, so I assume he caught his connection."

"Well, if I wasn't having dinner with Dirk and his parents, I would love to go with you."

"You *would*?" I wasn't even sure *I* wanted to spend the evening with my family. "Why?"

"I've always wanted to experience a proper réveillon dinner."

"Not me. The French colonists ate the feast after midnight mass, and just waiting until eight is killing me." My stomach rumbled, and I glanced at the Gingerbread Man. But eating pornographic baking on a religious holiday had to be a sin.

"I was referring to eating a traditional New Orleans meal in a private room at Commander's Palace. It's the perfect way to spend Christmas Eve with your family."

Not if your last name was Amato. "What does réveillon mean, again?"

"'Waking,' from the French word *réveil*, because the colonists fasted all day on the twenty-fourth and then stayed awake all night to feast."

"Then when did Santa supposedly come? While they were at church?"

My front door shot open with a thwack. A candy-cane-striped, stripper-shoed foot stepped inside, and a puff of smoke followed.

Santa it was not.

Nor was it a priest.

"Sorry to kick the door, Miss Franki," Glenda drawled from the threshold, "but my hands were otherwise occupied."

She held a Mae West–style cigarette holder in one hand and a gift bag in the other, but my eyes were glued to her outfit. Like my tree, she was wrapped in silver tinsel, but her ornaments were hung rather differently. "Um, the star goes at the top."

"I'm one of those inverted Christmas trees, sugar."

I shot a pointed look at the scads of wrinkled skin showing between the tinsel. "Without the branches."

"Are you trying to break my balls?" She shimmied, shaking the two strategically placed ornaments on her chest.

"I can promise you, I'm not."

She Cher-shook her long, platinum hair and dragged from her cigarette holder. "Where's your family? I've never met your daddy, or your brother Michael."

I froze at the mention of my oldest brother. He was an accountant in Houston, and I saw him so rarely that I'd actually forgotten he existed. He was the type who grew up and fled the nest, while my brother Anthony was the one who refused to leave. I tried to escape but kept getting pulled back in like Michael Corleone from *The Godfather*. "They'll be here soon, but Anthony's the only one coming."

"That's too bad, but at least your daddy will get to enjoy this." Glenda reached into the gift bag and pulled out a North Pole with a Barbie clinging to it—in pasties and a G-string.

"Woooow." I emphasized the *ow*. "That's...really.........festive."

"Isn't it *just*? I like to think of that Barbie as me back in my heyday."

I didn't like to think that at all, and I was sure Mattel wouldn't either.

Glenda strutted to the fireplace and rested a six-inch heel on the head of the bearskin rug. She placed the North Stripper Pole on the mantle between my Elves on the Shelf, and I half-expected her to produce tiny dollar bills for their hands.

My Mr. Grinch ringtone sounded, matching my mood. I glanced at the phone on the coffee table. "It's my mom."

Veronica looked up from her popcorn strand. "I hope they haven't run into that storm."

My laugh was a quasi cackle. "My uptight mother, grouchy father, meddling nonna, and slacker brother have been trapped in a car for five hours. There's a hurricane raging, I assure you."

She rose from the armchair and ushered our landlady to the door. "Let's go get a few more ornaments from my apartment."

I mouthed *thank you* behind Glenda's back and pressed answer. "Hi, Mom."

"Francesca?" Her normally shrill voice had a caged-animal element. "It's your mother, dear."

Irritation set in, and she wasn't even at my apartment yet. "I know that, which is why I said, 'Hi, Mom.'"

"Well *someone's* a scrooge."

I sighed and forced my tone to be merry and bright, like the holidays were supposed to be. "Where are you guys?"

"We just pulled in to— Oh, *Joe. Really.*"

"I can't help it, Brenda," my dad said in his tense driving voice. "I've got a sick stomach."

My father always had digestive issues. Even when he hadn't eaten.

"Can we at least get a courtesy window-roll-down?" she shouted.

He grumbled something I was glad I hadn't heard.

"Anyway." She turned on the faux cheer as easily as one turned on Christmas tree lights. "We're in Baton Rouge. This holiday traffic is unreal."

"Are you sure you don't want to stay there for the night?" The question was futile, but a girl could try. "Veronica said the storm is going to be pretty bad."

"We own a deli, Francesca. We're not the Hiltons. And after all the years I spent slaving over a stove for this family, I think I'm entitled to a nice holiday meal in a restaurant. We'll just have to ride out the storm together."

I feared fatalities, and not from the high winds. "Mom, you know I live in a one bedroom."

"We've been all over this. Your father and I will take your room, your nonna can sleep on the chaise lounge, and you kids can camp out on the floor."

She said it like Anthony and I were still in elementary school instead of thirty-two and thirty, respectively.

"Yo, Pops," Anthony boomed in his affected New Jersey accent. "Blow those burps in the *front* seat, would ya?"

"*Again*, Joe?"

I felt like the caged animal, especially since the chaise lounge I was sitting on was upholstered in zebra print. But I could always sleep on Veronica's bizarre tiki-adorned couch or in the giant champagne glass in Glenda's living room.

"Franki?" My father's voice burst in my ear. "The GPS is showing that it'll take two hours to get to New Orleans instead of one."

"Our reservation is at eight, Dad, so you'll need to go straight to Commander's Palace."

"We're not going there, dear." My mother spoke with forced merriment. "Anthony changed the reservation."

"What? You let *him* pick the restaurant?"

"Well he *did* work in hospitality, Francesca."

"Mom, he worked at a strip club in the Quarter for a week." Then he fled home to Houston to free room and board.

"Strip clubs are pretty darn hospitable," she sing-songed.

I couldn't argue with that. "What is this place?"

"Laurent, on North Rampart Street."

It didn't ease my concern that the name sounded like "low rent."

A hiss came through the receiver, followed by a low growl. It sounded like...*a catfight?*

"Let go of my phone, Carmela." My mother's tone had gone from shrill to dental drill.

"Not a chance-a, woman," my nonna rasped in her thick Sicilian accent. "Franki, is-a Bradley there?"

Her question was more loaded than one of Santa's toy bags. In accordance with a cockamamie Italian-American custom, my nonna had forced me to steal a lemon from a Saint Joseph's Day altar to land a husband within a year. That was nine months ago, and she reminded me daily that Bradley's time to propose was almost up. "Uh, he's meeting us at the restaurant."

A beep interrupted the line. It was Bradley.

"That's him calling, Nonna. I need to let you go."

"*Aspetta.*"

When she said "wait" in Italian, you did.

"Is-a he gonna pop-a the question? I'm in-a my eighties, and I don't have-a much-a time left."

My lips pursed, and the line beeped again like a game-show timer pressuring me for an answer.

"What did she say, Carmela?" my mother asked. "I mean, two years is certainly enough time to know if you want to marry someone. If Bradley waits much longer, I'll be too old to be a grandmother."

They had just encapsulated the main problem with my family. My single-and-childless status was about them, not me.

Another beep escalated my stress.

"Francesca," my mother shrilled. "Are you there?"

As an early present to myself, I seized the opportunity and hung up.

A text message appeared on my display.

Bradley's flight from Jackson had been canceled. He was going to rent a car and drive the three hours to New Orleans.

I sprawled on the chaise lounge and stared at the shiny gold *fleurs-de-lis* on my fuzzy blood-red wallpaper, hoping their brightness would lift my sinking holiday spirits. Because if Bradley was a no-show on Christmas Eve, my nonna would turn the réveillon dinner "waking" into a "wake."

2

"Bûche de Noël." Rhonda, a barrel-chested brunette waitress, presented the Yule log dessert in her French-Maid-meets-Hooters uniform. She placed it on the table so that Shawna, her petite blonde co-worker, could begin slicing and plating.

My mother smoothed her dyed-brown Sarah Palin updo. "Look at those marzipan mushrooms. Isn't that the most adorable thing you've ever seen?"

No one at the table replied, and it wasn't because the meal was almost over and Bradley hadn't arrived. The Christmas Eve kicker was that my nonna, who'd been mourning my *nonnu* for over twenty years, appeared to have a date. His name was Luigi Pescatore, an elderly widower who not only knew my grandparents back when they sold produce from a cart in the French Quarter, he'd also helped me with a vampire murder investigation.

My father, whose already sick stomach had worsened at the sight of his elderly mother with a man—and in a dress that was no longer decidedly black but an ambivalent shade of gray, swallowed a burp and waved away the blonde and the slice of cake.

Nonna sat as stiff as uncooked spaghetti and stared straight ahead, gripping the handles of the black handbag in her lap. Luigi mimicked her stance, sans handbag, of course. They reminded me of *American Gothic*, the painting of the pitchfork-wielding farmer and his wife, but in an *Italian-American Gothic* version.

The blonde leaned her corset-enhanced hooters close to Anthony, who'd donned his best black tracksuit and gold rope chains for the dinner, and put a candy dish in front of him. "I brought this for those caramels you're eating."

I gaped at her, incredulous. I'd been trying to get a clean knife for thirty minutes, and my brother got his own candy dish?

"Eyyy, thanks, dahlin'." Anthony puffed out his pecs and held up a clear plastic bag of individually wrapped caramels. "My nonna made me these babies. They got *cannellino* in 'em, which is cinnamon booze. It's like an Italian version of Fireball." He shoved one between his lips and chewed with his mouth open.

The blonde's smile was coy as she sashayed from the room.

I wished that he would follow her, as he'd done once before. Anthony had been eating the gooey caramels throughout the meal, even during the savory courses, and I couldn't take much more of his smacking and finger licking.

My mom, whose face was flushed with wine and the prospect of unloading her live-in mother-in-law of two-plus decades, raised her goblet high. "I'd like to make a toast before we open the gifts." She swung the glass toward a table full of presents beside the door behind me. "Here's to family and friends who may be joining us in the future," she beamed at Luigi and then frowned at the empty seat beside me, "or who may not."

Luigi raised his goblet. "Hear, hear."

My dad let out a resounding belch, and I skipped the obligatory clinking and chugged instead.

"Yo, I've got a toast too." Anthony raised a beer bottle. "Here's to Franki not cooking."

I leaned close enough to smell his hair gel over the stench of his musk cologne. "You wanna sing with the choir at midnight mass? Because I can arrange for you to be a soprano."

He scooted his chair toward my nonna. "Even you gotta admit, sis, this joint is pretty good."

Apart from a shabby Christmas tree, some cheap blinds, and green carpeting that smelled as though it had been salvaged from the post-Katrina floods, Laurent wasn't all that low rent. "The food is surprisingly delicious, but the décor is lacking."

"Whoa, what about all this red and green for Italy?"

I sighed. "They're the colors of Christmas, Anthony."

My mother turned to Luigi, and the sleeve of her black dress slipped from her shoulder. "Speaking of the holiday, I hope you'll join us for midnight mass and the gospel choir concert at Saint Augustine Church." She gave him a sauced wink. "Carmela's going to be there."

My dad moaned and clutched his gut.

"Pardon the interruption."

I turned to see a fiftyish woman with highlighted hair in a loose bun. Her bright red lips and nails popped against her white wool business suit. "I'm Yvonne Chenier, the manager, and I couldn't help but overhear you mention the concert. Might I also suggest the bonfires along the levees of the Mississippi River? They light the way for Papa Noël, our Cajun Santa Claus."

My mother's eyes were as bright as the bonfires. "What a charming tradition."

"If you have little ones," Yvonne said, "you won't want to miss the Teddy Bear Tea at the Royal Sonesta Hotel."

My mom shot me a side-eye, and the bonfires had burned out. "You need a grandchild for that."

"And-a you need a husband for that." Nonna gave a sharp nod. "Luigi has a young-a cousin, Franki. I can hook-a you up."

Luigi brushed a wisp of thinning hair across his scalp. "His divorce is still pending, but that's a minor technicality."

I didn't need to go the levee bonfires because they were burning in my chest and belly. I literally kicked myself under the table for not going to Boston with Bradley.

Nonna scowled at the manager. "I got a suggestion. Next-a year you stick-a to the menu and make-a the Italian food."

Yvonne clasped her hands. "I'm afraid that wouldn't go with our French Creole theme."

"French-a Creole?" Nonna gave me the evil eye. "You told-a me we were havin' a ravioli dinner."

"I said we were having a réveillon dinner. REV-ee-on is clearly not the same word as ravioli."

Anthony popped a caramel. "Lay off nonna, will ya?"

"Your brother's right, Francesca. Mind your manners."

I tossed my napkin on the table. It was ironic that I had to lay off a woman who pressed me harder than pasta dough.

Yvonne's smile was as tight as her skirt. "You all enjoy the rest of your meal."

She turned to leave and ran into the host, a tall bag of bones in a white suit coat and black slacks who reminded me of Baron Samedi, the Haitian voodoo loa of the dead. "I'm sorry, Maurice."

"That's all right, Miss Chenier." He approached my father. "The valet needs your keys, Mister."

My dad pulled the keys from his pocket. He'd demanded them from the valet after the car was parked, convinced that the guy would go for a joyride in his Ford Taurus station wagon. "Tell the valet to bring the car to the curb in twenty minutes. And no funny business."

Maurice's eyelids lowered. "Yessir."

"Santa," my mom batted her lashes at my father, "it's time to pass out the gifts."

"Give us all a gift-a," my nonna boomed, "and stop-a callin' him-a that."

My mother's face went as dark as her dress, and she refilled her wine goblet.

I rested my arm on the table and turned to the doorway to watch my dad pass out the presents.

He pressed a fist to his mouth and blew out a burp. "Hand this to your mother, will you, Franki?"

I grimaced but reached for the gift and spotted a couple of

caramel wrappers stuck to my silk sleeve. "Seriously, Anthony? You put your trash by me?"

"What'sa mattuh? Just pick 'em off."

I gritted my teeth and removed the sticky wrappers. Then I dipped my napkin in my water glass and tried to clean the brown goop from the silk.

A short, stocky man entered in chef's whites and a toque blanche. He had a thick brown mustache and pinkish skin the color of lightly seared tuna steak. He seemed like a stereotypical French chef who ruled his kitchen with an iron fist and a stainless steel cook's knife. His mouth in a pucker, he scanned the room and zeroed in on my nonna. "I am ze chef, Guillaume Gaston. Ze manager say you did not find ze food satisfactory, *Madame*?"

She gave him the onceover and pulled her handbag to her bosom as though he'd come to steal it. "*Signora*."

His mustache twitched. "Was it ze oysters Bienville or ze seafood gumbo, *Signora*?"

Anthony dropped his fork on his dessert plate. "Actually, my man, it's this log. It could use some booze, like my nonna's caramels heuh."

The chef's skin went from seared to sautéed.

I intervened to prevent another Franco-Italian war. "There was a mix-up, Chef. She was expecting Italian."

He bit his index finger.

And I scooted my chair back.

"Ze spaghetti and meatball, I presume?" He put his other index finger into his mouth and bit that one too.

I moved closer to my brother. The chef was unwell. "Um, ravioli and veal."

Chef Gaston gave a strangled cry, grabbed his throat, and lurched from the room.

No one made a sound until Anthony popped a caramel and started smacking.

My dad put a package at his place setting that was shaped suspiciously like a hammer. "Brenda, where's Franki's present?"

"It's with the other gifts, Joe."

"I don't see it."

"Well, check the floor." She reached for her goblet. "I know it's there because I put it on that table myself."

My dad shrugged. "Evidently, it's gone."

"The ring," she breathed. "Somebody stole it." Her eyes fluttered up into their sockets, and she undulated like a wave. Then she crashed down.

Right into the bûche de Noël.

3

"Yo, Ma looks like a mud wrestler with that brown icing all ovuh her." Anthony crossed his arms against his chains. "Am I right?"

If I hadn't been helping my dad hold up my unconscious mother, I would have smashed *his* face into the cake. "Would you stop standing around and go get some wet paper towels?"

He pulled up the collar of his tracksuit jacket and bounce-walked from the room.

Yvonne hurried in. "I brought smelling salts from our first-aid kit. This always does the trick."

My head snapped back. *How often did she have to administer smelling salts to her customers?*

She broke the vial and waved it beneath my mother's nose.

My mom jerked and grasped at the air. "Where's Luigi?" Blinded by icing and a marzipan mushroom, her head thrashed from side to side. "He didn't leave, did he?"

I moved the wine goblet out of her reach before the scene got even uglier.

"Oh, I'm not going anywhere, Brenda." Luigi turned to my nonna. "Carmela is too enchanting."

My nonna maintained her pillar-of-salt pose, but my dad belched and gave a groan.

I leaned across the table and took Luigi's goblet—and a half-full bottle of wine.

Yvonne approached my father. "I'm going to have a look around the room in case the gift got moved or fell in a corner."

He nodded but looked doubtful.

Anthony returned with a dripping wad of paper towels. "Heuh ya go, Ma."

"Thank you, son." My mother peeled off a towel and wiped her eyes. "You're always so thoughtful."

He grinned right at me.

I resisted the urge to grab a towel and wipe the smarm from his lips. After all, it was the season of good will towards men, even though I could make the case that my brother was a boy. "Mom, before you fainted, you said you got me a ring?"

"Your father gave it to me when you were born. I wanted you to have it."

My eyes misted. I was truly touched.

"Because I figured Bradley wasn't going to give you one, and it looks like I was right."

The mist vaporized. The woman wouldn't give it a rest even if she had only one breath left. "What does the ring look like?"

She twirled a paper towel in her ear. "You've seen it. It's the square-cut emerald on the gold band."

Luigi let out a whistle. "Emeralds aren't cheap. You got insurance on that?"

My mother swayed and gripped the table. "I let the policy lapse to cover Anthony's trip to bartending school in New York."

I looked at my brother. No matter how much experience I gained as an investigator, I would never be able to solve the mystery of how he conned women.

My dad's face had turned the color of the bûche de Noël. "Why wasn't I informed of this trip decision?"

We all stared at him. My mom's standard operating procedure was to exclude him from financial extracurriculars. *How did we know that, and yet he didn't?*

Yvonne cleared her throat. "In light of what's happened, Mr. Amato, we'll comp your meal."

My dad rubbed his hands together. "That's at least three hundred bucks. That should about take care of it."

"Um, no, it shouldn't." I didn't have a date, so I was getting that gift. "I need a moment with my family, Yvonne. Can I meet you in your office in a few minutes?"

"Certainly." She flashed a smile, but her green eyes flashed something else.

My father put a hand on my shoulder. "You're not going to investigate this yourself, are you, Franki? This is a job for the police."

"It's nine thirty on Christmas Eve, Dad. A stolen ring isn't going to be high on their priority list. And I think I can handle this myself."

"All right. I trust your judgment."

"I'm going to go talk to Yvonne about questioning the staff."

"Start-a with that-a cook." My nonna raised a fist. "He rob-a me of-a my Christ-a-mas ravioli."

"Réveillon, Nonna. Réveillon," I shouted as I exited the private room.

Laurent had closed at nine for the holiday, so the main dining area was empty. I followed the sounds of dishes clanking and entered the wait station at the back of the restaurant. It was a hallway with an exit on either end and a food pickup window shared with the kitchen.

Rhonda, the brunette waitress, scraped the contents of a plate into the trash and stacked it on a tray. She didn't look up. "Whaddya need?"

I eyed her "Do Not Cross" tattoo. "The manager's office?"

She pointed a dirty fork at the swing door to my right.

I should've known better than to expect polite conversation from a woman with a street sign on her arm. I entered the kitchen, but Chef Gaston wasn't around. The walk-in door was ajar, so I assumed he was inside cooling off from his run-in with my nonna.

A door marked "Manager" was next to the walk-in.

I approached and heard voices inside the office. I knocked, and they stopped. Abruptly.

A thirtyish male opened the door and motioned for me to enter the closet-sized room. He was so tall, dark, and hunksome that a trip to confession was in order.

Yvonne glared at me from her seat behind a beat-up wooden desk. "This is Declan, *my* bartender."

The *my* didn't escape me. "Pleasure," I said, and I meant it. "So, before I call the police—"

"No." She shot a panicked look at Declan. "You can't do that."

Her reaction convinced me that something lowdown was going on at Laurent. "I can, and here's why." I took a seat in a metal chair and rested my arms on her desk to drive home what I was about to say. "I have to spend the next week with my family after my boyfriend who hasn't proposed didn't show up for dinner, and the emerald ring in that missing package is the only thing that's going to get me through it."

"I've comped your meal, what else do you want?"

"Tell the employees they can't leave until I've questioned them. I'm a private investigator at Private Chicks, Incorporated."

Declan snorted. "That name's a joke, right?"

"It's a play on private *dicks*." I raised an eyebrow at him.

Yvonne opened her mouth, and her upper lip stuck to a front tooth. "Fair enough. I'll inform them that they have to stay late."

"Perfect. And then you can tell me whether you stole my gift."

She leapt to her feet and slammed her hand on the desk. "Where in the hell do you get off—"

"I'll tell you." I rose and leaned my five-foot-ten inches forward to show her I wasn't intimidated. "Everyone who came in that room is a suspect, and you seem reluctant to cooperate."

Her gaze met mine. "I didn't take your ring, and I have no idea who did."

Satisfied, I straightened. I believed her—not because she was trustworthy, but because she wouldn't have done anything to bring the police to the restaurant. "I'll start questioning your staff."

Declan stood.

"Thanks, pal. But I can definitely show myself out of this little box." I exited the office, closed the door, and ducked around a metal rack stocked with foodstuffs.

About thirty seconds passed, and the office door opened and closed.

As I'd suspected, either Declan or Yvonne had checked to make sure I was gone—a sign they were up to something. I tiptoed around the rack and pressed an ear to the hollow door.

"She's going to have to go." Yvonne's voice was as clear and acidic as the white vinegar on the rack next to me. "There's a bonus in it for you if you get rid of her. Permanently."

"Done," Declan said.

I took a giant step backwards.

Were they talking about me?

4

"**Y**ou sink you can snoop in my keetchen, eh?"

I leapt from a dry goods rack I'd been searching and turned to face the chef. He held a fistful of raw meat in one hand and a cook's knife in the other.

"Someone stole my Christmas present," I said to the knife. "I was looking for it."

"Bullsheet." He kicked the walk-in door with his clog, and it slammed shut with a dungeon-like echo. Then he tossed the meat on a chopping block and approached me with the knife. "You are a spy. Who sent you? Was it Hugo? Or zat rascal, Felix?"

I attempted a throaty laugh that came out a croak. "I'm Italian-American. We're not known for any of the major spy qualities, like blending in or being quiet."

He pointed the knife, and one-eyed my face.

I flattened against the wall with my hands up. I tried to stay motionless, but my nostrils betrayed me. The chef was cooking butter and garlic, and they were programmed by my DNA to flare at the aroma.

"Zen why are you here, *Mademoiselle*?"

"I'm a private investigator. I need to ask you a couple of questions about an emerald ring that was stolen from our private room."

He scratched his greasy pink cheek with the knife. "Do I appear to have ze time to chat?"

"Well, the restaurant *is* closed."

"But ze keetchen is open." He lowered the knife and approached the chopping block.

I relaxed until he picked up a stainless steel meat tenderizer.

"I must make ze food for ze staff and zat...zat *ruffian* who expect me, Chef Gaston, to make ze *Italien* food."

"Oh, that ruffian's my nonna. She's done eating."

"*Mais non.*" He came at me with the meat tenderizer, and I went back to my surrender position.

"Every customer, zey must leave satisfied. Before she go, she will taste my *ravioles* and *grillades* of veal."

"Might I suggest that you call them ravioli and scaloppine? Otherwise, she'll never put them in her mouth."

The chef's face turned as red as a Bordelaise sauce. Then he erupted in an expletive-laden tirade more explosive than the Bastille Day fireworks in Paris. When he finished, I understood why the phrase "pardon my French" had come about.

"Chef, my nonna is from Italy. What do you expect?"

"Puah, Puah," he faux-spat on the floor. "Ze *Italien* cook sink zey are *artistes* because zey put ze tomato on ze pasta, but zey are no van Gogh."

Maybe not, but I had a feeling that Chef Gaston was, because I could see him cutting off an ear. "Look, your French food is very good—"

"Ve-ry good? Ve-ry good?" He pounded the veal with the meat tenderizer in rhythm with the syllables. "*Mon Dieu!* I-should-have-a-Miche-lin-star, *Made-moi-selle.*"

"Wow, a Michelin star." I feigned admiration to get him to put down the mallet. "You're obviously a top-tier chef."

"*Oui.*" He paused to glory in the compliment. "But I did not earn it, and I had to leave Paris in disgrace. Now I must work in zis *merde* restaurant cooking *merde* food for *merde* clients." He held up his hands, fingers bent, and screamed at the ceiling.

I inched toward the swing door.

"Do you know ze reason I lose ze star?"

I didn't, naturally, and I sensed I didn't want to.

"I miss one rotten mussel, and ze Michelin inspector die of ze food poisoning."

I had a touch of hypochondria, and that revelation did nothing for my gut, which was full of a dozen oysters and a half pound of seafood gumbo.

"I must get ze money to go back and restore my *réputation*." He grabbed his cook's knife and stabbed at the meat.

He had a motive to steal my Christmas present, but there was no way I would question him while he was busy stabbing flesh. Instead, I did what every self-respecting PI would do—I fled through the swing door to the main dining room.

Like me in the kitchen, the blonde waitress, Shawna, was being cornered by a fruitcake. Her back was to the wall, and my brother leaned in menacingly, only instead of a knife his lips were the deadly weapon.

"I assume you're asking her about my missing Christmas present, Anthony?"

He turned. "Uh, what?"

Shawna dipped under his arm. "I'd better get back to work."

I followed her to the wait station, where Rhonda was refilling sugar caddies.

Shawna shot me a look more toxic than that mussel Chef Gaston had missed. "This area's off-limits to customers."

"I'm not leaving until I find the emerald ring that was stolen from our room. Do you have any idea who took it?"

She raised her chin.

"If that's the way you're gonna play it, you either show me what's in your apron, or I call the cops."

Her French Maid hooters heaved. She untied the apron and threw it on a condiment table.

I looked through the two pockets. An order pad, some pens, and a bottle of Visine. I held up the eye drops. "Are you putting these in customers' food? Or are these for clearing your eyes after you smoke a joint?"

She snatched the Visine and apron. "We don't do drugs."

I noticed she didn't answer the part about people's food, and my already alarmed gut gave a kick.

Rhonda wiped a caddy with a wet rag. "We get drug-tested." She glared at the kitchen. "By management."

That didn't mean they weren't dealing. Restaurants were often fronts for illegal drug operations. "What about my ring?"

Shawna slammed a container of Slap Ya Mama Cajun seasoning on the table. "I didn't take it, all right? And thanks for ruining my shot at a date with your brother."

"Trust me, honey. There's nothing any woman could do to ruin their chances with Anthony. But I urge you to try." I turned to Rhonda.

"Don't look at me, lady. I got a kid at home. I can't get arrested, especially on Christmas Eve."

She seemed sincere, but I was convinced that something illicit was going on at Laurent.

Chef Gaston placed several servings of the seafood gumbo in the pickup window and looked down his Gallic nose at the waitresses. "Here is ze slop, you mongrels."

"Hey, I ate that for dinner." I touched my stomach, waiting for the poisoning pains to start.

Rhonda jerked a bowl from the window, spilling it on the counter.

"Animal," the chef shouted, flinging bits of veal from his mustache. "How many times I tell you? My food is like a *bébé*. It must be coddled, stroked."

Like that veal he'd massacred on the chopping block?

The chef cradled his knife in his arms and cooed and rocked it like a baby.

My jaw dropped. The guy was crazier than a fruitcake. He was a full-on nut torte.

I left the wait station to check on my mother and spotted Shawna talking to Maurice, the host, by the entrance. I pulled back and peered around the corner.

She palmed something to Maurice. Without a word, he shoved it into his pocket and slipped outside.

It was either drugs or my ring.

5

Inside the restaurant, I crouched beneath a window overlooking North Rampart Street and did what Chef Gaston had accused me of—I spied on the staff.

Maurice and the valet, a wiry guy with slicked back hair, stood in front of a lime-green Chevy Impala lowrider smoking cigarettes and flashing gang signals. They could have been fooling around, trying to look tough, but I didn't dare underestimate them. New Orleans had gangs it wasn't wise to mess with, like the D-Block Boys, the Mid City Killers, and an unnamed group of transvestites who wore fluorescent wigs and showgirl attire.

Per my father's instructions, the valet had retrieved our station wagon and parked it behind the lowrider. My dad had been right not to trust him, or Maurice for that matter. They both seemed sketchy, casting furtive glances up and down the street as though they were waiting for something or someone they didn't entirely trust. I still suspected drugs, but they could have been involved in any number of illegal operations—selling guns, running an escort service, or fencing stolen goods like my ring.

Part of me wanted to forget the ring and leave Laurent. But if there was ongoing criminal activity at the restaurant, the PI in me couldn't leave that uninvestigated. And I wasn't in a hurry to go to church and listen to my nonna pray for me to find a husband. So, I rose from my hiding place and went outside to chat with the men.

North Rampart was quiet for ten p.m., not even the streetcar was in service. It was a two-way street with two lanes of traffic on either side of neutral ground, a local term for the concrete median that ran down the middle. Despite recent gentrification, North Rampart still looked kind of seedy, and the dim light of the old lampposts added to the dodgy atmosphere.

I approached Maurice and the valet, whose nametag said Reuben. It was a balmy sixty degrees out, and the air was thick with smoke, cologne, and suspicion. "Evening, fellas."

Reuben crossed his arms, and Maurice's black eyes bore into mine. They were deep set and lined with dark circles, which made them all the more unsettling. He exhaled a puff of smoke and flicked his cigarette butt into the street. Then he reached into his suit coat pocket and pulled out a pack of Pall Malls—a common voodoo offering to Baron Samedi.

The brand got me thinking. *What were the odds that the underworld dealings going on at Laurent were the work of the god of the underworld's lookalike?*

I needed to find out, but I had to tread carefully. "So, what're you guys doing for the holiday?"

Maurice lit a cigarette and stared at the empty street.

Reuben leaned against the lowrider. "My homeboy, Maurice, be gamblin' and hittin' the strip clubs."

Your average Christmas Eve. "What about you?"

"I'm goin' to a fancy dinner." He shoved his fists forward to reveal finger tattoos that spelled Taco Bell.

If that qualified as fancy, I couldn't fathom typical.

He grinned, revealing silver teeth. "You wanna come?"

"Uh, thanks, but my family's in town." I pointed at the restaurant, and a pain pierced my side. "Oh, no," I muttered. "The seafood."

Maurice and Reuben exchanged a lidded look—one that said, *she's a problem.*

I'd hit on something they didn't want me to know. But what? All I'd said was "seafood."

Maurice dragged off his cigarette, which he held between his thumb and index finger, and gazed at the street. "Maybe you should go back inside." His black eyes shot the corners to glare at me. "To your family."

"Yeah, man." Reuben kicked a foot onto the side of the car. "Y'all need to leave. The restaurant's closed."

They were trying to get rid of me before whatever they were waiting for went down. "I'm aware of that, but someone stole my Christmas gift from our private room, and I'm staying put until I get it back."

Maurice blew out a cloud. "We don't know anything about no ring."

Apparently they did, because I hadn't said it was a ring. And I never saw Yvonne leave her office to inform the staff of the theft, as she'd said she would do. "That's interesting." I mimicked his side glare. "Because I never told you what the gift was."

A click caught my ear, and my eyes darted to the lowrider.

Reuben had pulled out a switchblade.

I stood my ground and hid the fear that squeezed my lungs.

He opened and closed the blade against his thigh, as though it was a game. But the three of us knew otherwise, and the implication was clear—I'd get cut if I didn't go away and keep my mouth shut.

"I think she's accusing us of a crime, Maurice." Reuben's voice was soft, but sharp.

"It was a question," I said, "not an accusation."

Maurice stiffened and threw down his cigarette.

I stepped backwards, but he wasn't interested in me. He nodded at the street, and Reuben rose from the lowrider and followed his gaze.

A tricked-out Buick in glossy, candy-apple-red paint crept toward us. It had six wheels—four underneath and two on the trunk—with protruding wire hubcaps known as Swangas.

Because I'd grown up in Houston, I knew the car was a slab, a local Hip Hop acronym for a Slow, Loud, and Bangin' vehicle. What I didn't know was what a slab was doing in New Orleans.

Reuben tapped Maurice with the hand that held the switchblade. "What do we do, man?"

"We take care of it."

Was a gang war about to start?

Reuben popped the trunk of the lowrider, possibly to retrieve a weapon, and I leaned forward to see the contents.

A hand covered my mouth, and an arm encircled my waist.

I struggled, but my feet left the ground. I landed face-first in the trunk before I had time to kick.

The lid slammed shut, and everything went black.

I'd been kidnapped.

6

My heart raced like greased lightening as I squirmed onto my back in the pitch-black trunk. I was sure Maurice had dumped me inside, and he hadn't done it to protect me. Meanwhile, my phone was in my handbag in the private room, so I couldn't call for help.

Muffled voices were audible.

I stayed still and listened.

There were three, maybe four men. They weren't shouting, so I ruled out the gang war. A deal had to be in the works that they didn't want me to see. *But what happened afterward? Would they let me go? Or take me to a bayou and feed me to the gators?*

I shuddered and felt around the dark trunk for an emergency release. If the men did plan to kill me, Yvonne might have been involved. She could've called or texted Maurice and Reuben from the office and given them the same order she'd given Declan the bartender—get rid of me. Permanently.

Sweat formed on my face—not from the humidity, but from fear. I couldn't give in to panic. My life depended on it.

Dragging sounds came from the street, like crates being pulled over asphalt, and I went still again. The driver of the slab had brought either a substantial shipment of drugs or something larger, maybe illegal arms.

"No, man." Reuben was near the lowrider. "Load it in here for now."

I waited for the trunk to open or to feel movement in the backseat, but the car remained as motionless as I did.

After a few minutes, a door or a trunk slammed in the distance, followed by more voices and more slamming. An engine started, and a car sped away.

The slab must have left.

Locals believed that the voodoo loa Baron Samedi met the deceased in a top hat and tails to dig their graves. So, I had to get out of the trunk before his lookalike, Maurice, took me to meet him in person. "Help! If anyone is out there, please open the trunk."

Silence.

I pounded on the lid until my fists were numb.

No one came.

Where were Reuben and Maurice? Had they left in the slab?

Raindrops hit the car, lightly at first, and then leaden. Water seeped inside and dripped on my forehead like a torture tactic.

I gave up the search for an emergency release and pulled my knees to my chest. Kicking off my heels, I placed my feet on the lid and pumped as hard as I could.

It opened.

And so did the sky. A bucket's worth of water dropped on me like that dancer in *Flashdance*.

I grabbed my shoes and held the heels like weapons. North Rampart Street was empty except for a guy in fairy wings. But he was trying to punch the raindrops, so I wasn't worried about him.

I climbed from the trunk and ran into the restaurant. The kitchen and wait station were empty, and so was Yvonne's office.

Had the whole staff fled and left us alone in the place?

I returned to the private room. Chef Gaston and Shawna, the blonde waitress, stood near my nonna with two plates.

Anthony observed with interest—the French Maid hooters, not

the food.

My mother looked up from her compact and lowered her tube of lipstick. "Oh, Francesca," she scolded. "Where have you been? You've ruined your dress."

I clenched my fists. She acted as though I'd been playing in the rain instead of searching for my ring. "Uh, I've been looking for my Christmas present?"

My dad rose from the table. "Have you sniffed out the culprit?"

"Not yet, but there was a suspicious incident outside." I went to my purse and grabbed my phone. It was better to tell the authorities what had happened instead of alarming my family. "I'm calling the police—"

"*Silence*." Chef Gaston shot cook's knives at me and then nodded to Shawna, who curtseyed awkwardly and leaned forward to deliver the first dish.

Nonna eyed Anthony and then Luigi, and she took the cloth napkin from her lap and tucked it around the waitress's chest.

Shawna's eyes widened and darted to the chef.

He pushed her aside and kissed his fingertips. "Zis is a French-Creole specialty, Signora. Veal grillades over jalapeño cheese grits."

"Grits-a?" Nonna reeled as though they were maggots. "Why not-a polenta?"

He removed his toque blanche and used it to fan himself. "Because ze grits are ze traditional accompaniment to ze dish."

Nonna's chin went up, and her mouth went down. "What else-a you got?"

Shawna delivered the second dish, ravioli in cream sauce.

"That don't look-a like ricotta filling to me. And where's-a the tomato sauce-a?"

The chef's cheeks took on the hue of a crisp rosé. "One does not pair *fromage* with pan-fried lobster and scallops, Signora. Ze sauce is a white wine and lobster stock reduction, which complements ze filling."

My nonna pulled a rosary from her handbag.

His mustache twitched. "What are you doing with zat sing?"

"Prayin' someone teach-a you how to cook-a."

His face turned bordeaux. "My credentials are impeccable. And we are ze only restaurant in New Orleans with seafood of zis quality."

"Too bad-a for the seafood that you don't-a know how to use it."

Chef Gaston made a choking sound and grabbed his neck.

Nonna curled her lip. "And it smells-a like it's been outta the fridge since Thanks-a-giving."

He spun, rose to the toes of his clogs, and hotfooted it from the room.

I stared after him—not because he was strangling himself, but because of what he and my nonna had said. I didn't understand where a low-rent place like Laurent would get better seafood than any other restaurant in the city, or how they could afford it. But if the lobster and scallops smelled fishy, maybe they hadn't come from New Orleans.

Were the dragging sounds I'd heard outside crates of shellfish?

No. That was absurd. New Orleans was right by the Gulf of Mexico, so a despotic French chef like Gaston wouldn't need to get his seafood from Houston—and from the trunk of a slab, no less.

On the other hand, after I'd muttered the word seafood, Maurice and Reuben had branded me an enemy and locked me in the lowrider.

It was time to re-question the chef.

I returned to the kitchen, but Gaston wasn't at the stove. The walk-in was ajar, so I figured he was getting more veal ammunition for his war with my nonna. I walked over and peered inside.

Someone shoved me from behind.

I catapulted forward and dropped my phone, which skidded across the kitchen, and I fell across some crates.

The thick, metal door slammed shut, and the dungeon sound echoed in my head.

Once again I was trapped in a dark space with no means of communication. Only this one was a freezer, and the staff was gone.

Would my family find me? Or would I freeze to death in my wet dress on Christmas?

7

"Can someone please open this walk-in? My life isn't all that great, but I still want to live it." I slammed the ball of my fist on the door for emphasis and slumped onto the stacked crates. I'd been inside for about fifteen minutes, and my future was already in doubt. It was so cold that I could feel crystals forming on my dress, but I couldn't see them because the walk-in was darker than the lowrider trunk.

If only I'd been able to hold on to my phone.

My mind drifted to Bradley. I'd probably received a text or voicemail from him, telling me he'd arrived in New Orleans.

"Why, Franki?" I yelled at myself. "Why didn't you go with him when he invited you to Boston? It wasn't like you were going to have a Hallmark-Channel holiday with your family—or even a freakin' greeting-card moment."

But I couldn't dwell on my bad decisions. That would take hours, and I had to find a way out of the walk-in before I succumbed to hypothermia. Apart from an unlikely rescue, my best shot at survival was the overhead light. I hadn't been able to find the switch on the wall, so I assumed it was outside the freezer. But if I could get the light to come on, I'd be able to see the cooling fan so that I could jam something in it to break the motor. Failing that, my only other option was to use the boxed and crated food to make an igloo.

Slowly, I climbed onto the crates, and it wasn't easy because my toes were going numb. I ran my hands along the ceiling. It took a few minutes, but I found the light bulb.

And a pull-string.

Illogically, I closed my eyes and tugged.

Light filled the walk-in. Even though it was dim and yellowish, it was more beautiful than the light of any Christmas tree—and especially mine thanks to Glenda's decorations.

"*Buon Natale*," I wished myself.

Then I looked for the fan. There were two of them in a protective metal case attached to the ceiling—with protective grates that I would need a screwdriver to remove.

"Forget what I just said. This Christmas is just not merry."

With a sigh, I jumped down to look for something to pry the grates open, and my eye landed on the top crate. A long metal bar attached the lid to the bottom—perfect for prying and jamming. I worked to remove it and noticed that the crate was unmarked, as were the others. A reputable seafood distributor like Bumble Bee or StarKist would have branded them.

And then I knew what was going on at Laurent. Chef Gaston, undoubtedly under pressure from management to keep food costs at a minimum, was buying hot seafood. He'd admitted to poisoning a Michelin inspector in France with a bad mussel, so he apparently had a history of shoddy—and shady—purchases.

The question was whether Yvonne knew about the illegal seafood ring, not to mention Declan, the bartender. I didn't have to wonder about Maurice and Reuben. They were in on the scheme, coordinating shipments. The dragging crates were proof.

But what had Maurice and Reuben done with them? The crates in the walk-in were too cold to be the ones that had arrived a half-hour before.

Reuben's voice echoed in my head. *Load it in here for now.*

But where was 'here'? They wouldn't have brought the crates into the restaurant because my family was inside.

"OMG—the Taurus."

Reuben had the keys.

The stolen seafood was in my parents' station wagon—unrefrigerated. *And if it had traveled the five hours from Houston in the back of a slab, who knows how long it had been that way?*

A cramp pinched my side that turned into a dull ache—the oysters Bienville and seafood gumbo. *Had they been properly refrigerated?* If not, I probably had food poisoning and some sort of sea worm that fed on shellfish. And at that moment it was either swimming in my stomach or boring a hole in it. I had to get out of the walk-in so I could get to a hospital.

I yanked harder on the bar, trying to pry it loose. But my fingers had gone numb, and my toes were ice cubes.

I had to jog in place, get my blood circulating. I lifted my knee, and my dress crunched. It was frozen solid. I put my foot down and rolled my ankle—it was too numb to bear the pressure. For the first time in my life, I wished I'd worn pantyhose.

Desperate to stop the fans, I searched among the products on the walk-in shelves for something thin enough to jam between the blades. Cream, puff pastry, foie gras...

...a ring box?

Stunned, I grabbed it from the shelf and flipped the lid.

Empty.

I knew the box was mine, and Chef Gaston was the most likely ring thief, but I needed proof for the police.

I looked around the floor. Something shiny and red protruded from beneath a bag full of heads of lettuce. I moved the bag and found wrapping paper with a tag addressed to me from my parents.

The ring box was mine, all right. And it was all I was getting for Christmas.

Frustrated, I threw it—or I tried to—but the ring box stuck to my fingers. There was a sticky brownish substance on the sides.

"Please don't be fish guts or congealed cow blood." I was having a bad enough holiday as it was without getting E. coli. But...if it was the cow blood, I might be able to make a case against the veal-wielding chef.

I raised the ring box to my nose and sniffed.

And my fingers curled, crushing it.

The scent was unmistakable.

Cinnamon.

Cannellino.

8

"You know I'm right, Mom." I turned to face her from my seat at the end of the Saint Augustine Church pew, and a whiff of shellfish wafted off my damp dress. "Old sticky fingers Anthony took my ring into the walk-in to show it to that waitress, Shawna. And he did it because he was hoping to score with her."

"Hush, Francesca." She glanced around to make sure no one had heard me. "Christmas Day is in five minutes, and mass is about to start. You got the emerald ring, so spare me the dirty details about your brother."

Thanks to Anthony, I'd been ripped off, kidnapped, and nearly frozen to death, but my mom was mad at *me* for tattling.

She tugged at the shoulder of her dress. "Besides, Shawna is the one with the sticky fingers. You heard what that manager, Yvonne, told the police officer. She was stealing tips from Rhonda and the bartender and paying off Maurice to keep him quiet."

I'd been wrong about Yvonne. When she'd told Declan to "get rid of her," she'd meant fire Shawna, not kill me. But I wasn't wrong about my brother. "Then how do you explain the ring ending up in the walk-in with Nonna's caramels smeared on the box when Anthony was the only one eating them?"

"I never said he didn't take the ring into the walk-in. But it's obvious what happened. That crooked blonde tricked my sweet son into taking her the ring, and then she distracted him and hid it in that tub of pâté."

I picked at a fleck of goose liver nestled around the ring band and pressed my lips together. If I'd said what I wanted to in my current setting, I risked eternal damnation.

She patted her updo. "And don't get me started on that chef and those hooligans, Maurice and Reuben. I don't know if we'll ever get the fish smell out of the Taurus."

My brother strutted up the aisle and leaned over my mom and me to hand the keys to my father. "Yo, Pops. I parked down the street, but I left the windows up."

"Good thinking, son," he grumbled. "We *are* in New Orleans."

Anthony shooed me. "Move over, sis."

I didn't.

He slid next to my nonna, who sat with Luigi in the pew in front of us. "Is that the thanks I get for savin' your life?"

"You went to the walk-in to look for the ring, not to save me."

My mother frowned. "That's not fair, dear. I asked him to look for you."

"Thanks for sticking up for me, Ma." Anthony shot me a scowl over his shoulder. "Between that waitress and Franki, my Christmas Eve is ruined."

Seething, I leaned toward him. "While we're here, you'd better pray for your soul, because when we leave you're a dead man."

"Honestly, Francesca, making threats in church and on Christmas? I raised you better than that."

I pulled down the kneeler. It was going to take a lot of praying to get through the holiday.

My mom leaned forward and gave Luigi's shoulder a squeeze. She let her hand linger, probably to prevent him from getting up and running. "How are you doing up there?"

He turned and flashed his dentures. "Still doing good, Brenda. Just like the last time you asked."

My nonna, who'd been as still as the statue of the Virgin Mary overlooking the altar, turned to glare at my mother. Her black eyes bugged out, and she made the sign of the cross. "*Madonna mia.*"

"I'm so glad we found you all."

I recognized Veronica's voice and looked up from my kneeling position, expecting to see her with Dirk.

But she'd brought Glenda.

To church.

In a sheer black dress with her scanty undergarments showing.

"Um...what are you doing here?"

Veronica tucked a lock of hair behind her ear. "Dinner with Dirk's parents ended early, so I told him that I wanted to come by the church and attend mass with your family."

"Actually," I said, "the question was for Glenda."

My landlady pressed a hand to her breast. "Miss Ronnie invited me to come with her, and I figured what the hell? It *is* Christmas, sugar."

One of unholiest on record, but yes.

Glenda flipped her platinum mane. "Now scooch your butt over, Miss Franki. I want a good seat for the show."

I moved and kept mum about the "butt" and "show" references. For my landlady, all of life was a performance involving body parts.

Nonna rose and placed an open hymnal on Glenda's midsection and pressed a Bible to her bosom. "You'll need-a these." She moved to return to her seat but froze. Her brow rose, and her hand went to her mouth. "It's a Christ-a-mas miracle."

I turned to see Bradley striding up the aisle in a dark suit, and the events at Laurent faded. I climbed over Glenda and Veronica and wrapped my arms around him. "You'll never know how happy I am to see you."

He kissed me church-appropriately. "I'm sorry I couldn't get here in time for the réveillon dinner. I'll bet it was amazing."

"It definitely was...that."

His nose wrinkled. "What perfume are you wearing?"

"Uh, Eau de Ocean."

"Huh. I like it."

Everyone moved down the pew, and Bradley and I sat on the end. He tipped his head at my father and smiled at my mother.

She flushed and smoothed her hair. "This is so lovely, isn't it? We're all together."

"Yes." Bradley gazed at me. "Lovely."

I tingled all over—until the priest approached the altar. Then I stopped that.

As we waited for mass to begin, I stole a glimpse at my family. We were in a historic New Orleans church in nice clothes on Christmas Day. It could have been a scene in a Hallmark movie—except for the stink of seafood. But in our defense, the fish *was* a religious symbol.

Bradley leaned in. "That's quite a ring you're wearing."

I beamed at the emerald. "It was a present from my parents."

He smiled and looked pointedly at the altar. "Looks like I've got my work cut out for me."

I stared open-mouthed at his profile and then leaned back in the pew, marveling at the wonders of the season.

Not only did I get my Hallmark-Channel holiday, I'd gotten my greeting-card moment too.

ABOUT THE AUTHOR

Traci Andrighetti is the *USA TODAY* bestselling author of the Franki Amato Mysteries and the Danger Cove Hair Salon Mysteries. In her previous life, she was an award-winning literary translator and a Lecturer of Italian at the University of Texas at Austin, where she earned a PhD in Applied Linguistics. But then she got wise and ditched that academic stuff for a life of crime—writing, that is. Her latest capers are teaching mystery for Savvy Authors and taking authors on writing retreats to Italy with LemonLit.

To learn more about Traci, check out her websites: www. traciandrighetti.com
www.lemonlit.com

ALSO BY TRACI ANDRIGHETTI

Deadly Dye and a Soy Chai
A Poison Manicure and Peach Liqueur
Killer Eyeshadow and a Cold Espresso

Lightning Source UK Ltd.
Milton Keynes UK
UKHW010955280820
368951UK00004B/93